THE POWER
AND THE PRIZE

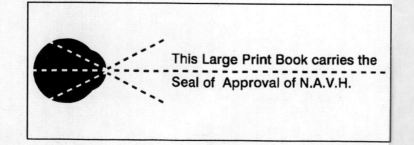

This Large Print Book carries the
Seal of Approval of N.A.V.H.

A MARTHA PEMBERTON WESTERN,
BOOK 2

THE POWER
AND THE PRIZE

CHET CUNNINGHAM

WHEELER PUBLISHING
A part of Gale, Cengage Learning

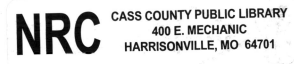
GALE
CENGAGE Learning·

Detroit • New York • San Francisco • New Haven, Conn • Waterville, Maine • London

GALE
CENGAGE Learning®

LIBRARY OF CONGRESS CATALOGING-IN-PUBLICATION DATA

Cunningham, Chet.
  The power and the prize / by Chet Cunningham. — Large print ed.
    p. cm. — (Wheeler Publishing large print western) (A
  Martha Pemberton western; bk. 2)
  ISBN-13: 978-1-4104-4553-7 (pbk.)
  ISBN-10: 1-4104-4553-4 (pbk.)
  1. Large type books. I. Title.
PS3553.U468P69 2012
813'.54—dc23   2012001656

Published in 2012 by arrangement with Chet Cunningham.

Printed in the United States of America
  1 2 3 4 5   16 15 14 13 12
FD122

THE POWER
AND THE PRIZE

CHAPTER ONE:
THE BASTARD

San Francisco, August, 1875

Martha Pemberton Dyke sat stiffly in an armchair in her father's drawing room. It was one of the few times she was totally oblivious to the luxury that surrounded her — the exquisite fabric that covered the chair, the huge window with its sweeping view of San Francisco Bay. Instead, her eyes shifted worriedly between her father and her older brother Randy, recently returned from Boston after graduating from Harvard University.

Randy was nearly as tall as his father, his straw-colored hair a little longer than it had been when he went away. But so much more had changed since then. She, Martha, not yet twenty-two, was already a widow. And Randy suddenly seemed filled with a constant, unreasoning anger. Now he stood with his chin thrust toward his parent.

"Father, you know perfectly well what I'm

talking about. I am no longer a child and neither is Martha. It is my firm conviction that we must have this out once and for all. It must be made clear to everyone, and especially to Martha. Good Lord, do you think that I *want* to shout something like this through the streets? No, of course not. I want it handled quietly and as a gentleman, but it definitely must be dealt with now."

Harold Pemberton wanted to take the boy by the shoulders and shake him until his head rattled. But he and his son were well beyond that stage.

Harold sighed. For the first time, he was feeling his age. Somehow he hadn't caught up with the fact he was fifty years old. Why is it the children seemed suddenly so young, and he felt suddenly so old? This certainly was one subject he didn't want to discuss and especially not in front of Martha. How had Randy stumbled across it in the first place? Oh, there were several around town who knew or thought that they knew. But he had managed to keep the lid on fairly well. The displeasure he could vent on anyone bringing up the point was enough to keep a lot of mouths closed.

Harold fixed a grim scowl on his face and rapped his silver tipped cane on the polished hardwood floor.

"Randall! I will not tolerate that tone of voice in my own house — especially from an untried and freshly hatched youngster like you. Get a degree from Harvard and you think you know everything. Be surprised how much you'll learn in the next four years. I've gobbled up boys like you for breakfast and been hungry an hour later. I told you last night that we would settle this between the two of us."

"No, by God, we'll settle it right now!" Randy thundered. The roaring baritone voice took his father by surprise, and the older man jolted a half step backward, toward the quietly burning oak in the fireplace.

"Right now is the best time, Father. I'll have it out here and now. The best way is the simplest and the kindest in the long run." He turned toward his sister. "Martha, the truth of this matter is that you are a bastard child. *My* mother is not *your* mother."

Martha gasped. Both of her hands flew toward her face, hovered in mid-air as her eyes widened. Then she sprang to her feet and slapped her brother hard on the cheek.

Instead of reacting with anger, Randy only smiled.

"Yes, I know. I quite understand. It caused me a great deal of pain the first time I learned the truth as well — a fight with a lout of a man who beat me into a miserable jumble of arms and legs. But, dear Martha, you simply had to know. I'm sorry."

Martha felt her knees starting to weaken. She stepped backward and slumped into the chair she had just left. Her mind spun and she fought to maintain her consciousness. She simply would not fold up like some flighty, half-witted girl. But her mother? *Her* mother was not the same as Randy's mother? Then . . .

She couldn't finish the thought. Somewhere a monumental trick had been played on her. She blinked, sniffed back the start of a tear, and looked at her father. His head was lowered, eyes on the crackling fire. He had not leaped to her defense. He had not struck Randy down with parental fury. Why?

She stared at her father again and, this time, his hand made a futile little gesture, then grasped his other hand at his chest. He turned slowly to look at her.

Martha did not need to ask her father if what Randy said were true. She saw it in his eyes. But there was also a pleading there for her to understand, and sorrow, sadness, and an urging that she not prejudge him too harshly.

For a moment, her anger was as great as Randy's. And then a flood of memories and love and a surging compassion flooded through Martha. She rose, steady and sure and walked to her father.

"Randy, leave us alone. I want to talk to Father. We'll call you when we want you to come back."

"I'd rather stay. After all, this has an important bearing on my future too, and . . ."

The look in her eyes stopped him. His mother had written in her letters these past three years that his little sister had developed into a strong, mind-of-her-own business woman. Perhaps it was true.

He made the slightest of bows and walked out of the drawing room, closing the heavy oak door as he left.

Martha went to her father and took his arm. They walked to the big leather couch and sat down close together. She held his hand.

"Randy is right, Father. It's time that I know. I have the right to know who my mother is."

Tears formed in his eyes. She had never seen her father cry. If anyone had suggested that he might be able to cry, she would have laughed. Now she watched a tear spill over his eyelid and roll down his cheek.

He sighed, then turned and looked at her. His eyes were more blue now than she had ever seen them. His hair had lost its golden tone, now blending strands of gray and white. Often she had wondered why she had dark hair while her brother and sister were both so blond. Her mother and father had light hair, too. However, beyond wondering, it had never worried her. But now . . .

Martha looked away, out across the bay at the ships moving on the water. She wondered if she could still see the wharf where the family's Pacific Steamship and Trading Company vessels tied up. Her father cleared his throat. She turned back.

His arms came around her and she leaned in and clung to him. Martha felt the hot tears behind her eyelids now and she let them come. A few moments later, she stopped crying and hugged her father tightly.

"Daddy, there isn't a way in the world that I could love you any more than I do right now. Nothing you have done or could do would ever make that change. If what Randy says is true, that my natural mother is someone I don't know, then I'll just have to learn to live with that. Nothing will ever

12

make me love you and Mother any less. And right now I love you both very much."

"This will make a difference, Martha. I know it will. And I know what you're thinking," he said. "You're wondering how I could take you away from your natural mother. How I could live a lie all these years. And the question that must be the most important to you right now: Who is your real mother?"

Martha found she couldn't talk. She looked up and nodded.

"Martha, your mother is a beautiful lady, a wonderful person I met in San Diego, twenty-two years ago. Her name is Maria Valdez, Maria Consuela Lucinda Valdez. I was down there setting up a small shipping office. Yes, I was married and I loved Abigail. But she was so very far away.

"I fell desperately in love with Maria. A short time later, she became pregnant. I was torn between two loves.

"We moved to San Diego for a year. I told Abigail about it and she forgave me. When we saw how Maria lived, we knew that we must take care of her and of you after you were born. Maria agreed to give up her newborn child and so it was arranged. For several years, we sent her money each month. Then I lost track of her. From what

I could discover, she was — is — doing very well without any help. Maria Valdez was always a proud woman."

Harold Pemberton slumped on the couch. It was as if the story had drained the last bit of strength from him.

"Martha, can you ever forgive me?"

She kissed his cheek. "Father, there is nothing to forgive. To be a child of love is the most wonderful heritage anyone can have. And I'm glad you brought me with you to live here." She paused. "However, if this comes out it could be embarrassing to you and the business."

"Yes, and to Abigail's social standing," he said. "You know how these society women gossip." He paused and watched her. "And what about you? Would you be crushed if the gossips heard about this?"

"Hell, no!" Martha said. Her father chuckled.

"Daddy, I've already raised a lot of eyebrows in the social set. They think I'm terrible now. One more little tidbit won't bother me at all. Of course, it might be a lot easier . . ."

"That's what I've been telling Randall. There are no serious legal problems, no problems at all. We're not a kingdom with rights of succession."

Martha stood and went to the door. She opened it and motioned for Randy to come in.

"If the tears and histrionics are done with, let's get down to business," Randy said, his face serious, but still tinged with anger at being expelled for even a moment. "Father, I presume that you will draw up papers at once eliminating Martha from any rights to the family company, businesses, properties and monies."

"No!" Mr. Pemberton roared. "I damn well won't! I'm running things around here for a while yet, you damn college know-it-all! This makes no difference just because you know. I've known for all these years. And legally — remember that word 'legally,' Randy — Martha is just as much my heir as you are. I have a court order dated almost nineteen years ago stating that fact. It's a legal document ascertaining Martha's parents. Now this is the end of the matter. You've blurted it out, and caused a lot of grief to your sister and to me."

"To my half-sister, Father."

"To your *sister,* and if I ever hear you mention this situation again in public or in private, I'll thrash you myself with a buggy whip."

Randy jolted backward, surprise, disbelief

on his face.

"But you . . . you are going to do nothing? The legal ramifications! The rights of legitimate heirs over illegitimate . . ."

Harold Pemberton slapped his son hard on the face, driving him to one knee.

"*There is no difference!* Martha is my daughter, Penny is my daughter, you are my son. There is no difference whatsoever — not in my love for each of you, nor in your legal standings."

Pemberton bent over his son, his finger almost in the young man's face. "Randall, you will not utter another word about this. I have made my peace with your mother years ago. Just now, Martha and I came to a complete understanding. It shall remain that way. If, at any time in the future, I hear of your communicating in any way a single word about this situation, I shall have you sent to Hong Kong as the last cabin boy on a Chinese slave ship. You won't see San Francisco for ten years. Do you understand what I'm saying? This subject is closed, the discussion is over and done . . . forever!"

Randy blinked, sighed deeply, then got to his feet slowly. Harvard had at least taught him that when you are beaten soundly in an impossible situation, you do not continue to fight. Rather strike your colors and get away and live to fight another day. He looked at Martha, whom he had watched grow from a scrawny kid into a beautiful woman.

"No matter what you say, Father, she's still my bastard sister."

Martha let out a cry of anger and frustration and stormed at him, beat through his surprise and ineffectual flailing arms and scratched deep furrows down his cheeks. She screamed at him as her father took her hands in his and calmly led her away.

Randy looked after her, blood on his cheeks and a combination of surprise and hatred in his eyes.

Martha calmed down almost at once. She had seldom been so angry, so savage, so mind-blindingly furious in her life. Now she softly kissed her father's cheek and ran up the wide staircase to the room which had once been hers on the second floor.

She lay down on the soft bed and, for a moment, wondered if she would cry. She found that she would not, and thought instead of her natural mother — Maria Valdez.

Martha knew that she must find her, see her, learn to know her and love her. Help her any way she might. It was a vital part of knowing who she really was. Oh, she was half-Pemberton, all right, growing up in this house with loving parents: the instruction, training, education, social standing, the environment. But she was also half Valdez, and that half she must discover for herself before she could marry Allen.

Allen! She had rushed away from him less than a week ago. It was only a week and four days since he and Johnnie Laveau had rescued her from that murderous Josiah West and his wife in Seattle. She had recuperated for two days in the hotel and Allen had been there the whole time. They had pledged their love and set the time for the wedding for three weeks hence. Then the sudden message had arrived on board a Pemberton ship. There was a crisis at home, Martha must come home at once, take the first boat south.

She rushed to the docks, held up a boat just ready to leave and hurried on board. She had kissed Allen goodbye and made him promise to follow her within a week. He said he would, and then they would be married as soon as possible. He had no intention of losing her again. He would ask to be transferred to the home office in San Francisco, and they would find a house and live in that beautiful city. It all sounded so wonderful.

Now this.

She simply couldn't let Allen marry her, knowing now what she did. Not yet. She had to investigate that other half of her ancestry. She had to know her natural mother.

Then she could tell Allen about it and, if he still would have her, they would plan the wedding. She would write him a letter in the morning and send it on the next ship going to Seattle. He might be on his way here already. She didn't know.

Martha felt fatigue settling in. She had not even been to her own house yet on California Street, the small home she'd shared with her late husband. Instead, she'd come directly to the Pemberton Mansion on the hill, where Randy had been waiting for her. Then Randy had uttered those terrible words which could rip her world apart, but only if she let them.

Martha turned over, thinking about the many happy hours she had spent in this room, growing up. For a moment she dreamed that she was a little girl again, running when her mother called. Then she came alert. Which mother? Which mother? She closed her eyes in frustration. She should have a nap. Tired, she was tired because she had not slept well on the ship. There had been worry about the crisis, about the letter. It had been signed by Randy, and she had feared that her father had taken sick or had even died.

But she had been the crisis. And Randy — what was he so worried about? He would be the one to take over the firm, the companies and run them. He would manage the larger part of the fortune their father had built up. Was he such a snob that he had to demand an illegitimate sister be publicly disowned?

Randy was thinking only of himself, of course, worried about his inheritance, not thinking what such an announcement would do to their father and mother. He was wrong, as usual. In many ways he was still a child, spoiled and pampered too long. If a young man didn't have common sense, not even four years at Harvard would help.

Martha turned over and looked up at the ceiling. She heard the soft knock on the door and looked up.

"Yes, come in."

The door opened and Penny stood there, concern on her pretty young face.

"I heard you run up the stairs. Are you all right?"

Martha nodded. "Yes, come in and let's have a good talk like we used to. I've been dashing around so fast lately I haven't had a chance to talk." She gazed at her young sister and shook her head slowly. "Penny, while I haven't been watching, you've grown into a beautiful young woman."

Penny smiled at her sister, not quite knowing what to say, or what to do. Martha suddenly seemed like a stranger. Then the stranger was talking.

"You know?" Martha asked.

"Yes, Randy told me. I wish he hadn't. He said I should know." Suddenly Penny ran to her, knelt on the floor and put her face in Martha's lap. Tears came down her cheeks, her soft blue eyes reddened and sobs shook her narrow shoulders.

"Why did he have to spoil things? What difference does it make now? Oh, I hate him! I hate that Randy!"

Martha stroked Penny's long blonde hair. It was so blonde. At least now Martha knew why her own locks were so dark . . . Mexican hair.

Martha suddenly remembered the thousands of incidents growing up with her brother and sister — the good times with hilarious joy and fun, interesting days they spent together, vacations, trips — but with Penny always slightly in the background, a little shy. She never had Martha's sense of adventure. She was never the "me first" type. But she was always there when needed — reliable, more considerate and kind than an older sister often deserved. A good baby sister.

"Penny, I don't see how this can make much difference to us. I'll have a long talk with Mother, and I'm sure it will be tearful. Oh, yes, she's still my mother, just as much as she ever was. Of course, now I know she did not actually bear me, but still, she has nursed me and cared for me, nurtured me when I couldn't do a thing for myself but scream and spit. Now I have two mothers. I'm very lucky because most girls only have one."

Penny's sobbing had stopped now and she sniffed, then used her handkerchief and looked up. "You've talked with Father?"

"Yes. He and mother worked this out twenty years ago, he said. I don't have any anger in my heart toward him, and I hope you won't either. Father is a wonderful man, absolutely brilliant in business. I have nothing but the greatest admiration for him."

Penny only half heard what her sister said. She frowned. Should she think of Martha as her half-sister as Randy had said? Somehow it didn't make any difference to her. Martha was still the same, still her sister. Penny sat up and watched Martha. She followed the line of chatter which wasn't important. She made the appropriate remarks but didn't understand it. Her very own sister was half-Mexican. But then she always had been, hadn't she? And Martha wasn't like the other Mexicans she had seen in town. They were so poor and filthy, and everyone was afraid of them. No, this had to be different.

But to think that her very own father had cheated on her mother and had this Mexican girl in San Diego! And not just once, but many times. Penny wasn't sure how many times you had to make love to get pregnant, but Rebecca Smith said it was five. Yes, she was sure it was five times.

Penny wondered what that would be like, to actually take off your clothes and be alone with a man who took off his clothes, too. She shivered slightly.

Then she realized Martha had asked her something.

"Oh, I'm sorry. I missed that, Martha."

"You certainly did. You were miles away. What I asked was, what are you planning to do now that you're all grown up?"

"Oh, the piano, of course. I've taken it so long. I'll never be on the concert tour, but Mr. Wyandote says I'm progressing nicely. I don't know if he means I'm any good or that I'm doing well enough so he can still collect his fee."

"And after your music?"

"Now you're starting to sound like Mother. I'm going on eighteen now and Mother has promised that I can have a big birthday party. After that, I can start accepting callers — courters! Of course I might just find somebody I like before that and run away and get married." She smiled. "Mother wouldn't like that a bit. Mother has her heart set on me going to Mrs. Bordeaux's School for Young Ladies. It's a finishing school, teaches all the social graces. But I certainly feel finished now."

Martha tried to listen to her sister critically. It was true that she hadn't seen Penny much in the past three years. Oh, Penny had been here all the time, but since Martha's marriage, it had been rarely that they'd seen each other. Now Martha wished she had spent more time with her. She should know her better. Penny had turned into a moody teenager, and Martha hadn't kept up with her. Somehow, Martha suspected a wild streak deep inside Penny that they would not be able to hold down forever.

"Look, Penny, one of these nights I'll have you over to my little house on California Street and we'll talk about just everything.

24

We'll talk about when we were kids, and about friends, and just anything *you* want to talk about. We'll even talk about boys. Okay?"

"Sure, Marty, whenever you say," Penny said. "You know I came in here all mixed up. I thought you would be prostrate with grief or shock or something." Penny shook her head, her blonde hair flying, her heart-shaped face and wide-set blue eyes filled with surprise. "I guess I'd forgotten how strong you really are. You should have Randy killed!"

"Penny, what a terrible thing to say!"

"Well, what he did was a terrible thing. If I were a queen, I think I'd have him flogged."

"I'm not a queen and I don't have time for that, Penny. My next job is to take leave from the store to try to find my real mother. I would guess she's in San Diego or down in Mexico somewhere."

Penny shook her head. "If I were in your situation, I don't think I'd ever want to meet my real mother. She did give you away, remember that. She must not have loved you."

"She gave me away, because she was very poor and she knew Father could take care of me and give me the advantages that she couldn't. I think that was very gallant of her."

Penny stood and walked toward the door. Martha noticed that her figure had blossomed, large breasts, tiny waist, wide hips. Her little sister was a woman already. All except her face which wore a slightly pouting expression as Penny waved and went out the door.

Martha frowned after her for a moment, suddenly worried that Penny might come to some harm before she settled down with a responsible and appropriate husband. But Martha couldn't take time to worry about that for long — she had so much to do. She had to get home to California Street and start making preparations to find her mother. She would ask her father where he had last heard from her and start searching there.

It wasn't the sort of mission she could send detectives on. Word would certainly leak out fast if she did. No, this was a task that she must do herself. She was sure that her father would insist that she take Johnnie Laveau along with her as a bodyguard, and she fit him into her plans. He had come back with her on the ship and should be at his little shack on the outskirts of town. He would be easy to contact. She settled into thinking about her plans for going to San Diego, and perhaps Mexico.

CHAPTER TWO:
MARIA CONSUELA
LUCINDA VALDEZ

San Diego, 1854

Harold Pemberton stood in front of the fire, and remembered another fire in the pueblo of San Diego, twenty-two years ago. He had been there only two days, and was staying in "New Town," right on the San Diego Bay. It was a marvelous natural harbor, but shallow near the shore. Light boats had to ferry goods into landings along the water's edge.

There had been the start of a long wharf into the bay, where ocean-going sailing ships could tie up, but it was not yet completed. It was 1854, and the area had only been won from Mexico in 1846. Along with the rest of California, it was still getting used to the idea of statehood, declared in 1850. There was no good hotel in town. The best place to stay was a hostelry named the Dupont House, and that was where Harold had registered. His interest was in opening a shipping office here and in getting the pier completed. He was negotiating to do both.

At dinner, in the small dining room of the hotel, he noticed a remarkably beautiful young girl, Mexican by her looks. She had flashing black eyes, shimmering raven hair that fell to her waist, and when she turned toward him and smiled, he saw her even white teeth and high cheekbones. All together, it made an enchanting combination. He sucked in a quick breath as he saw her stand, her breasts tight against her white blouse with its scooped neckline. The same evening, he asked some people who she was. The girl was Maria Valdez, daughter of Don Esteban Valdez, who owned the only real cattle ranch in the area, back in the hills toward the Laguna Mountains. Harold was married, but his wife Abigail, was so far away in San Francisco. He was lonely . . .

It took Harold Pemberton almost a week to arrange to meet her. They talked one afternoon in a courtyard, with an ugly old woman along as her *duenna.* The *duenna* interpreted what he said into Spanish, and turned the girl's Spanish into English. She sat between the two of them, like a good chaperone, and he could not even hold Maria's hand. It was a frustrating and futile effort. Harold gave it up as a bad attempt and went back to his work.

29

That same evening, at dusk, a woman came into his room at the hotel. She opened the door without knocking and stood just inside, leaning against the door, her eyes barely visible over a colorful silken scarf which shielded her face. She lowered the scarf and he saw it was Maria. She walked toward where he sat on the single bed.

"*Senor* Pemberton, do you think Maria pretty?"

"Yes."

"You like Maria, no?"

"Yes."

"*Senor* Pemberton, you want to marry with me?" She looked at him directly now, with her head held high, her eyes serious and a little frightened. He saw the tight blouse, her small waist, the tentative smile on her pretty face.

Harold Pemberton stumbled to his feet, hurriedly buttoned his shirt and stood in front of the bed. She came barely to his chest.

"Maria Valdez, it would be a great honor for me to marry with you, but . . ."

He had intended to go on at once, but the sparkling bright smile she gave him, stopped his words. She dropped the scarf and began opening the buttons of her blouse. She kicked off her sandals and stepped closer to him. Harold Pemberton was stunned at this reversal in form from the afternoon when he couldn't even touch her hand. Yet now she calmly unfastened the buttons, one by one, and she spoke English. He could say nothing, only watched her.

"*Mi padre* will be pleased. The whole *rancho* will be happy, too," she said, then let the sides of the blouse swing out. Quickly she let the white cloth slide off her shoulders. There was no other garment over her breasts. He could not stop staring.

Her smile was frozen now. "*Senor* Pemberton, am I pleasing to you?"

"Oh, yes, beautiful, just beautiful. But I should tell you that I'm . . ." He had intended to tell her right then that he was married and it would have ended it. Just one short phrase, just three words.

She walked to the bed and sat down, her breasts moving, doing a dance all their own that had his full attention. Oh, God, he had to tell her! How had it gone so far?

"Sit down, *Senor* Pemberton and we talk."

He sat beside her, making a deliberate effort to keep his hands away from her.

"Maria, you don't understand. Up in San Francisco . . ."

She looked up at him with those black eyes and smiled.

31

"You have business far up in San Francisco. Maria know."

She leaned out and brushed his lips with hers. Then she stood and, in one quick motion, unfastened her blue skirt. It slithered to her ankles. She bent and kissed his lips, then moved past him and stretched out naked on the bed beside him.

He looked at the exquisitely formed girl lying near him and she was more than he could deny himself. He slid off his shoes and lay beside her, then rolled toward her.

By that time, Harold Pemberton did not even think of telling her that he was married. He was only interested in the delightfully exciting girl on his bed, and his own surging needs. For the rest of the long night, Harold thought little of shipping or piers or tonnage.

In the morning, the girl was gone, as silently as she had come.

Harold went back to work. He had the office almost set up and an agreement signed to participate in building the pier, when Maria came back.

Her *duenna* was with her again, and Maria had put on her very finest lace blouse, a headdress and a brilliant skirt with a dozen petticoats. The *duenna* came right to the point. She faced this *gringo* with distaste.

She disliked this whole business. Had from the very first when they sat in the hotel for two days until they could attract Mr. Pemberton. But Maria had done it with gladness in her heart.

"*Senor,* you are Mr. Pemberton?"

"I'm Harold Pemberton, yes."

"And we have talked before. Are you quite ready to come to the *hacienda?*"

"The *hacienda* at your *rancho?* But why?"

"It is the custom," she said, a doubt growing. "The intent must be posted on the church door."

"The intent?" Harold rubbed his jaw. Surely this small, sexy Maria did not really think . . . She'd never even allowed him to protest — to tell her he was married. No, it could not be.

"The marriage contract, *Senor* Pemberton. It must be written and the intent posted. Surely you know this much about our customs."

She had been serious. By the look in Maria's eye, she was still serious. Harold took a step backward. The old woman glared at him.

"*Senora,* I'm afraid there has been a great mistake made."

Maria heard and looked up, her smile fading, her eyes turning cold and angry.

"No mistake," the *duenna* shrilled. "You say you marry with Maria, you go to bed with her. Now you must marry. No mistake."

"Oh, God, what is happening?" Harold said, as furious now with himself as he was with them. "She came to me one night, and we talked about marriage . . . but . . ."

"I not simply talking!" Maria said, tears in her black eyes. "You say you like me. You say you would be honored to marry with me. I accept and we are promised. It is our custom."

"Mr. Pemberton, Maria has four big brothers, all very good with knife and pistol, all very angry. *Por Dios!* I am glad I am not you. You must decide marry Maria, now."

"I can't marry her, I already have a wife — and a son — in San Francisco. I tried to tell Maria, but she wouldn't let me talk and something always stopped me."

"*Madre de Dios!* If I tell Maria's brothers, you will not live until the sun is born again."

"I assure you, madam, it was her idea. She came to my room, I didn't chase after her. She took her clothes off and came to my bed. It was all her doing."

The *duenna* looked at Maria sharply, muttered something and Maria nodded. The old woman whacked Maria with the back of her hand, nearly knocking the girl down. She watched Maria stagger backwards two steps and hang her head.

"Por Dios!" the *duenna* said, then turned to Harold. "You be gone before morning, or many men will be after your *gringo* hide to hang it on the gate posts of our *rancho!"*

Harold moved to the girl, caught her hands and turned her face toward him.

"Why did you do this? I never thought you were really serious about getting married. Why were you so insistent?"

Maria turned away. The *duenna* touched his shoulder.

"The *rancho*. We owe your *gringo* bank much *dinero*. We hear you have much money. Maria say she marry you and save the *rancho* and everyone happy. She say you *muy simpatico*."

They left then, and Harold never felt more like a heel. Once she'd stopped him from talking, he had had no idea she'd been serious. He thought she was just out to get away from her *duenna*, to show him that she really liked him.

That same night, he moved to the second hotel, taking a bed in a room with five other men. In the morning, he heard that three Mexicans had been run out of town when they came in drunk and angry, hunting for him. Harold spent the rest of his time in San Diego working from one of his merchant ships anchored in the bay.

It was two months later, on another trip to San Diego, that he saw Maria again. She was sitting in his room the second day, waiting for him when he came back just before dinner. He had food sent up to the room and she sat on the chair, very proper. Again, she was in one of her finest dresses, with much lace and many petticoats. In a flood of Spanish and English, mixed with torrents of tears, Maria confessed that she was pregnant, and that Harold was the father because she had never been with another man. He had to be the father.

Harold asked her what would happen when her own father discovered this. She said she would be thrown out of the house, disowned by the family, scorned and berated, excluded from polite Mexican society forever. Harold knew something of the situation and the customs. He had heard about this happening before. Now what the hell was he going to do about it? It was his fault. The whole damn thing really was his fault. He should never have talked to the girl in the first place.

She was still the most beautiful creature that he had ever seen, with her coal black hair, her dark eyes, and those demanding, surging breasts.

He asked her to sit beside him on the bed. Then quietly he told her what he would do. He would provide for her, a house there in San Diego, and a companion, a woman to care for her and to serve her. He would be down from time to time, and there would always be enough money. Then he tried to kiss her. She pushed him away.

"You are easy with promises. If it happens, then you may kiss again."

A month later, Harold had moved to San Diego with his wife and small son. The business in San Francisco was sound and his managers there could handle it. He went up the coast regularly to deal with problems and check on the firm in San Diego. He established the pier and docks and set up his shipping business, and later, he opened a retail store. He told Abigail of his total plans. He had confessed his infidelity as soon as he got home and knew the girl was pregnant.

Now he told his wife they would wait for the child, and then, if possible, they would take the baby back to San Francisco with them and tell everyone that it was their own.

As it turned out that proved to be the best for everyone. After the birth, Maria decided she should not keep the child, and she moved to a small Mexican fishing village well below the border. Harold gave her enough money to set up a small *cantina.*

Now, more than twenty-two years later, as he sat on the couch in front of the August fire, Harold Pemberton rubbed his eyes. It was cold this early in August in San Francisco. A sudden fog had moved in, but he felt a chill that had nothing to do with the weather. Was it a premonition? Somehow he feared that this quarrel in his house would have some far-reaching effect, that it would end in tragedy. Exactly what it might be he did not know. He did know that Randy was going to take some time and effort. The boy needed seasoning. Should he be sent to sea for a year or two to learn the feel of that end of the business? Or should Randy begin in the retail side?

Unfortunately, with the latter, Randy would be compared to his sister. She was good enough to make him finish second best. Perhaps in the bookkeeping part, or in buying of goods.

It would take time, but Harold would find the exact spot where Randy fit in and he would begin his apprenticeship. Randy didn't know it yet, but now that he had graduated from Harvard, he was ready to begin his real learning process.

CHAPTER THREE:
RANDY, BLOODY AND BOWED

Randy Pemberton had not stormed from the house in anger. After he did some cleanup work on his scratched face, he found that two short furrows had yielded most of the blood and that his face was not as bad as he had feared. He washed it carefully, patted dry the bleeding parts and stopped their flow with bits of paper. For the evening, he selected a clean white shirt, a broad tie, his best jacket with velvet at the collar and called for his rig. This evening, Madelyn would be the perfect antidote to his ruffled feelings.

He drove savagely, punishing the black, scattering a dozen chickens on one street, and nearly colliding with a heavy dray wagon when the stupid lout of a driver would not give way to him. Randy cursed the man all the way past and was rewarded with an obscene gesture. Randy returned it and ran the black hard for a quarter of a mile before he pulled to a stop in front of a cream-colored clapboard house, set back from the street and surrounded with a white picket fence.

The small gate was open, which was the signal. Randy tied the reins, jumped down from the buggy and barged past the gate. He closed it with a flick of one foot, and strode to the rear of the house, where he went through the back door without knocking. There was no one in the kitchen. He moved into the small parlor. Then he heard someone singing and grinned. Madelyn only sang in one place. He had caught the fair damsel at her bath!

Madelyn had the biggest bathtub in San Francisco — not a round metal one, but a long, wide sit-down tub. Many a time he'd teased her about it being a two-body tub, and she'd only giggled. Now he moved quietly to the bathroom door and edged it open a crack.

Sure enough, Madelyn, with her hair in a towel on top of her head, sat in the filled tub facing him, her pink tipped breasts glowing in the warmth of the water.

He opened the door silently, stepped inside, then snapped the bathroom-door lock in place.

"Well, look what I found in my bathtub!"

41

Randy shouted.

The girl jumped a foot out of the water, quickly tried to cover herself with her arms, then saw it was Randy.

She dropped her arms and pushed her breasts forward.

"Evening, love. Think of the devil and up he pops! You look all spiffed up, Randy-Dandy."

He peeled out of his jacket and put it on the back of the chair. Then unbuttoned his shirt. "Not spiffed up for long. As I've told you, that tub is big enough for two. A shame to waste all of your hot water."

Madelyn looked up quickly. "Oh, now, sir, that is wicked and naughty. You come bursting into my abode and accost me in my bath . . ."

"And don't you enjoy it!"

She laughed. Madelyn was just past thirty somewhere — she never would say where — and had let her girlish curves round out to what she considered as "pleasingly plump." Lots of men told her they liked their women with a little meat on them. They said there was that much more of a girl to love.

Madelyn's face was plain, with a nose a little too large, but her green eyes made up for that. They were cat eyes, interesting,

42

snapping, always changing. At times, they could turn cold and cruel. She claimed the biggest bosom in town, which could have been true, since there was no place for open competition.

She sat there, moving her breasts, which she knew excited this rich playboy, who always had a full wallet when he arrived and a much lighter one when he left. She didn't care if his appetites were a little strange at times. After ten years in the business, she could meet and match any sexual innovation suggested.

"Don't just stand there staring," Madelyn snorted. "Get off those duds and get into the suds." She laughed at her spur-of-the-moment rhyme and splashed water at him.

Madelyn had been delighted when Randy came back from college. He had been her only contact with rich society. When he first left, this source of contact — and information — had dried up. The thing she enjoyed second most was gossip, and she wasn't above using a tidbit for fun or profit whenever she could.

Now she hurried him out of his clothes. He had closed the gate, she was sure, so it would be an all-nighter. Good, and maybe he would let slip some juicy gossip.

Randy pulled off the last of his underwear

and stepped into the tub, sitting so he faced Madelyn. As he did so, he screeched at the heat of the water, then splashed her and reached out and grabbed both her breasts.

"Now this right here, folks, is why I keep coming back, to see the biggest breasts in all of San Francisco and surrounding territories. Yes, yes!"

Before the night was over, Randy had remembered his failure to have Martha disowned, and little by little he let some of the details slip out. Too late he realized what he had done, and as he tilted the whiskey bottle once more, he waggled his finger at the naked Madelyn beside him.

"Not one word about this to anyone, whore. If it gets out that Martha is a bastard, I'll wind up rowing last man on a Chinese slave ship. My old dad guaranteed me that, and he's good for his threats. So not one single little word!"

"That? About your half-sister? Half the town knows that already. Nothing new there. Anyway, you think I'm some kind of gossip?" She rolled over on the bed and caught the bottle. Oh, hot damn, but had she made a score tonight! This was the best bit of society dirt she had ever heard. There must be some way she could make it profitable. The newspapers? No, but maybe the threat of taking it to the papers would pry some hush money loose from that rich bitch. Madelyn would have a talk with her lawyer — customer friend, Mr. Lawrence Masters. He had a way with words — and putting them down on paper — that could do a lot to convince the swells to part with their gold.

Madelyn laughed and rolled over on top of Randy, smashing him into the feather-bed mattress and bringing a howl of glee from the drunken young man.

Morning produced the sun as well as a monstrous ache that tore at Randy's head with a mounting fury. Madelyn made him lie down, dressed him in spite of his lewd suggestions, and then fed him three cups of coffee.

All night she had been thinking of the grand things she would do when she had that snippety Pemberton woman under her heel. What was the slut's name now? She was married, a widow, a Mrs. something or other. Then she remembered: Mrs. Peter Dyke. Yes, Mrs. Dyke, dear — divinely rich, Mrs. Dyke — there is going to be a surprise for you. Oh yes, a real surprise. But Madelyn hadn't quite figured out just what it would be. Her lawyer was good at that.

By ten that morning, Randy could stagger

around the room. Then he had one quick shot of whiskey and went out to his carriage. An hour later he had patronized one early morning bar and then drove to the big building where Pacific Steamship and Trading Company had its offices.

His father was not in, his secretary said.

"Where'd he go?" Randy asked, aware of a slight slur in his speech.

"I'm sure that I do not know," Mrs. Tausch said, her nose tilted to indicate it was none of Randy's business.

Randy looked at her. She was about thirty-five, he guessed, and he couldn't tell from the dress she wore if she had any particular female parts or not. Dumb, stupid woman. He stared pointedly at her chest, and she turned, flustered, upset, unsure of herself.

Randy laughed at her and walked into his father's office, closing the door behind him. She was right. The old patriarch wasn't there.

Randy sat down in the big leather chair behind the square oak business desk and began pulling out drawers. He had just found the bottle of whiskey in the back of the lower drawer, and taken it out, when his father walked in.

"Get out of that chair!" Harold Pemberton roared. "When you earn the right to sit there, you'll sit, but not before. You don't know a thing about this company, do you realize that? You could be halfway to an expert now, but you spend all of your time whoring and drinking.

"No more, you hear me, Randall? No more whoring all night and drinking all day. You'll report to work tomorrow morning on the docks, hauling in goods, unloading ships, moving merchandise in wagons to various stores and warehouses. And you'll stick to it and act like a man, for a change. Do you hear me, Randall?"

"Yes, I hear you. I don't have any work clothes."

"Then go to a store and buy some. Do you have any money left after being out all night?"

"Enough."

Harold wrote a name and address on a slip of paper and gave it to his son.

"You'll report to this man in the morning at that address. He has complete authority to instruct, chastise or fire you, so watch your step."

"Yes, Father, I will. Now if you're through spanking me for being a naughty boy, I'd like to say something. I'll be taking an apartment of my own. It's past time I was out of your house. I have enough money, and I think it's time I do settle down a little. I'm really going to try to learn the business. Lord knows, I'm not fit to do anything else. I'm not a poet, or a philosopher, or even a teacher."

"Randall, I think that will be an excellent move, and getting your own place is fine, too. As for the drinking, there can be none of that while on duty. Company policy. About the girls, try to be a little more discreet."

"The way you were in San Diego, Father?"

Harold Pemberton lowered his head. "That's your last shot on that subject, Randall. We won't mention it again. I just hope that you don't make the kind of a mistake you'll have to live with the rest of your life. Always fighting — trying to make it all right again — but knowing that you have ruined a life and can never make it whole." Harold sat down at the big desk. Randy hadn't moved.

"Perhaps you should go see about your new quarters. The dock crew begins work at half past six in the morning. I suggest you get there a half hour early on your first day."

"I'll be there." Randy left and Harold hoped that he succeeded, that he showed up for work every day for the next three months. That was the stint that had been planned for Randy on the docks. Then three months in each and every department of the whole sprawling business.

It would take several years, but would prove invaluable in the long run, when Randy became manager and then president of the vast firm.

On his way out of the office, Randy went past the bookkeeping rooms. There had been a thin, winsome little girl working there who had caught his eye three years ago. She had been only seventeen then. That would make her twenty now. Inside the bookkeeping rooms, he saw her. The touch of red in her light hair was more pronounced now. Her hair was still long, which made him happy. She sat on a stool, working on a set of books. She was small, dainty. Her face had a tipped up nose, eyes of such delicate blue it seemed as if they would break if she even blinked, and a finely formed mouth.

He had never spoken to her, never squired her anywhere, had hardly seen her more than a dozen times, but he had remembered her. Oh, how he had remembered! She looked up and saw him, but at once glanced away. He relaxed. Her eyes had not shattered after all.

He would always remember her name, Amelia Borcherding. Amelia. He had never even said her name out loud, as though that might tarnish it somehow. He moved toward her aisle and deliberately walked past her. She did not look up. At the back of the room, he watched her for a time. Three years ago, he had made some discreet inquiries about her. She had a widowed mother and an older sister. They all worked. Her father had died in the smallpox outbreak in seventy-one. They had no social standing at all, which didn't bother Randy. He wasn't the snob he sometimes pretended to be.

Randy took one more look at her, then hurried out the door and down the stairs. He had to get ready to go to work. His outburst yesterday with Martha might have been a good thing. He was first in line to inherit the company. Of course, it would go in pieces and parts as stock to all of the members of the family. But it would be his responsibility to run the business and hold it together. At least now, he wouldn't worry and fret about Martha. It was out in the open with his father. At the time, it seemed that he had to make a point of it. Now it was behind them and he was glad.

Martha could take it. She was the tough one in the family. Much harder and stronger than he was. It probably was her Mexican blood. He had no doubt that one of the first things Martha would do now was to try and find her natural mother. It would be the type of action Martha would take.

Now to concentrate on work. His father at one time had said that if Randy ever came into the company, it would be at the bottom, and he would have to work his way up. From what he knew, there was no point lower in the company than a dock worker for Pacific Steamship. So here he was, right at the bottom. He would work hard at it, now that he was committed. Work hard and do well and learn everything that he could. Bottom or not, but he was determined to storm up the ladder as fast as he possibly could!

CHAPTER FOUR:
ALLEN CORNELIUS AT SEA

Allen Cornelius stood at the rail of the filthy scow wondering at the events that had brought him here. He was heartsick — filled with anger and resentment. He should have been on his way to San Francisco, to the woman he loved. Instead, he was a prisoner on this hell hole of a ship.

Allen couldn't believe it was only days ago that he'd stood on the dock in Seattle, watching Martha Dyke climb the gangplank, boarding the Pacific steamship *Enterprise,* bound for San Francisco. He knew then he should be going with her. Every fiber in his body longed to go. But there were a few things here he had to take care of first. He had to get the office straightened out and leave Caleb Jones in charge. One day for the office should be enough. Then another day to find someone to take care of his small son, a suitable boarding house to care for him for a short time. Then he would close up the house.

It was only three days later, that he should have been going up a gangplank himself, on the way to San Francisco and his marriage to Martha Pemberton Dyke. He had waited so long for that day, endured so much!

The rest of that first afternoon, the day he'd seen Martha off, Allen worked out the change of command with Caleb. The man had been his assistant but Allen had done much of the work himself. There should be nothing difficult coming up, so Caleb could handle it.

Allen implied that there might be a promotion shortly, and he would suggest someone from within the firm itself be named operations manager here in Seattle. Perhaps Caleb himself might be picked.

At the end of that day, the two men left the office and stopped at the Pine Cone Tavern. "Just two drinks to celebrate your new move, and your new bride — to a whole new life!" Caleb had said. Caleb wasn't a drinking man, and Allen was afraid before he got Mr. Jones home, he would be roaring drunk.

"Best damn boss in the whole Washington Territory!" Caleb said.

Allen grinned and relaxed as he had another drink with his friend. Caleb would

have a hard job trying to understand everything at once, but he could do it.

Before he realized it, Allen had downed
three shots of whiskey, and the lamps in the
dim tavern were starting to weave and waver
all on their own.

Allen ordered another round, but before it
came, Caleb toppled off the stool at the bar
and slithered to the sawdust floor.

Allen started laughing. He couldn't stop.
The barkeep slapped his face hard. Allen
blinked and the laughing ceased.

"You want your last drink, friend?" the
bar man asked. Allen waved his hand at the
man and stood, suddenly needing to find
an alley where he could breathe some cool
air. He aimed his body for the back door,
made it with only one small encounter with
a three-legged stool, and weaved into the
black Seattle night air. He stumbled against
something when he heard noises behind
him. There was a chuckle, then he felt arms
at both sides helping him stand. They were
friendly arms, swimming, blurred, friendly
faces.

"Hey, we going for another little drink?"
Allen asked.

"Sure, sure as hell are. One last shot," one
of his helpers said.

"Hey, I know you?" Allen asked, trying to focus.

"Doubt it mate, doubt it."

The trio walked another fifty feet and stopped. One man rapped on a side door.

Allen giggled. "Hey, this is a house of ill . . . house of . . . a whorehouse."

"Yeah, but they got good whiskey."

"Real good whiskey?" Allen asked.

"The best grog in the world, mate — the very best."

When the door closed behind them, a huge woman in a robe stalked in. Sweat beaded her forehead.

"Christ, is that another one? How many you getting tonight, anyway? How many do they need?"

"Whatta you care, Maude? Just open the doors for us."

The men propelled the unprotesting Allen through two doors, then into an alley where a covered buggy sat waiting.

"Time to put the lights out, mate," the large man said. He bounced an empty whiskey bottle off Allen's head. He sagged like a sack of wet flour.

When Allen woke up an hour later he was bound and gagged. It was dark. He had sobered up enough to realize he had been kidnapped. But where was he and why did they want him?

His prison was swaying, whatever it was. He listened closer and heard a horse and the creak of leather. He was being driven somewhere. Allen tried to cry out but the gag stopped that. He breathed shallowly, afraid he might gag on the strap through his mouth and vomit. He'd heard of men being drowned in their own vomit.

Allen's next thought was that he had been shanghaied. But if they were going to put him on a ship, why the carriage? No, it had to be something else. He tried to ease up to the edge of the carriage from the floor, to look out the window flap, but he couldn't make it.

A moment later, the rig came to a stop and the door opened. He was hauled out of the buggy like a sack of potatoes. Now Allen could smell the sea. Where were they? He couldn't see a thing and remained limp with the hope he might do damage to one of his kidnappers.

They carried him a few yards and draped him in the end of a small boat. A boat? Then he knew.

The shanghai experts had found a way to fool the Seattle marshals who were keeping a good watch on all ships about to debark. He would be put in a boat, rowed into the sound, where the small craft would come up on the water side of a ship. There the marshals couldn't see them.

Allen's foot lashed out suddenly, toppling one of his attackers into the water. The other guard laughed, and brought the empty bottle down on Allen's head again. Allen knew nothing more for over an hour.

When he awoke, they were at sea. He could tell by the gentle roll of the ship that they were still in the sound. Allen decided he was in one of the upper holds, cushioned on a set of sails, next to a dozen barrels. In the faint light he could only guess that the barrels were filled with rum. He was still bound hand and foot, but his gag was gone and his breathing came easily.

Ever since he had arrived in Seattle, he had heard about the hundreds of men each year who were shanghaied onto ships. In any port there were deserters, many of them men who had been forced to work on board a ship at some other port. The quota had to be filled and the old British legal system of press gangs couldn't be worked there in the Washington Territory. So they kidnapped drunks. Taverns and whorehouses remained the two best hunting grounds for the shang-haiers. A good strong man in the hold was worth twenty dollars to whoever delivered him. Many of the honest men in Seattle worked all month for twenty dollars hard cash.

Allen tested the knots. They were seaman tied and he wouldn't get them loose with his teeth alone. All he could do was wait and hope that he had drawn an honest master who would be fair with the crew once they were away from the Puget Sound islands. Many men would try to swim five or six miles to an island rather than be shanghaied. So all the new men were kept tied up until the ship was well out beyond the straits of Juan de Fuca, and until they had seen the last of Cape Flattery.

Allen tried to relax. Unlike most men who get shanghaied, he at least knew what was coming, what kind of a life it would be. With his two years at sea as a third mate on a Pacific Steamship craft, he had all of his maritime skills and a lot of knowledge about officer country as well. He knew one fact for certain. He wouldn't be going to San Francisco on Thursday. He quit fighting it and went to sleep.

"Wake up, mate, the joy ride's over. It's work your arse off sunup till dark from now on. Look alive!"

Allen came awake at once, saw that his legs and hands were untied. He stretched and rubbed at the chafed places on his wrists.

"What vessel am I on and where are we bound?" Allen barked out like a first mate who was accustomed to being answered.

The man who had untied him frowned and took a step back.

"None of your business. But I can tell you've been to sea before, mate. We'll have a talk with the captain about you. He's an honest man, but he'll work you hard. Up the ladder now. Get to the fo'c'sle and find a wedge to call your own. Keep your head about you, man, and you'll get along fine."

It was a long speech for the sailor who, Allen now saw, had only one eye and a left arm he carried in a constant crook because his elbow didn't work.

"The ship, what's her name?" Allen asked.

"*The Contessa,* that's what. A bloody countess," the sailor said with a laugh. "More of a whore if you ask me."

When they came on deck, Allen groaned. The smells in the half-filled hold had been normal enough — salt brine, old wood, sails, musty dampness. But on deck, the working half of the ship was strewn with trash and garbage. The lines lay in jumbled masses. A torn sail lay where it had been dumped by the men aloft. An empty water keg rolled around the deck. And the stench!

"You call this pigsty a ship? Smells like she hauls garbage out of Portland."

The sailor nodded. "Yep, you've got a nose on you. And you been to sea before. You should know enough to keep you alive — that is, if you know how to keep your mouth shut." He stepped over a jumble of rope and led Allen to the bow where the fo'c'sle held half of the working seamen.

"I'd like to see the captain," Allen said.

"Sure, I'd like to be President. Now get below and claim a bunk and be ready to work. This ain't no pleasure cruise for you, mate."

Allen stared into the man's eyes, then went down the ladder into the fo'c'sle. He'd seen many ships, but none quite as filthy as this one. The whole crew could work on cleanup and repainting for a year and not be done. The odor of unwashed bodies, human feces and urine assaulted Allen as he went below. There was no way to avoid it. Thirty men were jammed into the fo'c'sle, where fifteen might live comfortably. Bunks had been built floor to ceiling.

He took the only empty space, the top bunk. He was told he would be on the next watch unless they had to change sails. Then all hands reported to the deck at once.

He heard his name called and ran up the

ladder to the deck where a bull of a man stood with a short leather whip in his hands.

"Allen, is it?" the man said. "I'm third mate on board this scow. I crack the whip and you jump. Hear you've been to sea before."

"Yes, sir, two years." The mate was a seaman of the old school who had come up through the ranks. He had a broken nose and scars on both cheeks. He'd lost one finger on his left hand and showed the look of a man more at home fighting than being civil.

Now the mate frowned. "After two years, you should know port from starboard. What rate did you hold?"

Allen hesitated. "Seaman," he said.

The mate scowled this time. "I'd be saying you look more like officer country, mate, but we'll see, and we'll be watching you, remember that. Nobody in the whole world knows you're on board the *Contessa*. Your kith and kin don't have the slightest notion. You give us trouble and you go over the side like a dead codfish. Nobody is the wiser. You stay out of trouble on my ship and you stay healthy. Any argument with that?"

"No, sir."

The big third mate grinned. "Hell, you might work out all right after all. Remember, Allen. Here you're no better'n a stow-away. You shape up, tend to your business, and work hard and, in a year, we hit port and turn you loose."

"A year? That long a voyage?"

"That's right. Now no more questions. Just work those sails like you know how and you eat. Don't work and you don't eat." The third mate slapped the leather whip into his hand and stared at Allen for a moment more, then he let the five long leather strips fall from his hand so Allen could see how they were bound to the end of a two foot ironwood handle. It was a deadly weapon and Allen was sure the third mate could use it. He stared at Allen a moment longer, then turned and went back toward the quarter deck.

Allen dropped into the terrible smell of the hold. The only saving factor was something he had learned long ago. The human nose can react to a new scent only for about ten seconds. Then the scent is minimized and the body actually forgets it is there. It takes a breeze, a movement, something to change the air around the nose to bring new scents or reinforce old ones. This time in the fo'c'sle, Allen looked around. A dozen men were sleeping. Others lounged on the hard bunks. A young man Allen guessed to be eighteen came up.

"They catch you back in Seattle?"

"Yes."

"Welcome to this floating prison. Only eight of the thirty in here are volunteers. They caught me in a whorehouse down in Portland. They dropped me down through a trap door into a tunnel under the street and threw a cargo net over me. They had me tied up before I knew what happened. I didn't even have my pants on yet. Then they pushed me into a box and swung me on board and into the hold."

"What's your name?"

"Lonnie. Lonnie Jenkins." He held out his hand.

"I'm Allen Cornelius, from Seattle. Do you know where we're headed?"

"Not sure. One of the volunteers said he heard the officers talk about Hawaii, then the South Seas. Sometimes he hears right."

Lonnie seemed younger than at first. A tousle-headed youth with a happy grin, gangling arms, and a powerful upper body, he was five-feet eleven and wore jeans and a striped shirt.

"How long you been on board?" Allen asked.

"Over three months. We went to San Francisco from Portland, then up to Seattle.

They keep us locked in the fo'c'sle whenever we can see land. Use the voluntary men for tying up and handling cargo. But at least they feed us. How much were you worth to Shanghai Joe in Seattle?"

"Twenty dollars was the going rate."

"I brought fifteen in Portland. If I'd known that I'd have gladly paid the fifteen greenbacks myself and stayed on shore."

Allen nodded. From his study of the fo'c'sle, this was an unusually rough-looking group of sailors. The volunteers were together in the best bunks toward the middle of the fo'c'sle, where the roll and pitch would be felt least. His own bunk was at the very bow of the craft and he'd be rocked to sleep with every little pitch.

Allen began thinking about Hawaii. If they were headed there, it meant he had very little time to cook up anything before they came near the islands. He'd keep his eyes open and learn the routine of the ship. If they had any kind of favorable winds, they would be at sea for about two weeks before reaching Hawaii. It was precious little time to learn who his friends might be, and who would reval a plot for an extra few scrapes of dry bread.

Right then, he didn't have any planning time. He heard the pipe and the shouts. The wind had changed and all hands were called on deck. He saw the problem at once. A shifting wind had ripped one of the lower sails in half. A dozen men were already aloft, cutting the flapping canvas away so a new sail could be hoisted.

The first mate jabbed Allen's ribs with an ironwood club.

"On your way, on your way! Up those lines! Help on the upper cross arm. Lively, now!"

And Allen was running for the rat lines up the mast, then walking the lines out on the first spar, unthreading the weather-hardened rope as it snaked through the large grommets where they held the dead half of the sail to the spar pole. The four men barely had the task done when the new sail came. Five more men stormed up the lines to help hold the canvas in place, as they made the upper end fast to the spar and tied it securely. Then it was let out fully and caught the freshening breeze. The craft shuddered, then lunged forward with a new will, quartering into the wind, ploughing through the sea on course, as the sweating seamen went down the rat lines to the deck.

The outing gave Allen a chance to evaluate the craft. The *Contessa* was a three master, square set, with plenty of canvas, and he guessed about sixty men and officers. There was simply not enough time to work up a majority of the crew into any kind of a takeover before they got to Hawaii. But even if only half the crew were shanghaied into serving, it would make his work easier.

As Allen walked the rolling deck toward the fo's'cle, he saw the third mate backing Lonnie Jenkins against a bulkhead.

"And I say you're a yellow belly, Jenkins. You went up the lines all right, but then you just hung on. For a month, you've been shirking. Now take off your shirt, yellow belly!"

The boy shook his head.

"Take it off or I'll cut it off you!"

Slowly Lonnie unbuttoned his shirt and pulled it off.

"Turn around and take your medicine. The next time I tell you to get aloft, you not only run, you work!"

The whip sang through the air and the five thin strips of leather cut into the soft skin of Lonnie's back. He screamed and fell to the deck.

The third mate rolled him over with his boot and laid the lash to the bleeding back again, then kicked Lonnie in the side.

"Next time, son, you do like you're told."

The mate walked aft. Allen ran to Lonnie

and helped him stand, then half-carried him into the fo'c'sle.

They had no medicine to treat the cuts. Allen harangued a sailor out of his spare shirt and tore it into dressings. He found a cup of whiskey that he sloshed over the lash marks. Lonnie screamed as the alcohol burned away the danger of immediate infection, then passed out. Allen finished treating his back, then bandaged the welts and slashes. With help, he laid Lonnie in his bunk on his stomach. Allen shook his head and watched Lonnie. Why did the power of command turn some men into absolute beasts? He never had been able to figure that out.

The boy would recover, if they could keep the wounds from festering. Allen lay on his own bunk trying to work out some plans. Taking over the ship would be hard. Slipping overboard near some inhabited island would be best, but the chances were that whenever any land was in sight the shanghaied men would be locked below. He would have to wait and watch.

Twice that first day, after Lonnie's whipping, they were needed topside, and Allen made sure the boy was beside him. He helped Lonnie work, getting it done quickly, making the lashing right and fast. The boy learned quickly, but he held an abiding hatred now for the third mate.

"Blockton is like a mad dog," Lonnie said that night. "He should be killed and thrown overboard."

Allen looked around, hoping no one else had heard. "Easy! That kind of talk can get you killed. Each officer usually has a spy in the fo'c'sle. Talk softly, Lonnie, and stay alive."

The first few days dragged by for Allen. He kept thinking where he should be, what he should be doing. Then he shut his mind to such subjects, concentrated on doing everything right on board the ship, and staying out of trouble.

Food was worked in six-man messes. Each group drew rations and cooked the simple, often rancid food for themselves over small charcoal fires. A little salt pork and moldy bread made up their diet the first week.

Allen survived it. He'd had less and worse on some voyages when the winds refused to blow and rations ran low.

The fifth day out, he fashioned a fish hook from a strong nail and baited it with bits of thread and colored yarn pulled out of the men's clothes. A seagull landed on deck and one sailor threw a net over it, then scalded it and cooked it for his dinner. Allen picked up the discarded feathers and added more appeal to his lure. He covered the hook completely with feathers and red and blue yarn he salvaged from a pair of knit socks.

For fishing line, he wrangled fifty yards of heavy canvas sewing string from the sail maker, on the promise that he would share in the catch. Lead weights were added and the next time they saw what the sailors called "little whales" — porpoises, Allen once heard a man calling them — he was ready. He dropped his lure over the stern with half a pound of lead six feet up the line, then let the string play out.

When he served with Pacific Steamship, he had discovered that when they found the jumping fish the man called porpoises, there would often be a school of large hungry fish under them. They had let down deep fishing lines and caught large fish with yellowish fins. Often the *Star of the Sea* would alter its course to approach such schools of the jumping porpoise to try for the big fish underneath. Many times, they landed some. Their captain always claimed the choicest fillets.

Now Allen saw that the ship was cutting directly across the path of the jumping "little whales" and he tied the end of his line to the ship's rail and held the surplus in his hands, which he had protected with a pair of stout gloves bought with his day's food ration. Allen tugged on the line hopefully but felt no answering pull. They were almost past the school of porpoise when the line came alive, jerked out of his hand, and the rest of the spool of string spun off and tightened at the knot he had put around the railing.

With all the excitement of his first fishing bite, Allen reached for the taut line and gave it a gentle pull. Something tugged back. He tried to draw in his prize, hand over hand, and had a dozen yards of line on the deck when he felt a surge by the fish below. He had to let the line he had gained slip back into the sea.

Another seaman, a huge dark brown man who said he was a native of Hawaii, came and watched, then offered to help. Together they pulled in line, played it out when the pressure built too high, then worked the line in again when the fish tired.

It took them over half an hour to gain enough line so they could see the white flash of the fish's belly as it turned over and swam for the depths. The fish was getting tired, but so were the men on the line. They pulled again and, this time, worked the fish to the surface, where it splashed through the swells, made one more desperate dash for freedom, and then came alongside the big ship, exhausted.

The trouble was that the beast lay quietly in the water, ten feet below, and the string was not strong enough to lift the creature over the rail.

The big Hawaiian, who said his name was Kona, motioned for Allen to wait. He sprinted away and came back with half of a grappling hook tied to a long pole. He pushed the sharp hook under the fish and pulled.

There was a cheer from the crew watching on deck. The third mate was there, too, his hands on his hips, waiting.

Together Allen and Kona hauled the big fish over the side and dumped it flopping on the deck, its tail beating a tattoo on the boards. It was over four feet long and Allen was sure it weighed more than sixty pounds. This one, too, had the long yellow fins.

A dozen men charged, eager to get part of the fresh fish. Allen stomped on one hand, blasted his fist into another face and was aiming a kick when a pistol shot boomed into the late afternoon sunshine. Everyone stopped where he was.

"Stand back, all you scum. Your little fish will be on the officers' menu tonight.

Stand back!"

Blockton stood over the fish, pushed a knife through its head, killing it, then took the lure from deep in its mouth and tossed it back to Allen. "The next catch is for your mess. This one is for the captain."

"But . . . there's enough to feed sixty men there."

Blockton laughed. "A good officer enjoys wasting food while the scum in the fo'c'sle starve. No more backtalk, Allen, or you won't eat for three days."

Allen took the lure, saw where the fish's teeth had begun to cut through the tough sail cord. He cut off the lure, took off three feet of the line, then tied the hook on again with more knots than he had used before. That was the biggest yellow-finned fish he had ever caught.

Allen fished again, but this time the porpoise were gone. The lure was at the end of its length of line for a half hour before he felt the tug of a fish. By the pull Allen knew this one was much smaller. He had Lonnie help him pull in the catch, and assured Kona that he and his mess would share it.

"This one is for the fo's'cle," he said. "We'll feed as many men as we can." There was a small cheer and, as it quieted, Allen saw the captain taking his nightly walk around the small quarter deck. The man did so everyday to watch the sunset, whether the weather was cloudy or bright. This time, he paused in his rounds and looked at the fish the third mate showed him. For a moment Allen thought he saw a note of pleasure on the captain's face, then the look was gone and he motioned the man away.

Allen was disappointed that most of the big fish would be wasted. Entirely wasted on the officers of this ship. He hadn't seen an officer so far that he would let on board a Pemberton ship.

Rather than think himself into a fury, Allen concentrated on the smaller fish, and within ten minutes, had the prize on board. It was half the size of the other yellow fin. Kona took over and gutted the thirty-pound fish. Then he slid his sharp knife along the backbone, slicing from just in back of the head all the way to the tail, leaving the backbone intact. He flipped the slab of fish onto the desk and cut the fillet into three pieces.

Kona gave the three slabs of meat to three different fo'c'sle messes, then cut out the three-pound fillets from the other side and gave one to Allen, kept one himself and took the last one to the sailmaker. Someone eagerly pounced on the fish's head to cook for soup, and another man made off with the backbone so he could cook out the tender meat from around the thin slab of bones.

That night half the crew ate better than they had in weeks.

The next day, third mate Blockton found Allen on deck.

"How in hell did you catch those two fish, Allen?"

"I knew where to fish. When I was on the other ship, I learned how."

"Tell me how you did it or I'll use you for shark bait." As Blockton said it, he took out his new six-gun revolver and frowned. "I wouldn't want to have an accident with my new six-shooter, now, would I?"

Allen shrugged. "You should be trailing two lines all the time. One on the surface and one down about fifty feet. We found that whenever we saw a school of the 'little whales,' there was a good chance there would be a school of the yellow fin fish under them. An old man on the other ship said the big school of deep-feeding fish frightened many smaller fish upward where the 'little whales' would do their own eating."

The third mate rubbed his face. "Sounds crazy to me, but it worked. I'm making you our fisherman. First catch goes to the officers, then to the men. Whenever the lookout or the helmsman spots your 'little whales' on the top, we'll make a course change if we can to get close to them."

He paused. "Don't think this is my idea. The captain ordered it. I'd let you fish for the officers only if I could. The captain said it was the best-tasting fish he's ever eaten. Insisted that I give the rest of that big one to the men aft." He turned to go. "You're also authorized to get the ship's metalsmith to help you make some better hooks."

Allen smiled as the third mate walked away. At least his small experiment wasn't going to be a total loss. After that, they had two lures in the water in all but the foulest weather, and caught their share of fish. Allen had the metalsmith make him some hooks with barbs on them, and three points. The treble hooks were buried in larger feather and yarn lures that certainly looked good enough to eat.

The second afternoon of fishing, Lonnie was flogged again. He had spoken back sharply to Third Mate Blockton. This time Lonnie's hands were tied to the mast so he couldn't fall and he was given five lashes by Blockton.

Allen and Kona carried the bleeding

young man into the fo'c'sle. This time there was no whiskey to clean and seal the cuts. Allen washed his back with fresh water, then put on some salve one of the other men said he thought might help.

The next day was the fourteenth since they left Seattle. Kona said he could almost smell his home islands. He volunteered to take the lookout until darkness, hoping he might spot one of the first of the chain of the Hawaiian islands so he could dive overboard and swim for shore. But the islands did not appear.

There were four others in Allen's mess beside Lonnie: Halligan, an Irish rogue who had spent half his life at sea; Warnick, another shanghai victim from San Francisco, who had been sold to the boat because he couldn't pay a gambling debt; Rosales, a Mexican, who spoke little English but was the best seaman of the entire crew; and Arizona Smith, a man who had never seen the ocean before his trip to San Diego where he visited a brothel, and got drunk. Next thing he knew he'd been shanghaied and thrown on board *Contessa* — all within two hours after arriving in town.

Halligan would have stayed drunk all the time if he could have gotten enough whiskey. He said he was better on the sails when he was half-drunk than sober, because he knew no fear that way. Halligan finished the last bottle of whiskey he smuggled aboard, and now, as the dry spell lengthened, his belligerence increased. He was a voluntary seaman, but the pressed men did not resent him as they did the others. They felt sorry for Halligan and his continual battle with the bottle.

The men settled into a sea routine of work, eat and sleep. The weather was predictable and calm. More and more, Allen worked on his ideas for a plot that would allow him to escape. As yet, he knew only two men he could trust, Kona and Lonnie.

The boy had been flogged a third time, even before the wounds had healed, and now his back was looking ugly. Allen knew Lonnie needed real medical attention.

Kona kept telling Allen that they were very close to Hawaii.

"I can tell by the smell of the breeze," he said, "and the birds. I saw a bird yesterday that lives only on Hawaii."

The *Contessa* had been out of Seattle sixteen days when the first speck of land was reported by the lookout, just at dusk. The next morning, they would be locked below deck. There was no chance for a *coup* now.

Lonnie headed back from the stern where he had emptied the slop jar. He met Third Mate Blockton who was waiting for him. The mate yelled something at Lonnie. The youth had been angry all morning because his back was not healing properly, and because he figured that Blockton had singled him out as a whipping boy. Lonnie kept on walking toward the mate.

"Hey, scum, you forgot part of the slop," Blockton said. "A big turd is carrying the slop jar, why didn't you throw that one overboard too?"

Lonnie growled but kept his angry words inside.

"Lonnie, you're nothing but a stupid shit-head, you know that? You're so dumb you've got piss for brains. Your mother must have slept with a syphilitic goat to breed you."

Lonnie dropped the slop jar, roaring his anger he surged forward, clamping his big arms around the third mate before the surprised man could leap aside. The two crashed backwards, bounced off some gear and smashed onto the deck. Lonnie sat on Blockton's chest hammering the mate's face with angry fists. Blockton had clipped his head on a cask as he fell and was uncon-scious.

Two sailors sat near by watching. Neither

cheered, but there was no move either to part the pair or stop the fight. The second mate, Mr. Parmlee, ran up to them and hit Lonnie with both fists in the back of the neck, then dragged the younger man off Blockton.

The third mate was still unconscious.

"You and you," the second mate thundered, picking out two volunteers. "Lend a hand here. Carry Mr. Blockton to his bunk. Look alive, now!"

The sailors carried the limp form to officer country and stowed him in his bunk. They said he was still out when they left him, and his breathing was uneven. His nose was smashed, one eye closed and his face half purple, the men recounted with glee.

Mr. Parmlee ordered Lonnie into the lower hold where he was put in chains. He would have his trial the next day. Striking an officer on board the *Contessa* carried a punishment of death. Since Lonnie was shanghaied, there would be little danger of any challenge to the verdict if it were death.

Allen worried all that night. He had asked to give Lonnie's defense. He knew nothing of the law, but had sat in on a trial or two of this kind on board the *Star of the Sea.* Those had been proper trials, with rules of evidence, challenges, and proper procedures. Allen had no misconceptions that such would be the case here. This would be a mock trial, and he had to be careful or he would be in trouble as well. But he owed the lad a fighting chance. There was little doubt in his mind what the eventual outcome of the trial would be. Allen wondered if the whole thing would take more than ten minutes.

The trial was set for dawn, the traditional time for hangings on board ships. Allen stood near the quarter deck. Lonnie, still with chains on hands and feet, was placed near the aft mast facing the judge. The captain, who sat in a chair brought from his cabin, would preside.

The captain's name was Adrian, Captain Lucas Adrian, and Allen heard he had been at sea for forty-five of his fifty-five years. He was a medium-sized man given to overweight and, some said, half eaten away with gonorrhea. His face was round, with slightly puffy cheeks that wore a perpetual red tinge. His hair had entirely gone on top, but snowed gray plumes on each side. He looked down at a single sheet of paper with a scrawl on it.

"This court is called to order. The accused, one Lonnie Jenkins, step forward."

Lonnie shuffled up a step. The captain

looked at him, then at Second Mate Parm-lee. "Go ahead, George."

"Captain, yesterday I came upon the accused beating the prostrate and unconscious body of Third Mate Blockton, as he lay on the deck. Jenkins had to be forcibly removed from the body. Blockton was injured severely with what we think is a serious concussion, lacerations of the face and scalp and a broken nose. He is in his bunk and will not be ready to return to service for at least a day."

The captain looked bored. He glanced toward the west, but none of the islands the lookout thought he had spotted at dusk, the day before, now showed. It had been a false sighting, probably a low-lying dark cloud.

"You did then actually see with your own eyes this seaman striking his superior officer, one Third Mate Blockton?"

"Aye, Captain, that I did. Struck him repeatedly."

"Thank you, Mr. Parmlee. Is there any defense?"

"Aye, Captain, sir. Mr. Allen acting for the defense."

"Proceed."

Allen looked at Lonnie and winked, then walked toward the captain. He stopped ten feet away so he could not be accused of assault upon an officer.

"Captain, the accused, Lonnie Jenkins, is a boy under eighteen. He is serving as a prisoner and against his will on this craft, having been illegally kidnapped from his hometown of Portland. He is in involuntary servitude aboard this vessel and has every legal right to demand his freedom, and to bring charges against the officer and owner of this vessel for his abduction. At the present time, Mr. Jenkins does not ask that such a charge be brought. However he retains his right to bring such complaints later.

"As to the charge itself, the only problem involved here was a minor scuffle, a small fight, a disagreement between two men. Lonnie Jenkins is not a sailor, he is not bound to duty or service to his nation's navy, nor is he legally bound by any arbitrary laws of the sea, or specific and unreasonable rules of this ship. A scuffle between two men is not just cause for taking the life of one man, even though he is not here accused as the perpetrator of the fight.

"Added to these facts are those that the third mate did, without just cause, use his whip three times on the accused in the past two weeks, and that the third mate did continually harass and harangue Mr. Jenkins. It seems plain that Mr. Jenkins had just and due cause for defending himself when he was again verbally assaulted by the third mate. He defended himself in the only way he knew how."

Allen watched the captain carefully. He seemed almost asleep.

"Therefore, Captain, sir . . ." — Allen shouted this, and the captain stirred and stared at him — ". . . it is our contention that Lonnie did not attack the third mate. Rather that Lonnie was simply defending himself against a repeated and continual unlawful attack upon his mind and body by the third mate. It is a clear and simple case of self-defense. Therefore, Captain, we plead that the accused is innocent of striking a superior officer, since it is a matter of self-defense, which is a stronger and more legally binding law than that of striking an officer.

"Added to this the point that Jenkins is not legally bound to obey any laws of this ship, either legal or illegal, since he is not here lawfully or willingly, but through trickery, deceit and kidnapping, so such a charge is illegal and immaterial in the first place and has no legal justification.

"With these facts in mind, the court has no alternative but to find for the accused, and judge him not guilty."

Half the crew, which had been assembled for this spectacle, cheered. They stopped suddenly when the captain turned and glared at them. He stood and approached the prisoner.

"Son, you struck Third Mate Brockton?"

Lonnie could only nod. His eyes were wild with fear.

The captain belched. "Hell, he admitted it. Nothing else I can do." He turned to the second mate. "Guilty, Parmlee. The verdict is in. Hang him, and be quick about it. We'll make our first landfall anytime now, and I want these wharf rats locked below deck or we won't have a crew."

Parmlee already had a hangman's noose fashioned from three-quarter-inch line. He ordered two seamen to move Lonnie under the forward yardarm and stood him on a fifty gallon hogshead. He then fixed the rope over the lower spar and tied it off tightly so it was the proper height to fit over Lonnie's head. The noose was placed, adjusted, and Parmlee stood back. He had put a rope around the bottom of the big barrel.

Allen watched in horror. He had never seen a man hung. It was inhuman. It was monstrous. But he couldn't turn away. He vowed that it would not go unpunished.

Everyone involved would pay a terrible price for what he was doing to this innocent boy.

"All ready, Mr. Parmlee?" the captain asked, his voice bored.

"All ready, sir, aye."

Parmlee nodded and the two seamen pressed into duty heaved suddenly on the rope around the barrel. It pivoted backward and shot out from under Lonnie's feet.

There was a gasp from the assembled crew as the youth dropped, the rope stretched for a split second, then tightened and his neck snapped from the pressure of the hangman's knot. It sounded like a spar breaking in a heavy wind. Lonnie's tongue came out of his mouth and his eyes bulged, then stared, unseeing.

Allen turned away from the twitching body as Lonnie's nerves continued to function after the brain had ceased sending signals. His chain-laden feet twitched again, and his body turned slowly in the early morning breeze.

The captain walked in front of the dead boy and stared at him for a moment. "He's dead, Mr. Parmlee. Cut him down. Get him over the side and let's put this ship back to work!"

"Aye, aye, sir."

Allen plunged through the hatch into the

fo'c'sle. He would watch no more. There would be no burial, just a body thrown overboard. No last words, no good thoughts. He had seen enough of the mock trial to fill him with anger and desire for vengeance. Now more than ever he wanted to take over this ship. To take command. To mutiny! And by God, he would figure out a way to do it, or he would die in the effort!

CHAPTER FIVE:
MOVING SOUTH

"It just doesn't make sense, Father," Martha said. She paced to the window in his office, then back to the big chair. "There is no reason why Allen should disappear. None. There are many reasons why he would stay in Seattle, finish his business there and then come down here. The lady who is keeping his son says she hasn't seen Allen. He told her one morning that he would be around the next day to make some kind of permanent arrangements for the boy, then nothing. That simply isn't like Allen. It must be foul play."

Harold Pemberton filled his pipe slowly and nodded. "I agree with you, and we have the best man investigating. When the report came through yesterday, I sent a detective up there on the return boat. We should know in two weeks. But from the report by this Caleb Jones, Allen has just vanished. He didn't specify if it was voluntary or involunary."

"Can we trust Caleb? He is in line to take over the job there, isn't he? And he said he and Allen stopped by at a tavern for a drink after work to celebrate. Caleb says the next thing he remembers is a friend helping him go home."

Martha forced the tears back. She would not cry. Instead, she walked to the window again and looked out over the port.

"This may be a small blessing in disguise for me, Father. At least, I won't have to face Allen before I go to Mexico. And I am serious about going, I assure you."

"I wish you wouldn't, but I can understand your reasons," her father sighed.

"Now, I'm sure it isn't as dangerous down there as all the stories we hear. You said it wasn't more than a hundred miles below the border. And I will take Johnnie Laveau with me, as you suggested. He can more than handle a few rowdy Mexicans."

Harold Pemberton watched her, and reflected for a moment how quickly, how easily he had misjudged a strange custom in a strange land, and the life of regret he had suffered for it.

"Martha, just remember that you will be in a foreign country, and one that is not well known for its law and order. The Baja peninsula is sparsely populated. Some say it's a wild land where only the gun and the knife rule. You've already suffered enough in your young life, Martha. I don't want anything else to happen to you."

She went to him, kissed his cheek and hugged him tightly.

"Father, I appreciate your concern, and I will be as cautious and careful as practical. But I want to find my mother. You said you were certain she was in Todos Santos, near the big bay, on the ocean side. That's where we'll go, and it will be fine. I'll take along enough money to buy our way out of any small problems and I'm sure that's the only kind we'll find.

"I read once that the fear of the unknown is the most unrealistic terror man has. At any rate we will be careful, and will come home within a month."

"You'll go by boat to San Diego, and then pick up your horses and buggy there."

Martha smiled. "Yes, Father. I'm sure by now our San Diego office has everything all planned out."

It wasn't until Martha was at home that evening, packing, that the full impact of Allen's disappearance hit her. Was it possible that he had *wanted* to vanish? He had left her once before when he could have stayed. Now, he was gone again. Had he faced the idea of returning to San Francisco and marrying her realistically and found it more than he could accept? Was it possible that he was actually afraid to marry her?

She thought about it calmly and dry-eyed for several minutes, then threw herself on her bed, pounded the pillow and cried.

Why? She had given him no reason. She thought she had made it absolutely plain that she loved him and wanted him. Surely that last night in the hotel, before she came home, when they had made love so tenderly, so completely — surely that had not frightened him. She thought it would have had exactly the opposite effect on him, and make him want to be with her all the time.

She sat up, more furious than tearful now. She wasn't sure if he had run away, or if something more drastic had happened to him. But the detectives would find out. Until then, there was nothing she could do. She was sure the detectives would talk to everyone in that tavern that evening. They'd discover exactly what Allen had done, how many drinks he'd had, who he talked with, where he went when he left, and what really happened.

She finished her packing, trying to put the problem into the proper perspective. She shouldn't be premature about condemning Allen. She would wait and hear the reports from the detectives.

But that would be after she came back from Mexico. Once more, she thought Allen's disappearance might be a disguised blessing after all. If Allen were there right now, asking that the wedding be next week, what could she tell him? What would she say? Just blurt out that she was a bastard and she was going to try to find her real mother? Tell him that she must do this before she could think of marrying anyone? It would be awkward at best. At worst — she didn't even want to think about that. Instead, she concentrated on the problems at hand.

Martha was aware that there were bandits in Mexico. Carefully, she stitched two diamonds into her blouse, then another one into the skirt. She removed two of the stays from her light corset and enlarged the area where the stiffeners rested. Then folded two one-hundred-dollar greenbacks around each stay and sewed them back in place. There was no way to tell where they were. She marked the involved stays with a stitched 'X' so she could find them quickly.

Now, with the gold in her purse and what she would have Johnnie carry, they were ready. She selected one ring, a large ruby worth five hundred dollars, and put it on. She would turn the stone so it was inside her hand and could not be seen. That done, she checked everything again, and went down for a long talk with Mrs. Larson, her housekeeper.

The trip to San Diego by coastal steamer took almost a week, with a short stop in Los Angeles. The little town of San Diego clung to the side of the bay, and more houses and businesses were going up each day.

Martha and Johnnie stayed in separate rooms at the Horton House, the magnificent hotel built in 1870 by Alonzo Ernesto Horton, who had bought up nine hundred and sixty acres of "useless land" for twenty-seven cents an acre. He established "New Town," and soon, San Diego was busy building itself on the Horton land, which he sold at amazing profits.

Horton poured $150,000 into his hotel. It had heated rooms, hot and cold running water, and was so luxuriously furnished that, for many years, it would remain the finest lodging place anywhere on the West Coast.

The Pacific Steamship office had made the arrangements. Johnnie looked at the Democrat Buggy with a top. He would have preferred a closed carriage, but there wasn't one to be rented. He tied a saddle horse on behind with a lead rope. That way, if the buggy broke down, they would each have a horse to ride to their destination.

They had a rifle in the buggy and Johnnie sported a new gun belt and a six shooter. He went to the outskirts of town and learned how to shoot the weapon. The new one-piece cartridges were quick and easy to use, lots better than the flint-lock pistols he had fired before. And now he had six shots without reloading!

That evening they had a last dinner in the sumptuous dining room at the Horton House. They ate fish, duck, steak and lobster, and Martha could not remember ever having such a grand meal. It might have to do them for a long time.

Early the next morning, she had the hotel kitchen workers pack them a basket of food, enough for three days, including bread, cheese and wine as well as fresh fruits, and some fried chicken and cured ham. Martha looked over the basket and decided it would have to do. They left just as the warm September sun lifted over the hills behind the southern end of the San Diego Bay. The road they took skirted the large natural port and went south, where the international boundary was marked only with a cow fence on one side and the village of Tijuana on the other.

There was a small building at the border, but it was siesta time when they arrived, so no one was manning the station.

They wheeled the buggy through on the dirt street and kept on moving south. There was little chance to get lost. They simply followed the dirt track nearest the ocean, and they soon were away from the village and into a barren, burned, brown stretch of land, where Martha wondered if even a weed might grow.

It was a desert region, plain and simple. Martha had heard it received only three or four inches of rainfall a year. San Diego had only ten. She was sure that San Francisco had more than twenty-five inches of rain, and now she could understand the many benefits.

They stopped for lunch on a rise from which they could see the ocean. There was not a sign of a house, a barn or a cow. Nothing but an occasional rattlesnake that slithered out of their way from its warm spot in the dirt road. They ate bread and cheese and shared a bottle of port wine, then were back in the buggy and moving.

Johnnie estimated that they had covered

almost thirty miles by the end of the first day. They had not seen any other travelers on the road, passed one lone shack a half mile seaward from the trail of a road, and had spent the day enjoying the harsh realities of the desert. Martha was impressed with the strange barren beauty of it all.

Johnnie set up a small tent, pounded stakes into the ground and erected the pole. The tent was not tall enough for Martha to stand in, but served her well. He rolled out blankets for her and used one for himself, sitting in the buggy with the pistol and rifle close at hand. He had built a small fire from dry cactus and small branches taken from a dry water course, and boiled coffee and heated water for Martha to use for washing. He put out the fire as soon as it became dark.

"Mon make us target in fire," Johnnie said. "Mon see fire many mile away."

She was glad her big Jamaican friend was along. Johnnie had been a watchdog and bodyguard for her for over two years now. He had been a sailor, until her father put him in charge of the docks.

She met Johnnie while she was launching a ship, and soon her father had assigned him to her as a personal bodyguard during her stays around the docks. He had been with her to Seattle, and had saved her from a slow, freezing death at the hands of a former employee of Pacific Steamship who hated the company. Now he was with her once more, with stern orders from Harold Pemberton, himself, to guard Martha with his very life.

As she lay down to sleep, Martha thought again about her trip to the small Catholic Church in San Diego, at the Presidio. There, she had seen the birth record that had been entered in the big book twenty-one years ago. The parents of a girl child, Martha Louise Pemberton, were listed officially as Abigail L. Pemberton and Harold L. Pemberton.

She had worried about it, but decided it would do no good at all to have it changed. It might even do harm to someone. So she left it alone. Instead, she said the name of her mother over and over. Maria Valdez, Maria Valdez. She would never forget it, and she would remember forever the first meeting with her natural mother.

With the dawn, they were moving again. They had been urged to take no more than three days for the trip, and to drive smartly and get through the areas that were sometimes frequented by highway bandits as quickly as possible. However, since there were so few travelers, the robbers could no longer make a living at such work, and did not watch the road the way they used to.

The second day passed with no incident, except getting mired down in one short swampy section they had to cross near the beach. Johnnie got out and pushed, and Martha touched the reins to the horse's head to move them forward.

With the start of the third day, Martha thought she noticed a change in the land. Was it a little greener here? Had there been a recent rain to bring a flush of grass to the slopes? They followed the beach for a distance, and Johnnie stopped the buggy on the hard sand and ran into the surf. Then, in the backwash of the waves, he dug furiously and came up with three huge clams as big as his hands. He opened them with his knife and dug out the delicate meat which made an impromptu lunch.

They had just left the beach and rounded a turn in the road, past a wide wash in the finger ridge that extended almost to the water, when Johnnie heard a shot. Before he could draw the six-gun, two horsemen were on each side of the carriage, pistols drawn. A third man held the head of their horse.

"*Buenos dias, gringos,* and welcome to

Mexico. We hope you are very rich and that the *senorita* is very beautiful, for we are going to enjoy both your gold and your company. Give me the *pistola* please, *muy* carefully."

Johnnie handed him the six-gun, then the man slashed his own weapon down across Johnnie's head, tumbling him from the buggy and into the sand.

Martha gasped with the sound of the first shot, then sat, unable to move as the *bandidos* stormed around the carriage. She couldn't help but shiver as the bandit who hit Johnnie leaned into the buggy and stared at her.

"Ah, si, muy bonita, verdad? Muy hermosa." He grinned, doffed his hat, and showed blackened teeth.

"*Senorita Gringa,* welcome to my country. We will be most good hosts, I guarantee." He leaned in and patted her breast, but pulled back when she slapped his hand.

"Ah, a chili pepper. That is good. It always makes it more interesting that way, no?"

He backed away and the buggy started moving again, led by the man beside the buggy horse. They turned away from the sea, and drove up the wide wash. Martha screamed.

"Stop! Stop! Where is Johnnie?"

The leader of the group rode to her side and pointed to a horse over which Johnnie had been draped. His hands were tied and he appeared to be in pain. At least he was alive.

Martha scowled at the Mexican *bandido*. "If you hurt Johnnie, I promise you that I will slit your ugly throat."

The bandit roared with laughter. "Ah, the chili pepper again. I like that. I will make you my favorite *puta*." He laughed and turned, speeding up the little caravan as it wound deeper into the foothills and toward a high peak on the horizon.

Martha did not know how long they twisted and turned through the ravines and ridges, but they kept working higher into the hills. At last, they came to a point where the buggy could go no farther. She was helped from the vehicle by the bandit chieftain and put on the trailing horse.

"No side-saddle here," he said, laughing. "You would fall off. Straddle the animal with those delicious legs, *senorita.* Your delicate parts will not be harmed."

Martha hated the blush that colored her face as she straddled the horse, trying to keep her skirts tucked under her legs to protect them. If only she could get his pistol. But that would have to wait.

The men took everything from the buggy and carried it with them. They unhitched the buggy horse and brought it as well. Then they all rode into the hills. After what seemed like an hour, in which Martha was sure her thighs were chafed to the bleeding point, they came to a narrow valley mouth where a guard waved as they passed.

The ravine opened into a quarter-mile-wide green valley, with a small lake at one end and a flowing stream that vanished into the sand before it left the meadow. To one side stood three buildings made of a few logs, but mostly cactus branches plastered with adobe mud to make them windproof. She had seen many shacks like these in Tijuana. They stopped in front of the shacks and she was handed down off her horse.

The bandit leader bowed and held his hat at his waist in an outrageous parody of courtesy. "Pardon, *senorita,* let me to introduce myself. My men call me *Jefe,* which in your language means chief. That's what I am, their leader. I am also your chief, and your master. You will do what I tell you to, or you die. It is simple, no? Do or you die. Don't think you are special — I get all the *senoritas* I want. You *do,* or you die."

She turned, the fury in her eyes enough to make him laugh again.

"Do not worry. You will get used to it. After six months or a year, you will speak Spanish as good as we do, and you cook good Mexican food for us, too."

She turned and tried to slap him, at the same time grabbing for his pistol, but he was ready and caught both of her hands. He held them in one of his and with his other hand rubbed her breasts through the light blouse.

"Ah, *muy magnifico,*" he said to the other men who watched. They hooted and laughed, and one said something rapidly in Spanish which sent the listeners into screams, roars and catcalls. She tried to pull away but he held her fast still stroking her breasts.

"Do not worry, little chili pepper. I will not let any of them touch you, at least not until you have me, no?" He pulled her to him and his mouth covered her in a move so unexpected that she couldn't fight it until it was too late. She hated the smell of his breath, the scratching of his black moustache. Then he pushed her away and led her to the smallest of the three buildings. Inside was one big room with a small cooking fireplace at the far end, a bed of blankets on the floor at one side, and a small table and three chairs.

"Mi casa," he said. "You may live here in pleasure or in pain, whichever you choose."

"I will never stay here willingly."

"Oh, I know that, *Senorita Puta,* that is why I have guards who shoot very well, and that is why I have kept all of my friendly rattlesnakes in the canyon, so you will not want to walk among them. They do not like strangers and rattle their tails and strike quickly."

He watched her shiver and knew he had scored a telling point.

"*Gringa,* you will stay here as long as I tell you to. You will do what I say. I no can make you like it, but I can make you do it."

He reached for her and loosened the blouse at her waist, then began unbuttoning it.

"No," she said.

He slapped her hands hard. "Yes. '*Si*' is our word. You will say '*si*' every time, no matter what I ask, no matter what I tell you to do. Is right?"

"No."

His smile came back, bigger than before, and he took off her blouse, leaving only her loose-fitting chemise covering her.

"Bueno," he said. "Come to bed."

Her eyes were frightened now, but also respectful. She nodded.

102

"Si," she said.

She started to move. He stopped her. "The word," he demanded.

"Si," she said, her face blank.

Martha slumped on the pad of dirty blankets. She knew she was going to die. She had heard many stories about the Mexican *bandidos* since she'd decided to come. They were rapists, killers, cutthroats, unprincipled men who lived by the gun, taking what they wanted, killing and robbing everyone they met.

He dropped beside her, looked at the thin cloth which covered her, but made no move to touch her or take off the rest of her clothes.

"Why you travel?" he asked sharply.

"We are going to Todos Santos to visit my mother."

He looked at her closer. "Then you are part Mexican."

"My mother is Mexican, my father a gringo."

"Well said, *linda.*" He grinned. "No wonder I like you so much. No wonder my breeches bulge out. You mostly Mexican. I can tell by your chili pepper temper."

He laughed again, then pushed her back on the blankets and bent to kiss her mouth.

"Remember, little one, you will say *'si'* to

everything I say, everything I tell you to do. Is not right?"

"*Si,*" Martha said. She remembered his huge hand around her throat and, at that moment, had decided nothing would be gained by dying. She would live. She would do here whatever she had to do so she might live, and one day, she would have her vengeance on this bandit chief. She frowned now as his hands caressed her.

"Johnnie, is he all right?"

"The Negro? He has a hard head. He is bound and held." *El Jefe* smoothed the sides of his heavy black moustache. "Is he your slave, or your lover?"

"There are no slaves in the United States, not since President Lincoln freed them in the war in 1863."

"Then is he your lover?"

"No, a good friend, a protector."

"Then Negro do one hell of bad job, no?"

"*Si.*"

He ripped the thin chemise from her and stared at her breasts. There was no way she could turn. Martha felt as if she had been soiled, violated by his eyes. She hated him, despised him, but he held life and death control over both her and Johnne. She closed her eyes, felt his hands roam over her body, then his surprisingly gentle fingers removed the rest of her clothes and she shuddered.

"Do not fear, small one. The act of love must never be a thing to fear or to bring pain. Rather a time for joy."

Martha hardly heard his words. She was astounded by her response. There was repulsion, yes. But she was also fighting the surge of some automatic response in her body, a warm glow, the reaction of her breasts to his touch. She would not welcome him, she would not let him know that he moved her — but neither could she fight him.

Martha kept her eyes closed and sensed his growing excitement. His hands explored farther, lower, touching her legs, then her very private place. His swift entry brought a gasp of surprise from her, mingled with pain. She would not open her eyes, she would not react.

When it was over he lay beside her, playing with her long black hair.

"You must be half *Gringa,* woman. You do not enjoy it like a real chili pepper should. You were there, you want to, but nothing happened."

"I don't enjoy being raped."

"Raped? Who raped you? We made love."

"With a death threat if I refused?"

"Half-*gringa,* you have much to learn about men, about me."

The week that followed was one of intensive learning for Martha. The two other women in camp were Mexican, fat and dirty and about thirty, she thought. Martha worked with them from the first day, helping to cook, washing the greasy pots and tinware the men ate from, bringing in wood for the fires, and washing the clothes that were given to her.

She saw Johnnie from time to time. He was shackled with a ball and chain around one leg. He had to carry it everywhere he went and it almost eliminated his chances of running away. His main job seemed to be splitting wood and sawing up limbs from the trees. They had also taken away his boots which would be another hazard if he tried to run away. The wound on his head seemed to be healing, and she saw that he was not seriously hurt. They could not communicate, but she was sure that all the money he carried had long since been discovered. Her own reticule had been emptied on the table in the shack the first day and *El Jefe* grinned at the dozen twenty dollar gold pieces. He counted them three times and tried to compute the amount. She told him how much it was in American dollars and he grinned again. He brushed aside the stack of eight one-hundred dollar green-backs and several smaller denomination bills. To him, the gold was much more important. However, he did take the paper money and push it into a long leather purse with a snap on it. This he hung around his neck on a silver chain.

It was now after the evening meal. Martha had finished washing the dishes in the big building, and had been led back to the smaller one where *El Jefe* lay on the filthy bed, smoking a hand-rolled cigarette. One coal-oil lamp gave off a sooty light.

El Jefe motioned to her when she came through the door.

"Come here, *puta*," he said.

"Si." She walked to the bed and stood over him. She still wore the same white blouse and blue skirt she had on when she was captured. He would not allow her to change.

"Take off the top one," he said.

"Si." She removed her blouse and stood bare to the waist.

"Sit, we talk."

She sat beside him on the dirty blanket. He was cross-legged. She followed his example. The bandit chief made no move to touch her.

"This Negro, is he very rich?"

"No, he is a working man. He guards other people. He has no money, but he does have some magic."

"Magic?"

For a moment, Martha was almost as surprised as her jailer. She'd nearly forgotten about Johnnie's magic. But he did have it — if only . . . An idea began to form in the back of her mind. "Yes, if he has certain things — some herbs and potions — he can work magic. He would need a cat, I believe."

"Magic!" *El Jefe* stood and walked to the door where he called loudly. Soon someone came and they talked in whispers for a moment, then the chief clapped his hands in delight and went back to the blankets.

"Magic does he have? We see." He reached for her then, and Martha wondered what strange form of sexual gratification this insatiable Mexican outlaw would demand tonight. Each night, since they had arrived, she had served him, and in some of the most unusual and disgusting ways. There were times she wanted to die — but the will to survive was stronger.

"Ah, my little chili pepper, you will be very good tonight, no?"

"*Si,*" she said.

CHAPTER SIX:
A SWIM FOR SHORE

For the first week of his internment at the docks, Randy Pemberton worked hard. Good Lord, he never knew any human being had to work so hard, and so long! He went home at night after his nine hours and fell on his bed, barely able to summon up enough energy to get anything to eat.

He had rented a small flat not far from the downtown area, and now walked to the docks each morning. He had bought work clothes, and thought he was fitting in rather well. He wasn't as adept at moving the bundles and stacks of goods as the more experienced men, but he learned quickly and by Tuesday of the second week, he was feeling more human than dead. That evening, on his way home from work, he stopped at a tavern and lifted a few beers, then had a shot or two of whiskey and slowly got drunk.

"Damn bastard!" he shouted to no one in

particular. He had been sitting at a table by himself. His drunken logic seemed so remarkably clear: here he was working his ass off on the docks, and his half-breed of a half-sister was living it up in luxury in some San Diego hotel! She was having a royal time of it on the Pemberton money, and she didn't deserve a penny of it!

"Lousy bastard! Should throw her right out of the family, that's what I should do!"

The bartender had seen young Pemberton before but never in working clothes. He knew his name and his relationship to the richest man in town, and now listened with interest to the young man. He took a bottle of whiskey and a glass to Randy's table and poured him a shot.

"I agree with you, young man. She's a bastard if there ever was one and she should be kicked out of the family. What's her name again?"

"Sister, damn sister of mine! Martha." He tipped the glass of whiskey, emptied it, and then reached for the bottle. It fell off the table and bounced on the sawdust floor. The barkeep helped Randy to the door and told him to go home and sleep it off.

Coming back inside, the tavern owner paused for a moment. So Martha Pemberton, daughter of the great wealthy son-of-a-bitch Harold Pemberton, was a bastard! Now that would make interesting talk for the bar and its patrons. None of the men in this place had much love for old moneybags Pemberton anyway.

The man with the apron was Amos I. Kilarney. He was shorter than most men, built wide like a bulldog, with a face that looked like a pug. His arms were stout and strong, and many a bigger man regretted trying to settle an argument with Kilarney using his fists.

Amos had more than a touch of the sneaky about him as well. He scratched his thinning hair and wondered if this might be a bit of information he could use somehwere else.

A letter to the great Mr. Harold P., asking for a stipend to keep quiet? No, his only gift there would be a boot in the mouth.

The newspapers? No, they would want only facts, and would pay only a pittance for them.

The young lady herself? She probably didn't have much money of her own.

Kilarney picked up the half-filled whiskey bottle from the floor, wiped off the top, put the cork back in it and went behind the bar. Hell, why was he fooling around? He'd go directly to the great Mr. Pemberton in person. Yes, he'd walk in, lay his proposition on the table and ask, no damnit, he'd *demand,* a thousand dollars a month to keep quiet or he'd take it all to the newspapers. Now there was a good plan! Amos took another drink in celebration of his new-found good fortune.

The next morning, the door of the President's office was open and his secretary, Mrs. Tausch, hesitated to close it. The man she had just let in, Mr. Kilarney, was not the usual caller, and she was sure he wouldn't be there long.

She went back to her desk and arranged the other projects she was supposed to be working on. But she kept one ear aimed at the door, hoping to catch some of the words. As she suspected, the unkempt man with the red cheeks and old jacket came out the door quickly, looking behind him. He was a short man, stoutly built and now in a good deal of a rush. He didn't stop until he was through the outer door. Then Mr. Pemberton followed him, anger still evident on his usually controlled face.

"Find Mr. Nelson and have him come up here as quickly as possible. Also send a messenger to the first floor and have Brideley come up at once."

"Yes, sir."

He turned and stalked back into his office without his usual smile or thank you. Mr. Pemberton was extremely upset about something. At least that man Amos Kilarney was gone. He smelled of beer, and Mrs. Tausch didn't like him.

Ten minutes later, Harold Pemberton looked across his desk at the two men he had sent for. Both were heavily muscled, and one had an eye partially and permanently closed from bare-knuckle fist-fighting in the ring. Both now worked for Mr. Pemberton on extremely "delicate" matters.

"You will meet my son Randy at the docks where he is working and tell him you have a special assignment for him. Then proceed to take him, calmly if possible, but by force if necessary, to the berth of the *Abigail P.* Restrain him in a cabin, with strict instructions to the captain that Randy is not to be allowed out of the room until the vessel clears the port day after tomorrow. I'll give you sealed instructions for the captain, and a letter for Randy as well."

He handed them the two envelopes. "Any questions?"

There were none and he dismissed them.

Two days later, Randy stood at the rail of the ship he had been imprisoned on as it moved out of San Francisco Bay. He had asked special permission to come topside so he could at least wave goodbye to the city.

The captain knowing Randy's position, and knowing he someday might run the firm, reluctantly granted the request. But a guard was with him at all times, until they were well out to sea.

A letter from his father told Randy that, in a drunken tirade, he had shouted the information about his sister's birth, and already a lout had come with a blackmail demand. No more such chances would be taken with him. He would be gone two years, working first in the Hawaiian office, then on board a ship sailing to the Orient and back again to Hawaii. His father said he was certain that, after Randy thought it over for a few days, he would see the wisdom of this "transfer."

Randy had been furious, but did not let on to anyone in the crew as he sat in the cabin awaiting the ship's departure.

Now the *Abigail P.* was leaving the wide mouth of the bay, and moved a half mile off the nearest point of land. Randy noticed the guard relaxing more and more. Randy pointed to one side.

"Look, a whale!" he said.

The seaman looked. Randy pounded his

fist against the man's chin and drilled his left into the man's stomach, bending him over. Randy pumped his knee upward at precisely the right moment, connecting with the seaman's jaw, and dropped him unconscious on the deck.

Randy didn't waste a second. He vaulted over the rail, hit the water fourteen feet below, feet first, hardly making a splash.

He didn't think anyone on deck saw his escape, but he stayed under water as long as he could, stroking downward and away from the ship. When he could hold his breath no longer, he surged for the surface, but let only his face come out of the water in the three foot swells.

Greedily he sucked in air for a dozen breaths. Then he sank again, and swam underwater toward shore for twenty yards before surfacing, only showing his face. From a hundred yards away, he would be impossible to locate, he was sure.

He turned and looked at the ship. It was still under full sail heading for the open sea. No one had seen him. Now he realized he could never swim to shore fully clothed. He did a jelly fish float by ducking his head and letting his back rise out of the water. As he floated this way, he bent and unfastened his boots and let them sink, then pulled off his pants and let them go. Before his escape, he had put all of his valuables in a purse and tied it with a boot lace firmly around his neck.

He surfaced and stroked easily toward shore, stopped again and let his shirt float away, then settled into a leisurely crawl stroke toward the closest point of land he could see. He had always been a strong swimmer and a half mile swim would hardly make him breathe hard. He saw that the movement of the wind and tide would carry him further south, but it didn't matter.

Before he reached shore, Randy had to stop and rest twice. He realized that since his swimming program ended at Harvard, he had not been in the water. He would have to correct that and swim more.

Randy walked out of the water more tired than he had expected, and found that he was near the old ruined fort. He shivered in the blustery end of August weather. He checked his purse and found it completely soaked. The paper money would take some drying out, but the gold coins were intact.

Even in his underwear and dripping wet, he had little trouble stopping a horseman who was riding past. After a few words of explanation about falling off an outbound vessel, Randy convinced the man he should give him a ride into the downtown area. A five-dollar gold piece completed the deal.

When they came to the first few houses, Randy watched carefully. At the fourth one, he saw wash on the line. He ran to the line, snatched a pair of pants, and scurried away just as the housewife came out with a broom and a scream.

The pants were much too large, but covered Randy for his ride into town. A short time later, another gold piece hired the horseman to deliver a message to Randy's friend, Blake Townsend, a merchant.

An hour later, Blake met Randy at Madelyn's place, a bottle under one arm and a bundle of clothes under the other. He laughed all the way through the house until he found Randy, being properly consoled by a naked Madelyn, in the back bedroom.

"You've really done it this time, bucko," Blake said. "Your old man was shipping you off to where?"

"Japan, China, Hong Kong, and Madelyn wouldn't even be there!"

Blake bent over and rubbed Madelyn's breasts. "I'd hoped to keep all this tit here for myself. How in hell did you get in so much trouble with your father so soon?"

"Don't bother asking, just help me get down to the bank before it closes so I can get some cash. I'll even pay you for the clothes." He began dressing.

"You both going to leave me?" Madelyn said, faking a sob as she lay in a provocative pose on the bed.

"True, love, for a time," Blake said. "But I'll be back. We can't let all of that go to waste. I don't know about our swimmer."

"I won't be back for some time and that's the truth of it," Randy said. "I've got to take a long trip down to Mexico to investigate a few things."

"You said your sister went down there."

"True, and I'll probably have to rescue her from some Mexican army officer, who knows? Now, come on. We'll be late."

That afternoon Randy Pemberton withdrew five thousand dollars in cash from his account at the Pacific Coast Bank. Half of it was in large denomination greenbacks, the rest in smaller denominations and 300 dollars in gold. That evening, he stayed in Blake's bachelor apartment and, early the next morning, set sail for San Diego in a ship that did not fly the Pacific Steamship flag.

Five days later, he landed at San Diego and inquired about the best route south, paying special attention to stay as far from

Pacific Steamship vessels and people as he could.

It took him two days to check into the cost of hiring a pair of horses and guides, and when the discouragement mounted and the stories of increased activity lately by highwaymen and *bandidos* came out, he wondered if he should go at all.

Then someone told him Todos Santos was on a large bay. Why didn't he hire a boat and sail down, or catch a ride with one of the small merchant ships or fishing ships that stopped there?

A day later, he sat on a thirty-foot, twin-masted sailer. "Dom" Domingo was her master, owner and entire crew. He was twice as old as death and his pock-marked face was wind- and sun-stained until he looked like an Indian.

"Ha, you try to ride to Santos now and you'll get stripped clean and your hide dried into jerky. Them *bandidos* down there are a murderous lot. Pirates could learn hell of a lot from them bastards. Seen a fire on the beach going down that way once. Not a living thing within twenty mile that place, so I moved in for a closer look. Got me some old bi-noculars and I checked it out good from a hundred yards offshore. Had been a carriage, and a horse. They burned the carriage. Horse musta' got shot in the fight. They was two dead men and to one side, a woman who had been stripped naked and staked out on the sand. These bastards must have lined up and gone around twice with her before she died.

"Just as I got my canvas up to pull away, a musket ball twanged past my head and I prayed for a good wind."

"You go down often?"

"Whenever need to. Whenever somebody wants to go. I got no schedule. I ain't no stage line nor railroad."

"How much does it cost to ride down?"

"How much can you afford, friend?" The old man chuckled. "Get used to bargaining with these Mexes. They like to haggle, start high, come down, go up. Just so it's a haggle."

Dom Domingo probably wasn't his real name. His eyes told Randy that he had seen the inside of more than one jailhouse, and that he wasn't above making a quick dollar, honest or not. But the eyes, squinty and dark, set in a face that was shriveled and brown from the sun, also told him that a deal was a deal. Randy woul not have to worry about being knocked on the head while he slept, and his body relieved of its valuables before being thrown into the sea as shark food.

Randy grinned. "Old man, in this leaky tub, half-rusted away, and with bed sheets for canvas, I'll do you a favor. I'll give you ten dollars paper for the ride."

"Ten!" Dom exploded. "My last passenger was a real gentleman, he paid fifty-five for the privilege, and he provided all the food for the six-day cruise."

"He wasn't a gentleman, he was an idiot," Randy growled. "I'll come up to fifteen and half the food, but that's absolutely the highest I can go."

Dom laughed and shook his head. He had asked for bargaining and he was getting it. He knew he had a fare and he liked the cut of the jib on this youngster.

An hour later, they arrived at a fair price — twenty dollars and half the food. Randy intended on buying all the food, and went to a grubby little street called Fifth Avenue. There he found a groceries and dry goods store. The street was dirt, half lined with horses hitched, flat-bottomed wagons and four-wheeled buggies. But the street sported wooden sidewalks, carefully laid down and extending ten feet out from the business establishments.

Randy bought two baskets of supplies, one of canned goods, new on the Pacific coast market. There was canned peaches and applesauce and the like. He filled the baskets with fresh fruit, long loaves of bread, cheese, six bottles of wine and two jugs of sweet water. There were crackers and small tins of sardines and a dozen eggs at a ridiculously high price of twenty-five cents the dozen.

When Dom Domingo saw the food, he nearly cried.

"My God, no! You trying to fatten me up for the kill? I ain't seen that much grub since the time I rustled that little grocery store in Kansas. We did eat good for a few days."

As they moved out Randy saw that Dom was an excellent sailor, and that his craft, while a little shabby and worn, was in excellent condition and sound as railroad stock. They cleared the long run out past Point Loma, seen by Juan Rodriguez Cabrillo in 1542. When the Portuguese sailed into the bay and landed he became the first European to set foot on California soil.

Dom turned the little craft south, once out of the harbor, and leaned back, a chaw of tobacco in his cheek, a grin on his face.

"Now ain't this one hell of a lot easier than bouncing around on a saddle for a hundred dusty miles?"

Randy agreed that it certainly was.

It took them five days to sail down the coast. Admittedly Dom was in no hurry, and he never moved after dark, sliding into some sheltered harbor or in back of a point and dropped a sea anchor.

The fifth day Dom sailed close in to one area, near a point, searching for the exact spot he wanted. Then he dropped his anchor. He pulled out two fishing poles and they fished for half an hour using some small fish as bait. Soon they had a two foot square wooden box filled with flopping, spiney, big-mouthed bottom fish.

"So far we're getting red rock cod, red-stripers, salmon groupers and sheepshead," the old man said. Soon he hoisted two more fish aboard on one lift. Without a word he put the fishing gear away and pulled in the anchor. Randy didn't have the slightest idea why they had been fishing.

Fifteen minutes later, they rounded the big point and sailed into Todos Santos.

"Here it is, young Pemberton. A damn sight easier than busting your butt on some nag. I'll be around for a week or so in case you want to go back. If not, when you're ready, leave a notice down on the dock, and first boat heading back will look you up."

At the dock, a cluster of black-haired children saw the boat and came running.

Dom opened the box of fish and let them take their pick, one to a customer, and soon the box was nearly empty and twenty children ran off shouting for glee, and hoisting their prize fish for dinner.

"Children," he said and shrugged. "Always there are the children. They are so easy to please."

Randy rubbed his jaw with one hand. This tough old sea dog was as soft inside as a new-born puppy. He wished him well.

"Where can I find a Maria Valdez. Do you know her?"

"Ask at the *cantina. Senora* Valdez is the owner."

With his small valise in one hand, and a curious squint to his eyes, Randy walked up the sunbaked, dusty lane toward a cluster of a dozen buildings that made up Todos Santos. Not more than fifty people could live in the whole village. It looked like the last outpost before Dante's hell, and twice as hot. He felt wetness run down his arms, his nose seemed to dry up and turn to sandpaper. Twice he coughed in the powerder-like dust which whipped up as a breeze, lost its way, and passed him.

At the *cantina,* he sat at a table. At least he was out of the sun. The building was slightly cooler, but not much. It was a square room with two tables and chairs and a short bar with a small rack holding six liquor bottles. No one else was in the room. He thought of shouting for service, but did not really have the energy to do that. The door and windows were open, all un-screened, so the most breeze possible would blow through.

Randy stood, left his bag on the table and went to the bar. He could not read any of the labels on the bottles, but reached for one when a voice stopped him.

"*Si, senor?*"

"A drink. You have any whiskey?" He turned and saw a young girl, no more than fifteen, with long black hair, a thin figure and a sudden fear on her face.

She stepped quickly back through the door leading into the next room. He heard excited voices, then a short, heavy-set woman entered. She was all Mexican, a shade lighter than the younger girl who crowded behind her.

"*Si, senor.* American?"

"Yeah, right. I need a drink. You got anything worth drinking around here?" He made a glass tilting motion.

"*Dinero?* You have money?"

"Well, damn right!" He took a five-dollar gold piece from his pocket and dropped it

125

on the hard wood of the bar, letting it ring and spin until it lay quietly.

The woman came, looked at the coin, bit it, and when it did not dent, she dropped it back on the bar and took a bottle from the group.

"*Gringo* whiskey?"

He nodded. Randy watched her. His guess was that she was about the right age, thirty-eight or forty. But had she ever been pretty? Her face was a little flat, eyes sad, her young girl's figure had long since given way to corn tortillas, beans and the rest of a starch-rich diet. Her arms were heavy, hands work-worn and one finger twisted from an injury. Now she poured a small glass of whiskey and set it before him. Yes, she could have been pretty once.

Randy tasted the drink, smiled, then let half of it burn the dust and dirt and salt from his throat. It was good whiskey.

"*Senora* Valdez?"

She looked on with a question unvoiced, then lowered her head once in assent.

"The boatman said that was your name. Do you have any rooms? You do speak some English?"

"A little," she said, her accent heavy.

"From a long time ago?"

Her eyes came up. Had they once been

126

snapping, eager, alive? She said nothing. For a moment, he had forgotten that he must look a lot like his father had twenty years ago when he was in San Diego. It was possible that she had made such a comparison. Did she wonder if her youthful lover had returned, not a day older than when they had met? He must find out now.

"Maria Valdez? Maria Consuela Lucinda Valdez?"

Her eyes pinched and narrowed, then her eyebrows lifted in either futility or resignation. *"Si,"* she said.

"Did you used to live in the United States, near San Diego, on your father's *rancho?"*

Her stare this time was longer, somehow softer, and her eyes seemed to be remembering. Then they hardened and she looked away quickly.

"Un dollar," she said, motioning at the drink.

"For one drink?"

"Si, for you, one dollar. Next drink, five dollars. You go away. Maria not feel well."

Randy smiled at her. Now he was certain she was the one he was looking for. She had nearly fainted when he asked about the *rancho* in San Diego. This was the woman, all right.

He gave her the five-dollar gold piece. "Do

I look a lot like him — like Harold Pemberton?"

She covered her face with her hands.

"You go! I no want you here!"

"I know Mr. Pemberton very well. He's
my father. I've come to find you, see how
you're doing. Is there anything you need?"

"*Senor.* Please go away. I do not know
what you talk about. Go now."

She turned and walked toward the door
she had come from. Randy moved just
behind her.

"Please, *Senora* Valdez. I mean you no
harm. My father does not know that I am
here. He tried to send me far away across
the ocean so I would not come. I wanted to
meet you. Has your daughter arrived here
yet?"

Maria Valdez stopped, and turned slowly.
"*Mi hija,* my pretty one?"

"Yes, she's a grown woman how, twenty-
one years old. She has long black hair just
like yours. Hasn't she come looking for
you?"

"No. No *senorita* come from *Los Estados
Unidos.* When?"

"She must have left two weeks ago, or
more. She should be here by now."

"How she come?"

"I don't know, I've heard there are *bandi-*

128

dos on the road."

"*Si,* many, many bad *bandidos.*"

"*Senora* Valdez, I'd like to take you back to San Francisco with me. Then you could see my father again, and your daughter will be there. We call her Martha. Wouldn't you like to see that small baby you gave up so many years ago?"

"Oh, *si, si!* But no can go. *Mi casa. Mi niños.* Must stay."

"Ridiculous! You can get someone to take care of your *cantina* and your children. Domingo will go back up to San Diego in a few days. Then we can go on a boat to San Francisco. We'll go right around all the *bandidos.*"

"No! No can go."

"Maria, do you realize Mr. Pemberton is very rich? He owns many *casas,* many businesses, much gold, *mucho dinero.*"

Maria Valdez came back a few steps and sat on one of the chairs. Tears seeped from her eyes. "*Si,* I know all this. *Senor* Pemberton is *muy* rich. He give me many dollars to start, to run *cantina* for many years. He help me *mucho.* He is a good and honest man. But it was so many years ago."

"That's why you sould come up and say hello, get to know him again and the rest of the family. He's still married to the blonde woman."

"You must go." She was crying openly now.

"No, you don't understand. I want to help you. Look, I'll pay you to come up north with me for a week or so. I'll give you a thousand dollars in American gold, if you'll only come up on the boat with me for a visit. You can bring your young daughter with you. It would be exciting for her!"

Maria Consuela Lucinda Valdez shook her head and walked out of the room. This time he did not follow her. He finished the whiskey, poured another shot and drained it quickly. Then, leaving the five-dollar gold piece on the bar, he picked up his small valise and walked out of the *cantina* into the blistering hot sunshine and the ever present dust.

A half hour later, in the bay beside the small dock, he swam in the warm water and tried to make Domingo understand.

"No, dammit, I'm not trying to go to bed with her daughter. All I'm asking *Senora* Valdez to do is take a week's vacation in San Francisco. Now, why is that so terrible? She refused my offer without a reason. Wouldn't even talk about it."

"Maria is a proud woman. She has two children here in town, both by different fathers. No one would marry her. I know the story well. Some *gringo* ruined her. Excellent family, all that. Everyone knows."

"So what's so great about staying here? It's hot, it's filthy and dusty. It's dry. There must be all of fifty people living in this rundown shack town."

"*Si,* but it's their home."

"Domingo, is this your home, too?"

"Sometimes. Now I sleep only on the boat."

"Looks like I'll sleep on her, too, if I may."

"Pick out a chunk of deck."

Randy turned over in the water, opened his eyes under the surface and watched a small startled fish dart away. He swam lazily toward open water, then turned and churned the return trip with a fast backstroke, and coasted to a stop near the small, white sailboat.

Randy got out of the water on the dock and looked in the fish box on the boat. There was one left, a three-pound red rock cod with a gaping mouth in the warm salt water.

Ten minutes later, Randy had a small metal grillwork set up over a cooking fire on the sand. He fed sticks into the blaze six inches under where the two slabs of fish Domingo had filleted away from the backbone

131

lay cooking. Randy wondered if he should turn them over yet.

Domingo came and looked through the smoke. "Turn them," the old sailor said.

"Not done yet," Randy countered and left them another two minutes. When he turned them over they almost fell apart.

When they finished eating the fish and chunks of the bread they brought with them, they polished off the last of the *vino,* then sat back and watched the small waves.

"You met Raoul yet?" Domingo asked.

"Raoul? Who's he?"

"Maria's son, her older one."

"You know him?"

"Know everybody in town."

"Why should I meet him?"

"You shouldn't, but you gave his mother a bad time today and Raoul will not like that. He will be angry with you."

"He takes care of his mother?"

"He thinks he does, and he is not a polite man. Raoul is large, and ugly and mean. He is not a polite *hombre. Comprendo?* He'd just as soon gut you with his long knife as he would stomp on your head. Raoul is not real smart."

"Ugly sounds like the word. I'll watch out for him."

"You better more than watch out, if you

intend on talking with his mother again. You better take along that little toy gun you brought."

"You old son of a bitch," Randy flared, "you looked through my gear when I was sleeping."

"Son, you never told me not to. I had to know if you was ready for middle Mexico here."

Randy went on board the boat, found his valise, and took out the new Derringer. It was a .44-caliber and held two shots, over and under. The barrels were only three inches long and the whole thing could be hidden in one hand. He checked to see that it had two rounds in the chambers. Then he closed it and slid it into his pocket. He was sure there would be no real need for it, but if it would make Domingo feel better, he'd carry it. He could always bluff one of the black-haired kids who ran around the boat.

"Domingo, tonight you come with me up to the *cantina*. Maybe you can make her understand what I want her to do. You're good with the chattering Spanish."

Dom scratched his balding head. "Hell, only if you're buying the booze. You tasted tequila yet?"

As soon as it was dark, they walked to the *cantina*. A dozen men were there. Someone had a mouth harp and was wheezing away. Dom knew most of the men, nodded, called welcome to others. When they sat down, Dom ordered tequila for them.

Randy watched the men, wondering if one of them was Raoul. He doubted it from Domingo's description. Randy was not looking for the man. Dom said he was nineteen or twenty. He sipped at the tequila, and could guess at its potency.

Maria Valdez came through the room serving bottles of warm beer. Randy had no idea where it came from, perhaps from a supply boat of some kind from further south or from the States.

Someone produced a fiddle and began to play. A table top served as a drum and with the harmonica they had a foot-tapping orchestra. A young girl with clicking castanets came out and the men clapped as she did a traditional Spanish dance, her skirts swirling and flapping, her hard heels tapping on the wooden floor.

At the end of the dance, the young girl hurried back into the side room, and Randy guessed she was Maria's daughter, the girl he had seen before.

Before the music started again, a huge bear of a Mexican came through the outside door, looked around, saw Randy and walked directly toward him. Two men moved out of his way, a third hesitated and was pushed aside.

The man was over six feet tall, with bushy eyebrows, and a full black beard. He wore no shirt and only a pair of faded blue pants. His boots were caked with mud and, in his right hand, he held a machete.

The weapon's blade was now only two inches thick where it had been repeatedly sharpened until it was one third worn away. The steel gleamed like fire, reflecting light from the half dozen coal oil lamps, which burned around the *cantina*.

Domingo stood up, pushing in front of Randy. He began talking to the big man before he arrived and went on talking rapidly in fluent Spanish, greeting him, saying how glad he was to see Raoul, complimenting him on his health.

Then quickly his tone changed. He became a teacher, scolding Raoul for bringing his machete into a *cantina*. Someone might get the wrong idea. Someone might think Raoul was threatening him and shoot Raoul with a pistol. A pistol can reach farther than the longest machete, and farther than a strong man can throw a blade.

Gradually, the fire in the big Mexican's eyes began to dim and then simmer. Domingo went on talking, quietly now, motioning the others to go about their business, for the music to start again.

"Raoul, it is true, the *gringo* did come to talk to your *madre*. But many people talk to her, even I talk to Maria Valdez. She is my friend. Why can't the *gringo* talk to her as well?

"I am sorry that your *madre* was crying. Who knows how women think? Perhaps she was remembering a time long ago, before you were even born. Perhaps she will cry no more. You are a good son to your mother. You must go back to your nets in the bay, back to where the large clams lay hidden in the sand. The bay and the sea are your friends, they can be relied upon and understood."

Raoul stared at Domingo. Then his eyes moved to Randy, who had not understood a word of the Spanish conversation, but he knew a threat when he saw one.

"What the hell does he want?" Randy asked quietly.

"Can't you tell? He wants your head on a platter, your guts spread all over the floor. He's not the brightest lad on the coast, so don't do anything to rile him."

"Him? Hell, he's the one riling me!"

"Don't let him see that gun in your

pocket, and don't show it unless you're ready and willing to use it — and only if there's no other way."

Domingo called for a drink for Raoul. His mother brought it, patted his shoulder and smiled. He tried to smile back, but couldn't quite complete the task. She retreated to the back room. The drink was weak tea, the strongest anyone let him have anymore. Raoul sipped at it as Domingo talked. He told Raoul about the ocean trip, about how they had stopped at the reef just around the head and caught a box of fish for the *ninos*. Here Raoul showed his half-smile again.

Gradually, Randy began to understand. Raoul was the local idiot, not right in the head, and he was evidently monstrously protective of his mother. Anyone who made Maria Valdez cry or hurt her would answer to Raoul. Randy began to sweat. What the hell should he do now? He had made Maria Valdez cry, evidently by reminding her of her lost love, her lost child, her ruined life.

Randy put his hand into his pocket, his fingers closing around the Derringer, which had two shots. He would use the gun if he had to. He was sure it would take both shots to stop the giant and his machete.

There was no more time to think about it. Raoul surged forward and motioned for

Randy to stand. Randy rose, and as he came up, he took the Derringer from his pocket and held it unseen at his side. At least he was ready.

The big Mexican lunged for Randy, who jumped back. Domingo slanted in front of the suddenly furious Raoul. One of the Mexican's big hands slapped Domingo aside as if he were an irritating fly, slammed him into a table and rolled him across it to the floor on the other side.

Raoul took a step toward Randy.

"You bastard, you hurt my mother," Raoul shouted in Spanish. He brought up the two-foot-long machete, swinging it menacingly. To prove it was sharp, he slashed at the back of a chair, and cut the inch-thick dry board in half. Raoul jumped a step closer, the machete poised to deal a death blow.

Randy lifted the small pistol, showed it to the man. "Stand back, or I'll shoot you, you raging maniac," Randy shouted.

The Mexican didn't understand the words, but he knew what the pistol was. He lunged forward again. Randy leaped back. He almost escaped, untouched, but the tip of the razor sharp machete caught his left forearm, slicing it a half inch deep and two inches long. Blood gushed down his arm.

Randy screamed in pain, fright and surprise. He aimed the pistol at the big man's thigh and fired. The roar of the .44 cartridge in the small building sounded like a thunderous explosion. Men covered their ears and ducked, but the two principals never wavered. Randy watched the slug pound into Raoul's thigh, and jolt him back a half step. But the big man recovered and came forward again with only a slight limp.

Randy watched the deadly blade swing toward him again. He pulled up the Derringer and fired once more, without time to aim, hoping for a chest hit, something to slow down the damned giant. As soon as he fired he dove to one side, going over a chair, tumbling to the floor, scrambling away.

He never saw the bullet strike. When he lifted the weapon it came higher than he thought. The big .44 slug slammed through Raoul's nose, slanting upward, broke into a dozen chunks of hot lead and bored through vital motor nerve centers of his brain. The swing of the machete faltered and ended in mid-stroke. Raoul's hand relaxed and the blade slanted forward and sank the tip an inch deep in a table top.

Raoul's legs went next, his knees buckled as the power lines from his brain lost their energy. His eyes glazed, a spatter of saliva came from his mouth, and with all the involuntary muscles relaxed, Raoul's bowels emptied as he crashed through a table and rolled to the floor. Raoul had ceased to exist.

For several seconds there was total silence in the *cantina.* Then a sob ripped the stillness, followed by more and a scream as Maria ran into the room and dropped to her knees beside her son.

Domingo sat on the floor where he had fallen, holding his shoulder. He wondered if it were broken or only bruised. He was still groggy when he stood, but he realized what had happened. The Mexican was dead, and his new friend was in *mucho* trouble.

Randy stared down at the dead man, then at the blood still flowing from his own arm. He took a handkerchief from his pocket and wrapped it around the wound, then held the cut with his hand to slow the bleeding. He knelt beside the woman and looked at her.

"I did not mean to shoot him. He was trying to kill me."

Maria looked at him for a moment, a touch of anger quickly melted away. Tears came to her eyes again and she touched Randy's shoulder.

"I know. It is not your fault. It is part of the cross I bear. For I have sinned mightily and must say a thousand Hail Mary's every day for the rest of my life. I am wicked, and the wicked shall beget of their own kind. Go. Go quickly now and sail away with your friend before . . ."

She looked up and saw a man coming toward them. Fresh tears burst from her eyes and she moaned and wept for the dead and for the living as well. Would her sin never be propitiated?

The man who touched Randy on the shoulder wore no uniform, carried no weapon, but Randy knew who he was as soon as he came.

"*Senor,* I am Estrada, *policia.* I must put you under arrest for the death of Raoul Valdez."

"Arrest? But it was plainly self-defense. I'm lucky I'm not the one lying there with my head chopped off!"

"In that case, I would be arresting Raoul. You must come with me to *la estacion policia.*" Randy looked for Domingo, saw him standing, still dazed and called to him. The old sailor walked over with his rolling gait and shook his head.

"I heard. There is nothing I can do right now. Tomorrow, when my head is cleared, I will think of something. Go along with him, now."

"But it was self-defense. You all saw it! He came at me. He cut me. I warned him. The idiot was about to chop off my head!"

"*Senor,* in any death, there must be investigation. Then perhaps a trial. You should be free quickly, perhaps six months."

Randy Pemberton swallowed. Six months! There was no place to run, his gun was empty. Six months in some dusty jail in this filthy village! He'd never live a month. Randy shook his head. There was nothing he could do.

CHAPTER SEVEN:
BREWING THE PLOT

An hour after Lonnie Jenkins was cut down from the spar and pushed overboard, Allen had been summoned from his bunk and escorted into officer country to the captain's cabin. He stepped inside the room as ordered and stared with unconcealed belligerence at Captain Lucas Adrian. The man was not fit for command.

Up close Allen could see the man's sour complexion, the over-red of his cheeks that might indicate a rum pot, and he took pleasure in finding one of the captain's legs resting on a cushioned stool — evidently a victim of the gout.

"Allen, they said your name was. Last name I would guess. Frankly we don't get many men who can express themselves quite as eloquently as you do. Are you a lawyer?"

"No, I'm a slave. A shanghaied victim on board this craft illegally, and held against my will, which constitutes kidnapping, a serious crime, and I'll declare it so as soon as I'm a free man."

"And the lad we just lost was a friend of yours, I know. Too bad, but he should not have struck the officer. Discipline must be maintained. As a man of the sea surely you must recognize that."

"Captain, when you feed men enough, give them reasonable work, and treat them like human beings and not animals, there are never any problems with discipline. This is not the eighteenth century British navy. We are not under that type of primitive regulations."

"Yes, Allen, and more's the pity, more's the pity." He studied the man who stood before him and he was sure his information had been correct. Yes, the man would do nicely, if he could be enticed. If he could somehow break through to him.

"Mr. Allen, we have an opening for the right man in our company as an officer. A new third mate, we're needing, after promotions, and if my eye doesn't deceive me, you're a man who's been to sea — and in officer country before. At least a second, I'd say. What would you say to a quarter share and forty in gold a month and found?"

For a moment Allen considered it. It

might be a chance to make the lot of the men better, to turn things around on board this floating pigsty. Then he shook his head. "No, Captain. I wouldn't fit in with your other officers. I'd not be a good man for this ship. I've never sailed under canvas pulled by unwilling hands."

"Pity, Allen. You might have been good. If you'd been third mate, that young lad you liked would have been alive right now, wouldn't he?"

Captain Adrian groaned as he lifted his swollen foot off the stool and put it on the deck.

"A word of advice to a former officer, sir. Never talk again on my ship the way you did today. It leads to trouble. And trouble you can't afford. You've enough already. Blockton!" The captain bellowed out the man's name. The third mate pushed open the door and stepped inside.

"Aye, sir!" Blockton was not quite recovered. His face was black and blue, his nose smashed, and his eyes showed pure hatred.

"Tie this seaman to the mast and give him two with your whip. Put it in the log and call it general insubordination. Two of your best, Mr. Blockton."

"With pleasure, sir!"

Allen started to say something, then shook

his head.

"No comment, Mr. Allen? Nothing about being fair and reasonable, and a comment on discipline? Your usual glib tongue has left you speechless? And a good thing or it would have been four strokes. Now, off with you and watch your tongue or it will be two strokes a day until your flesh peels off your back!"

At the mast, Allen felt his shirt ripped away and his hands tied to the tall timber.

Blockton stretched it out, testing his whip, waiting until Allen turned to look at him. With the glance came the singing of the leathers and five welts purpled across Allen's back. He kept his sudden scream inside his chest. The pain was furious, unlike anything he had ever felt in his life. It didn't come and fade, it surged into life and grew in intensity, exploding into a red haze as he sagged for a moment against the ropes that held him upright. He battled it away, biting his lip until blood seeped into his mouth.

"Like that, do you, Allen. Taste one with some muscle behind it." Again there was a pause, but Allen did not turn toward the voice. He heard a grunt and tried to steel himself for the descending lash, but he was not in time.

This time the leathers sliced through his

flesh, searing his back with five red lines that sparkled bright with droplets of blood which pooled quickly and ran from stripe to stripe until they surged down his back in red streams, making a giant checkerboard of red squares.

This time he could not force the red haze from his head. It closed around him, surging over his consciousness and blasting him down, down, down, until he could no longer feel the pain, and then he found release in unconsciousness.

Allen awoke on his bunk, screaming. From deep in his own bag Kona had produced a small bottle filled with whiskey, which he now dabbed with a cloth on each part of the red, opened flesh. Two men held Allen down as the big brown Hawaiian wiped again and again and each time bringing a new surge of pain. The eternity of agony ended at last, and Allen was sobbing into the comfort of his folded arms. Now he could hear Kona's words come drifting through the haze.

"That's the end of it. It's all over now. The worst is done, my friend. It's downhill now, all the way to Hawaii."

The other men had been locked in the fo's'cle for two hours before Allen was cut down and taken below. The last man through the hatch had reported a half dozen small green islands. They had to be the first specks of land in the chain that formed the Hawaiian islands.

Huge tears crept down Kona's cheeks. He began chanting to himself, his hips swaying, and his hands making strangely graceful motions.

"Home," the big man said softly. "I'm home again."

It was two full days before Allen could get out of his bunk. He listened to the progress of the ship moving into port, heard the men called. The shanghaied men were locked below, of course. But the non-impressed men scurried topside and worked the big sheets, staggered back to their bunks exhausted from overwork. At last, the hull bumped gently against piling and they were tied up.

Allen tried to sit, but Kona gently pushed him back down.

"Tomorrow," he said.

"I'm one big scab back there, anyway, isn't that right, Kona? Are there any yellow places, and pus forming?"

"No, man. Your back have five cuts, all healing. One more day, then you get up and not break it all open again."

They stayed in port for three days, with

almost no activity on board. The men in the fo'c'sle guessed most of the officers and loyal men were on shore leave. Kona tried the hatch, but there was no way it could be opened. They had no tools, not even a marlinspike, and now they understood why. It was the perfect time to escape with the others gone, but there simply was no way to get through the locks or six inches of wooden hull.

Enough food had been left in the fo'c'sle for three days, and on the fourth, the men straggled back to the ship. The fo'c'sle hatch opened for an hour with an armed guard and a steel grating locked over it. Then they sailed with the three o'clock tide.

Kona sat beside Allen, working a salve into his back. The pain was subsiding now, but the deep soreness was still there. The lashes had cut more than a quarter of an inch into his flesh. But the cuts would be healed completely in two or three weeks, if they did not turn sour with pus.

The big Hawaiian told Allen how he came to be on the ship. He had been going from one of the big islands to another, with a fisherman friend, in an open dug-out canoe with a sail. A sudden squall tore away their sail and capsized the craft. As the boat went over, the end of the mast struck his friend and he sank beneath the waves. Kona swam to find him, but the body was swept away in an instant.

Kona barely made it back to the water filled dug-out canoe. Since he was alone, he could not tip it over and get the water out. He floated in the canoe full of water for two days, until the *Contessa* found him. They were outbound and he agreed to work on the ship until they reached a port where he could get another ship back to Hawaii.

That had been two years ago, and he had been kept a prisoner ever since.

"Officers now get worse," Kona said. "Five men die on this ship since Kona come. Three hanged, two from whip. Now hang young Lonnie. Kona very angry." He leaned closer to Allen. "We must take over ship. We must mutiny!"

Allen's face broke into a grin and he nodded. "Yes, yes, but when, and how? Who are our friends? One day out of port, we all will be working the sails again. They are short on officers. The first mate is sick in his cabin. If the second mate should have some kind of an accident . . ."

Kona laughed softly. "My old friend Ba, the small one from China, will help us. He cooks food for the second mate. When you wish, the second mate will become much ill . . . very sick."

Allen laughed. Now they were beginning to get it put into form. He mentally ticked off what they needed to do. There must be a weapons locker somehwere. Until they found it, marlinspikes would have to do. Twenty-two of the thirty men in the fo'c'sle were shanghaied. All of them would support a mutiny, he was sure.

When? He needed at least another week for his back to heal, but they might not have that much time. They had to be able to get back to land. Two days out of Hawaii would be ideal.

Third Mate Blockton would be a big problem. If he could be eliminated early, it would help. An accident? A broken leg tripping down a ladder? No, Blockton was tough as a white shark and twice as agile. He'd miss the trip and skin the man who tried it.

Have him flogged to death? A knife in Blockton's guts or a marlinspike through his head would be better. Allen had no stomach for murder, but with Blockton he could make an exception. The third mate did not deserve to live. He had killed many men in his time, and now the odds were catching up with him.

Night would be the best time to mutiny.

Midnight would be a fitting hour. The watch and helmsmen — if they were friendly, so much the better.

That afternoon, when they were still locked in, Allen talked to half the men, quietly, two or three at a time, sounding them out on the chance of a takeover of the ship. He never used the word mutiny, and the men he spoke to smiled and laughed and urged him on, giving him their co-operation in any way they could. Not even in one eye did Allen sense a hint of betrayal. He felt now that he had a base for moving against the officers.

The second day out of Hawaii dawned sunny, clear and calm. The sails shivered in a windless sky. The pressed men were let out. The third mate swore at the heavens. Men lay in the sun laughing guardedly at the mate's frustration.

Kona sat in the stern and stared eastward toward the islands and home. Quietly Kona and Allen talked to the men they wanted to use in the takeover. They emphasized this was a legal move to take control of a ship by those who worked her.

By the end of the second day the calm had broken and they were moving again. Allen was ready to strike. He winked at Ba, who caught the signal. That noon, the second mate, Mr. Parmlee, dined on tainted pork and beans, with a touch of powder from Ba's mysterious sea bag. He was ill and unconscious before sundown. Confined to his bed, with no ship's surgeons aboard, he was left to either live or die by his own strength.

Food at the men's messes had not been good, even though fresh supplies should have been taken on at Hawaii. The men had seen a dozen chickens and two pigs put in the hold, but they were for the officers only. Allen's fishing lines had not been productive, and during the calm, they had not caught a thing. They averaged one fish a day during most of the run, and soon the officers tired of it and the fish became a staple for the crew.

Kona had selected two men to help him in his job of taking over the wheel and the watch.

Allen and Ba would lock the loyal men in their bunks aft, and take care of the third mate. Ba had stolen a knife from the mate's mess and said he could use it well.

Allen went over everything again, hoping he had it all worked out. There was nothing more he could do now.

Just before dark the men were herded into the fo'c'sle and counted, then an iron grill

153

clamped shut and locked.

Blockton grinned through the grating. "Like rats in a stinking hold, you are. Captain's orders that all potential trouble-makers be locked up from now on. Pleasant dreams, lads." He laughed as he pranced away.

So they would wait a day. Allen adjusted his plans. They would have to strike just at dusk, just before they were locked in. Evidently the captain had smelled trouble. With his first mate disabled, and now his second mate suddenly getting food poisoning, the situation looked dangerous. The old captain knew he had an unhappy crew, knew that the shanghaied men would cause trouble if they could. So he struck first.

All day Allen went over his plans, but could find no holes, no trouble spots. He concealed himself well, just before dusk, near a sail locker aft of the fo'c'sle. Ba was on the other side.

When Blockton had locked them in the night before, that scurvy little cripple, Hadderlee, the captain's steward, had been along so he could report the deed in detail to the captain. Allen suspected it would be the same way tonight. Kona was waiting to trap Hadderlee as he came out of his domain.

154

Dusk gathered as Blockton swept the ship, rousting a dozen fo'c'sle men who had purposely dallied on the deck. The mate was shouting and angry by the time he had pushed and kicked fifteen men into the compartment. He was so furious, he forgot to count, which was part of the plan. As Blockton reached for the padlock, Ba threw his knife. It was a six-inch blade, heavily made and it struck on the point and vanished half way to the hilt in the third mate's back.

Allen surged from his hiding place and brought an iron spike down hard on Blockton's head. The third mate's face went suddenly haggard as the knife wound began draining energy from his body. The surprised face flashed at Allen as the heavy iron came down. Blockton reached up with strong arms, clawing at Allen's chest. But his hands lost their force, and he fell to the deck with only a slight moan. Two men from the fo'c'sle rushed out, picked up the massive body and lugged it to the rail.

They flopped him over the rail, then pushed him off and watched him splash into the sea. To a man, they felt like cheering, but they did not.

Hadderlee saw it all from his position near the aft mast. He turned, rushing toward the captain's cabin when Kona's big hands closed around his throat, picked him up and carried him to the rail.

"Little worm, do you want to live another ten seconds?"

Hadderlee's wild eyes caught Kona's large brown ones. He nodded quickly.

"Then you will go to the captain's cabin at once, as usual, and say that all men are locked in for the night. Do you understand?"

Hadderlee's head had slumped and Kona pulled his hands away from the cripple's throat. He revived the small man and repeated the instructions.

When Kona was sure Hadderlee knew what he was supposed to do, he put his short knife to the small man's side and they walked the companionway to the captain's cabin.

In his usual croaky voice, Hadderlee did as he was told.

"Captain Adrian, sir. The fo'c'sle crew is safely locked away for the night. Is there anything else, sir?"

"No, dammit. Leave me alone!"

"Aye, aye, sir."

Kona hauled him back out of the foreign area to the deck, where he wanted to throw the scum overboard. But Kona checked himself. Authority and command must not be abused.

Kona left the small man with two men on deck and ran to the big wooden spoked wheel, where the helmsman stood. The man in control was Allen. He had taken over the helm and was putting the ship into a gradual turn that would bring her about and set her on a return course to Hawaii. Men scampered up the lines, hauling in sail when ordered to, and setting new sails as the ship turned, and the long tack began working back to the islands.

The lookout had fought the takeover and had been knocked off his lofty perch, falling into the sea. Allen gave the helm to Kona, who looked immediately at the stars, changed the heading slightly, and settled back with a smile on his big face.

Allen ran to the captain's cabin. There was no answer to his knock. He tried the door and found it bolted. Allen moved to the first mate's door and knocked. He was told to enter. Allen went in quickly and slapped the mate's hand away from his pistol. The man lay in his bunk and was not dressed.

First Mate Al Hanson was too sick to be angry.

"I told Adrian he was working too many pressed men," the mate said. "He's been asking for a mutiny for six months. Block-ton caused it, I can wager. But Adrian wouldn't agree, because he pocketed the wages of every man he's shanghaied. I won't fight you, but neither can I condone a mutiny."

"Sir, do you have any other weapons?"

The mate nodded and pointed to another pistol and a dagger on his sea chest.

"Now, can you leave your bed? I need you to get the captain to open his door."

"To prevent bloodshed, I'll do that, even though he'll brand me with your stripes."

Hanson rose from the bunk in obvious pain and hobbled into the companionway to the cptain's cabin. Allen pounded on the heavy wooden door with a pistol butt. When they heard mutterings, the first mate spoke up.

"Captain Adrian, I need your help."

There were more half-asleep mumblings.

"Captain Adrian, this is Hanson. Can you open up? I need your help!"

A moment later, the door opened, and a pistol came out. Allen slammed his own pistol butt down on the captain's wrist.

He could hear the bone crack, then the six-gun roared, the bullet missing both men. The weapon fell to the floor and Allen retrieved it. Kona ran up, took the first mate back to his cabin and locked him in. They then searched the captain's quarters and found a dozen pistols, of all types and vintages. The captain lay on his bunk in agony, holding his right wrist. When they were sure there were no more weapons in the cabin, Allen turned to the man.

"Adrian, you are not fit to command a rowboat, let alone a merchant vessel like this one. I am relieving you of that command for the good of the impressed men on this ship. You will be put off near the first bit of land we sight. All those who wish to go with you, may. All those who choose to stay with the ship and again become free men, may. If it were my choice, I would hang you from the yardarm at dawn, but my own good judgement has saved your diseased, rotten neck for a different kind of justice — one which will give you more time to suffer. Death is not the ultimate punishment, it is over much too quickly. I hope you suffer for twenty years. And if the authorities catch up with you for kidnapping — perhaps you shall."

They rifled the cabin, took out a large quantity of food and wine, and a strong box, then locked the captain in his cabin and posted a guard outside with a loaded weapon. They checked the second mate who was too ill to protest. Kona found two pistols and a quantity of shells, shot and powder for the flintlocks.

Back on deck, the impressed men lay in the early moonlight. They ate what they wanted from the officer's stores and each man had a bottle of wine.

With morning, the winds picked up, and Kona stayed at the helm. He had no compass, did not want one. He guided the ship by the sun, by the current in the ocean, by the birds he saw and the slant of the clouds in the sky. Some of the men said he also sniffed the air.

One by one, Allen talked with the twenty-eight men locked in the aft bunks. None of them had been shanghaied. Some expressed sympathy for the impressed men. Others said the lot of them should be hung. Allen picked out those he could trust and let them work the ship as usual. The rest, sixteen, remained loyal to the captain and were locked up.

Allen could not understand the men. The captain and his officers had flogged them, starved them, fed them rotten pork and little else, but now the seamen were loyal to him.

Allen ordered the men kept in the lockup until they reached land. With any luck that should be within a day or two.

The free men moved around the ship, exploring areas where they had never been. Then one or two began cleaning up the vessel, just to have something to do. When sails needed to be set or hauled in, the free men leaped to the tasks, singing. They tried to outdo one another with their skills as sailors, because they knew each bit of work they did brought them closer to freedom in a free port.

The third day of the return trip, Kona dozed near the wheel when the lookout spotted the first landfall. Allen had felt earlier that they had turned a little more to the north than they needed to. But then he remembered that the Hawaiian string arched out, angling northwest. Kona had wanted to sight the islands at the first opportunity.

Kona came out of his nap and scanned the horizon, the tiny spot growing larger, until it turned green. He sailed straight for it and, when less than a mile off, he smiled.

"Yes, Niihau. Good. No white man lives there. Only a few of my people. Plenty fruits, taro, fish."

Allen called for the main topsails to be hauled in and the *Contessa* slowed. The hands put the longboat over the side and made it fast. Then the sixteen men straggled up from the aft hold and were ordered into the boat. One tried to change his mind, but Allen would not permit it.

"You made your choice. Stand by it. Down the side and into the boat!"

All three officers had to be lowered by slings from a spar. The second mate had recovered somewhat from the poisoning, but still could keep no food on his stomach. When all were safely stowed aboard the longboat, the seamen lifted the oars ready for orders.

"You'll hang for this, Allen, and all with you," the captain warned.

"You're living a hundred years in the past, Adrian. No legitimate court would touch us. When they hear how you kidnapped your crew, starved them, and put the money for the wages and food into your own pocket, you'll be the one hung." The men cheered behind him.

"Oh, we found your strongbox. Don't worry about it, the goods will be divided among the men who were shanghaied. And, Captain, pay attention that you don't lose your head out there on that island. Kona tells me it's called Niihau, and as he says, that means 'cannibal.' So watch yourself."

The men in the longboat looked at one another in surprise.

162

"Then give us some weapons, Allen!" the captain demanded.

"Cut them loose, Kona," Allen called, and the longboat drifted away.

The crew of the *Contessa* was busy then, setting more sail, changing course. When Allen had the vessel well on its way, he looked back at the small boat and saw six oars pulling in rhythm as the craft moved toward Niihau. He smiled about his little joke on the captain. It served him right.

Allen and Kona talked about their route. Their strategy had been to sail into Honolulu Harbor, sell the goods aboard the *Contessa* for whatever they could get, divide the money among the men and abandon the ship. Her rightful owners would be notified eventually, and would collect her. It wouldn't be right to sell the ship. No, a quick sale of goods, a division of funds and the men would blend into the scene at Honolulu, waiting for passage on an honest ship or working their way back, to various homes, from San Diego to Seattle.

When the vessel was on its new course, Kona said it was about one hundred and fifty miles from Niihau to Honolulu.

"If wind hold, we be there tomorrow, before dark," Kona said.

Allen thanked him and began his rounds

163

of the men, asking how long each had been a shanghaied victim on the *Contessa*. It ranged from a little over two months to two years. Allen gathered the shanghaied men around him and told them of the plans to sell the trading goods, abandon the ship, and scatter before anyone knew it was a mutiny ship.

All hands agreed.

"You said something about the captain's sea chest, Mr. Allen?" one man said.

Allen signalled and Ba brought it.

Rather than a sea chest, it was more of a strongbox — very heavy and with a sturdy lock. Hammers swung and the hasp broke from the chest. The men crowded around as Allen opened it.

Inside the box were two compartments and two cloth sacks. In the first compartment, they found stacks of bills, mostly greenbacks, but some Hong Kong dollars, a few British pounds sterling and some French francs. One man set to counting it and soon had the sum.

"Six thousand and two hundred dollars!" he shouted. A cry went up from the men. Allen had counted thirty-four men who had been shanghaied. It indeed was something to cheer about.

Allen opened one of the cloth sacks and

found it filled with double-eagles — twenty-dollar gold pieces. The count there was faster: three thousand dollars even.

The second sack was made up of smaller gold pieces, another fifteen hundred dollars American.

The last compartment contained the ship's log and important papers, those of ownership, and data that was highly incriminating for the mutineers. Allen took all the records and threw them overboard.

Someone did some fast figuring — ten thousand, seven hundred dollars in hard cash money in the strongbox!

"A share for each man shanghaied, Captain Allen?" someone asked.

"That's *Mr.* Allen," he insisted. "Let's take a vote. How many for a share per man?"

Thirty-four voices thundered out "Aye," and it was decided.

There was some figuring again, and, a moment later, they came up with a sum. "That's three-hundred and fifteen dollars per man, hard money," the fastest figurer said.

The sum seemed huge to most of them. Many had worked for years at ten dollars a month and food on ships, or for twice that and no found in stores and on farms. Cattle ranches paid cowboys only twenty to twenty-five dollars a month and found. So much money all at once boggled their minds.

Allen considered it again. "Men, perhaps we should forget about the goods on board. Legally, we could get into trouble over that. Perhaps we should slide into port just at dusk, tie up, pick up our pay, and fade into the night. What do you say?"

Again a chorus of "yes" carried the motion.

Allen turned and caught the familiar sight of jumping porpoises.

"Look alive with the fishing gear! Over the side with all lures! Rig for deep running! Kona, close haul the mainsails and slow us to five knots. I want to eat yellowfin for dinner!"

And so they did. They caught four of the fish, all thirty-pounders, and cooked them on the deck. They washed the fish down with the last of the fresh mangoes, papayas and coconuts from Hawaii. They planned on eating the chickens the next day, but gave up on the pigs because no one wanted to butcher them.

Kona did not have any of the fish, except a small slice he had cut off raw. He could almost smell his islands. He could see the fish, watch the birds he knew so well, and he could practically taste the fruits of his lovely islands. After two years away, he did not want anything to deter him from guiding the ship safely into the great port on the next day. He would not sleep until sunrise.

At dawn, he checked their position again, watched the sea birds and the waves. He looked where the September sun was and made one last adjustment on his bearing. With a compass point to follow, he turned the wheel over to Allen, and went to sleep. Each hour he awoke to take a new look for the signs that he knew would bring him home.

He settled down near the wheel just after sunrise and slept better than he had in two years.

That afternoon the *Contessa* worked her way around the island the natives called Oahu. There was no room at the small docks in port for the large ship. So, as was the practice, the *Contessa* put down her anchor in the southern arm of the bay to await dock space. The men were given their share of the found money, and then rowed ashore in the remaining longboat.

It took two trips to get them all ashore, and on the second one, Allen and Kona went. On shore, they shook hands. Then the big Hawaiian hugged Allen and told him to come see him anytime he was in the islands. Anyone would know where to find Kona.

Allen remembered the small clapboard building that had served the Pacific Steamship Company in Honolulu three years ago. He wondered if it were still there. He was sure it was, or if not, a better one. Once there, he would have no trouble in getting a ship home.

When he arrived at the office, he found everything exactly the way he had seen three years before.

CHAPTER EIGHT:
THE CALM AND THE STORM

The *bandido* camp where Martha and Johnnie Laveau were held prisoner was called
Arroyo Seco, not for the small lake and bubbling stream, but rather for the dry wash
they rode along to get to the green valley.
Life drifted from one day to the next with
little change. Scouts reported few travelers
on the road, and these were stopped,
robbed, but seldom held for ransom. Ransom was a risky business, and *El Jefe* did
not like to take risks. He and his men had
lived in *Arroyo Seco* for over ten years, with
little outside interference.

Some of the men had wives and families
in Todos Santos, but it was here that they
made their living. From time to time, they
stayed in town for a week or a month, then
returned to "work" at the dry-wash camp.

El Jefe had tired of the new half-breed
senorita. Her novelty soon faded and he
used her only when he had a need.

Martha welcomed the change in his sexual demands, and worked out elaborate codes and methods to communicate with Johnnie Laveau, but somehow they never worked. Johnnie was treated like a slave, doing the most menial tasks, digging latrines, chopping wood, cleaning out the horse corral, taking the horses to water each morning and evening. His head wound had healed and he kept waiting for what he hoped was a favorable chance to escape.

On the surface, Johnnie gave his captors no cause to worry. He carried his ten-pound iron ball wherever he went, his right arm supporting the weight. He never complained and he was more than willing to make a try at some magic when the *bandido* chieftain asked him to.

"But, mon, need many things: black cat, dozen feathers, droppings from bat, two small apples."

El Jefe laughed when he heard the list, and had his men find the items. Johnnie told the chief that it would take him at least a week to work up the materials into usable form.

During that week, Johnnie obtained clippings from *El Jefe*'s beard, which he hid, in a special place near his bunk, at the far end of the largest building.

Johnnie knew he did not have a hundredth of the materials that he needed, so he concentrated on the apple, carving a man's face in it, and letting it shrink and shrivel in the warm sun. Soon it took on the shape of a head, and a face, and onto this he fastened the clippings from *El Jefe*'s beard. Next, he made a crude stick body and put the head on it. Then he used a piece of string and wound it tightly around the apple head. That night, in the pale moonlight, Johnnie set out his materials and whispered an incantation. He then buried the bearded apple-head doll in a shallow dust grave behind the corral.

The next morning, *El Jefe* had a pounding headache he could not stop. He was furious.

"Headache! I never have the headache!"

The following evening Johnnie did his magic act for *El Jefe* and Martha. It was a display of old sleight of hand tricks. Using *El Jefe*'s deck of playing cards, he threw them into the night sky, and proceeded to apparently retrieve them from *El Jefe*'s ear, his pocket, and from under his chair.

When Johnnie was through, he told *El Jefe* he was sorry that none of the other magic worked, but he didn't have the right ingredients.

"Maybe mon do good next time," he said.

That evening, *El Jefe* went to bed early, agonizing over his aching head. As he lay beside Martha, he tried to think what was the matter with him. He had always been strong, never sick.

"Your wizard," he said, touching her shoulder. "I was fine before your wizard did tricks."

Martha laughed. "Doing card tricks and causing you great pain are much different. How could a quiet man like Johnnie do that? Anyway, your headaches started the day before the tricks." She patted his aching head and rolled away. "I think I am too much woman for you. *El Jefe* is becoming an old man who must be careful now that he has been brought down to size!"

He grabbed her and in spite of his headache they made love three times that night. Even that did not help, and his hurting head grew steadily worse.

That night, while *El Jefe* battled his pain, Johnnie slid out of his bunk, slipped past the other sleepers and quietly clubbed the outside guard into unconsciousness with a thick stick. He looked around. Everything was quiet. No one seemed to have heard him. Johnnie carried the ten-pound ball automatically now, allowing for it in his walk, in his work — in his escape.

Like a ghost, he moved toward the corral. He was not sure if there was more than one guard outside, but he didn't think so.

Johnnie had planned this move for weeks. It was his one chance to get away, his chance to get out and bring back help for Mrs. Dyke. He must. He had promised Mr. Pemberton.

Johnnie moved like a shadow from one darkness to the next, running when there was a cloud over the moon, walking the last twenty yards toward the corral. The ten-pound ball was still in his hand, the chain stretched so it would not hit against itself and make noise.

At the edge of the horse enclosure, he rested. One mount was always left saddled, just outside the fence, in case a quick trip was needed to the lower guard. Johnnie found that horse and pushed it against the poles of the corral. He climbed up and slid into the saddle. He looped the chain around the saddle horn and for a moment he was free of its weight.

Carefully he untied the reins, and nudged the horse toward the gate. No use in leaving if he would have immediate pursuit. He opened the gate, swung it wide, walked his mount inside and around to the far side where he began prodding the nags toward the open gate. He wanted them to walk out if possible, but soon gave up on that idea. He waved his arms and slapped his hands, driving the horses out.

One horse broke into a canter and then a run. A moment later, the thirty horses were pounding out of the enclosure and through the edge of camp toward the trail.

There was a shout behind him, but it was lost in the pounding of one hundred and twenty hooves. Johnnie was right behind them, flapping his arms, herding them together, turning them into the narrow trail toward the valley mouth two miles below.

He knew there was a guard there, but he was probably sleeping. No one had ever come looking for *El Jefe.* Why would they come tonight?

But the horses had wakened the guard. As Johnnie slammed past with the other horses, he lay low against the mount's neck, hoping he would not be seen.

Again he heard some shouts, and this time one pistol shot. Then he was past, and still driving the herd of horses along the water course, forcing them as far as he could from the bandits. It would take some time to regain their mounts and pursue him.

He pushed the horses for over an hour,

then let them slow down. A few began to wander away, to tire. But he held a dozen together and herded them on down the water course, hoping it would lead him to the ocean and the trail he had been following with Martha Pemberton Dyke. The trail to Todos Santos now seemed faint and far away.

Sometime, just before daylight, he lost the last of the horses, and let his own mount rest. Then he moved again at a walk down the sandy, dry riverbed, toward the sea. There were fewer hills in front of him now, and that was a good sign.

As he rode, Johnnie made his plans. They had been in the third day of travel from Tijuana, and that meant they must not have been more than twenty miles from the little town of Todos Santos. He would turn in that direction when he found the trail, and ride into the settlement. There, he could have the shackle taken off his ankle, report where the *bandidos* lived and take some soldiers back after them. Or, if there were no soldiers there, he could find a boat, sail back to San Diego and send word to Mr. Pemberton. It was a decision he would soon regret.

Johnnie had been riding for two hours after the sun came up, and had worked through many of the hills and dry creek beds. But he always kept moving toward the ocean, following a fairly easy trail that the bandits had worn in the ground with constant use.

Then the dry river course turned around a small hill — and before he knew it, there were two horsemen riding toward him. He stopped. Then, not able to figure out a better defense, he rode straight at them. Only when he got close did he realize they were *bandidos* from *Arroyo Seco*. They figured out who he was about the same time and drew their pistols.

Johnnie lay low against the horse's neck to make as small a target as possible and continued to ride at them. There was no place else to go in the narrow gorge.

On signal, the two bandits split apart so they could come at him from slightly different angles. He heard the shots of the six-guns, but nothing hit him.

Johnnie turned toward the smaller of the two men. Still lying low against the horse, he unhooked the ten-pound ball from the saddle horn. The horses snorted and reared as they came close. The maneuver threw off the bandit's aim, and by the time his horse had come back with all four feet on the ground, Johnnie's mount was on him. The other horse lunged aside, undirected by the rider. Johnnie surged so close his stirrup grazed that of the other rider. The tactic had left the bandit surprised — with his gun pointing in the wrong direction.

Johnnie held the chain and swung the heavy ball at the man's chest as he passed. The ball crashed into the *bandido,* crushed his ribs, jamming them into his lungs, driving them through his heart killing him instantly.

As his horse tore on past, Johnnie almost lost his grip on the chain, but held on as the ball came flying past the bandit. It was all he could do to lift the ball and put it back around the saddle horn.

The other rider had changed his course. He now rode hard at Johnnie from the side, trying to hit him with his pistol. Two more bullets slashed past Johnnie's head and missed. But the next one hit the horse in the head. It went down in a floundering confusion of man, beast, legs. But Johnnie had managed to pull the ten-pound ball free of the horse. He found himself unhurt and, carrying the ball, ran for a scattering of brush twenty yards away.

The pursuing bandit saw Johnnie's horse, down and dying, and looked back at his friend sitting slumped over in his saddle.

His horse had stopped moving. The bandit raced back to find out what had happened to his friend. After all, the Negro could not get away on foot.

Johnnie looked around him. There was no place to run. But he had to get away, to hide. The bandit's brief ride to check on his friend gave him a chance, but what was he going to do with it?

He looked around again, grinned and went to work.

The bandit Valquez reloaded his new *pistola,* as he rode toward his friend, Pedro. Why was Pedro simply sitting there on his still horse? Was he loco or hurt?

Valquez could not see anything wrong with Pedro as he rode up.

"Pedro, you loafer, come on. Let's kill that Negro, and *El Jefe* will give us a reward." He cuffed Pedro on the shoulder. The bandit leaned away, and fell out of the saddle, his body limp as it crashed to the ground.

Valquez couldn't believe it. He jumped from his horse and touched his friend's eyes. The lids stayed open. He started to bend to listen to Pedro's heart when he saw the man's chest caved in, his shirt stained dark red with fresh blood.

Valquez gave a shrill cry of anger and loss.

He mounted his horse and charged at the place where he had last seen the black man. The Negro would die, but he would die slowly! He would pull out the Negro's fingernails, cut off his toes, gouge out his eyes — and then he would start to get cruel. The Negro would die a thousand deaths before this morning was over!

Valquez found the Negro's dead horse, then rode to the small patch of shoulder-tall brush. A dozen times Valquez rode through the brush, but he did not flush out the Negro. He was not there.

Valquez rode off a dozen yards to each side and studied the land in every direction. Impossible! The black gringo could not have run away. It was too far. He carried the ball, and was barefoot. There were sharp rocks and dead cactus and rattlesnakes all over the arroyo. There had not been enough time for him to get out of the gully. He had to be hiding in the brush.

Again and again Valquez tramped his horse through the brush and weeds, rode a dozen yards in a large circle the way he had seen the trackers do. The black had not walked away. There would have been tracks. He was not a god, nor a bird, so he had flown away.

Nor, Valquez thought, were there any

small hoofprints of *diablo* to show where the Negro had turned into a devil and walked away so no mortal could see him.

He had to be here! Once more, Valquez covered the ground on foot, worked through the brush, *nada!*

He got on his horse and, leading Pedro's as well so the black could not use it, he rode a circle around the spot a half mile out, climbing up and down arroyos, watching from high points. Nothing moved in the desert — nothing that was black and human and lugging a ten-pound ball and chain.

At last, Valquez gave up. The Negro was a miracle man, or he was already dead. But the story he would tell *El Jefe* would be quite different. He'd say he caught the Negro, shot him and buried the body. No, *El Jefe* would demand that he come and show the body.

At last, Valquez decided to tell the truth. He shot the Negro's horse from under him, went to help Pedro, and when he came back two minutes later, the injured Negro had vanished. But he was twenty miles from town, and twenty miles from any water. He was on foot and alone. The Negro was as good as dead. *El Jefe* would believe that. He had to.

Three hours later, Valquez met *El Jefe* and ten of his men who were riding hard toward him. They had herded up most of the scattered horses. Now they stopped at a wide turn in the arroyo.

"You are hunting for the Negro?" Valquez shouted.

"You have seen him?" *El Jefe* asked.

Valquez nodded and they rode back the way Valquez had come. On the way, the *bandido* told his chief exactly what had happened. He added a lucky shot in the shoulder to the story to make it more reasonable.

El Jefe glared at his rider. The man was stupid or he would now have the Negro back in his grasp, where he could strip the black skin off and watch him die in agony.

Nearly three hours later, when they arrived at the point where they could see the dead horse and the body of Pedro, *El Jefe* stopped his eleven men and told them to dismount. Then he went ahead on foot, closely followed by Valquez. They walked to the dead horse, then to the brush. *El Jefe* did not look at the sparse growth, nor did he pay any attention to Valquez and his protestations about how hard he searched.

Instead, *El Jefe* stood and looked over the edge of the dry wash, the banks, the upthrust of the arroyo to the top. He did the same thing time and time again. Then he grunted.

"Now *stupido,* I will show you where *El Negro* watched you in your search, laughed at your stupid mistakes."

They walked forward to the center of the wash, where a dozen riffles of fine sand had been deposited during numerous sudden rains that sent water flooding down the low places to the sea. At the very edge of one of these riffles. *El Jefe* stopped. At his feet lay the answer: a man-sized depression scooped hurriedly out of the soft sand. A man had lain in the depression and covered himself with sand, probably allowing only his nose and eyes to remain above the surface. Impressions of the man's heels still showed in the dry sand, and the imprint of the heavy steel ball was plain to see.

"He was there, under sand, watching me?" Valquez couldn't believe it. "I rode so close to him. See? Two feet from his head my horse's hooves hit. Why was he not afraid and leap up?"

El Jefe knocked Valquez down and kicked him twice in the ribs.

"Did you shoot the Negro or not?"

"I think I hit him, *El Jefe.* He rode right at us. We separated. He swung heavy ball at Pedro. I think I hit him."

The chief kicked Valquez again, called for his best trackers and told them to follow the footprints.

Then minutes later, the trackers gave up. "The black gringo moved from the sand to the hardness of the rocks," the trackers said.

When *El Jefe* examined the dead horse, he saw part of the saddle was gone. The saddle blanket had been stripped away and some of the leather straps cut off. A moment later he discovered that Pedro's body was missing its boots and shirt. A knife, canteen and pistol were also gone.

When Valquez formed up with the riders for the return to camp, *El Jefe* knocked him off his horse with a thunderous clout to his head. Valquez sat in the sand, knowing there was no response he could make.

"Valquez, you will walk back to *Arroyo Seco.* Until we find *El Negro,* you will do his duties. You will wear his ten-pound ball, and you will clean out the corral. *Vamos!*"

Three men were sent to track down Johnnie. All had rifles, double canteens and strong horses. They were given two days to find him. In that time, he would be able to walk to Todos Santos. If he got there, it would endanger the whole *bandido* camp.

At the camp, *El Jefe* was still furious with everyone. Two men killed, and the Negro was still not captured. The guard who had been beaten had died during the night.

But worst of all, the Negro was still free. He had to be captured, or he could bring back the soldiers.

El Jefe called his men together, explained how serious the situation was, and asked for three volunteers to ride to Todos Santos, and station themselves around the town to watch for this Negro. If he tried to get into the town, he was to be shot dead. He must be killed at all costs before he could talk to any soldiers or any federal police.

The three volunteers left as soon as they were fed and given fresh mounts.

El Jefe returned to his shack and lay on his bunk. He was still plagued by headaches. It was a continual throbbing now and seemed to be getting worse. It was a mystery to him. It seemed as if someone had tied a wire around his head and was tightening it every few days.

Now he turned to Martha.

"Your Negro friend is a clever man. He escaped today, and is one very smart *hombre,* but we will capture him. My six men will find him and kill him and life here will be as it was before. If he died twice, I will still not be satisfied."

"No, *El Jefe,* Johnnie will not be captured

and he will not die. He is a magician, remember? I think he is causing your headaches. I remember now that he has done it before. He calls it voodoo. He is from Jamaica, a black land where voodoo is common. If he is causing your headaches, you better ask him how he does it before you kill him. Otherwise it will get worse and worse. It will end only when he takes the curse off you which he has applied. Black magic and voodoo can be very strong."

"Nonsense! I am *El Jefe.* That Negro cannot hurt me. I can cut him to pieces if I wish."

"Yes, but he has hurt you. You said you never had headache before. Now you do, and it is getting worse. You are being a victim of voodoo, no doubt about it."

El Jefe slammed his hand down on the blankets. "No! No! It is all mumbo jumbo. There is no voodoo here. I am *El Jefe* and I will not permit it!"

The next day, good news came to *El Jefe.* The scout said that two wagons and a carriage were moving down the road along the coast, evidently heading for Todos Santos. They would be in an ideal position to be attacked late that afternoon.

El Jefe found his good spirits again. He kept putting cold cloths on his head, and it even felt better. Carefully, he organized an attack party. As he did, he eyed Martha. "Take off that filthy blouse. Put on something clean!"

Martha ran to her two valises and took out the blouse with the diamonds sewn into it and showed it to him. "This?" she asked.

He nodded and waved her away, then watched her dress.

El Jefe thought about the situation. Yes, he was right. The lookout reported at least two women in the party, and four men had also been seen. It was possible there were other persons in the two covered wagons, a grand party, probably rich.

He would approach them a little differently than before — in the buggy! Yes, and the *gringa* would ride up in the buggy with him, meet them politely, then pull the shotguns on them and his men would sweep in. It would be a neat trick, catch them totally by surprise, and the *gringas* in the group would not be damaged.

El Jefe tossed Martha a bar of soap. It was sweet-smelling and she realized it had come from her own valise.

"*Gringa,* go wash yourself. Take a bath, wash your hair. You must be *muy hermosa* for this afternoon."

"A bath?"

"In the stream or in the lake."

"Oh, yes. Now?"

"Now."

"Si."

She found a towel, again from her valise, which she had not been permitted to use before. She went to the far side of the small lake, undressed in some bushes and slid into the cool water. It was delicious.

She had washed her hair and just soaped her arms and shoulders when she realized someone was watching her. She promptly slid under water to her neck and continued to wash — not as efficiently, but it was better than nothing. But after a while, she became so cold that she shivered uncontrollably in the water. She left the lake, walked openly to her towel, ignoring the several pairs of eyes now watching, and wrapped the towel around her. She sat down and dressed.

Martha walked back toward the shack feeling more refreshed and alive than she had in weeks. For no reason, she thought about the small calendar she had scratched on the wall of the shack with a nail. This must be near the end of October, the 24th or 25th. She had been gone from home for almost two months. Her father would be frantic.

Back at the shack she brushed her hair, and when it was completely dry, she arranged it with some combs and pins on top of her head.

El Jefe did not like it.

"Do not look like cheap *puta.* Let it fall down around your shoulders."

She took it down and he nodded. *"Muy bueno."*

He picked out the blouse she had shown him before and a long skirt. When she was dressed, he smiled and led her to her horse.

She knew at once that they were going on a raid. Each man in the party had two pistols and a rifle. There were fifteen men and they looked eager to be started.

It had been well over a month and a half since she had ridden up this trail from the ocean. But she had no delusions that she would be able to escape. *El Jefe* was too strong for any group of travelers.

She realized she must be going along as a decoy or a show piece of some kind to help catch the travelers off their guard. But if possible, she would scream or fire a gun to warn them somehow. If there were any women in the group, she would be doubly sure to give them some indication that they were in danger.

The riders wound down the trail and

stopped to hitch one of the horses to the Democrat buggy. A test showed the horse would pull the rig without any trouble. Then *El Jefe* ordered Martha into the buggy, climbed in himself, and the group continued its journey toward the main trail that wound down the 1,000 mile length of Baja California.

She was surprised how close the bandit camp was to the road. When they came in, it seemed that the bandits had led them in the buggy for several miles from the track before they left the rig.

Now she realized it was little more than a mile off the main trail where the buggy had been left. As they approached the track through the barren desert and rolling grassless hills, the men split, half moving on each side of the trail and heading north. *El Jefe* drove the buggy slowly forward in the direction of Tijuana.

"You're attacking a party coming this way?" she asked.

"*Si.*"

"And I'm the camouflage, the bait."

"*Verdad.*"

"I'll spoil it for you. I'll scream and tell them to run for it."

He grabbed one of her breasts with his big hand and squeezed hard. "You do, *gringa,* and I cut this *pecho* off. You want that?"

Tears filled her eyes. She shook her head. Then she shivered and one sob escaped her. He relaxed his hand.

"You no like that?"

"No."

"Then do not be foolish."

"You would do that to me, cut me?"

"*Si, puta,* everywhere. Two new ones on these wagons."

Martha realized he meant exactly what he said. Despite the few actually tender moments they had experienced together, he would maim her if it served his purposes. He would throw her aside like a worn-out toy, break her or kill her as it fit his plan.

She knew at that moment that she could not risk warning the strangers coming down the trail. If she did, surely she would die.

Martha Pemberton Dyke was not ready to die, not yet, and not without making a real mark in the world!

They drove half a mile and stopped. A mirror flashed from the left, picking up the sun and bouncing its rays directly into the buggy. It was the signal. The buggy began to move ahead again, then quickened and was just past a turn in the trail on the near side of a steep ravine.

The first of two covered wagons came down the far side. A woman sat on the outside driver's seat beside a man. The buggy plunged down the steep trail to the ravine bottom.

At the center of the ravine the roadway narrowed and *El Jefe* pulled the buggy far to the side as they drove along the trail. He over corrected and the off wheel dropped into a deep hole, jolting the buggy to a sudden stop. The wagon driver pulled up at once, a look of concern on his face. He was young and the woman beside him looked young, too. But not pretty, and strangely masculine.

El Jefe swore in Spanish, and Martha didn't try to understand him. There was nothing she could do to warn them.

The next covered coach came down the ravine, and too late saw the traffic jam at the bottom. It skidded to a stop as the driver applied the foot brake and stopped with the two horses touching the first coach.

Almost at that instant, a shot sounded from the rim of the gully. *El Jefe* pulled up a double-barreled shotgun from the floor of the buggy and had it almost to his shoulder. Just then, a .44-caliber pistol round caught him in the forehead and drove him against the back of the seat.

For a moment, *El Jefe* looked more surprised than he'd ever been in his life. Then the slug continued into his brain and his whole body twitched with death contractions. This jolted his fingers which set off the double triggers and emptied both rounds from the shotgun into the side of the buggy horse, which went down in a scream of pain, thrashing its way to a quick death.

Pistols and rifles opened up from the ravine ledge.

Martha dropped to the floor of the buggy and prayed.

The covering canvas fell from the coaches and revealed iron sides, with firing slots in them. They bristled now with a dozen rifles that fired again and again, picking off the poorly concealed *bandidos* on the rim of the ravine. They thought they were going to have another easy fish shoot in a barrel, which had made them careless.

The third vehicle in the convoy, a wagon, had stopped on the edge of the ravine. Four men scrambled from the rig and took positions behind rocks to support the fire coming from below. Using careful shots, the sharpshooters on the wagon began silencing the bandit guns. Two bandits ran for horses, but were cut down by the repeating rifles.

Martha nearly fainted from the sound and the smell. Then something hit her in the shoulder. She couldn't cry out; she couldn't move. The hot sudden thrust through her shoulder made her whole body go limp, and she was sure she had died.

Then the pain told her she was still alive, so thundering, so sharp, so frightening, until the gunfire faded away and she heard nothing more.

In the gully, the man who had been driving the first coach lay on the ground not moving, evidently the victim of an early volley from the rim. The "lady" in the seat had been ready and, when the first shot came, she did a neat backwards roll into the iron protection of the wagon, and survived. Both the drivers on the second wagon had pivoted backward out of danger and helped fire from the wagon slots.

A yelled command from the first wagon came dimly to Martha's ears, and the rifle fire stopped. Two men in the wagon above untethered saddle horses from the back of the rig and rode off, hard in pursuit of two bandits who had made it to their horses.

From the first shot to the last, the fight had lasted only forty-one seconds. Martha came back to consciousness from her faint and could have sworn the shooting lasted for at least twenty minutes. Her head ached, her shoulder pounded with pain, she had dirt in her eyes and her nose burned with the gagging cordite powder. She had never been so miserable in her life.

The man who drove the first wagon, and had shown concern over the buggy wheel in the hole, lifted off the ground, dusted off his clothes and laughed quietly. His captain told him that playing dead in an ambush situation was a risky business, but as long as he had to be the only man without protection, he could try it as long as it worked.

Lieutenant Ernesto Costa called to his men in the two coaches, and found that no one had been wounded. He ran to the buggy, peered carefully over the edge of the floor, his six-gun ready, but what he saw made him realize he hadn't been mistaken. She was a real girl, not a dressed-up male, as he had used on the drivers' seats. And she was beautiful.

He saw the blood on her shoulder staining the expensive blouse, and shouted for the medical kit. A moment later a private ran up with the kit.

"Madre de Dios!" the young man breathed when he saw Martha. "She's real."

Lieutenant Costa had torn her blouse at the shoulder, and saw that the bullet had entered just under her shoulder and high over her left breast. The girl was unconscious again. He lifted her, looked under her shoulder and saw where the lead had come out her back. An ugly wound but certainly not fatal. He put compresses on both wounds, stopping the flow of blood. Then he wound white bandages around and around under her shoulder and around her neck to hold the bandages in place.

A half hour later, his men came back with two captives. Costa helped his men moved the *senorita* to the first covered coach and laid her on a soft pallet. Sergeant Norte bathed her forehead with cool water as the lieutenant interrogated the two prisoners. After an hour, and with only one broken arm between them, the two prisoners agreed to lead the soldiers into *Arroyo Seco.*

Lieutenant Costa was torn between two duties. He should take the beautiful woman to Todos Santos and rush her to a doctor. But he also should take his men into the stronghold and wipe out the rest of *El Jefe*'s men who had remained behind. This band had been terrorizing the area for ten years. At last, he chose the less pleasant course. He left Sergeant Norte in charge of the vehicles with three men to drive them. They moved the wagons as far as the turnoff to

Arroyo Seco. There the lieutenant checked on Martha again, kissed her pale cheek and motioned them forward.

"Be very careful, watch her all the time," Lieutenant Costa warned. "Drive at a safe speed, but get her to Todos Santos as soon as you can, and take her at once to the doctor. We will be there at the first possible moment with our prisoners."

Sergeant Norte saluted and watched his commander ride off. He would take special care of this pretty one. The lieutenant was clearly smitten with her. He waved his men forward and they drove down the dusty road toward Todos Santos.

Once Martha stirred and tried to sit up, but the sergeant gently pushed her back on the pallet. She knew she was dreaming. She imagined she was in a buggy again, and they were moving, but somehow she was lying down, and her shoulder still hurt. What had happened to her shoulder? She couldn't remember. Only the ravine, and the three wagons, and then the shooting.

Oh, the poor horse! It had cried so when the guns went off. And *El Jefe,* where was he?

She couldn't get up strength enough to open her eyes. This fuzziness would pass. She just needed a rest, one little nap and she would be up and around and find out what happened.

The poor travelers! They wouldn't have a chance! Had one of them pushed her down? What did happen back there? But she was so tired. Just a little nap . . . It all slipped away, and she was sleeping again.

The sergeant shook his head. He had seen lots of bullet wounds, but never anything like this one. There was no clean hole in front. He had helped the lieutenant dress the wound and it looked to him like the bullet had hit something and came down sideways, but still had enough power to blast on through her shoulder. She wouldn't be feeling very well for a long time, not with that.

He watched her, changed the wet cloth on her forehead, and knew that a fever was starting. How could it come on so quickly?

She was the most beautiful woman he had ever seen. She might be twenty or twenty-one, and she didn't look all Mexican. The thrust of her breasts, even as she lay on her back, was enough to draw a sigh of admiration from him. But he looked away quickly. When she was well, she would be for the lieutenant. He had seen that much in the officer's eye. If he let anything happen to her, it would be his stripes, Sergeant Norte knew.

He called sharply to the driver of the coach to be more careful, to hit fewer holes in the road or to slow down. At once, the sergeant noticed that the driver did both, and the three-striper grinned. A sergeant also had some power.

CHAPTER NINE:
LOVELY SPANISH GUITARS

It was three days before Lieutenant Ernesto Costa rode into Todos Santos. He had lost two men dead, four wounded, had killed ten bandits, captured their camp and taken four men and two women prisoners. He had suffered a bullet wound in the thigh and a saber slash on his left arm, but he was smiling. *El Jefe* was no more, his camp discovered and neutralized, his men dead, prisoners, or run into the hills. And the prize of all, Lieutenant Costa had found two valises which could only belong to the *senorita* he had rescued from the villain. This should all stand him in good stead with her when he called.

There was no medical doctor in Todos Santos. But the local *curandera* had visited Martha shortly after her arrival, had made several chants and offered three kinds of herbs to help Martha in her healing.

When she left, Sergeant Norte took over

the treatment, kept the wound clean and once a day washed it off with the purest alcohol he could find. Already her fever was fading. He hoped she would waken soon.

Martha lay on a real bed in a small house that had been taken over from the owners for a short time by Sergeant Norte. He told the family he had a seriously sick lady who needed a good bed.

"This *senorita* is a favorite of the lieutenant, and you would make him very happy if you were to offer to let the lady stay here until she gets well."

The family moved out at once and Martha lay on the soft bed struggling with the fever. The second day, the fever slackened more, and she ate some broth the sergeant served. She was not fully conscious but seemed to want the food.

By the third day, when Lieutenant Costa came to see Martha, she had grown worse. Lieutenant Costa sat beside her the whole afternoon, putting cold clothes on her forehead. The *curandera* came again, studied her for a time, left some more herbs and laid her hands on Martha's forehead.

By evening Martha was feeling better and that night her fever broke. By morning, she sat up and asked the surprised Sergeant Norte where she was, and who he was. She spoke in English and he didn't understand a word she said. He had assumed she was Mexican. Quickly he ran for Lieutenant Costa, who knew English.

Lieutenant Costa came into the room, his dress uniform on now, his boots polished, his buttons shining. He saluted her smartly, then sat down in the chair beside her bed and smiled.

"Permit me to introduce myself. I am Lieutenant Ernesto Costa, of the Mexican national army. You have been rescued from *El Jefe* and you are completely safe. I fear that you were hit by a stray bullet in our battle with *El Jefe*."

Martha watched him for a moment, then she began to cry. Huge tears dribbled down her cheeks and she sobbed openly for a moment, as the soldier sat watching her.

"Even when you cry, *senorita,* you are the most beautiful woman I have ever seen."

She heard, dabbed at her eyes and automatically brushed back her hair. She choked back the sobs and tried to talk. It took her a few moments to find her voice. "I know . . . I know that I'm a mess. My hair, everything." She blew her nose on a handkerchief he hastily offered.

"Thank you. And I know I sound just terrible, but I want to thank you . . ." She stared at him closer. "You're the driver of the first coach! I thought you were dead with the first shots at the wagon." She hesitated. "I guess you're not dead after all." She stopped, her face twisted in pain. "Oh, God, I remember seeing *El Jefe* killed, and the poor horse." Her eyes misted again.

"*Senorita,* I too wept for the horse. It died in agony only a few feet from me. I shed no tears for *El Jefe.* He was a murdering outlaw, and Mexico is better off now that he is no more."

"I know. I was with him . . . I know."

He bowed slightly. "Excuse me, *senorita. Lo siento mucho.* I am a rough soldier, too long in the field with rough men. The delicate, refined ways of a beautiful woman make me act like a schoolboy."

"Oh, no, no. You rescued me! That's the most wonderful thing in the world. I'll appreciate that for as long as I live. Really. You are gallant, and gracious and the most handsome man I've seen in a long time."

He bowed, a slight flush tinging his neck and face. When he looked at her again, he smiled. "Now, I must not tire you. What would you like to eat? Some broth, an omelet, fish? You must eat to gain back your strength."

They talked for a moment more and just

before he left, Martha remembered what she wanted to sk him.

"Have you seen anything of Johnnie Laveau? He's a Negro, a black man from the island of Jamaica who was my body-guard. He too was captured but escaped two days before you arrived. It was my thought he would come here."

The lieutenant frowned. "Why have we not found him? We will search the surrounding countryside. Were any of *El Jefe*'s men chasing him?"

She told him of the six men sent to find him, and that he did not even have a horse. The soldier left at once to mount a search party. He ignored his limp and the pain in his arm. If the *senorita* wished the Negro found, he would do everything he could to save the man from the *bandidos.*

Johnnie Laveau lay in the narrow water course that had been cut in the soft soil a quarter of a mile from the beach by a recent cloudburst in the mountains. He wished he had some magic to make the two *bandidos* stalking him go away, or even to make himself vanish. But his voodoo was not that strong.

Johnnie had survived the past five days with a large helping of luck, a desperate will to live, and his instinctive skill at the game of kill or be killed.

When he took the full canteens, boots, shirt, knife, blanket and pistol from the dead man, he had left at once, trotting down the watercourse heading for the coast. The trackers caught up with him while he was still five miles inland, and Johnnie had killed the first with the pistol while the man studied a complicated series of tracks and backtracks and other signs Johnnie had left to confuse them. With the captured rifle he had killed the other two and headed toward the coast on one of their horses. But the beast had stepped in a hole, breaking its leg and he had to kill it.

Now, in the fifth day of his flight from the bandits, he had run out of ammunition and discarded his weapons, hiding them so the two remaining trackers would not find them. This way, they thought he was still armed and would be cautious. If they were careful enough, he had no chance. Otherwise, it had been a good fight. A battle to the death!

He lifted to the very edge of the trench and watched the two horsemen approach. For the past three days, Johnnie had filled his belly with the meat of the giant clams from the sea. He had rationed his water and still had a small amount in one canteen. He had accepted the gift of water from each bandit he had dispatched.

Johnnie lifted his only weapon and laughed in spite of his somber mood. No one in his right mind would use such a weapon against two pistols and two rifles. But no one claimed Johnnie Laveau was in his right mind.

His weapon was a rock the size of his fist. He had looked for two hours to find the right one. Then he had tied it tightly to a braided rope he had fashioned from crawling vines which he had discovered in a swale near the sea. The vines had not been strong enough singly, but when twisted and braided, they formed a serviceable rope to swing his rock. He had hoped to find some tough, strong bull kelp at the beach. But none had washed on the shore. He could have used a twenty foot long stem of the kelp to trip a horse, or knock off a rider.

Now he lay wishing he had the knife back. It had served its purpose, flying straight and sure, sinking to the hilt in a tracker's chest. But then the knife was lost.

The horses were closer now. It was his plan that they would separate, each following a double set of footprints he had left. Only one set came this way, and would put the rider out of sight of his compatriot. That would cut down the odds.

Across the narrow trail in this water course he had scooped out a two foot deep ditch three feet wide. He had used the blanket to cover the hole, weighting it down around the edges with rocks. Then he'd sprinkled sand over the dull brown blanket so it would blend in with the rest of the sand and rocks. It worked very well. He hoped the horse would hit the ditch with either its front or rear feet and pitch the rider off.

If it did not, it was Johnnie's plan to leap up suddenly in front of the horse, making it shy to one side. Then Johnnie would swing his rope around and around and knock the rider off the horse before he had a chance to shoot.

That was the hope, the gamble. He had no other choice. But all of life was a gamble, and so far he had won.

As the sun dropped lower on this fifth day of his struggle, he had little hope that he could eliminate both of the bandits. If the one on this side had no ammunition in his weapons, Johnnie would not have gained an advantage, but he would have cut down the odds again.

The riders came closer, stopped near the division of the tracks and talked. Then they separated. The larger one with the heavy moustache rode Johnny's way.

The *bandido* walked his horse, watching the tracks. Johnnie hoped that he hadn't made them too obvious. The rider came closer. Johnnie crouched in the ditch now, his vine rope and rock ready. Twenty feet . . . ten feet . . . five feet . . .

The horse walked confidently toward the section of the trail which held the hole. The camouflage looked good. Then, the wind whipped up the edge of the blanket, exposing the side of the hole. But the rider's eyes were fastened on the set of footprints three feet to the right.

Now!

The horse's front feet plunged into the hole. The animal whinnied in alarm. The rider tried to hold his seat, but the jolting drop pitched him forward. The horse screamed in pain and terror. The bandit's rifle was still in the boot. The horse crashed to his knees in the ditch and the rider vaulted over his head. The bandit's hands flew out and his pistol hit the dirt ten feet away.

The screams of the smashed up horse ripped through the silent desert heat, as the bandit scrambled, trying to gain his feet, looking for the pistol.

Johnnie came out of the ditch, running toward the bandit at the first stumble of the horse. As the black man ran toward the bandit, he swung the rock around his head faster and faster, in a ten foot circle. The *bandido* rolled over and got half way to his feet when the tethered rock slammed into the back of his head with the force of a freight train.

The man's head split open like a dropped melon, and Johnnie watched him flop to the ground. He ran to the pistol and checked it. Three rounds in the cylinder. He rushed to the horse and jerked the rifle from the scabbard. The long gun was out of bullets.

Now the question was, did the other bandit have any rifle ammunition. Johnnie was sure that the other man had heard the scream of the horse. A shot rattled through the brittle-dry air, confirming his suspicions.

Johnnie dropped to the ground, but realized that he had not heard the whizzing of the bullet itself, felt nothing, seen no spout of dust.

Before he could pull up the pistol, there were two more shots, then half a dozen more. Johnnie frowned, then heard horses riding hard. He ran to the narrow ditch, jumped in and crouched low out of sight and waited. The horses came nearer.

Six or eight mounts, Johnnie guessed. Had *El Jefe* brought up his whole army to wipe out one black man? He could not go back to that camp. He would not let himself be captured again. That he had decided two days ago. He had three rounds left in the pistol. With them, he would send two of the bandits to hell, and use the last round on his own black forehead.

But when Johnnie looked over the edge of the ditch, he saw a strange sight. There were no *bandidos* racing toward him. Rather a lone man in a uniform of some kind, with a saber lifted, rode cautiously toward the whimpering horse and the dead man. Behind him, a dozen mounted and uniformed men formed ito a waiting line.

"Soldiers?" Johnnie asked himself out loud. He lifted slowly from the ditch, holding the pistol by the barrel and both of his hands high over his head.

The officer rode toward him, smiling. Quickly he saluted with the saber and slid off his horse.

"*Senor* Laveau. It is good to see you. We have done you the small favor of dispatching the other *bandido* who chased you. *El Jefe* is dead, his camp wiped out. Your charge, Martha Dyke, is safe, though wounded. She sent us to find you."

Johnnie Laveau's face did not change.

"Gracias," he said, then walked to the horse which still thrashed around in agony on the ground. Johnnie put the creature out of its mistery with one pistol shot, then handed the weapon to the officer. They walked toward the line of troopers.

As soon as the mounted party arrived in Todos Santos, Johnnie's ankle iron was removed. He asked to see Martha. When he stepped into her lamp-lit bedroom, frown ridges rimmed his eyes. She was so pale. At first, he thought she was sleeping. He knocked softly and she turned.

"Oh, Johnnie!" She tried to sit up, made a small cry of pain and slumped back down.

He was at her side in an instant, looking at her injured shoulder.

"Johnnie, it's so good to see you. How on earth did you ever escape all of those bandits?"

"Long story. Mon no tell now. You hurt?"

She told him quickly about the raid on the wagons and how it was a special, innocent-looking ambush designed to overwhelm *El Jefe.*

"Your wound, hurt bad?"

"Yes, it does hurt, Johnnie, but it is getting better every day now. Soon I'll never know it was there, except for a small scar."

Her eyes held a touch of tears. "I'm so happy that you're here, safe and well. If I'm crying, they are happy tears."

"No cry. When you well, we get ship, sail home. No more Mexican *bandidos.* Johnnie sail. Many ship stop here."

She caught his hand and kissed it. "Oh, thank you, Johnnie, for being here, for helping me. I just don't know what I'd ever do without you!"

His eyes flashed for a moment, remembering one amazing night with Mrs. Dyke that now seemed so long ago. Then the sparkle dimmed in his eyes and he bowed.

"I always take care, Miz' Dyke."

He left, went to the moonlit bay and dove in, scrubbing his skin with the fine sand. He dressed and fell into the bed in a warehouse which the Mexican army had appropriated for its stay. Johnnie slept the clock around.

The next day, and most days after that, Johnnie spent at the docks or in small fishing boats, swimming, talking with the children in an amazing mixture of English, Spanish and hand signals. They loved him.

When Johnnie had left Martha's room, Lieutenant Costa knocked on Martha's door. He held a guitar, wore a smile and carried one yellow rose for which he had bargained with a woman for a half hour before she let him pick it. He presented the rose to Martha with a little flurry and a bow.

"This rose pales in your presence, but it is the best one in all of Todos Santos."

Martha smiled, took the rose and sniffed it. "Delightful," she said, filled with a sudden gratitude. "Lieutenant Costa, I appreciate everything that you have done for me. I don't know how I can ever repay you. I certainly will pay this poor family for letting me use their house."

"There is no need to pay anyone. The people appreciate our army. We keep them safe. But my small company must patrol this entire upper half of Baja California peninsula, more than five hundred miles long, so we cannot be everywhere at once."

"Then shouldn't you be off on a patrol?"

He smiled, took the guitar, and strummed a few chords.

"The men are tired, and they deserve a rest, no?" He smiled again.

She listened then as he began to play. After a while he sang, too, and she could tell his voice had been well trained. It was a rich baritone, and she was sure he was good enough to be a professional performer. He laughed at the idea.

"My father was a soldier, my grandfather was a soldier, so I, too, am a soldier. My father would consent to nothing else."

He played again and, before she knew it, Martha drifted off to sleep.

During the next week, Lieutenant Costa was in her room almost every waking moment. They talked about his home in Mexico City, and how he missed it. He was not married, and he would be on patrol here in the Baja for another two years before he was relieved, then promoted to captain and returned to Mexico City.

The second week, Martha was feeling as strong as ever, and could sit up easily. Her shoulder pained her when she moved her arm, but she found that she had a complete range of movement with it — up, down and to both sides. She was sure there would be no lasting problem with it.

Sergeant Norte came and examined the arm and shoulder, had her move it around and smiled.

"Es muy bueno," he said, beaming. He then told the lieutenant that it appeared she would have total and natural use of her arm. She should be up and around now, out into the village. It would be good for her.

When Sergeant Norte left, Lieutenant Costa told Martha what he had said and explained he was the closest thing they had to a doctor in their company. He had studied to be a doctor for two years, then had to give it up because he ran out of money.

Lieutenant Costa apologized because he could not come and see her that afternoon. There was a trial that had to be started and, since he was the highest federal official in the area, he was required to act as the judge. It would be a preliminary hearing.

"A killing of the village crazy man happened here a few weeks ago. A very nasty thing. It should be a simple case. But in Mexico, our justice is different from yours. A killing is a very serious offense."

They talked of other things, and Martha was genuinely sorry to see this gentle man leave. He looked so dashing in his army uniform, and his saber.

She reached out quickly with her left arm, testing it, but felt only twinges. In another week, she would be ready to travel.

But first, she had to locate her mother. This was a very small village, it shouldn't be hard. However, she had wanted to be recovered from her wound. Tonight or tomorrow, she would ask Lieutenant Costa to help her find Maria Valdez.

That evening, Lieutenant Costa played a dozen soft, Spanish songs of lost love, and while Martha didn't understand most of the words, she caught the general idea. When he finished one, she motioned for him to come closer. He sat on the edge of the bed and smiled at her.

"Ernesto, you have been remarkably kind to me these past two weeks. I am deeply grateful. Now I must ask still another favor of you."

"You have only to ask, beautiful lady."

"I'm searching for my mother. I've never seen her. It's a long story but I believe she is living here and that her name is or was Maria Valdez. Do you know of such a person?"

He sat back in surprise. "Then you are part Mexican. I knew it. Such beauty could not be all *gringa*." He smiled as he said it, and laughed softly. "Yes, of course, your mother. One woman lives here by that name. She runs the cantina. She is old enough to be your mother. That was where we had the trouble . . ." He stopped.

"I must see her. Could you take me to see her?"

"No, it would be better if I brought her here. Tomorrow, when you are fresh and rested. I'll bring her tomorrow morning."

Martha covered her face with her hands. The moment she had thought about, wondered about, worried about was almost here. "I don't think I can wait!" she cried.

"*Si,* you can wait. You will want to fix your hair and put on your best dress. You should be out of bed now, up and moving about. Do you want her to think you are a cripple? Tomorrow morning, you will get up and dress. By ten o'clock, I will have Maria Valdez here to meet you."

That night, it took Martha a long time to get to sleep. When morning came, she woke early, before the small strutting red rooster from the house next door could crow to greet the sun. She sat up on the bed and looked at herself in the hand mirror from her valise. Ernesto had brought all of her things back to her. She couldn't find a single thing missing.

Her hair! It was a fright. So dull, dingy. But she didn't have time to wash and dry it now. She brushed it a hundred tmes, which helped.

Then she used the water on the small dresser and washed her face. Her shoulder twinged and ached a little, but it seemed as nothing now. She was going to meet her real mother!

Martha tried on three different dresses, but none of them was right. Then she looked at a simple white blouse and full red skirt. It was the only thing she had with her that looked even slightly Mexican. Why hadn't she brought something more appropriate?

She ate a quick breakfast and hurried the dishes away. Then she tried on the blouse and skirt she decided they were the best she had. She cleaned her nails for the third time, and waited.

A half hour later, Lieutenant Costa knocked, and opened the door on her bidding. He stepped in and motioned.

"She's just outside. Maria can speak some English, but she may pretend not to. I think she's about forty years old. She didn't want to come, and I didn't tell her what it was about. I only said I had someone I wanted her to meet."

He stepped back and ushered the woman to the doorway. Martha looked curiously at the small lady who stood there. She was short and plump and very Mexican, her black hair long, her face dark and slightly flat. She could have been pretty once.

"Maria Valdez?" Martha asked.

The woman nodded.

Ernesto motioned for her to come into the room. She glanced at him with respect and caution. At last, she stepped inside and Ernesto closed the door.

"Maria Valdez, I want to talk with you,"

Martha said. "Would you please sit down?"

The woman sank into the chair and Martha sat on the edge of the bed, smiling at her.

"I understand that you speak English very well, Mrs. Valdez."

"Some."

"Is it true that you once lived in the United States, near San Diego?"

Maria's face froze, her eyes went dull and she lifted one hand then let it drop. There was defeat on her face, in the way she held her hands, in her body position. At last her eyes lifted and she nodded.

"Mrs. Valdez, I'm not trying to make you unhappy, or to make you remember things that you would rather forget. But it is all tremendously important to me. While in San Diego, did you have a child?"

"Si." Her voice was listless.

"Mrs. Valdez, I know it has been a long time, but does the name Harold Pemberton mean anything . . ." Martha stopped.

Maria's head came up abruptly. She turned to Ernesto and spewed out an angry, rapid barrage of Spanish that Martha could not understand. Only the anger was certain.

Mrs. Valdez rose and, without looking at Martha, walked out of the room.

Ernesto held the door for her and, when

she was gone, he closed it and held up his hands to Martha.

"She is a very proud woman. There is little more I can do for you now."

Martha watched him, her eyes unsure. "But she did react when I asked her about San Diego, and again about having a child there. Then, when I used the name of Harold Pemberton, she froze. She shut herself up completely. What did she say before she left?"

Ernesto frowned. "She was very angry, and scolding me for doing this to her. She said the old lieutenant they had before I came would never have insulted her this way. She said she was going back to her *cantina* and would appreciate it if I did not step my boots in it. Under no circumstances would she come here to see you again."

Martha listened, her frown fading, and at last a smile came to her pretty face. "Ernesto, I am sure now, sure that Maria is my mother. It will take some time, but I will go to her and convince her that I am not trying to hurt her, or to change her, or to make her go anywhere. I only want to come to know her and to love her as a daughter should love her mother."

Ernesto shook his head and sat in the chair. "It is not right that a poor stupid man like myself should ever understand the thinking of a woman. It is beyond a simple field soldier like me. However, if you would like, I can arrange a short sail for you around the bay later this afternoon. It will blow the last of the desert dust from your lungs, and would be a good change of scenery for you."

Martha smiled. "Yes, Ernesto, I would like that. And then, after our sail, we will stop by at Maria Valdez's *cantina* and I will have a glass of port wine."

Ernesto smiled, said he would pick her up at two o'clock and left the house.

Now he was sure. Before he had only guessed. But the name made the difference. When Martha said she was here hunting for her mother, he wondered if there might be some connection between her and the *gringo* in jail. But the names were different. So he forgot it.

But now there was no doubt. The name Pemberton made the connection. Randy Pemberton, Harold Pemberton. The latter must be the father of both of these *gringos,* perhaps by different mothers. So he had a double problem. The trial of Randy Pemberton was a week off. The *gringo* would have legal counsel. But if the state proved that he killed Raoul, even with extreme provocation and only to save his own life, he could still be sentenced to five years in prison. That was the law.

Ernesto decided to handle one of his problems at a time.

When he left Martha, he went to the police station and made sure that the prisoner was being well cared for. Ernesto had Randy moved to a larger cell, one with a barred window, through which he could see. A bunk with a mattress was put in. Ernesto talked to Mr. Pemberton and told him that his case was receiving special consideration since the man who had been killed was mentally unbalanced, and since he had already assaulted Mr. Pemberton with a deadly weapon.

Ernesto hinted that some kind of pre-trial arrangement could be worked out, given a few more days. Would the good Mr. Pemberton be in favor of such a suggestion? Randy said he was more than willing.

On his way out, Ernesto gave orders that Randy be given special meals from the *cantina,* and that they should be charged to the rations bill for his company. This done, he went to see Maria Valdez, but she would not come out of the kitchen to talk to him.

The sail around the big bay was delightful. Ernesto handled the small boat and the single sail as though he had been a sailor all his life. The craft was a fishing boat, but worked well. They went out a mile to sea, then came scudding back before the wind, the spray flying in their faces. Martha loved every moment of it.

A hundred yards off the dock, Ernesto dropped the sail and the boat came to a stop, bobbing in the subdued swells.

"Martha, I must tell you that Maria is going to be very hard to talk to. She would not even come out and see me this noon. We can go to her *cantina* but do not be surprised if we do not see her. Her daughter will serve us."

Martha nodded. "Ernesto, I am willing to stay here for a month, or two months, if I must, until she will listen to me."

At the *cantina,* the young girl served them, a tequila for Ernesto and a port wine for Martha. The port had lost everything it ever had except its color, but Martha bravely sipped at it. She asked the girl to tell her mother that Mrs. Martha Dyke would like to talk with her. Ernesto translated the request and the black-eyed youngster hurried away.

She came back a moment later, shaking her head. Her mother was too busy and could not come out. Perhaps tomorrow.

They drank, talked and waited for an hour before they left.

Three days in a row, they went to the *cantina,* drank and sat. The second day, they waited two hours, the third, three hours.

The fourth day, they arrived in the evening. The *cantina* was filled. When Maria Valdez went into the back room, Martha followed her. The first room was a small one, used to put orders together. The kitchen was just beyond.

Maria turned when she sensed someone behind her. When she saw Martha, she put her hands over her face and sank into a chair.

"No, no, *por favor.* I am a strong person, but this I cannot live through."

Martha knelt at her feet, took the woman's hands and looked at them. "Mrs. Valdez, you have worked very hard in your life, no? You have supported yourself and your children. I admire that. I like people who do things for themselves. I am impressed by a person who can stand on her own two feet, even after the fates have been unkind and unfair to her. After a strange country and unusual customs did not turn out to be exactly what an eighteen-year-old girl thought they were going to be."

Martha felt the hands tremble. She was

not sure if the woman could understand all of the words or not. But she went on.

"Mrs. Valdez, I know that a great wrong was done to you, and that there were misunderstandings on both sides. I know that you were trying to help your family, to save the *rancho* from ruin. I can understand that. You were very brave then, even as you are now."

For a moment, Maria looked up, the tears in her eyes drying as she watched this young woman talking to her.

"I am not trying to hurt you. I do not wish to make you feel sad, but there are two questions I must ask. You did know Harold Pemberton in San Diego, some twenty-two years ago, didn't you?"

Her head moved slightly in a nod.

Martha smiled. "And was there any mark on your baby daughter, that might still exist today? A scar or a sign?"

Maria thought a moment, then the hint of a smile touched her plain face. Her eyes sparkled for a second. "*Si,* a small mark. A birth mark on ankle. *Muy* small, shape like 'L'."

Martha gave a shout of joy. She reached up and hugged the woman tightly, then kissed her cheek. Tears of joy poured down Martha's cheeks. She sat on a bench and took off her shoe and the short cotton hose she wore. She showed the woman her right ankle. On the inside, just below the ankle bone, there was a small purple birthmark in the rough shape of an 'L'.

Maria stared at it for many moments, then looked up at Martha. Her face filled with such a joy as she had seldom known.

"Mi hija!" she said. She put her arms around Martha and rocked her back and forth, saying the two words over and over again. Tears flowed as both women cried.

Maria's younger daughter came up and asked her mother something, but Maria waved her aside.

When Lieutenant Costa heard nothing from the back room after several minutes, he moved cautiously to the doorway and looked in. The two women sat near a table in the corner of the room, arms about each other, talking. Lieutenant Costa grinned, took off his uniform jacket and helped the young girl serve the drinks.

Long after the *cantina* was closed, Maria, Martha and Lieutenant Costa sat in the restaurant, talking. The officer listened to the women, translated a word, an idea now and then, and sipped his drink. He had a smile on his face so broad that he had almost forgotten his other problem.

The woman talked about the big *rancho* in the United States. It had been in the Valdez family for three generations. Then came the Mexican war and, suddenly, the whole family was in a new country, *Los Estado Unidos*. Things were done differently. It led to all sorts of troubles and a bank loan, and soon they lost the whole *rancho*.

Her father took them all back to Mexico, and they lived just across the border for a time. But her father died of some sickness she did not understand. She received some more money from *Senor* Pemberton and with it she bought this small *cantina* in Todos Santos. She had been here ever since.

It was well after one in the morning when they said good night. Ernesto Costa walked with Martha back to the small house where she was staying. No one else was there. They went inside and he lit a lamp for her.

"Ernesto, I want to thank you again for all the help you've given me. You have been remarkable. First you save my life, then you help me find my real mother."

Her smile dazzled him. He stepped a bit closer. "Then would it be asking too much if I sought your permission for a kiss?"

"Of course not. A kiss and a toast, then you must go. No?"

He brought the glasses, then took her in

his arms and kissed her soft lips. For just a moment, Martha spun back over the years, remembering another kiss from a man she hardly knew in a San Francisco rented room. She clung to Ernesto, and felt him responding.

The kiss lasted a long time, too long, she knew, and when he at last pulled back, she sighed softly.

"Ernesto, you shouldn't kiss a girl that way."

"But I enjoy it. Did not you enjoy?"

He kissed her again and this time held her closer, pressing her breasts hard against his chest. She struggled for breath, then felt those little bundles of resolve melting within her.

She pushed him away and shook her head. "Ernesto, please don't spoil it." That soft warmth built in her body and she did nothing to stop it. A minute later, she wasn't sure what had happened but he had moved slightly and now his hand crept inside her blouse. He should not be doing that. She told him to stop. Didn't she tell him to stop?

She heard herself sighing again and his tongue probed at her lips, and before she knew why, her lips parted. For a brief moment, Martha felt that everything was perfect. She had found her mother, she had been rescued from the *bandidos,* even her shoulder was almost healed.

Somewhere her mind was telling her to make him stop. To push him away and scold him. But the right connections simply never got made. She felt his lips leave her and he picked her up and carried her through the small living room to the bedroom, placing her gently on the bed. A second later, he stretched out beside her, his lips covering hers again.

The kiss was long and Martha felt warm and wonderful. What was she going to tell Ernesto? She couldn't remember. His mouth moved from her lips to the soft fabric over her breast and Martha gave a moan of surprise.

"Oh, Ernesto!"

CHAPTER TEN:
A SIBLING RESCUE

When morning came, Martha turned over, not wanting to come fully awake. Slowly, her mind cleared. She never had been one to spring wide awake in the morning.

But suddenly she sat upright, staring around the room, looking at the bed beside her. She gave a long sigh of relief. She was alone. For a moment she had been afraid that . . .

Martha shook her head slowly, remembering last night. *"Whore, puta!"*

She dropped back on the bed and slammed her hand against the pillow. What in the world had she been thinking? She was not so intoxicated that she had been able to resist. Now he would never speak to her again. He would laugh and jeer at her, telling everyone about how easy it had been, really no contest at all.

Martha sat up slowly. Why should she blame herself? It was his fault. He had seduced her. She had never said that he could go ahead and make love to her. Why not blame him? Yes, it was his fault. She would be the one not to speak to *him!*

Martha lay down and shook her head, changing her mind again. Why in the world was she trying to *blame* anyone? They had made love and enjoyed it. Neither one of them were virgins, so what difference did it really make? She was sure she wouldn't get pregnant, so what had been hurt? Her pride?

When she saw Lieutenant Costa again, she would be natural. She was sure that he would be, too. It had been a marvelous night and she was not ashamed of it.

With that put in its proper place, she rose, washed her hands and face in the bowl, and dressed. She decided to walk to the *cantina* for breakfast. She was trying to decide what she would have to eat when she stepped out of the small house, and almost collided with Lieutenant Costa who had been sitting on the steps.

"Buenos dias, Senorita," he said with a touch of a question in his voice.

"Buenos dias, Senor."

"It is a beautiful morning, no?" he said. "For me the most beautiful morning that I can ever remember. They say the new day is often tempered in one's mind by what happened the previous evening. Would the *senorita* agree?"

She smiled at him, her eyes playing the game.

"I have heard that said, yes. And for me, this is an outstandingly happy morning, a day filled with great promises and expectations."

He sighed. "Good, for a moment I was afraid that you might be angry. We never really decided . . . what we were going to do. I mean, I gave you little choice . . . you know."

"You mean you are a conceited man and you think you can seduce any girl you want to?" She shook her head. "No so, big army officer. You merely indicated your interest in a certain activity. It was I who made the decision, and let things progress. The woman always determines what happens, whether you big strong men know it or not."

He looked around quickly to see if anyone else had heard her. "Are you always so open, so frank?"

"*Si.*"

He glanced at her and they both burst out laughing.

"Now, enough of this, let's have breakfast. Then I want to spend the whole day with my mother. We have so much to talk about."

She looked up and saw him frowning. "Isn't that all right?"

"It may not be, *bonita* Martha. But first, breakfast, then we will talk about it."

They ate eggs and beans and slabs of hard bread and wine at the *cantina.*

"The wine is not good, but the water here is even worse. To drink the wine is safer for a sensitive *gringa.*"

She kicked him under the table and he laughed. Martha and her mother talked for an hour as they ate. Then Maria said she must get back to work. Martha looked up at Lieutenant Costa and waited. When his eyes turned to her, his face was serious.

"*Senorita,* do you remember days ago, when I said I had a trial to attend to."

She frowned, remembering. "Vaguely, but I was not concerned."

"Yes, you are. Several weeks ago in this village, a man was killed. It was clearly a case of self-defense as you would say in your country. But our laws are much different from yours, and here such a defense is totally worthless. The man who was killed was not normal. He was mentally slow, strange, a little crazy. Everyone here tolerated him. I had talked with him many times. He was devoted to his mother. Anyone who bothered his mother was visited by Raoul,

232

and at once brought to his kind of justice by being beaten up, and sometimes killed. The law is more lenient toward this kind of a person."

"I need to know all of this?"

"*Si*, you must listen. A man bothered the strange one's mother, made her cry, tried to make her go somewhere with him. She was *muy* upset.

"Raoul found out and went to the *cantina* to find this man. He would not listen to reason and tried to kill the man with his machete. The *gringo* was cut on the arm, and saved his life only by shooting Raoul twice. Now the *gringo* is in jail. The charge is killing Raoul, and it happened in front of fifteen witnesses."

"Ernesto, I'm sorry for Raoul *and* this other man, but what does all this have to do with me?"

"Raoul is Maria Valdez's son. And the man who shot him is your brother, Randy Pemberton. Randy is in jail now."

"Oh, my God!" She stared at Ernesto for several seconds. Then she looked away, rubbing her hands over her face as she tried desperately to beat back the tears. "My God, Randy! He came here and tried to talk mother into going to San Francisco? Why? And then he had to kill Raoul!"

"Yes, but do not blame him for the killing, Martha. If he had not done so, then Randy would be in a shallow grave here in Todos Santos right now."

"I must go see him. Can I visit him? Please take me to see Randy right now. He must be wild with anger and fear."

On the short walk to the police station, Ernesto explained that he had only made the connection between her and Randy when Martha had mentioned Harold Pemberton to her mother. Martha nodded, only half-listening. How was she going to get Randy out of this mess? A good lawyer, somebody from Mexico City or Tijuana? No, there was not time for that.

"Martha, you must understand why I waited a few days to tell you about Randy. He was safe and nothing would happen to him. I did not want to burden you with two problems at once. Today, I thought it was time."

Martha touched his hands in thanks.

She would wait and see just what the situation was with Randy. Then she would have a talk with the jail officials. Something could be done. If it was truly self-defense, there was no good reason why it couldn't be worked out.

Then the real truth came through to her.

234

Randy had killed her own half-brother, a man she did not even know!

The jail was only another poorly constructed building, and looked so fragile that anyone with a kitchen spoon could soon dig his way to freedom. It had been a house, evidently, before being turned into the jail.

Randy's cell was a room with a regular door with a hasp and padlock. The police chief, who was also the jailer, opened the door.

Randy lay on a single bed. He looked up, saw them and sat up.

"Martha! So you finally got here. God, what took you so long?"

"No greeting, Randy? Not a 'good to see you,' or 'welcome to Mexico,' or anything? It looks like you haven't changed much."

"I'm not in the best of moods today. I feel all closed in somehow. I suppose you've talked with your real mother?"

"Yes, we had a long talk, and she's a very nice lady."

Randy laughed. "I guess you'd have to think that. She's really nothing but a . . ." He stopped, looked at Martha, then at Lieutenant Costa, who walked up behind her.

"Hey, what's the judge doing here? What the hell you doing here? It isn't trial time."

Lieutenant Costa stared at him, but did not reply.

Martha let the frown build on her face. "Randy, you don't seem to realize that you're in serious trouble. You have killed a man. Doesn't that mean anything to you? It's more than breaking a window or stealing a buggy. You killed a man."

"But only in self-defense, dear half-sister. He came at me with a machete, almost cut off my arm. And he would have severed my head from my neck if he could. I barely escaped with my life."

Martha looked at Ernesto.

"That is what witnesses say. It seems to be true."

"Damn right, it's true. In a civilized country, I'd be given a medal for killing that wild animal."

"Raoul was my half-brother, did you realize that?"

"He was also an idiot, the village crazy man that everyone was afraid of."

"Have you sent word to Father about all this?"

"No, and I won't. He thinks I'm in Hawaii, on my way to Hong Kong and Japan."

Martha saw she was getting nowhere with him. She changed tactics and let her frown vanish. "Are you getting good food, Randy?

Do you have a comfortable room?"

"Room? It's a cell, with bars on the window. Yeah, it's all right, I imagine, as jails go. But I'd lots rather go home."

"You could spend five years in the Baja prison," Ernesto said.

"Five years for eliminating that crazy man? That is crazy."

Martha shushed them with a glance. "Now stop that, both of you. I must do some thinking. Randy, you're my brother, and I'll do everything I can to help you. I'll come see you, tomorrow."

"Yeah, sure you will. Your misguided sense of loyalty again. I bet you're just going to rush around to help me." He lay down on the bed and covered his eyes. Randy didn't look up as they left.

Outside Martha stared at Lieutenant Costa for several seconds, then pinched her eyes and led the way out of the building. She headed back for her small house.

Lieutenant Costa stayed behind her. "Your brother is very young," he said.

"Yes, and sometimes not too smart." At the house he held open the door and she smiled. "Ernesto, would you come in for a moment? I have to think this through."

He bowed and followed her. Inside, she sat at the small table and motioned for him to use the other chair.

"A few days ago, when you mentioned a trial, you said that since you were the highest government official in the area, you would have the job of being the judge. Did you mean the trial for Randy?"

"Yes, the same one," he said, tight-lipped.

Martha was surprised. "I detect a bit of anger in your tone, Ernesto. Why?"

"He is a *gringo,* a foreigner who has killed a Mexican. Why should I not be angry. He has violated the federal law and God's own law."

"But anger. It is not like you, Ernesto."

"You know little of me, *bonita.* Anger can often be put to good use."

"Ernesto, I have heard that Mexican justice is not blind, that in special situations, justice can be tempered with mercy. Is that true?"

"Justice and mercy should always go hand in hand, Martha. I believe that."

"And in this case, if there is no mercy, what happens to Randy?"

"He is tried, and when convicted, he will spend the next five to ten years in the Baja California prison. No time off for being a *gringo.* He must spend the full term. Then he is released, escorted to the border and told never to come to Mexico again."

"Five to ten years is a long time."

"*Si.*"

"Ernesto, am I right in saying that you have considerable control in this trial? That you might find the man guilty or innocent, regardless of the testimony, or that perhaps the charges could be reduced or dismissed . . . if the presiding judge thought that it would serve justice?"

"Pretty one, in Baja California, we have few people. We can afford only the most simple of legal systems. It is true that in some cases, we look to the will of the people. We find out who was killed. If he were a *bandido,* there would be no charges. If he were the village priest, there would be no chance of an innocent verdict. So, it is true, the good of the people is most important to our Mexican law."

He moved closer to her, caught her hand. "My pretty one, there are many ways to read the evidence. If the sister of the man charged with murder were to tell me of the wonderful qualities of her brother, this would help. If the beautiful sister of the killer were to explain to me in helpful, friendly terms . . ."

His hand brushed her breasts.

Martha closed her eyes. So he was getting to it at last. What she had given freely once, would now become a bargaining point.

239

When she looked at him again, his face was out of focus, close to hers, his lips reaching out. His kiss was hard and demanding, his hand rubbing harder now, working inside her blouse to her bare breasts.

Martha let him kiss her but did not respond. His other hand moved to her knee.

"If the sister of this man were to show the judge the delicate and marvelous ways of making love for the next seven days, the case would be simple to resolve without a trial. The *gringo* would be found guilty, sentenced to serve the time already in jail, and a few more days, then expelled from jail within the week."

Martha did not flinch as his hand worked higher on her inner thigh. Now she *was* a *puta*. She was bargaining with her body for the favor of this important man. She was selling herself. She was . . .

"Beautiful lady, why don't we go into the bedroom where we can think through this mutually attractive suggestion in much more proper surroundings?"

He caught her hand and she rose when he did and, with each step, Martha knew she was nailing down a decision, that there would be no turning back.

He smiled at her. "Do not be so harsh with yourself. I make the proposition there is no way to refuse. I save your life from *El Jefe,* I give you medical care, I even find your *madre.* How can you refuse such a kind and generous *hombre?*"

He stopped at the bedroom door and opened her blouse. Her hands were at her sides, as he kissed her once more, then laughed.

"Oh, sometimes I hate myself when I do this. But with you as the prize, and to have you for a week, lying all naked and ready and anxious beside me — for this I would sell my very soul to *el diablo!* You are the most fantastic woman I have ever made love to. And for the next seven days, I will own your body. But I will also give as well as take, and if you do not find satisfaction, if you do not agree that it has been an even exchange of passions, then I will be surprised."

Inside the bedroom, they sat on the quilts and he kissed her, then pushed her back on the bed and forced her legs apart. With his knife he cut off her underwear and without removing his or the rest of her clothing, he took her there rough and harshly, as if she were, indeed, a cheap *puta* under a desert tree.

Martha cried.

■ ■ ■ ■

Four days later, Lieutenant Costa was exhausted. He walked slowly to the police station, held a quick hearing for the *gringo*, and found him guilty of involuntary manslaughter. Randy was sentenced to the time already incarcerated, plus four more days. Then he would be put aboard a boat and expelled from the country.

Ernesto found Domingo at the dock and told him what had happened to his young *gringo* friend, and that he must take him back to America four days hence. There would be two more passengers, a Negro he probably already knew, and Mrs. Martha Dyke, Randy's sister.

Martha had spent every evening with her mother in the *cantina*. They talked about dozens of things, and Maria assured Martha that she never wanted to go to the United States or see Harold Pemberton again.

"These are my people here. They need me in their way. I understand them. I am too old to learn new ways."

Martha said that every three months a ship would stop in the harbor and deliver to her a large shipment of goods: food, clothes, a whole general store full of merchandise that she could sell or give away as she wished, and there would be money enough so she could hire three barmaids to do the work in the *cantina*. As a start, Martha took apart her corset and found the four one-hundred dollar bills. She gave two of them to her mother, and saved the last two to pay for the passages back to San Diego and then home. Ernesto told her the boat ride with Domingo had all been arranged, and that they would leave the following Saturday morning.

Late that night, Martha lay gasping on the bed. She had just experienced a thundering climax within herself at exactly the same instant that the man-thing inside of her erupted. Ernesto groaned and rolled away from her.

"Now, I am really a *puta*," she said to him. "You bargained for a *gringa* lady to adorn your bed for a week. But, Ernesto, you have been cheated. Now I do not feel like a lady — either half-*gringa* or half-*Mexican*. Now I know I am a whore, and you have been short-changed."

Ernesto laughed and sat up, rubbed her breasts, kissing them and quickly shaking his head. "Martha, you will never be a *puta*. You have too much heart, too much love, too much *caring.* Who else would do this for a brother who seems to hate her? Who else but you could do this for a brother who brought this all down upon you and even killed your half-brother? Not a *puta.* A real *puta* would have sailed away, not caring, and let the *gringo* rot in his jail cell." He kissed her mouth gently, then began dressing.

"I will not see you again, pretty one. Tomorrow morning, we ride south. We have been here too long, and have much work to do. Perhaps some of us will die. You will still leave on Saturday. I shall always remember you, and I will think that you would have made love with me these past few days, even without the bribe and the threat."

He kissed her lips once more, gave her a smile she was sure was hiding his honest regrets, and then he slipped out the door.

She lay there a long time, then got up and washed her face and cleaned herself before she went back to bed, and this time to sleep.

The next two days, she spent with her mother. They traded stories and secrets and plans. Martha would come down twice a year to visit her. She would buy her own sailing boat and leave it in San Diego. The big ships would stop often and send in goods, and life would be more pleasant for all the people of Todos Santos. There would be plenty of money to send Consuela, her younger half-sister, to Mexico City to school.

Martha remembered the two diamonds. She found the blouse and tore open the seams, revealing the two gems. She gave them to her mother, and told her to send them to be sold in Mexico City.

Martha had secret plans. Next summer, she would arrive with a shipload of building materials and bricks to build a fine house. She would also put down a well for pure sweet water, and pipe it to the house. She would keep up with the latest developments to be sure that her mother and her people benefitted from them as quickly as possible.

Saturday morning, she went to the jail and watched as they unlocked the doors and let Randy walk out a free man. He was strangely subdued. His cockiness was gone, his bravado and anger were missing. They found Johnnie Laveau at the dock, stowing supplies on board Domingo's boat.

When Dom saw Randy coming he ran to him and threw his arms around him, hugging him.

"Don't do that," Randy said.

"Hell, I'm just happy to see you. You don't know how close you come to rotting in some Mex prison for the next ten years. You be damn happy you got off." Dom looked at Martha but she said nothing. He knew. Probably everyone in town but Randy knew how he escaped a long prison term. But now Martha did not care who knew. It was her business, not theirs. To hell with them!

It was going to be a good trip north, she knew. They pushed off, and stopped just around the point and caught four rock fish.

"Any more than that would just spoil before we could eat them," Dom said. "We'll catch more when we need them, and we'll dig some clams."

"This mon, clam chief," Johnnie Laveau said. And he was.

They made the trip up the coast in three days. When they pulled into San Diego harbor, Martha had never been so happy to see the United States flag in her life! The thirteen stripes and thirty-seven stars had never looked more wonderful. She wrote a long letter to her father explaining everything and had Johnnie and Randy take it on the first boat they could get heading for San Francisco. She stayed in the luxury of the Horton House for three days, then followed.

When she was at sea again, beating up the shoreline in a small coastal steamship, Martha wondered at last about Allen. She had pushed that problem from her mind until she had everything resolved about her mother.

Now she was at peace. She knew who she was, and she knew that she still wanted to marry Allen Cornelius more than anything else in the whole world.

But what about Allen? Did he still want to marry her? Had Allen vanished on his own, or had foul play been involved? She resolved that if her father knew nothing more about it than when she had left, she would go directly to Seattle herself and see what she could discover.

She must know for sure what happened to the man who was her one true love — no matter what!

Two days later, Martha paced the deck of the *City of Portland* as the steamer belched smoke from her stacks, rounded the point and nosed into the big San Francisco Bay. It was November 2, 1875. Deliberately, she walked along the rail as far as she could go, turned and went back the other way, willing the steam ship to move faster. Somehow, she wished it could cut across the San Francisco peninsula rather than having to sail around the end of it to the sheltered dock areas.

A thousand questions still pounded in her head. Would Allen have been found yet? What would the report from the detectives who went to Seattle have to tell? The biggest question still hovered over her like rain-filled clouds over a Sunday picnic, ominous and threatening: did Allen run away because he didn't want to marry her?

At last they rounded the tip of the land and turned toward the docks. As the big ship moved slowly in, Martha thought she saw a familiar face on the wharf, but then it was gone. It had been one of the men from the store, she was sure. But why would he leave so quickly?

By the time the ship was tied up and the gangplank down, she saw her father's big black carriage come rushing up to the dock. Someone had been watching for her to come in and raced to tell him!

He came running up the gangplank to greet her and they hugged each other on deck as tears misted their eyes.

"It's so good to have you back home, Martha," he said, emotion choking his voice. "When Johnnie told us all the trouble that plagued you, I wished I hadn't let you go." He couldn't go on. He blew his nose, then gave instructions for someone to look after her luggage. They hurried down the gangplank to the carriage.

Martha leaned her head against her father's strong shoulder and tried to realize that she was safe and at home and with her family and everything would be all right. For the moment, she couldn't risk asking him about Allen. Not yet. She would ask soon.

Martha didn't pay any attention to the direction they took, just closed her eyes and tried to relax. It did seem a long ride if they were going to the office, but she decided they were going to the mansion instead.

Harold Pemberton talked rapidly, about what Johnnie Laveau said happened, about the shipboard ride home, and about her brother Randy.

"No, we won't discuss Randy at the moment. He's home and seems to have the wind dumped from his sails. We'll see how he recovers and then we will all have a dignified and gentle talk. Did you see Maria?"

Martha told him about it, about meeting her, about how difficult it had been at first. She said she was going to visit Maria twice a year, and she would send a big ship down with lots of goods.

The carriage stopped then and her father got out and made a big show of helping her down the step. When she looked up, she was surprised to see that they were at the small house on California Street.

She looked a second time, and then she was running. Someone had opened the door and stepped out on the small porch. At first, she wasn't sure who it was. Then her heart leaped and she ran as fast as she could.

"Allen!" she called, and ran all the faster. He met her near the front gate and swept her into his arms.

He clung to her and she to him and, for a moment, Martha was so filled with happiness she thought surely that she would explode.

"Allen, I'm never ever going to let you out of my sight again!"

He kissed her and smiled, and kissed her again. "I'm thinking of putting shackles around our ankles, forge us together so we can't be more than two feet from each other, ever, for the rest of our lives!"

They turned and walked slowly back toward the little house.

Harold Pemberton stepped back into the carriage and ordered it to go home. It had been quite a day, and he was feeling old today. No, he shouldn't say old, just a little tired.

The ship had arrived in San Francisco

well before noon, and Allen and Martha spent all afternoon becoming reacquainted, and making love so tenderly and with such strong feelings that Martha wept softly in total joy.

Martha grinned when he told her he had been shanghaied. "I remember your telling me you were in no danger of that in Seattle. You claimed that all the body merchants knew you, and anyway you never got drunk. You said that only a fool was ever shanghaied."

Allen laughed and kissed her. "That night I was a fool, but I'm back and settled and I've made arrangements for my son in Seattle. I've been transferred to the corporate office down here, and I'm ready to marry you tomorrow afternoon, or just as soon as we can — if you'll still have me."

She kissed him for five minutes as she accepted his proposal, which led to more complicated maneuverings and they made love again, slowly pushing each other to the very peak of ecstasy.

Then they dressed and both knew what was next.

"Darling, we do have to go see Mother. I think they will expect us tonight. I must have a long and understanding talk with Mother, to take some of the sting out of this whole affair. I want to be positive that she understands why I had to go to Mexico, and that now I'm more proud than ever because I have two mothers, and I don't give a fig who knows it."

She looked at Allen closely. "Father did tell you why I went to Mexico?"

He nodded. "And I understand completely. You'll need to talk to your mother about the wedding, too. Convince her that it should be very informal and private. Forestall any grand plans she might have for the ceremony. A reception is fine, but I think a judge should do very nicely with your parents as witnesses."

Martha agreed. But for once, she couldn't say a word. She sat there and looked at Allen, and suddenly she couldn't even remember what that lieutenant what's-his-name looked like.

"Allen, it is going to be wonderful. At last, it is going to be perfect and I'll really be married to you. Do you know just how long it has been since I first fell in love with you?"

Allen reached for her and kissed her cheek. "Yes, darling, I know, exactly. Now, I think it's about time we started mending some fences and getting the next few hectic weeks planned out so everything isn't all a jumble."

"Yes, Allen," she said. She had no inclination at all to say *si*.

Chapter Eleven:
A New Direction

San Francisco, January, 1877

Martha Pemberton Dyke Cornelius, better known now as Mrs. Allen Cornelius, looked out the big parlor window and saw the bay and the hills beyond spread out before her like a beautiful picture. It had been a cold, blustery, rainy day, but now the sun had broken through and stroked the landscape with brilliant shafts of light.

Martha could scarcely believe she'd been Mrs. Cornelius for two years. How quickly the time had passed since she had come home aboard that steamer from San Diego. Her chilling experiences in the Mexican wastelands seemed only yesterday. But the two years since had been filled with joy and growth and tenderness. She had never been happier.

She and Allen were married two days after she arrived home, with only the family there and a judge presiding. They did not take a honeymoon trip, but stayed two glorious weeks in the little house on California Street. Then Allen went back to work in the family business, the Pacific Steamship and Trading Company. Martha officially retired from the firm, and spent her time at home, trying to be the perfect wife and mother to Allen's young son. She soon became involved in the social whirl and the society "charitable" works that seemed to help the society matrons as much as the recipients of those goods works.

But Martha had worked hardest at trying to become a natural mother herself. Three months after her marriage to Allen, she still was not pregnant, so she went to a doctor. His name was Dr. Paul Patterson. He was new in town and was an expert on women's special problems and diseases.

Martha blushed even yet, remembering how he examined her and the probing measurements he took inside her. For a moment, she had wondered if Dr. Patterson was enjoying his work. But then she saw his face and she knew that he had done this so often, he no longer looked at a woman's body in the way other men did.

He had been unusually frank with her. "Mrs. Cornelius, it is going to be extremely difficult for you to have a child of your own.

You have a tipped uterus. Oh, it's nothing that can hurt you, or that needs surgical correction."

She was dressed then and sitting in his office where his framed medical degree hung on the wall behind him. Dr. Patterson was tall and thin, beardless, and had the look of a man who worked too hard. She guessed he was about thirty-five.

"Now, mind you, Mrs. Cornelius, I'm not saying that it is impossible for you to become pregnant. The fact is you might fool me this very week. What I want to impress upon you, and what you should tell your husband, is that it will be harder for you than most women, and that you will have to try more often." He smiled at her. "Most men don't mind this part in the least."

When she didn't laugh or even smile, Dr. Patterson went on. "The best time for a woman to conceive is at the time of ovulation, when eggs are produced and in position in the uterus. For most women the peak time for easiest conception is the thirteenth to fourteenth day after the start of her last menstrual flow. Thirteen to fourteen days. For optimum results, I suggest you have intercourse once every twenty-four hours on the tenth through seventeenth days —"
He stopped short at the sight of Martha sit-

ting there, blushing bright red. He touched her hand across the desk and she jumped.

"Mrs. Cornelius, please don't be embarrassed. I understand you've been a business executive. Look at this as a simple business problem of logistics. All you have to do is have the right material at the right location at the right time. The workings of the female body are my business. You're an intelligent woman, you've proved that just by coming to inquire about your situation. Now let me go over those days again, so you are sure that you remember it."

Dr. Patterson handed her a pad of paper and a pencil.

"Please write down the pertinent facts so you'll have them for your records."

He went over it once more, and this time Martha found she was less embarrassed and could understand it better. It all was logical and made sense.

Now, nearly two years later, Martha smiled remembering that first talk with Dr. Patterson. She had seen him many times since, and the Pattersons had become good friends with Martha and Allen.

At any rate, the advice or luck or chance or good planning worked, and her son, Harold Allen Cornelius, was almost a year old now. He was a lively child, and had been spoiled. It was understandable, being the first grandchild in the Pemberton family. But Mrs. Larson, Martha's long-time house-keeper, had pointed out certain trends she was noticing with Hal, and Martha had moved to curb the excesses at once. She would not have a spoiled child. He would be loved and cared for, but he would be disciplined when he needed it and he would be trained in proper manners.

The small house on California Street was not Martha's and Allen's home for long. For nearly six months, her father had been building a new place for her on the hill, less than half a mile from his own mansion. Indeed, the new house was a mansion in its own right. It had all of the latest developments — gas lights, running water in two inside bathrooms, and a host of other luxuries. The mansion was Mr. Pemberton's wedding gift to her and Allen.

Martha had been content to stay home during her pregnancy, and help her newly conceived baby grow for the first nine months of his life. She read everything she could find on pre-natal care. She hounded Dr. Patterson for anything that might affect the health of her unborn. He simply told her to stay healthy and, as an afterthought, he told her not to use opium, tobacco or any other strong drug.

After considerable soul searching Martha decided that all alcoholic beverages and wines also were drugs, and so she concentrated on milk, and water, foregoing tea and coffee as well.

She didn't know if what she did helped or not, but Hal was born fit and healthy, weighing six pounds and seven ounces.

During the first year of Hal's life outside her body, she concentrated on being the very best possible mother. She nursed Hal for five months, then weaned him and took delight in the fast growth of the small bundle. They had a nurse in the house for Hal. She would give way to a governess in another year. They had two women in the kitchen and one driver and of course, Mrs. Larson, who'd run the house on California Street, came along as head housekeeper in charge of the other domestics. As usual, she did a remarkable job.

Allen excelled at the firm. A little over a year after their marriage, he won a promotion over two other men, and they themselves agreed that he was the best for the spot. Less than a year later, word came that Allen's father had died in Boston, and he was one of three to share in the huge Cornelius estate. He had told Martha about his father's firm, much like the Pemberton group of businesses, also in the shipping and marketing field. Allen inherited a large sum of cash and securities and a thirty-three percent interest in the shipping business. For a time, he thought of moving back to Boston and taking over his share of the management, but his two brothers discouraged him. They told him it might upset the delicate balance they had forged. He would be kept informed of all of the important business developments, and get his share of the profits.

They sent letters of credit to him in staggering amounts, and he appointed a conservator in Boston to handle the rest of his stocks and affairs there.

Martha never knew what any of the final figures were. She said large amounts of money embarrassed her, especially when she knew so many people who were barely finding enough to eat and clothes to keep themselves warm. She knew that the totals were well over a million dollars. There was more money than she and Allen would never need or be able to use.

In a sudden splurge, she hired one of her father's ships and sent yet another load of canned food and well-drilling equipment to Todos Santos. Also on the ship were clothes and blankets, enough for everyone in the village.

This was the fourth shipment she had made and the largest. One of the main cargoes was a huge quantity of red brick, mortar and lumber, doors and windows enough to put up a six room house for her mother and to build a new *cantina.* There were also two masons and two carpenters aboard. They were instructed to hire the local workers they needed and train them. Then they were to put up the buildings. The *gringo* foremen were paid double their usual salary for the job.

Maria had written a long letter to her daughter, thanking her for the supplies, and expressing gratitude that she was allowing the men of the village to work on the buildings so they could earn money.

Martha had performed her duties well, both as a daughter and a mother, over the past two years. But now, as she watched the shafts of bright sunshine stabbing through the mists and the rain as the squall broke up, she felt restless. Her main duty was done now at home. Her stepson was at boarding school, and she didn't want to go on being a one-child mother and a society *grand dame.* She had loved her days working at Pacific Steamship, but now she knew that it would not be right for her to go back now. Both Allen and Randy would resent it. Even if Allen said nothing, he would feel threatened, always comparing his work with hers. No, she must find some new activity, some new service she could do. Perhaps a social work for the poor, but something not run by the San Francisco social elite.

She was, of course, already active in a dozen charities, foundations and movements. They all seemed so good and noble, but when the actual dollar amounts, or the work performed came down to those who needed it, the net value seemed so low, so inadequate. The society women themselves benefitted by only thinking they were really helping!

There must be something she could do, something she could promote, could help.

Nothing came to her, no inspiration. She picked up the newspaper and leafed through it. The paper had grown in just a few years. What was the population there now? Well over a hundred thousand people, she thought. There must be something. . . .

She saw a story in the paper which stopped her.

Salt Lake City Women Vote for winner. Word has come from Salt Lake City, Utah, where women are permitted to vote in state and local elections but not in federal, that in a straw poll taken on the Presidential race, eighty-seven percent voted for Samuel J. Tilden, the Democratic candidate who apparently has won the contest over the Republican candidate Rutherford Birchard Hayes.

Utah women were given their voting franchises in territorial elections and local elections in 1870. However, the turnout at the polls has been far under that predicted.

The only other territory where women may exercise their vote is in Wyoming, which granted women that right in 1869.

Martha read the item again. Why couldn't women vote? They were certainly as smart as men, could be just as good in business, were certainly better than most men in school. She'd proven that herself. Martha read the article again. Then she remembered Susan B. Anthony, whose name had been in all the papers a few months ago. She was fighting for women's suffrage — women's rights to vote. Susan B. was a real firebrand.

It was eight or nine years now that Susan B. Anthony had been upsetting men and campaigning for women's rights. The more Martha thought about it, the more she liked the idea. Why didn't she investigate what was being done right there in San Francisco about women's rights, women's suffrage! Had there been any activity? She didn't know of any, but she would certainly find out.

Martha put on her fur coat and a hat to keep off any sprinkles, then asked Mrs. Larson to call her carriage around. She was bent on going to the San Francisco *Bulletin* newspaper office to find out what had been printed in town about the women's suffrage.

At the *Bulletin* office she soon found that there was no file of clippings kept on women's suffrage. One of the women, who heard her question, came back and offered to help her. Martha was in the paper's morgue, filled with years of the daily *Bulletin* editions, neatly squeezed together between wooden rods and hung on racks.

The woman who'd volunteered to help held out her hand. "I'm Wanda Bellmarner."

"Mrs. Cornelius. Can you help me?"

Wanda smiled stiffly. "We ran a story on the local suffragettes about two weeks ago. One of the men writers looked up all the local enthusiasts and asked them the same dumb questions. But at least it will give you some names." She hesitated. "Are you interested in the idea of women's suffrage?"

264

"I think so. At least I want to find out all I can about it so I can make up my mind."

Wanda looked at Martha leafing through the past week's editions. This lady was upper crust, that was for sure. That fur coat would be worth half a year's salary, and the dress under it wasn't exactly a cheap piece of chintz. Wanda didn't even want to think about the rings.

"Be glad to help you any way I can, Mrs. Cornelius. Was that Mrs. Amos Cornelius?" Wanda tried it even though it was the oldest way in the books to get an identification.

"No, I'm Martha, Mrs. Allen Cornelius. Where did you say that entry was?"

Wanda found the item and watched as the woman read it. She had at least come with a pad and pencil, and she wrote down names and addresses. There just might be something here after all, Wanda thought.

When Mrs. Cornelius was through writing, Wanda asked her if there was anything else she might do. Martha shook her head.

"If you really want to learn about the movement, talk to the second woman listed there, Susan Stone. I hear she really knows all about it."

Martha glanced up curiously. "May I ask how you know so much about all this?"

"I work here and get to know most everything. I'm a proofreader. I check to be sure the typesetters set the words down right that the reporters wrote."

"Oh, I see. Are there any more articles about the suffrage movement?"

Wanda found one more, a small one, then waved. "Well, I've got to get back to work. You see Susan Stone. She's the one."

When Martha walked out of the *Bulletin* office, Wanda went back to the morgue. She was not surprised to find that Mrs. Allen (Martha) Cornelius had her own file folder in the clipping room. And she found out why. Martha was a Pemberton, one of *the* Pembertons, and that spelled only one thing, m-o-n-e-y!

As soon as she left work at six, Wanda took a hack and rode over a mile down the peninsula to Susan Stone's house. Susan should know as soon as possible that this rich woman was interested in the suffrage movement!

Chapter Twelve:
A Company Man

Since returning from Mexico, Randy Pemberton had really settled into the business. He accepted his father's ultimatum that he would either go into an executive training program and stick to it, or he could not come into the firm at all. Randy stuck to it. In the past two years, he had worked in fifty-two vital departments of the corporation, spending two weeks in each one. In each, he had absorbed as much of the operation as he could, and related it to other departments in the business as a whole. It was a learning period that should have taken ten or twelve years, but Harold Pemberton felt that he simply didn't have that much time.

Randy was twenty-five years old, and had firmly convinced his father that he was both interested and devoted to the business. And, as he put it, he was a Harvard man, after all, and could tackle any job and get it done correctly.

Randy now stood an inch taller than his father at an even six feet. He wore his light hair slightly longer than most men, letting it billow upward in a natural wave, then fall to brush his collar in back and hide part of his ears. His eyes were blue and clear, and he had learned to hold his whiskey as well as most men. He was not known to gamble excessively, was not given to wild talk or action. He had given up his open liaison with the city's wide variety of prostitutes and, due to this new image, he was considered one of San Francisco's most eligible young bachelors.

More than once, Randy's father had hinted broadly that it was past time that Randy should find a wife and raise a family.

"Randy, what you need is a strong woman, who is easy to get along with, who can provide you with at least two and preferably three male heirs. Right now, you're the last of a short Pemberton line. Do you realize that? Don't let it die out on us. I always want a Pemberton to be running this company!"

But Randy had no intentions of getting married, not yet. He was enjoying himself too much. Now and then, however, he did think about Amelia Borcherding. When he worked in accounting, he arranged it so he could be near her and face her work desk. Twice he said hello to her, but something held him back from going further. She seemed so tender, so naive, so pure that he didn't want to touch her, to spoil her. He tried, but he could not forget her.

He always side-stepped the hint of scandal. It wasn't an easy thing to do, but by working hard at his role, he had managed.

In the field of business, Randy had mastered a few basic elements of management. One was that he became efficient at delegating work to various individuals and departments. He would then gather the pieces, put a finishing touch to them with a conclusion, and present the package. He never actually said that it was all his own work, but neither did he give credit to those who helped. Who was going to complain? Who would stand up and do battle with the corporation president's son? And especially when everyone knew Randy would take over the firm someday. Nobody could challenge him, and Randy knew it.

By the end of the second year, Harold was well satisfied with his son's progress. He put Randy in his first permanent, responsible position: vice president in charge of retail sales. The job was one step higher than Martha had held when she was with the firm. That pleased Randy, but he quickly found that the new job took much more time than he wanted to devote to the work. Again, he used his talent for delegating work.

Now, Randy looked at his watch, a gold one he kept in his vest pocket, on a gold chain. It was nearly two-thirty.

He picked up his hat, overcoat and umbrella and went to his outer office.

"Miss Wendell, I have a three o'clock appointment. It will probably tie me up the rest of the afternoon. Take messages, and if there were any appointments set for the rest of today, please re-schedule them for later. This came up suddenly, and there is no possible way around it."

Miss Wendell bobbed her head. She never smiled. She was absolutely the ugliest woman Randy had ever seen, which was why he asked for her. She was about forty and not a very good secretary, but she fit in with his plans. There would be no danger of any unseemly advances by him toward Miss Wendell.

Outside, he found that his carriage had been brought around as per instructions from Miss Wendell. Whenever he intended to leave the building, she was to send a runner to the company stable area and have his

270

carriage sent to the front steps.

Randy ignored the stable boy, took the reins and drove away smartly. Just off Market Street he stopped and went into a small retail fish market. He walked near the back and saw her standing near the display of lobsters.

As he came up beside her, she glanced over and smiled. She was not the prettiest woman in town. But he had challenged her to meet him here today and she had accepted.

"Mrs. Barclay," he said quietly. "It's good to see you."

"Randy . . . I . . ." She stopped.

"You're glad you're here," he filled in for her. Without saying anything else, he took her by the arm and helped her out of the market. She pulled her hat low over her face and stepped into the carriage. There was no rain but the fog was heavy as he worked his way through the streets and stopped a half mile from the fish market. He had pulled into an alley just off Merriweather Street and parked behind a small house.

The woman had not said a word as he drove. Now she touched his arm.

"Randy, I know what I said at the party, but the wine . . . you know I was just a little too full of wine . . ."

Randy reached over and kissed her lips gently. He had never touched her before, and it gave him a surging, wild thrill. She murmured something and he kissed her again, this time with more force, and he sensed her response.

"Now, Mrs. Barclay, let's not play games. You met me in the fish market because you were curious to see if I would show up. But you came with me because you are looking for something else — some romance, some forbidden fruit. Right now, it's time we go into the house and get out of this miserable fog."

Without another word, he stepped from the rig. Then he reached in and helped her down, and held her arm as they went in the back door of the small frame house. They went through a kitchen to the front room, where they found the shades pulled, a lamp lighted and a fire burning in the hearth.

She looked at him quickly.

"Randy Pemberton, you planned that I would come all the time!"

"Of course. I wanted you to. You wanted to." He took her in his arms, and kissed her lips and held her close. Then he helped her off with her coat, removed his own and his jacket and led her to the couch. Her dress was blue and gold, closely fitted at the top and swept wide at the skirt. He admired it for a moment, then he looked into her eyes.

"Mrs. Barclay . . . Becky . . . I brought you here to make love to you. We both know that, so why should we try to deny it?" He kissed her again, pulling her close.

She pushed him away. "Randy, the only reason I came was to see just how far you would go. I mean, you should be ashamed of yourself. I am a married woman."

Randy reached out and put his finger against her lips. Then he kissed her and as he did, cupped one of her breasts in his hand and rubbed gently.

She gasped, but his lips sealed the sound on hers and he held the kiss a long time. When he let her lips move away, he caught her other breast. "Becky, dear, sweet Becky. We both know why we're here." He kissed her again and this time he bent her sideways on the sofa until he was lying on top of her. One hand pushed under the bodice of the expensive dress. His kisses came quickly then and she had little chance to protest.

He had the blue and gold dress open to the waist when he lifted his lips from hers, and she did not scream or cry out. He picked her up and put her down on the big rug in front of the fireplace.

With her help he lifted the blue dress from

her shoulders, then removed her petticoats.

Two hours later, they sat sipping coffee next to the fire. Both were naked. She shivered and he put his shirt around her bare shoulders.

"Randy, I never dreamed that when we arranged our little meeting that you would try to . . . I mean even suggest . . ." She sighed. "Randy, you are exciting." She laughed. "Then Shirley was telling the truth. Shirley has been on your rug in front of the fireplace, too. I thought she was just making it up, trying to shock me. You know how she is. Do you ever! I guess that's why I hinted I might have lunch with you." She looked up. "Would you be angry with me if I said I actually hoped that you might get a little fresh with me?" She groaned. "Oh, God! My husband! Wally would kill me. You've got to promise never to tell him."

Randy laughed. "You think I'm going to brag to the assistant treasurer of the company that I've been making wild love with his beautiful wife? You think I want to fight a duel?"

"Oh, no! Anyway, duels are illegal now — have been for twelve years." She paused, her finger twirling the blond hairs on his chest. "But, you really don't want him to find out any more than I do!"

He kissed her. "That's a smart girl." He looked at her, pulled the shirt open. Her breasts were much smaller than he had guessed. The way women wore dresses these days you couldn't always tell. He bent and kissed both breasts and then pushed her down on her back.

"Since you're still here, and it isn't time to go yet, and the fire isn't out yet . . ."

At six o'clock that evening, Mrs. Wallace Barclay came out of the public library and tapped her foot impatiently. Her driver was supposed to pick her up promptly at six. Then she saw him swing around the corner and she walked toward the carriage. What an afternoon! She was insane to agree to meet Randy again. Next Wednesday afternoon at two o'clock in the same fish market. It would happen again, and already she was looking forward to it, remembering this afternoon with a shiver. The things they'd done — strange, wonderful things.

Before they'd left, Randy had turned down the lights, put a screen in front of the fire, and locked the back door. Then he'd driven Mrs. Barclay to within half a block of the public library and let her out.

He hurried down two more streets. There was one small item he had to take care of and it couldn't wait. Mrs. Barclay had been more entertaining than he expected. Any woman was good, Randy believed, but some were just better than others. His game of cuckolding as many officers of Pacific Steamship and Trading as possible continued to give him remarkable diversion. But this business at hand was more serious, and would take his total concentration.

He parked his rig next to the waterfront and ran back a block, then walked up one more street to the warehouse he wanted. The Pacific Steamship sign showed plainly in the soft winter night. He moved along the side of the big structure, found the door, and inserted a key in the lock. It opened easily. Inside, he moved cautiously through the darkness, remembering the layout and where the material was he wanted.

The large shipment of paint had arrived only that morning, and would be moved out to retail stores the next day. Nearby were boxes filled with wooden and bamboo items shipped from Hawaii and Japan. The paint would work fine for what he wanted. Using a screwdriver he had brought from the carriage, Randy pried off the tops of two five-gallon cans of paint. He tipped one over, spilling the paint across the other cans and into the cardboard boxes.

Quickly Randy took a packet of "stinkers"

from his pocket. These were sulphur matches pasted together in a round form. He tore one of the stinkers off and scratched it on the wooden floor. It lit and gave off a bright, sudden flame that smelled strongly of sulphur. Randy edged the burning stinker into the paint on the floor. It caught fire, burning rapidly along the river of paint.

The flame surged to the cardboard boxes, igniting them. Now Randy lit another five-gallon can, still right side up.

The smoke and flames billowed higher. The paint would provide a hot fire, generate enough heat to blow the tops off the other cans of paint, adding more fuel to the fire. It would be impossible to quench.

Randy ran toward the back door. There were no windows showing on the street so the fire would have a good start before anyone noticed it. He watched the flames eating into the boxes. Some furniture caught and kindled as the inferno spread.

A curious, pleased smile flashed across Randy's face. Then he ran from the warehouse, locking the door carefully behind him. He forced himself to walk casually toward his carriage two blocks away. Inside the rig, he turned and stared back at the warehouse. Nothing unusual showed yet.

A half hour later, the fire broke through

the roof of the warehouse and Randy touched the reins to the horse and moved down the street away from the fire.

He began to sing a little song, a nameless ditty he had learned when he was small. Probably one of the nurses or governesses had taught it to him. They watched over him day and night until he was twelve. God, how he'd hated them — all of them. They ordered him around and scolded him like they were his mothers. His own mother had been too busy to do it.

But he had repaid one of the biddies. She had been about thirty and an old maid. She insisted on tucking him in, and every night she bent over him, pushing in the covers and letting him look down the front of her loosely worn blouses.

He knew she did it just to frustrate him, to get a little thrill of her own. Even at twelve, he knew that much. One night, he kept his arms out of the covers when she came in. When she bent over him, he pushed his hands inside her blouse and grabbed both her breasts. He thought she would scream and hit him, but she didn't. She smiled and just stood there, nodding, letting him play with them. She talked softly to him, and all the while she had one hand between her legs, rubbing herself. He

278

wondered at the time what she was doing.

The next day, she quit and he never saw her again. At least he had gotten even with her. Or had he? Now he realized he had done her a favor! So he still owed them — all of them!

Randy thought of the fire. He had wanted to stay there and watch it burn right down to the ground, but he realized that would be dangerous. Someone would recognize him and wonder why he happened to be there. But the fire would do its work.

In the past three days, ships had unloaded more than ten thousand dollars' worth of merchandise at warehouse #3. He knew how much was there because the papers had come across his desk only that morning. For one small delicious moment, he let the satisfaction of it surge through him. Be condescending to him, would they, the son-of-a-bitches! Try to make him over in their image, would they!

If they were going to allow his bastard sister to participate in the corporate profits and stock, in the benefits, then he was going to do everything he could to put a large hole in that corporation.

Some of his revenge tactics had begun almost by accident. He had been at a company party, twelve or fifteen couples in the big house of one of the vice presidents. During the course of the evening, he remembered something in his overcoat. When he went to the room where the coats had been left, he got lost, and wandered into a bedroom. A soft light was on, and someone lay on the bed, a woman. He moved closer and saw it was the youngish Mrs. McCardle, the wife of the head of purchasing.

Randy had secretly hated Lon McCardle for over a year. Some small thing in his department had proved highly embarrassing to Randy, and McCardle had teased him about it for several months. Now Amy McCardle lay there, breathing evenly, sleeping. She was a pretty thing, lying on her back, her big breasts pushing hard against the fabric of her dress.

Randy almost laughed. Why not? It would serve McCardle right to cuckold him. If he could manage it. Randy closed the bedroom door and locked it, then went back to the bed and gently began to caress Amy. She groaned softly and smiled. He stroked her breasts tenderly. She said something, turning more toward him. Her breathing seemed to quicken and deepen. Randy became bolder and pushed one hand under the dress, fondling the bare breast and she smiled in her sleep. Randy moved one hand to her leg and worked it up under her dress.

It was nearly five minutes before Amy Mc-Cardle came fully awake. She had been dreaming that she was about to make love with Lon. Now she looked up and saw Randy kneeling between her parted thighs, her dress around her waist, the top of it open and her breasts exposed.

His hand went over her mouth before she could cry out.

"Amy, sweetheart, don't worry. Nobody will never know. You and I are going to make love, right now. And if a word about it ever gets back to the company, I'll get Lon fired and black-listed, so he'll never get a job anywhere in San Francisco again. Do you understand?"

She nodded. He took his hand off her mouth and put his lips there. To his surprise, she nibbled at his lips, and her hands reached between his legs.

He took her quickly, roughly, not trying to please her or to give her any pleasure. It had to be that way, poetic justice. He was raping the wife in the company which was raping him of his rightful heritage!

The next day, there were no repercussions, and it solidified his idea. He would bed as many of the wives of the corporation officers as possible. That was only fitting in his plan of revenge.

However, he decided early that he would make no move directly against his half-sister. That would be too obvious and he would be at once suspect. If he could use the devious route, a long campaign, be the hidden detractor, he could at least bring the whole company down, he could divest it of its riches, and leave nothing of value for his bastard sister!

He rejected the point that by so doing he would also eliminate any inheritance for himself. He was so crazy and blinded by unreasonable hatred, it didn't seem to matter. Nor did he think about the fact that his sister's husband was a millionaire in his own right, with his Boston money. Instead, Randy concentrated on the drive to discredit and disrupt Pacific Steamship and Trading Company, while appearing to be a dedicated company man.

For six months, he had concentrated on seducing the executives' wives. Now only two remained, and both were so old and ugly that the prospect nauseated him. What next? Should he begin sending anonymous letters to the cuckolded men and give dates and times when their wives had been unfaithful? He could upset and demoralize the whole upper management team at once.

Sign the letters, "A Friend." And the notes would go on company stationery, through the company inter-office mail, so the men involved would know their humiliation was witnessed by someone within the firm.

Yes, now it was coming together! But again, he would do it so there could not be the slightest suspicion thrown on him. The wives wouldn't talk. They knew it would mean the end of their husbands' careers if they said who was involved. There would be a dozen domestic crises among the top executives!

He thought again about the fire. It had excited him, seemed to be so right, so natural, as if he'd expected to do it all along. But he had planned it all carefully. That was the secret, of course: to set up everything, think it through and then lay it out in detail. Planning was the secret of any successful activity. They would never find a single bit of evidence to tie him to the fire.

By design, Randy slowed his horse outside a tavern and looked at the name. "Kilarney's," the sign read. He parked his rig, tied the reins, and went into the tavern. He hadn't been there for over two years. At once, he recognized the owner, Amos I. Kilarney, a stout man with reddish cheeks, hair straggling down over his collar and wearing a soiled towel around his waist.

Kilarney looked at Randy and hesitated, then drew a beer for him and took the dime. He knew the lad, knew him from before, and for two years he had thanked his Irish luck that he didn't get in any trouble with the Pembertons because of it.

With the second beer, young Pemberton motioned for Kilarney to sit at his table for a minute.

"Mr. Kilarney, remember the last time I drank in your pub?" Randy said, so softly Kilarney had to strain to hear.

"Aye, lad, that I do."

"And remember the trouble you got me into? You tattled on me to my father about what I said. Ran to him for some blackmail money is my guess. And all you got for your trouble was the old heave-ho.

"Me, I got trouble by the yearful that you brought on me. Shanghaied by my own father, and banished, sent to sea. And nothing but bad times afterward, a prisoner in a stinking Mexican jail. A good deal of trouble you caused me, Amos I. Kilarney, and it's time to settle your debt."

As Kilarney listened, Randy outlined what he wanted the man to do, and the tavern owner pulled back in surprise.

Kilarney smiled at the man then. It was so

little, and he could even turn a neat profit doing it. There were still many sailing ships working the port that needed able-bodied men to pull the canvas, and they paid twenty-five dollars a man to the procurer.

"Mr. Kilarney, this is your debt. Remember our transaction must be in the strictest of confidence, even your wife should not know. If you ever slip a hint of our talk, your body will suffer grievous damage, and your little business here will be consumed by a disastrous fire. Do I make myself clear, good Mr. Kilarney?"

"Oh, yes. Yes sir. May I bring you another drink?"

"Strong drink is bad for a man, Kilarney. You won't see me here again, and you will report to me your results."

Randy left and drove back to the alley, just off Merriweather Street, where he had been that afternoon. It was one of two homes he maintained in the city. This one for afternoon trysts, and the informal comforts, another much larger house had a staff of four servants, and he stayed there half the time and used it for his formal entertainment.

He parked the rig in the back, unhitched the horse and put her in the stall, unlocked the rear door of the house and went inside.

Two lamps burned in the living room and a small white cat curled contentedly on the bear rug near the fire. On the couch sat identical twins, small girls with exquisite figures, beautiful hair and pretty faces. They were eighteen years old. Randy had found them through Madelyn, in a high-class brothel, and bought them a week ago. When he came in, both stood and smiled. One took his hat, coat, and cane, the other brought his pipe and slippers.

Randy chuckled at the way his new "staff" scurried around to please him, and patted them both on their round little bottoms.

"Thank you, pets, but not tonight. I have some deep thinking to do. I'll see you both in the morning."

"Yes, Mr. Pemberton," one said.

"We'll have breakfast with you at seven as usual," the other said.

Randy watched them walk to the door of the second bedroom and go inside. They blew him kisses. Then he was alone, staring into the flames of the fireplace.

He quickly reviewed his efforts, and went over his work so far. It was good. Now he had to work out the next few steps in his little campaign. He was looking for a real shocker, something with power, something that would attract a lot of public attention.

Whatever it was, it had to bring discredit on Pacific Steamship and Trading Company.

CHAPTER THIRTEEN:
A BRIGHT PENNY

Martha sat at her writing desk, planning a dinner party, when she heard the front door chimes. A few moments later, Mrs. Larson brought in Martha's younger sister, Penny.

"Hello, Martha!" Penny said, then threw her arms around her sister, hugging her and pecking Martha on the cheek.

Martha said hello and stepped back. "Penny Pemberton, you certainly are not my *little* sister any more. You're all grown up and a remarkably pretty young woman."

"Thank you, Marty. You don't mind if I call you Marty, do you? It's been such a long time since we've seen each other and I wanted to come and have a good talk."

Even before she finished the sentence, Penny's smile began breaking up. Tears welled up and spilled down the younger girl's cheeks. She leaned toward Martha, who put her arms around her, nestling the blonde head on her shoulder. Penny sobbed, a moaning heartbreak wail breaking through.

"Oh, Marty, I'm so miserable I could just die! I could die!"

The tears came again, racking sobs tore at her body and she moaned in despair.

Martha caught by surprise, hardly knew what to say for a moment. Then she smiled over her sister's blonde hair and tightened her arms around her and led Penny to an upholstered couch where they sat.

"Penny, why don't you tell me exactly what's troubling you? Tell me anything and everything. That's what sisters are for. Remember, I'm a girl, too, and I just might understand. Is it about boys?"

Penny pulled back and stared at her sister. "How did you guess it was about boys? I mean, I never said a word . . ."

Martha laughed and pushed some strands of long blonde hair out of Penny's face. "I know because I was once a girl, too. And not so long ago, remember? And I probably once felt the same way you do now. So tell me what's the sudden tragedy?"

"Just being a girl, I expect. I remember when I was about fourteen I felt so strange one summer. All of a sudden I wanted to run out and grab every boy I saw and kiss him. It was so weird and upsetting. Then in three or four months, that was all over. Oh, I guess the idea was still there, only it was a little bit easier to control, to live with. I still wanted boys to notice me and to like me, only I wasn't sure just what I wanted them to do about it."

Martha nodded, smiling, remembering her own days of instant tragedy and tears at the slightest hint of rebuff, or imagined injury. She called Mrs. Larson, who brought tea and cookies, and left.

"Go on, Penny. You were telling me how you feel."

"Yes. Well, now I know how I feel, I think. I know what I want . . . you know . . . what I'd like a boy to do. But usually, I'm so afraid that I just freeze up whenever something like that happens."

"Penny, don't push it. Don't rush. Remember, boys are people, too. That's easy to forget when you're this age. They have feelings and are offended and shy and bashful, just like you are. What you need is to have boys respect you. You must learn to enjoy them as people. You want to be fun to be with, right?"

"Well, yes, but I like to be kissed, too."

"And then after kissing, Penny?"

"That's what I get confused about. I tried to talk to Mother. But the first time, she got a sick headache, and the next time, she had an urgent committee meeting. She never talked with you about any of this, right?"

"Oh, my, you're right about hat." Martha laughed, remembering. "That mother of ours is so shy about sex I'm surprised she ever got around to having children. Yes, Penny, it's all right to say the word 'sex' in my house. Sex is natural and normal, but it is for adults — *married* adults. It is definitely not for blonde and beautiful nineteen-year-olds who are unmarried, and have their whole lives ahead of them." Martha looked at Penny sharply. "Penny, have you ever been to bed with a boy?"

"No, of course not. Sometimes I wish I had. Two of my friends claim they have and they know all about it. They're always telling me how good or how awful it was. It seems to be always one way or the other."

"Are either of these friends pregnant?"

"No."

"And probably most of their wild sexy times were only in their imaginations, just to impress you. Penny, most girls want to be virgins when they marry. And think of all the risks and the shame of getting pregnant before marriage."

Penny scowled at her sister. "Marty, I didn't come here for a lecture on morality. I want some answers."

"Then give me the questions."

"All right. Should I let a boy touch my breasts?"

"That's a complicated question. Usually I imagine that you would say no to that question. Not the butcher, or a man on the street or a suitor the first day he came calling. But it isn't always that easy. Say you're promised to some man, and your wedding date is set, and he's getting demanding. Then you might need to let him touch you and feel you, just a little to keep him interested, right up to your wedding night."

"But I'm not engaged."

"Yes, so my answer really doesn't help much, does it? I don't know what else to tell you. Penny, you simply have to use your common sense. Your body is not a toy to tease men with. You try that and you'll find out that men are stronger physically than you are. They will turn your tease into a seduction or rape and walk away laughing at you for your foolishness. That could turn out to be the most costly mistake of your young life," Martha sighed. "Penny, this is something that you simply have to live through to know about. And if you make any mistakes, pray that they are small ones that can be corrected easily. For a woman, sex is not a game, not a contest between her and a man, and your body is not a toy for someone to play with and then throw away."

"What does it feel like, Marty . . . you know . . . when you do it?"

"Do it? The polite word, Penny, is intercourse." She shook her head. "That's for married folks, Penny. Which is not answering your question, I know. What does it feel like? Penny, what did it feel like when you were kissed, when a boy kissed your lips?"

"Oh, well, I don't know, it's kind of hard to describe. First I was mad, then it seemed kind of nice, but it's hard to put into words."

"It's the same with intercourse, hard to describe. Penny, has a boy ever rubbed your breasts?"

Penny looked at the floor. "Well, once, yes. At a picnic. We were wrestling a little and he sat on top of me and held both my hands and reached inside and . . . you know . . . rubbed me. That was last summer."

"How did it feel?"

She smiled. "Yes, it is hard to describe. And you mean intercourse is a lot like that, only more and stronger."

"That's pretty close, Penny. When your suitors start to get out of hand, simply send them home. Call for the maid, or if Father is home, shout for him. That will scare them right into the bay. Play it safe, and stop with a kiss or two. Believe me, Penny, that's the best way to stay out of trouble."

Penny nodded. "Well, it sounds like it. I've known that, but I just wanted to talk about it. You know Mother. One more question. I was talking with a friend the other day and she said she was sure that it took three times . . . having intercourse . . . to get pregnant. Is that right?"

Martha reached out and hugged Penny. She laughed softly. "Penny, now that one I can answer. You wouldn't believe how hard it was for me to get pregnant. I'll tell you about that some day. But your friend is wrong. More than one girl has found that out. One time is all it takes if the conditions are right. Please remember that, Penny. Being pregnant and not married is the most tragic thing that can happen to a woman."

Penny looked properly impressed. "Just one time!"

Martha took both of Penny's hands and looked into her lovely face, her soft blue eyes.

"Little sister, I've never tried to give you any advice before. Maybe I shouldn't now. But I'm going to try. Hang on, just hang on. Don't let this sex thing worry you to death. Don't let it get out of hand. It can easily ruin the rest of your life."

Martha tried to lighten it a little. She laughed and then took a sip of her tea. "What you need is an outside interest. How would you like to have a part-time job? Oh, not one that you got paid for, but something worthwhile to do that will really help people. You would be a marvel at this. I used to do a little of it, and it's simple, easy, you can have a lot of fun, and meet people you never would meet any other way. Sound interesting?"

Penny frowned, then shrugged. "Might be."

"I have a friend who is a nurse at St. Andrew's hospital. They have this organization called the Pink Ladies. You dress in this attractive pink and white smock and go around to the patient wards offering them books to read, or you can write letters for those who want you to, arrange flowers, provide a little special attention that the nurses just don't have time to give. No training is needed, and it really is fun. Will you try it?"

"How long? How often?"

"Some of the women go each day from ten to four. Most spend one day a week from ten to six. Whatever works out best. I used to spend each morning from nine to one there, remember? It's really one of the most worthwhile things I've ever done."

Penny smiled. "All right, I'll try it. I'm not doing anything else anyway. I'll be a Florence Nightingale right here at home. Mother will like that."

They went on talking. Much later Martha gave Penny a note to take to the hospital introducing her. She was sure the Pink Ladies would welcome Penny with open arms.

By the time Penny left, she had regained her bright smile, her enthusiasm, and her optimistic outlook. Martha was pleased. She knew it was a sensitive time of life for her sheltered sister. Martha shivered, remembering her own first few introductions to sex. She wished that it could have been softer, less traumatic.

Tuesday, Wednesday, and Thursday, Penny worked at the hospital. At first, the smell of the building almost made her sick. But she got used to that. The people were the reason she went back. She had never met so many different kinds of people: children, old grandmothers, foreigners who couldn't speak English, one woman who cried all the time. They all felt so alone, frightened and in need of a friend. By the end of the first week, Penny was so involved and enthused, she talked two of her girl friends into joining the program. They all worked the same hours, and came and went together. The hospital was pleased at the addition of the bright, young, happy faces. The patients seemed especially glad when the three girls bounced into a ward.

On Saturday morning, Penny remembered that she would have two beaus calling that afternoon. She was not interested in either one. Hans Miller was a nice enough boy, and was from what his mother would call "good stock," meaning his family had lots of money. He was nineteen and would be leaving San Francisco to go to Harvard soon. That would interest her father. Hans was also the best looking of the two callers. Two inches under six feet, he was six inches taller than Penny, strong and wide-shouldered. He said he enjoyed swimming and sailing small boats on the bay. Several times, he had offered to take her sailing, but her mother said only if one of the parents went along, which ended that idea.

The other boy, Penny didn't even think about. She could scarcely remember his name.

It was near the end of January, which meant they couldn't play croquet. She'd watch the boys shoot pool for a while, then perhaps one of them could play the piano. She played a little. If she was at the piano she couldn't dance, and she loved to dance. The music and the movement — and then, too, she could be held in a boy's arms that way and not even her mother could complain.

Penny thought about Hans more seriously. He certainly was the best prospect she had right then. She could always get married. Then she would know all about it. Of course then she would be stuck with that person for the rest of her life. No, she wanted to be sure. She would marry only once, she knew.

Still, it might be interesting to see how bold Hans was. Her mind raced ahead, trying to lay out a situation where she could be alone with Hans, but only for a few minutes. How?

The cookies and punch! Cook always had something for them to nibble on. Today Penny would tell cook to keep it in the kitchen, then she would come and fetch it for the boys when they were ready. Yes, that might work. Not too long. She couldn't get trapped with him for more than three or four minutes. That way it could be thrilling, and at the same time safe!

She combed her hair and began dressing

for the suitors. She would wear the newest dress she had, the one with the long sleeves and the neckline that scooped so low her mother had the maid sew some lace on the bodice so none of her cleavage could show. Still, she could show some if she had to. She had a good figure, pinched in waist, womanly hips and breasts that were not as big as Martha's but better than any of her friends'.

She sighed. Sometimes she wished that the next year of her life was over. Then she would probably be all married and settled down *trying* to get pregnant. It seemed that's all women could do. Get courted, get married, get pregnant.

She made an ugly face at herself in the mirror, giggled and then tried to remember the name of the other lad who was coming today. She had to think hard to remember him, a boy named Louis Streib who had been to see her only once before.

Louis was shorter than Hans, and heavy. Oh, yes! He was the one who did play piano. He played very well and said that for a while he wanted to be a concert pianist, play on the stage in front of thousands of people. But he had decided not to when he discovered how much more training and practice it would take.

Penny put the final touch on her long blonde hair and wished that she could use some rouge, but her mother would have a fit. Someday, when she was married, she would use face makeup. Some perfectly respectable women did nowadays.

Two hours later, her mother met the boys at the front door and ushered them into the library. That's where the piano was. When Penny heard them coming, she began playing, and doing it badly so Louis would hold his ears in pretended anguish. It worked.

"Ah, here she is! Now, Mr. Miller, and you, Mr. Streib, I have to go attend to some things. I'm sure that both of you will be perfect gentlemen. If you're not, you'll never set foot in this house again. Now that I've said that, I hope all of you enjoy yourselves." She waited for some response.

Hans bowed slightly and clicked his heels. "Mrs. Pemberton, you can rely on me to be the very model of decorum."

Louis grinned. "Yes, me too. Your daughter is certainly safe in our hands."

Mrs. Harold Pemberton smiled and left the room. However, she made sure the library door was wide open.

At first, they sang around the piano with Louis picking the songs. Then he played a waltz. Hans immediately asked if he might have the honor of the dance. Penny curtsied and they swung around the room, barely missing the chairs. It was delightful, and she enjoyed the feeling of strength in his arms. For just a moment, she looked down at his waist, then glanced away, embarrassed.

Louis insisted on having a dance, too. He showed Hans how to play four notes continuously, in a little pattern. Louis sang the melody and Penny danced again. It left them all laughing by the time Louis came to the end of the stanza.

"Well, after that, I think we all need some refreshments," Penny said. "Oh, they aren't here yet. I'll go get them. You both sit there and rest." She headed for the door, then turned back. "No, I can't carry it all. Louis, you work on another waltz for us, and Hans will help me bring back the punch and things."

Hans moved quickly toward her, and Louis said he already knew a dozen waltzes, and began playing one as they left.

In the hall, Penny caught Hans' hand. She ran down a dozen steps and turned into the next room. It was her father's study, and had only one door. She motioned Hans inside and then closed the door quietly. Penny turned, leaning against the door.

Hans chuckled and stepped toward her. "Did you plan this, or was it a spur-of-the-moment inspiration?"

"I planned it carefully," she admitted.

He leaned down at once and brushed his lips across hers. When she did not slap him, he kissed her solidly on her mouth. She made a low, soft sound and his lips came away and he watched her.

"I liked that, Hans," she said, looking up at him.

He kissed her again. This time his arms came around her and held her close. When their lips parted, he held her still and she could feel her heart beating faster and faster.

"Hans, that was beautiful." She turned her head so she could see his eyes. "It's hard being a girl. I have feelings, too, and I can't explain those feelings. What I want you to do is help me. If I ask you to do one thing for me, then not go any farther, would you?"

"Sure."

"No, I'm serious. I want you to kiss me and touch me and then stop."

"Yes, I understand. You say stop, we stop."

His hair was almost as light as her own, and his blue eyes shone as he watched her. She caught his hand.

"First, kiss me."

He did and was surprised to find her lips

slightly parted. As he tried to work his tongue into the opening, he felt her lift his hand and place it over her breast.

It took him by surprise, but only for a second. He squeezed gently then rubbed. His hand edged upward and over the top of her blouse and then inside to her bare breast, pushing the inside cloth down.

Penny held the kiss. She moaned and started to sag. Never had she experienced anything so amazing, so wonderful, so warm and just . . . just . . .

She felt her knees give way. He caught her and pushed her solidly against the door, his hips pressing hard against hers, and for a moment, she was sure she felt a hard bulging near his waist.

The sensations kept coming. The kiss kept warming her, and his hand on her skin brought the surging wave of a warm glow that built all the way through her body. When he rubbed her bare breast, she felt something deep inside of her suddenly explode. Her hips seemed to jolt and she shivered, trembling for ten or fifteen seconds in a splurge of such brilliant ecstatic feeling that she knew she was going to faint.

She had never felt anything so wildly exciting and so all-consuming in her life! It was like she was sitting on top of an erupting volcano, like diving off the tallest bridge into a pool of sparkling water. She wanted to go on experiencing that marvelous sensation for as long as she lived!

Numbly, she broke off the kiss.

"Stop," she mumbled. She pushed him away. His hand was still inside her blouse. She lifted it away and blinked up at him in amazement. It had all happened so fast she wasn't even sure what had taken place. Then she saw Hans with the strangest look on his face. He turned away from her, pumping his hips forward five or six times. Then he gave a low groan and leaned against the wall.

It was another two minutes before he turned around. She simply watched him, her back still against the door, so shaken, so numb, feeling so like a large lump of jelly that she knew she couldn't move if the house were burning down.

He turned and looked at her. He tried to say something, but couldn't. Penny couldn't talk either. Silently she reached for his hand and held it.

"I'll be goddamned!" he said, softly, at last.

He moved back toward her but she held up her hand. "Stop," she said and he could almost understand her word. She adjusted the top of her dress, feeling her legs return to her own command. She could stand again. Penny saw a wet spot on Hans' trousers, near his belt. She sighed, took his hand and opened the door. She looked out, saw no one and they went into the hall and toward the kitchen.

"Thanks, Penny," Hans said, his face serious.

"Not a word!" she said, and he nodded.

In the kitchen, she told the cook they were ready for the punch in a voice that almost sounded like hers. The goodies were waiting.

Neither of them said a word as they carried the punch and cookies back to the library. Almost there, she touched his arm.

"Hans, I just wanted to . . . I mean to find out . . . what it would feel like if you did that. Thank you."

He grinned. "I understand. And any time you want to try that again, or anything else . . . you let me know."

She nodded and walked ahead into the library where Louis pounded out another waltz.

They danced again, not mentioning what happened. Hans played his one-fingered waltz and she danced with Louis. Then they went to the pool room and she watched the boys rolling the balls around the green felt tabletop.

But it wasn't the same. Penny still felt in a daze. She stood and motioned to the boys. It was such a haze, such a glorious feeling, she didn't want to be around anyone else for a while.

"Hey, Penny, you look like you put something bad in that punch," Louis said.

She shook her head. "No, but I do have a headache that is making me furious. Why did it have to come today? I think I better go lie down until it fades away."

She asked the boys both to come back on Sunday. She promised she'd be feeling better and maybe they could play croquet if it was warm enough, or darts. Louis went out first. Behind him, Hans squeezed her hand secretly. Then he was gone.

Penny told her mother the boys were gone, she had a headache, and wanted to rest a while. On her bed, Penny went back over the whole amazing thing. She was still in a kind of soft after-glow. It had been the most joyously jolting experience of her life. Was that what happened when a boy caressed her breast? Then what would the rest of it be like?

Penny closed her eyes, still so exhausted she wasn't sure if she were thinking straight. She went back over it again, trying to relive each fraction of a second. The slow build, the sweeping emotion, then the sudden explosion of something within herself that she had never experienced before. How long had this been going on?

Over and over she thought about it, remembering everything she did, and what Hans did. When he turned around and humped his hips forward, what was happening? She didn't understand that. Could she ask Martha? Hardly! One of the other girls might know. She could say a friend of hers wanted to know. Yes.

Again, she wondered why she didn't want to ask Martha. Marty was her sister and had been through it. She would know. But Marty was married and a mother, and she would scold Penny. Marty might even tell their mother. That would never do. Then Penny would get courters only when her mother was present.

Penny sat up and looked down at her breasts. She loosened her blouse and stared at them. From now on, she would be very careful who she let touch her there. She had no idea that they held such power.

She got up from her bed and stared out the window, looking over the sweep of San Francisco bay. But she wasn't seeing the view. She was wondering what they would do tomorrow when Hans and Louis came courting again. She would have to make certain that she was not alone with Hans again. Penny shivered just thinking about him.

CHAPTER FOURTEEN:
STEADY, STURDY SUSAN STONE

The day after Martha heard about Susan Stone at the newspaper office, she rode in her carriage to the woman's address and knocked on the door. It was a small house in a poor neighborhood, slightly less well cared for than the surrounding houses, though at first Martha couldn't pin down exactly why she thought so. On the small porch, she saw a broken board, which confirmed her first instinct — there was no man living at this house.

The door opened and a small woman faced Martha. She was not over five feet tall, with hair tied back in a knot on the back of her head. Her brown piercing eyes stared at Martha from under thin brows. Her face was round and she looked at Martha critically.

Before Martha could say a word, the woman stepped back and beckoned her inside.

"You must be Martha Pemberton Cornelius, right?"

Martha frowned for a moment, then found herself nodding. She was surprised. She wasn't that well known.

"Come in, come in. You must be interested in woman's suffrage or you wouldn't come here to see me, correct?" Without waiting for an answer the woman turned and walked into a sparsely furnished parlor.

It was painfully obvious that the family was poor. The furniture was old, worn out, of various styles and Martha was sure most of it had been bought used.

Without waiting for Martha to sit, or even offering her a chair, Susan Stone dropped into her favorite wooden rocking chair with a crocheted pillow top and began rocking.

"Well, so you're Mrs. Allen Cornelius?"

"Yes, and I'm interested in how you knew?"

"No secret. You went to the newspaper office yesterday to read up on the suffrage movement. My spies told me. I expected you here today or tomorrow. Sit down. I'll tell you anything you want to know about me, about the other members mentioned in that article, or about our movement. We have absolutely nothing to hide because we're working for the betterment of all women, for our inalienable rights, and the franchise of the ballot."

Martha mentally lifted her brows. This woman certainly wasn't bashful about speaking out, and she seemed to care a great deal about what she was doing. She had a real cause, a crusade!

"Mrs. Stone . . ."

"That's *Miss* Stone."

"Oh, yes, thank you. I've had some experience in management, in organizing a business and making it go. Perhaps I could be some help to you and your group. Is there any thought toward putting together a series of chapters around the state? With a statewide organization we could have some real power!"

Susan Stone looked toward the heavens. "Thank you, Lord, for sending down one of your angels to help us. Oh, yes, Lord, I knew all the time there were women angels." Susan looked at Martha, a grin edging her mouth. Then both women burst into laughter.

"Really, Mrs. Cornelius, I have twice the work I can do, and you're right, we do need organization. I'm no good at that sort of thing. I'd rather get up on a soapbox and yell at people and argue with them and try to convince them about women's rights to vote. I'm a talker."

Martha understood that very well. "Do you have any kind of literature, any printed tracts that you hand out? Any donation slips, membership forms? What do you have in the way of printed material?"

Susan Stone put her hand over her face and then pulled it down, revealing her sad expression. "Lordy, Lordy, you *are* organized, aren't you? We've never printed a thing. I can see now that we should. Here, let me show you what we've been doing. I have kept a scrapbook of our newspaper clippings, and everything I can find about Utah and Wyoming women voters. Of course I have a lot of material about Miss Anthony."

For the next two hours, they looked over the clippings, the reports from Utah and Wyoming where women could vote. Martha read two letters from Susan B. Anthony herself to Miss Stone.

"When is your next meeting?"

"Oh, well, we haven't any regular meetings."

"Don't you think that you should?"

"Yes, I imagine so."

"How many members do you have?"

"Well, not too many, but we've just started here."

"How many?"

"Six."

"Only six?" Martha shook her head. "We'll never be able to convince anyone of anything until we can get at least five thousand women to a meeting. That's our goal: five thousand women in a huge hall and a speaker — Susan B. Anthony herself if we can talk her into coming out here. Now, I want to sign up as your seventh member. I'll make a thousand-dollar donation to get things moving. You'll have to keep total, complete and accurate books. Who is your treasurer?"

"You, I guess. I wouldn't know a ledger from a beggar."

"All right. Let's have the next meeting tomorrow night, here at your house. We'll keep it hushed up for now, but be thinking of some plan. We want something big that will let us break out into the open, some parade or a march or a demonstration where we can attract a lot of attention, but not get arrested."

Susan Stone sipped at the coffee she had served them both. "You are organized, aren't you, Mrs. Cornelius?"

"Call me Martha."

"Yes, thank you, I'd like that. I'm Sue. I'm afraid I've been so angry that I haven't even thought about an organization. With your help and encouragement, we're going to accomplish something really good."

"I know we are, Sue." Martha looked over at the Seth Thomas clock and saw that it was almost four in the afternoon. She stood.

"I really must be heading home. Why don't we meet again tomorrow night at eight, here at your home? You arrange to have the others here and we'll get organized. All right?"

Sue smiled. "Yes, and I'll have a form worked out for members. Do you think we should have a membership fee?"

"Yes, of course. Let's make it two dollars a year. Then everyone can join. Of course, larger contributions will be welcome. I'll get some of my friends interested in this, too."

They said goodbye and Martha went out to where her driver waited. That night, she was bubbling with plans and ideas for marches, legislation and all sorts of demonstrations, but she didn't say a word about any of it to Allen. He was sweet and precious and honorable and she loved him with all her heart, but this was something that he might not understand. She wasn't keeping secrets from him, not really. When she came back from the meeting tomorrow night, she would tell him all about it.

Now, what could they do for their first act, their first big public display? The more she thought about it, the more she centered on one idea. It would work. The idea they presented wouldn't be approved, but the newspaper people would be there because she would tip them off. Yes, they would get a lot of good publicity. It would be a fine opening gambit. She would bring up the idea the next night at the meeting.

As she fed little Hal, she kept working on the idea, expanding it, refining it. They would burst like a bombshell on the town, she was sure, and it should get outstanding newspaper coverage.

The next evening, Martha told Allen she had a committee meeting. He was busy reading the *Bulletin,* and a packet of other newspapers from Boston that had come in on the train. It seemed hard to imagine that there was a railroad that you could get on and ride all the way across the whole United States! But it was there and had been linked up now since 1869. The telegraph system was now working, too. Messages could go from San Francisco to Boston in just a minute or two. Amazing! Martha didn't have the slightest idea how a telegraph worked, but it did. She had seen it, and it brought in the news from everywhere. All you had to do was be able to decipher those dots and dashes that sounded over the telegraph wire.

Martha was driven to the Stone house again and told her driver she would be ready to leave at ten that evening. He helped her from the carriage, then saw her to the door before he returned to his rig and drove away.

Two of the women were already at Susan Stone's house when Martha arrived. One was named Harriet, the other Beth. But Martha didn't try to remember the names. She was more interested in getting their ideas about the movement.

When all six were there, Sue began the meeting, then gave the floor to Martha.

"I think we should start by nominating — and electing by acclamation — Sue Stone as president of our group." The suggestion brought words of approval and much clapping. Sue then suggested that Martha be named treasurer the same way — and that was done.

"Madam Chairman, I wish to join this group and I offer my membership check to you." She handed the draft to Sue for a thousand dollars made out to the San Francisco Woman's Suffrage Association.

Sue looked at the check and gasped. True, Martha had said she was going to do it, but

316

Sue had never seen one piece of paper worth that much money in all her life. She didn't know what to do with it.

While the other women made small noises of surprise and appreciation, Martha said, "I suggest, Madam President, that I open an account in a bank. We can withdraw funds as we need them, and put other membership money and donations we receive into the account."

"Yes, let's do that," Sue said. She recovered enough to launch into a short pep talk about why they were here and what they wanted to do. Then she looked at Martha.

"Now, Mrs. Cornelius has suggested that we launch our crusade with some kind of demonstration or march that will bring us to the attention of the general public, as well as to the estimated forty thousand women out there. The newspapers are the best way to get publicity, but this time, instead of writing out what we want them to print, we want them to come see us in action. The only thing is, I haven't been able to think of anything we could do to stir up the town!"

No one else had a suggestion either.

Martha stood. "I did have one idea. I know one of the men on the City Board. I could request a citizen's comment time at their next regular meeting. I'll tell him it is about a new general charity that would benefit the city. I've spoken to them before and I know we could get a hearing. Then what we do is present a little drama. I thought we might have one of us come in costumed as a slave, with a fake ball and chain and a kitchen pan. Sue could say that women should not be slaves in the kitchen, that we're people, too, with intelligence and reason and so on.

"One of us might come in wearing an academic robe, and say that women are intelligent, too. Some of us could be university professors and brilliant scholars. So why are we not given the right to vote?

"Then we'd go on like that and, in the end, we could present our reasons for wanting a local city ordinance that in all future elections women would be granted full rights of voting for city laws and elected officials."

She sat down. For a moment, there was silence. Then everyone stood and cheered. She was crying. The others clustered around Martha, laughing and smiling and telling her how brilliant the idea was.

It was nearly ten minutes later before they could settle down and begin to plan out the presentation, decide on the subjects they would use for costumes to which Sue would key her talk.

They spent the rest of the evening working out what they would do, and decided that each woman would make her own costume.

At ten, the meeting ended, and Martha saw that some of the women had driven their own buggies. That was certainly being self-reliant and independent, but Martha decided she would just as soon not be in a buggy alone after dark.

The next few days were busy ones, dedicated ones. Martha worked on her own "slave" part in the demonstration. She made chains out of gray and black paper, then worked up a large papier mache ball and painted it black. She created a slave costume from old clothes and put a scarf over her head. She found one of her coats that would cover everything before the unveiling.

One afternoon, she went to the city offices and talked to the representative from her own fourth district, Charlie Matson.

"Ah, Mrs. Cornelius," Matson said as he met her at his office door, grasping both her hands in his. He was a pompous, emotional man, and she wondered how he kept getting elected year after year. It probably was because he knew and understood his people.

"How are your mother and father these days? I haven't seen much of them lately."

"Just fine, Mr. Matson, they'll be pleased you asked about them. What I wanted to talk to you about was a special favor. I need about five minutes to talk before the city board at your next meeting. Could we arrange that?"

"I'm sure we can, Mrs. Cornelius. Oh, we'll need a subject for the agenda, but if it isn't anything controversial, I don't see any problem at all. What will you be talking about?"

"One of my pet projects. It's not quite a charity, more like general welfare. That's a term you politicians use all the time."

"Well, that should be enough to get you on the agenda. I'll put it down as a personal privilege, and there won't be any question at all. Those meetings get so blasted boring that most of the men would enjoy something different. A pretty face like yours will really brighten up the whole day. We'll be meeting again on next Friday, and I'll put you down for five minutes."

"Yes, that should be enough time. Thank you, Mr. Matson." She looked at the fancy grandfather clock in his office. "Dear me, I'm going to have to hurry to get to my next meeting. Thank you so much, Mr. Matson, and I'll see you on next Friday, on February sixteenth."

Martha felt smug and satisfied when she left the city offices. If he only knew what they were up to, he would never give them a second of time! It was sneaky, but if they had to be sneaky to get the suffrage message across, so be it! She knew that she would probably never have another chance to talk before the city board. But she didn't care. If this would do the job, it would be worth it. This just might be what the suffrage movement needed in San Francisco to get things moving!

They had three more meetings before the big afternoon, and practiced their parts, wore their costumes and had it down perfectly. They all were nervous as they met outside the building then went in and sat in the last row. Each had on a bulky coat to cover up her costume. Two of them carried shopping bags to conceal some of the props for the demonstration.

There was a half hour of city business, and then Mr. Matson took the floor.

"Mr. Chairman, I would like to ask for a point of personal privilege to present a matter on the general welfare. It will require about five minutes of time."

The chairman, a craggy-faced man in his

late sixties, snorted, shook his head in annoyance and nodded. "Matson, I just hope you have something worthwhile to say, this time."

Matson turned. "To make this presentation, I call on one of my constituents, Mrs. Martha Pemberton Cornelius, from one of this city's most illustrious families."

Martha stood. "To start our presentation, I yield the floor to Susan Stone."

Sue walked to the front of the chambers, turned and smiled at the people, then faced the city fathers.

"Gentlemen, it's our honor to be here today to present to you a subject which in a way is very near and dear to every one of you, and which is, at the very same time, rejected, pushed away, kept in the background and which becomes the butt of your crude, offensive and unintelligent jokes."

Martha had taken off her coat. In one hand, she carried a heavy looking ball, from which chains of paper extended to her ankles. In the other hand, she held a large kitchen kettle. She stood, stepped to the aisle and shouted at the top of her voice: "I am a woman! But you men have made me a slave!" The audience gasped. Martha walked to the front of the room to stand beside Susan.

"I am a slave to the kitchen, to the home. I am a slave in legal dealings, and have to fight to maintain my inheritance, my control over my children. I am a slave if my husband wants to beat me. I do not want to be a slave any longer!"

The chairman thudded his gavel, but the shouts from the audience drowned him out.

Sue's strong voice now rang over the top of the other noise.

"Yes, Martha is a slave. I am a slave. Every woman in this audience is a slave. All women are nothing but slaves to a flood of unfair laws, of unfair customs, of shameful and ridiculous treatment which were out-dated even in Martha Washington's time. Give women the right to vote and they will bring about true equality between men and women. Suffrage, the right to vote, should be equally shared by both men and women. How else can women stand up for their rights?"

"Shut up, *woman!*" the chairman of the board shouted.

Sue turned, fury and scorn in her voice, as she walked toward the man. "Did you hear that? Did you hear what that miserable thing called a man, said? He shouted *'woman,'* like it was an unspeakable slander, like it solved the problem because I was telling him what he was doing wrong. But since I am a woman, then I must be mistaken, crude, stupid and out of place. This man is the epitome of this unfeeling and disgraceful prejudice against women.

"Did you people know that in the territories of Wyoming and Utah the women have the right to vote in all territorial, local and city elections? It is true. And in all these years, those two territories have not suddenly dissolved into chaos. There, women are free to help elect officials, to help create the territory and local laws."

Another woman from the back row of seats threw her coat off and jumped up.

"I want to be free, too!" she shouted. She wore academic attire, a huge black robe with stripes on the sleeves. "It is a fact that women are just as smart as men, often more intelligent. In grammar school, girls outdo boys in studies. I want to be free to study and learn!"

The woman marched down the aisle and stood facing the city officials.

Sue picked up the thread. "Why aren't there more women professors in our universities? Easy. Most universities won't even accept women *students*. Harvard, Yale, dozens of others are for men only. The only reason women are not in the upper brackets of government and business is that men continually and cleverly push us down. Men deny us a chance.

Put women into college and they will do just as well as men. Famous women's schools in the east have proved this. Fifteen years ago, back in 1861, a school called Vassar opened in New York state. It's now a great college and the only students in it are *women*. Many of the graduates are brilliant and outstanding. They have had an academic chance.

"Most girls get very little schooling after the eighth grade. 'She's a girl,' they say. 'She doesn't need to go on to school. How much does a girl have to know to have babies, to cook and wash and clean?' My God, you people! Don't you understand a woman is more than just a household slave?"

Another woman ran down the aisle with a hanger full of clothes and an order book in her hand.

"I don't want to be a slave to clerking in a store all my life. I want to be a buyer, a manager."

Sue took up the cry. "How many of you men have businesses? How many of you have women in your top executive level positions? None of you! None! I investigated. Now, isn't it remarkable that all of the women in your businesses are dumb oxes, so stupid they can't even be head accountants, or in charge of purchasing even women's clothing, or housewares? Isn't that amazing? You men, really know how to select intelligent clerks, don't you? You hire the dumbest women you can find, right? So there is no *chance* or reason to promote them.

"Think of your own wives and daughters. Yes, I've met some of them. One of them could have been a mathematician. She had a natural ability and facility better than any man's I've ever seen. But she was a *woman.* She was married off early, at seventeen, and now has four children, with another one on the way, and the closest she ever gets to mathematics is trying to figure how to make her husband's low salary pay all the bills. She was brilliant, and men killed her intellectual future. Your wives, are they all drudges, baby machines, child raisers and little else? I know better.

"Give us the right to vote! Right here, in San Francisco, we have the right to pass a city statute that would give all women over the age of twenty-one, who are citizens of this state, the right to cast their ballots in city elections. Make a start! Let us help you with an ordinance that would let women register and vote and become a part of the community life for the first time. Let us become equal partners with men in life. Let us help run our city. Utilize this great potential, natural resource, woman-power. There are forty thousand women out there who could vote, who would help our city become truly great. Please don't let the woman power of this great city go to waste!"

The chairman of the city board waited for her to go on, and when she did not, he banged his gavel. "There being no other pertinent business to come before this board, I declare the meeting adjourned."

Fifty women from the audience crowded around Susan and the others, shaking their hands. One of the costumed ladies handed out membership blanks and information leaflets to every woman in the room.

Charlie Matson left his chair behind the railing and worked his way to Martha. He shook his head.

"Martha Pemberton, you tricked me. You said it was for a good cause. That we could debate. But remember, women never voted in Athens or in Troy, they never had a hand in the government of Rome or spoke in the Roman senate. Nor did they cast ballots in England or France. Men run things, always will. I think I've more than evened up the favors I owed you." He turned and stalked away from her.

Martha stuck her tongue out at his retreating back and Sue cheered. The women gave out all the membership blanks they brought with them.

All the women met back at Sue's house afterward. They decided the promotion was a rousing success. Sue said she had seen at least two reporters from newspapers there writing like crazy. There should be good stories in the next day's papers.

When the women were gone, Sue had a good hot bath, put on a wrapper and read again Susan B. Anthony's letters. She was such a good person.

Sue had a light dinner and then read until about nine when she let the wood fire die down and went to bed. She remembered what one man said to her as she walked out of the city chambers. He whispered something about knowing exactly what she needed and he'd be glad to push it into her anytime. Disgusting! He was stupid and disgusting!

No, Martha had the right idea, they would talk and talk and talk — and they would organize — and they would win.

Sue felt a warm rush of affection for Martha. She was a rich woman who *cared* about the program. Sue smiled, thinking about Martha. What a pretty girl — and so young. She looked twenty-three. And what a rich one! She gave a thousand dollars! For just a moment, Sue thought of Martha's remarkable figure, her good hips, tiny waist and full bosom. Sue wondered what Martha would like like undressed. She shook her head and knew she should not think that way. Martha was a friend.

No! But the idea was already born, and lay there nurturing itself in Sue's imagination. She daydreamed that Martha was beside her and they were both taking off their clothes.

No! She would not think that way. Not tonight. That was for losers and they had won today. They had shown the city board that the movement had some power, some big names, some influence as well.

Yes, it was glorious. Maybe this should be a little celebration. Yes, a celebration. Sue's hand found her breast and she stroked one, then the other, then both. Now the only thing she could think of was Martha Cornelius. What a beautiful girl, such lovely breasts. The more Sue thought about it the lower her hand slid until it was between her thighs and she probed for the exact spot that would bring her a surging desire and a beautiful release of all her tensions.

CHAPTER FIFTEEN:
SATURDAY'S CHILD

It was Sunday afternoon in the big Harold Pemberton mansion, and Penny's mother had just checked on the young people around the piano. Hans and Louis seemed like such nice boys. She felt perfectly safe in leaving the three of them alone, so she could go back up to her sewing room where she was trying to get through a slim volume of Elizabeth Barrett Browning's poems.

Downstairs, only moments after her mother left, Penny announced that it was time to go after the refreshments.

"Hey, do I get to go this time?" Louis Streib asked.

"Oh, Louis, we need you to play the piano for us," Penny said, beaming her dazzling smile at the boy. "You're so good at it and we just love to hear you play. We'll be right back. I wouldn't take either of you, but that punch pitcher is so heavy."

Penny went into the hall with Hans close

behind her. When they were out of sight of Louis, Hans caught her hand and they ran down the hall. When they came to the study door, Penny tried to go on past it. But Hans held her, opened the study door cautiously, then slipped inside, pulling her with him.

"Hans, we aren't supposed to be in here!"

He grinned, closed the door and pushed in the bolt, locking it. He moved closer to Penny.

"Hans, you know we both could get in a lot of trouble if anyone finds us in here alone."

He paid no attention to her words, simply put his arms around her and covered her mouth with his hungrily. When she felt his tongue pressing against her lips, she tried to push him away.

"Hey, little Penny, you like to do this as much as I do, so stop pretending." He kissed her again, and this time, she didn't struggle. His hand pushed toward her breasts, but she caught it and held on. He crushed her body against his as he finished the kiss.

"Now, that's better, that's the Penny I know." He still held her tightly against his chest. He kissed her again, and this time, his hand sneaked under her bodice before she could stop him. Penny scolded herself.

She shouldn't let him do that. He must not. But she didn't have time to stop him. She had tried. Now she pushed feebly against him, knowing it would do no good.

Suddenly she felt his hand close around one of her bare breasts. It gave her a tingling sensation, a growing warmth that felt simply wonderful. It was so good, so marvelous. But he shouldn't! What if her mother came hunting them?

His hand rubbed and fondled her bareness and she knew he should stop, but he didn't. Then his lips left hers.

"Hey, I'm feeling you. You should feel me. Here." He took her hand and pushed it down between them until it rested over the bulge she had seen just below his belt. It felt huge and so hard and warm.

Then Hans was kissing her again, and she was lost in a swell of delicious feeling, so warm and fine. His hands were rubbing both breasts now and she waited, knowing that the whole sky would explode pretty soon, the way it had last week.

But it didn't happen. Instead, she felt flushed and hot and nervous. His hands opened the top of her dress, and the next thing she knew, he was kissing her bare breasts. Kissing them!

Her lower body jolted suddenly, and her

legs seemed to dissolve. She slid to the floor. He lay beside her and she trembled and shook and felt as if she would shake to pieces. It was that wonderful, spontaneous feeling again, so tremendous that it was like a million rockets and firecrackers going off inside her body all at once, in every part of her whole being!

He watched her as she shivered, then kissed her exposed breasts again and she felt his hips push against her. He caught her hand and put it over the lump in his pants and pumped hard against it. Then he groaned and gasped and trembled, and at the same time, she felt a wetness through his trousers on her hand.

When he stopped, she realized that he was lying on top of her. He moaned softly, kissed her breasts and stood up. He helped her stand.

"We better get that damn punch," he said, laughing.

Penny shook her head, trying to chase the fuzziness from it. She didn't want to go anywhere. She could go, but she wanted to lie there with him against her and remember how wonderful it had been. It all happened so quickly. They hadn't been in the room for two minutes. She fixed her dress, adjusting it and closing the three buttons he had opened. Then she stood up straight and he unbolted the door. No one was in the hall. As they walked the rest of the way to the kitchen, neither of them said a word.

They picked up the punch and cookies and started back.

He stopped her. "God, but that was good, Penny! You just don't know. One of these days, we're going to have more than two minutes, and I'm going to undress you and do it all slow and fine, the right way."

The warm glow was almost gone from Penny now. She shook her head. "No, Hans, I don't think so. The day you see me undressed will be the day you marry me, and I'm not going to marry you, so that won't work out, will it? Now, you just be a gentleman and forget all about this. If you don't, it will be all your fault and you'll be in a hell of a mess."

He laughed when she swore. "Penny, I'll never forget it and I'll never forget you. But I won't tell anyone. You can count on that. Your father would have me whipped through the whole British fleet."

She stopped him. "Hans," she whispered, "boys must know more about these things than girls do, right? It wasn't the same for me that time, not like before. It took longer."

"Oh, that happens with girls," he said,

whispering, too. "The best way is to let me touch you down below, you know, down there. It's always better then. A girl told me so. She even showed me where to touch, and I rubbed it for her and she went wild, just absolutely wild."

"Now, Hans, you made that up." They were still whispering.

"No, honest. She said there's a little kind of a button, a hard place and you rub on it."

The maid came toward them and they stopped whispering and moved on toward the library. When they got there, Louis Streib was still pounding out a waltz. They put the tray down and Louis headed for the cookies at once.

For a moment, Penny questioned if he were more interested in the food and the piano than he was in her. She wondered what he would do if she kissed him and reached down and touched his button. He'd be the one to go wild.

She watched him and now she was sure that Louis was not really interested in her. She decided he came along with Hans only because Hans asked him to, so the three of them could be alone, and not have a maid or Mrs. Pemberton herself as chaperone. That Hans was a very sneaky fellow. She would watch herself with him.

Hans told her about getting ready to go to Harvard. He had half of his clothes packed and had run out of suitcases, so he switched to a steamer trunk.

As he told her about Harvard, she listened with only half an ear, making automatic responses. But all the time, she was wondering what he had meant about a little hard place down there. At first, she dismissed it as more foolish boy talk. What did they know. But a girl had told him.

Penny tried to forget about it. Someday she would find out everything. By then, she would be married and wouldn't have to worry about it. Someday . . . Penny said. "Louis, isn't it time we had our dance?" So they danced to the three-note music Hans produced, but it wasn't fun this time. It wasn't the same as last week, not the same at all.

Penny endured a long game of checkers, then dominoes, and won both. Perhaps next week it would be warm enough so they could go outside and play lawn croquet. Penny tried to relax but she couldn't. The rest of the afternoon, Hans didn't have a chance to pull her into a room. She teased both boys scandalously until the courting time was over at four. She waved goodbye, not really caring if she ever saw either of them again.

Across town, Martha sat in her own library where she stared at a calendar. Here it was March fifth already, over two weeks since their big splash at the city board meeting, and they were still hearing the reverberations. The newspapers had jumped on it, playing up the story far bigger than it actually was. Headlines blazed: "WOMEN DEMAND THE VOTE HERE," "WOMEN SAY THEY'RE NOTHING BUT SLAVES," "WOMEN CHALLENGE CITY BOARD."

Stories abounded in the *Bulletin* and in every other newspaper in the city. They kept a running front-page story on it for days. Five different papers sent reporters to talk to Martha. They were interested in her position as part of the social elite now that she had joined a common, riffraff type of movement.

"No responsible woman would have anything to do with the suffrage movement," one reporter told her. Martha threw a vase at him, missed, but broke the vase. She then chased him out of her house. But he wrote the best story of all, giving both sides fair treatment.

338

Martha wrote a note of apology to him. That, too, was printed.

Martha looked forward to her morning mail because almost every day there were two or three letters with invitations to speak to various groups around town. All were women's organizations and most enthusiastic about her stand. For the moment, she had taken the spotlight away from Sue Stone, and she had no intention of doing that.

Sue was their leader. Most of the letters she took to Sue, who made arrangements to talk to the clubs herself. Martha did speak at a few when Sue had conflicts. Their membership was growing by leaps and giant steps. The week after their big demonstration, they had thirty-seven new memberships, each with the two one-dollar bills attached. Then things tapered off until the talks began. She always took another member along to act as a membership chairman. At each of the talks, they averaged ten new members, all signed up and paid.

Now, three weeks later, they had one hundred and forty-six members. Sue was astonished. They had nine hundred and forty-two dollars in their bank account, even deducting cash for printing and expenses. And new members kept adding to their income.

Martha thought it was moving along nicely, up to this point. But now the excitement was wearing off. They needed a new incident, some new program, something that would attract attention again — and grab some newspaper space.

Martha had been worried about Allen's reaction after that first day at the city offices. Would he be furious or understanding? Or would he ignore the whole thing?

That first night, he came home and kissed her then picked up Hal and played with him in the sitting room.

"I understand you talked before the city fathers today," he said.

"Well, yes, I was there, but I didn't say much."

Allen laughed, then looked up at her seriously. "But what you said, and what you started, has made a lot of the members of the board furious. It's also caused a stir among some of the other members of our business community."

Martha turned, not sure how she should react. Then she saw the edge of a grin creep onto Allen's face and they both broke out laughing.

"It was so much fun! Honestly, Allen, we just said a lot of the things I've talked over with you, and they were shocked, absolutely scandalized. I suppose the newspapers are going to be full of it tomorrow. Oh, Allen, you should have seen them." She paused for a moment, then asked, in all seriousness, "Should I have asked you if I could talk to them?"

Allen stood and walked over to her, with Hal in his arms. His face was just short of a frown, eyes narrowed. "Woman, you certainly should have! You realize I'm the head of this family, and what I say goes." But he couldn't maintain his composure any longer, and he laughed. Martha giggled and then the two of them were hugging each other, with little Hal in the middle, trying to poke his fingers in their eyes. They dropped on a couch and laid Hal between them.

"Now, young lady, you tell me all about it! Every syllable, every glance, you bold, brazen woman! I want to know everything that happened."

Martha curled up beside Allen and went through the afternoon for him, told him about how it started and her visits to Susan Stone. He chuckled in spots, became serious when he realized what she said was so right.

"And so we gave them one final appeal on

women's rights, and they cut off the meeting. We knew there wasn't a chance that they would even talk about passing an ordinance for women's suffrage in the city, but it was a good opening barrage."

"Opening? Then you plan other such events?"

"Just as many as we can. What if you couldn't vote, Allen? How would you feel? What if you couldn't go to the bank and get a loan — unless I came along and signed the papers, too? There are thousands of discriminations that women have to put up with every day. What if Sue wanted to obtain a mortgage to buy a house? She couldn't 'qualify' for a loan. She isn't married, and besides she's only a woman."

Allen kissed her and held up his hands. "Whoa there, stop! You don't need to convince me. I've seen you in action in the company, remember?" She relaxed. He went on. "Of course, there are always two things a woman will never be able to do."

She bristled, then giggled. "I know one, sire a child, but what's the other?"

"Why, raise a good full beard!"

She tried to hit him but he jumped up, waved, and went into his study to read the newspapers.

Martha remembered that day with fondness now. Allen had reacted just the way she hoped he might. He was an intelligent man who knew there was a lot of woman power that wasn't being utilized. He wasn't afraid of competition with women as many men were.

Not all the husbands had been that understanding. Four of the new women members had written asking for their fees back and cancelling their memberships. Their husbands had demanded it. Sue had taken a write-up on it to the newspaper, including the names and addresses of the men involved. That made another good follow-up story.

But now there was nothing in the papers. They needed more good publicity. What should it be? Martha stood and paced the length of the room, stared out the window, then paced back again. She did it several times and — suddenly realizing what she was doing — had an inspiration.

Marching, walking, a parade! Why didn't they stage a small parade on the streets. They could get out every member, all make signs, and carry them. Maybe they could find a band somewhere that would play — no, a buggy in front and a buggy in back, and in between, women marchers, all wearing black skirts and white blouses and black hats. They would make a wonderful picture!

That same afternoon, Martha went to Susan Stone's house with the suggestion and Susan liked it. They worked out details. Susan would speak at the end of the march in Prospect Park. Sue's two more talks had gained them fourteen new members — more marchers!

As they worked out the plans for the march they built up each other's enthusiasm. Sue appointed a march committee with Martha as chairman. They would figure out the rest of the plans, notify all members, and have them at the march site at 11:30 a.m. next Friday, March sixteenth.

At the door Sue kissed Martha's cheek. "Martha, dear, I just don't see how you keep coming up with these ideas. They are outstanding. I still thank the good Lord that He brought you along to work with us."

Martha smiled, said goodbye, and hurried out to her buggy. She and Allen and little Hal were going to see the proud grandparents that evening for dinner. Since it would be the first time she had talked with her mother or father since the women's suffrage activity had been in the newspapers, she wasn't sure what their reaction would be.

But that evening turned out to be a love feast.

"I couldn't be happier with the whole thing," Harold Pemberton said as dinner began. "And just for your information, young lady, we once had a department head in our organization who was a woman, before she retired. You may remember her." He smiled then went on. "As for buyers, we do have several women in our retail division who are buyers now, and we have one woman who is head of personnel in the Pemberton Mercantile. I think we stack up pretty well."

"Yes, Father, you have a few, but only a few. And besides, you're a good man, you're liberal in these matters. Don't you know hundreds of businesses where the highest office a woman holds is secretary, clerk or maybe bookkeeper? Those are the firms we're after."

"But, Martha," her mother said, "surely being a woman, being a kitchen slave as you suggested, isn't that what a lot of women want to do?"

"I don't know, Mother. Neither of us has ever had to do that work, have we? We don't scrub floors and keep house or cook meals and wash clothes. We hire it done by other women. But for the millions of women who simply want something more than that, why should they be denied at least the chance of trying for it? I think that's what we're really saying. If a woman wants only to be a housewife, a clerk or a maid, that's fine, let her do that. But there should not be laws, nor practices, nor rules that keep her from being a doctor if she wants to be, or a lawyer, or even a United States Senator if she can get elected."

Her mother nodded. "Oh, yes, it does seem like you have a good argument."

"It all gets back to women's suffrage, the vote, which is the root of the whole argument, as I understand it," Allen said.

"Yes, exactly. If we had the vote, then we could help legislate a lot of this discrimination right out of existence. Is that so unrealistic, Father?"

Her mother shushed them all then and said grace before the meal began. From long practice, there was little conversation as they ate. After a course, and before and after dinner, were the fashionable times to talk.

Friday morning, Martha had two sign painters working on large cardboard placards attached to sticks which the women would carry. She had the men paint a hundred of the signs with all sorts of slogans: "THE VOTE NOW," "SUFFRAGE

NOW," "WE WANT TO VOTE," "WE'RE PEOPLE, TOO," "WE'RE NOT KITCHEN SLAVES," "I WANT TO BE A U.S. SENATOR,"

"*YOUR* WIFE IS A PERSON," "DO YOU WANT YOUR DAUGHTER TO BE A BABY SLAVE?"

Friday morning, shortly before eleven o'clock, Martha had the placards loaded in two carriages. They were to be transported to the meeting point halfway down Market Street, near the new hardward emporium. Martha parked the buggies on the cross street and began welcoming the women. Sue was there waiting when Martha arrived.

"How does it look?" Sue asked.

"I think we'll have over a hundred women," Martha said. She knew the membership was almost two hundred, and figured half would be a good turnout. Each member had been sent two letters and had been visited and urged to attend the rally. Martha asked for volunteers to drive the buggies and picked two women she knew could handle the rigs.

Martha took each woman's name and gave her a sign, asking her to bring it back so they could use it again.

Sue and Martha talked about the lineup and decided to stretch out their women so it looked like as many as possible. "I like that idea you had of chanting the slogans. The same ones on the signs. Martha, those signs are just tremendous. I don't know how I can ever thank you enough."

"Sue, I'm the one who should thank you. Now, you take the lead and start lining up the women as they come. We want them three wide and stretched down the street. Tell them to stay about six feet between the rows. My carriage will lead the parade and clear the wy. I have another buggy coming behind so none of our women will be run over."

The women arrived in bunches, almost all with their black skirts and stiff white blouses. They looked like a regular army.

By the time they were ready to move, Martha had signed up one hundred forty-nine women, and they started walking down Market. There was a noontime crush on the main thoroughfare. Buggies, fancy coaches, wagons, Democrat buggies, men on horses and big, heavy dray wagons loaded down with goods.

The lead buggy driver, Emma Davis, broke into the traffic and led the women into the street. Almost at once Sue started the chant at the front of the line.

"Give us the vote! Give us the vote! Give

us the vote!"

The women picked it up down the line, and by the time they were all on Market, it was a loud chorus. Chanting the slogan, the marchers stepped down the street past some of the biggest and most important businesses in town, including Pemberton Mercantile.

People stopped along the way and watched them. A few men laughed, but some women cheered. One man staggered toward the women, waving a bottle, but somebody in the crowd along the sidewalk pulled him back.

"We're not kitchen slaves! We're not kitchen slaves!"

The new slogan rang out as the procession continued. Martha had worked her carriage towards the rear of the marchers, and she motioned for her other buggy to stay close and protect the end of the line. She didn't want any incident. Nothing could go wrong. It had to run smoothly, perfectly, without any trouble, to prove that they were intelligent, practical and efficient.

They marched farther down the main street, buggies and rigs giving way on each side, many stopping until the marchers moved past. Martha noticed a uniformed policeman staring at them. She ignored him, but watched as he walked along pacing them, then spoke to a sergeant of police who hurried off. Martha wondered about it, but then forgot him as the slogan changed to:

"Women's suffrage now! Women's suffrage now!"

Martha watched the crowd. What was the mood? In some places the women waved at them, laughing, shouting agreement. One woman ran out and got in line, joining them. Many other women stepped back into store doorways. A buggy came careening down the street toward them. Emma Davis pulled her rig directly in the path of the wildly driven buggy, and screeched at the driver until he stopped. Then Emma moved her rig back into the line of march and continued.

The chanted slogans changed every minute now, until they had run through ten of them. They were three blocks from the park when Martha began to relax. She hadn't expected any type of counter move by the men, but it was a calculated chance that she had taken. Some of the men were still boiling mad, and an attack was still possible. But they would have to move quickly to get it into operation before the march was over. Fifteen minutes, Martha had guessed for their trek, and now she could see the park. They were almost there.

A fire siren wailed. Martha didn't know what it was, at first. Then the wailing increased, and she realized it was the hand-turned siren on the new San Francisco steam fire engine that pumped water from its own tank and could send a spray of water over a hundred feet into the air.

The sound grew louder. Then she saw the slashing, prancing feet of the big fire-engine horses, as they pulled the engine around a corner a block from the park and came straight down Market. Martha climbed down from her carriage and ran toward the head of the line. She charged past the marchers and ran to the buggy.

"Hold fast, Emma," she ordered her driver in the buggy. "Swing to the side now just enough to let him past, but don't stop, and don't let him bluff you. It's a trick!"

The flashing white legs of the fire horses came closer. Emma grimaced and held the reins firmly. There was room at the side of the street for the emergency rig to drive past. That was the law. Fire engines had the right of way.

Emma looked at Martha. Hold, she had said. The big heavy fire wagon team would knock down her one small mare and their big hooves would bite through the mare's hide, then stomp over Emma in the seat of the buggy before they could be stopped. The fire horses were used to having the whole wide street!

The big horses were half a block away. The women's chant continued. Most of them weren't aware of any danger.

"Give us the vote, now! Give us the vote, now!"

Closer. Emma felt sweat running into her eyes. She was frightened, more so than she had ever been in her life. In an instant, she realized that she had never been closer to a violent death.

The big horses were scarcely fifteen feet from the mare when their driver jerked the team of six to the right, and the fire wagon slashed past the buggy and roared along the line of marchers. A few women jumped away, but there was no actual danger.

The fire wagon turned to the right at the next street and was gone. Martha jumped on the buggy, her black skirt flying. She wanted to dissolve in tears. That had been so close! Instead of weeping, she lifted her chin.

"Very good, Emma. You deserve a medal for that, or at least a written commendation." Martha smiled at her, jumped to the street and went back to the march line.

Martha stayed near the lead of the column, and it wasn't until it was too late to change their direction that she saw the trap. The fire rig had made two more right turns, circling the block and coming back to Market, a block ahead of them now. They stopped at the intersection, and Martha could see the steam boiler fired up and the horses out.

It was going to be another training exercise for the firemen. Already a stream of water slashed onto Market street, and a dozen firemen were out clearing that section of the street of all rigs, horses and pedestrians. A few moments later, the street was ankle deep in muddy water.

Martha saw the trick, but there was no way around it. She ran back to the lead buggy and told Emma to drive right on through the water and past the firemen. Told her not to back off. Emma set her jaw and touched the reins to the mare, who picked up the speed and stepped into the water which had drained their way.

"Keep marching! Keep going, right through the water!" Martha shouted as she ran back along the line. She rushed back to the front of the column and stepped into the water, slipped and almost fell but caught herself and walked forward.

The hose men kept the water just ahead of the women, hoping to discourage their march. But when they saw the lead buggy almost through the wetness, they lifted the angle of the hose and water splashed the horse, buggy and Emma, bringing a roar of laughter from the crowd. Then Martha and Susan Stone were up to the hose. It shot a two-inch torrent of water at a ninety-degree angle to their line of march. Martha stepped out strongly toward the water and felt it hit her side like a runaway horse. She staggered, stumbled and fell to her hands and knees.

She could hear the laughter, the roaring amusement of the predominantly male audience. Martha struggled up, and saw that the hose was working along the line of the march, knocking down half the women, turning their clothes into a muddy, sloppy, wet mess.

Martha looked around. She began to run again, this time straight at the two firemen who held the hose. Their sides were toward her now and they couldn't see her or hear the shouted warnings. Martha didn't know what she was going to do when she got to them. She had seen rugby matches where players knocked men down by throwing themselves at each other. She decided her momentum was her best weapon and she ran faster, lowered her shoulder and smashed into the man holding the hose. Her shoulder caught him in the side just under his bent arm.

Surprise and the force of her small body combined to jolt him against the second man who wasn't braced for a force from that direction. The joint weight bowled over both men, who slammed to the street and dropped the hose.

The unattended high pressure hose whipped and snaked around, spraying firemen and spectators now, instead of the marchers. Two more firemen ran out and fell on the writhing hose to control it. But by that time, Sue Stone had swept her charges past the intersection, picked up the wet and confused women, and had everyone safely marching into the park.

Martha lay on the ground in the soggy street, and looked up at one of the firemen who had a big grin on his face.

"Lady, that was a damn nice block. You ever play rugby?"

Martha jumped up and ran into the park, where Sue was mounting the speaker's stand and looking out at the audience. She was soaked to the skin, her clothes plastered to her body, her hair fell in strings and ropes down her back, but the enthusiasm on her face was far from dampened.

"Ladies and gentlemen, you have just seen a prime example of desperation — of male desperation. Will they discuss suffrage with us calmly and openly? No, they resort to underhanded, dirty tactics, which shows how desperate they are, and reveals their total lack of honesty and the falseness of their logic. They use the fire department and charging beasts to try to unnerve us, to do their battles. It's typical male desperation. They can't fight fair. They can't even meet us and talk over the problems. So they try to run us down with draft horses, and then wash us into the bay. Now is that fair play?"

The crowd of women, and two or three hundred others who had grouped around, shouted a loud chorus of "No!"

Martha listened in amazement, as Sue went on with her speech, adapting it to what had just happened. And tying it in with a logical, reasonable argument why women should have the vote now.

Just before Sue's talk seemed to be winding down, someone tapped Martha on the shoulder. She turned to find two uniformed policemen standing next to her. One nodded.

"Aye, Captain, that's the one. That's the lass who upset the firemen."

The captain of police bowed slightly.

"I'm sorry, Miss, but you'll have to come along to the police station with us. You're under arrest."

CHAPTER SIXTEEN:
ONE AMELIA, TWO AMELIA

Randy Pemberton paced the seven steps to the window of his office in the new Pemberton Building on Market Street. It had gone up only last year and now held all of the corporate offices of Pacific Steamship and other related and non-related Pemberton companies and interests.

Randy stared down at the city for a moment, then went to a small mirror in the coat closet and checked his appearance. Perfect. His hair was combed exactly right, his shave close and clean, and he wore just a touch of bay rum and rosewater shave lotion.

He closed the closet door, flicked a small spot of lint off his deep blue suit, and walked back to the big window where the heavy drapes were half-closed.

The room — was it right? He glanced around. Two original oil landscape paintings, and one oil of a pair of clerks waiting on a customer in the men's department adorned the walls. The sales graph on the wall was subdued enough not to be garish, and the couch was against the other wall.

The table with two chairs set for lunch did look out of place, but it couldn't be helped. Then there were various chairs, lamps and his big desk with his chair next to the window so his visitors and guests could not see him quite as well as he could see them.

Everything was perfect. Sweat popped out on his forehead as he wondered about his fingernails. God, had he cleaned them? He looked, remembered. Yes, he had cleaned them for the second time five minutes ago. Where was that idiot of a messenger? How long did it take to go down two floors and escort a young lady to the fifth floor?

Oh, Christ, maybe she would refuse to come! He had spoken to her almost every week lately, just a hello or good morning. So he was sure she knew who he was. For five years, he had been watching her, wanting to be near her.

She wasn't coming. He knew. Why was he trying to fool himself? He simply knew she wasn't coming. It was almost ten after twelve. The boy would arrive there in two minutes, would give her the note, and she would have seven minutes more to work. Then at twelve the messenger would lead her back up the stairs and, at three minutes after twelve, at the very latest, they should have been here. Where were they?

She wasn't coming, and the messenger was too frightened to come back and tell him. He would expect the traditional fate of the bearer of bad news. Randy would have that messenger's neck for this, break him in half, or hire somebody to break him in half. It just wasn't fair that the kid could take advantage of a vice-president this way. Yeah, he was a Pemberton, too, a goddamned Vice President Pemberton. He'd show that snot-nosed kid. What the hell . . .

Randy listened intently. He thought he heard the outside office door squeak. No, it was nothing. He had imagined it.

Randy went to his desk and slumped in the big chair. So this was what rejection felt like? Was this why he hadn't done anything more about her than say hello for five years? Five long, wasted, yellow-belly years! Christ, what a waste! He could go out to Madelyn's house, and if the gate was open, he could go in and goddamn well not be rejected.

What the hell was he worried about? This fluff was just another girl. Girls were all alike, easy to find when he wanted one. They were all over the place.

The outer door closed with a definite, recognizable sound. Randy jumped to his feet, wanting to adjust his tie, wishing he'd had time to brush his teeth again. His shoes, were they polished? Had he . . .

The inner office door opened slowly and she stood there looking at him.

"Mr. Pemberton?"

"Ah, oh . . . yes." He had to swallow three times before he could get out that much. His voice sounded like a boy soprano.

She smiled and he wanted to run over and kneel at her feet, to kiss her feet, to . . .

"Mr. Pemberton, the note said you wanted to see me and that I should come right in. Is that right?"

Randy nodded, he motioned her inside and came around from behind his big desk. She looked at the office in wonder and he realized this was the first time she had been here.

"Would you . . ." He stopped.

She turned and looked at him. Beautiful. The red glints in her light hair had taken over until the long, shimmery cascade shone like copper. He had almost forgotten how small, how dainty she was. Not over five-feet one, she looked even shorter with a slim body and a round pixie face. She had a slightly tipped up, finely chiseled nose, and eyes so faintly blue that he used to think they would break if she blinked.

Amelia Borcherding smiled now as she took a step toward him.

"I was wondering if . . ." he said, then stopped, and motioned toward the table. "Lunch?"

Her smile came quickly, lighting up her face with surprise and pleasure that so dazzled him. Randy, who prided himelf on his perfect manners, almost forgot to go forward and hold her chair.

As she sat down, he marveled at the erect, straight way she held herself. Her hair smelled delightful and he wished he could remain there near it. He went to his side of the table for two and sat down, then lifted a small silver bell and rang it.

From the other door, leading into his inner private office, came two men, both in formal waiter's attire, and wheeling a small cart with trays on two levels.

One man served the wine, letting Randy have a sip in a glass to test for bouquet, color and taste. When Randy nodded approval, the waiter poured the light red wine and set long-stemmed cut-crystal goblets in front of them. Then the waiter moved back, standing at attention as the two sipped-their wine.

Amelia wrinkled her nose in surprise.

"Don't you like it?" he asked.

"I'm sorry, but I've never tasted wine before. We never have it at home."

"If you don't want it . . ."

"No, let me try it. A person should try new things, don't you think, Mr. Pemberton?"

He could only nod. Her voice was much lower than he guessed it would be from such a tiny girl. It fascinated him. For just a moment, he realized that he looked at her in a way that was different from the way he observed other women. The first thing he did when meeting any woman was automatically to check on the size of her bosom. He wasn't sure now if Amelia even had breasts. He didn't want to look. Her eyes held him captive.

"Oh, yes . . . new things. I agree." He snapped his fingers and the waiter came forward with chilled fresh crab salads on boats of lettuce, all mixed with a tangy tomato and horseradish sauce.

He watched her test it with the outside fork. Her face brightened. "Oh, that is delicious. Is it crab meat? I've eaten it once or twice. It's very good."

Somehow this was the best thing he had ever heard her say, and his smile was growing. But he could say nothing.

"Mr. Pemberton, may I ask you something?"

He nodded.

"I keep thinking that I saw you a long time ago. Then the other day, I remembered. Back at least four years ago, I saw someone in the accounting department and he looked very much like you. We both were much younger then, of course, but could that have been you? We never did speak back then."

"Yes, that was I. I thought . . . I liked to watch you work."

"Well, thank you. I don't know why I'm chattering away like this. Usually I'm not a big talker." She laughed. "I imagine it's because I'm so nervous. You see, I've never even been up here on the fifth floor before, let alone eaten lunch here."

"I'm glad you came."

"So am I."

The salad was gone, their plates vanished like magic and were replaced by the luncheon plates. On one side of the bone china lay a large square of baked salmon fillet; on the other side a tender, just broiled steak. Side dishes of baby peas in butter sauce, baked potatoes and asparagus were added.

364

"Oh, my!" Amelia said. "There's so much food."

"I wasn't sure if you liked salmon. Eat whatever you want." He watched her, and for a small girl, she ate a lot. The salmon vanished, and half the steak, all of the potato and peas and half the asparagus, as well as a dinner roll. She sat back and sipped at the delicious coffee.

"Mr. Pemberton, you realize I won't be able to lift my pen all afternoon!" she laughed softly. "What a meal!"

He had hardly touched his salmon, and took only a few bites of the steak and asparagus. Mostly he watched her every movement, still captivated by this small, charming, innocence.

"Dessert?" he asked.

"Oh, my, no."

Amelia had been tremendously surprised by the messenger's visit and the written invitation to have lunch with Mr. Randy Pemberton on the fifth floor. Yes, she had remembered him these past few years. She felt sure two years ago that he would make some move toward her — talk with her or invite her out but — he did not. She had followed closely news of his affairs and his troubles. For a semi-public figure like a Pemberton, there was very little of his life that he could hide. She knew he had a reputation with the girls in the bawdy houses, that he had been in trouble with his father over something, and had even been in jail in Mexico for killing a man in self-defense.

Then for two years, she lost track of him as he was in what everyone called a "son-of-the-boss, management-training program." He was in and out of the offices, went to sea for a while, and then came back. She knew the first day he got his promotion to the fifth floor and his new assignment. Lately she had seen him, and about once a week, he came past her desk and said hello. Nothing more, a nod, sometimes a smile and a good morning, or some simple greeting. Then he was gone.

Now this luncheon.

Amelia watched him and marveled that he was so tongue-tied, so shy, so nervous. He seemed half-frightened out of his wits. Even here, in the familiar surroundings of his own office. What a contrast to his public reputation.

Idly she wondered just who the real Randy was. There was no doubt that he had lived a wild life for four or five years. But now? She watched him eating, picking at the food really, and it left her in a quandary. Was this the real Randy Pemberton, or was the real Mr. Pemberton the man who fired a clerk in her department because he stepped on Randy's just-shined shoes?

Amelia had thought of not accepting his luncheon invitation. She had visions of herself stripped naked and compromised on the carpet of his office, or in a bed in his private quarters. She knew for sure that he would kiss her and try to fondle her, and she would probably have to use all of her persuasive powers to retain her virginity. But even understanding that, she knew at once that she would come. It had been such a long time in happening. And she had based all of her arguments against coming on his public reputation. That was unfair. Randy and his reputation might not be one in the same. And she could always run out of his office, screaming.

From the very first glance, Randy Pemberton had been a total surprise. He hadn't even touched her hand. He had never touched her, not even to shake hands, she realized. And it had taken him three years before he would say hello. This was tremendous progress, but at this rate, she would be in her sixties before he asked her to marry him.

Vaguely, she was aware he had asked her

something about dessert.

"Oh, my, no," she said. "No thank you, I've no room for any dessert, but thank you very much. I couldn't eat this much every noon or I'd be fat in a week."

His smile was warm, genuine, not as forced now as it had been before. She was glad.

"I really should be getting back to work."

He made some small move with his hands. "Not really. You could be late. I do have some small influence with your superiors."

"Yes, I imagine you do. However, I work for a very strict taskmaster, an R. Pemberton. And he is strict and just and I always make sure that I give him a fair day's work." She stood, smiling. He jumped up almost at the same time, seriously jeopardizing the stability of the pedestal table.

"May I see you back to your office?" he asked.

"Oh, no, Mr. Pemberton, thank you very much. I appreciate this chance to talk and to have lunch with you. I'm glad that at last we have started to get to know one another a little better. There has never been a meal that I've enjoyed more. Perhaps we can do this again sometime." She paused, then hurried on even at the danger of his misunderstanding. "Perhaps one of these days I can share my lunch with you."

"Yes! I'd like that, Miss Borcherding. I'd like that very much." For just a moment, he reached for her, then he drew back.

She extended her own small right hand and waited for him to take it. She felt a marvelous tingle when their hands touched.

"Mr. Pemberton, I thank you again."

"Miss Borcherding, the honor and the privilege were both mine, I assure you." He bowed slightly and walked with her to the outer door.

She turned, nodded at him, and was gone down the hallway.

Back in his office, the luncheon things were gone, and only a faint fragrance masked the cooking odors. Randy Pemberton felt good. He nipped the end off a long cigar and lit it, then sat back in his big chair behind the desk, with both hands laced together in back of his head. He smiled, and slowly made up his mind. Of course, he would have to pick exactly the right moment to tell her, but as far as he was concerned, it was definitely decided.

At the other end of the fifth floor executive-office complex, Harold Pemberton scowled at the man sitting in the upholstered chair beside his big desk.

"Wally, do you realize what you're saying?"

Wally Barclay hunched lower in the chair. His hair was now mussed, his shave not the best in his life, his tie was crooked and his dark suit coat looked like he had slept in it.

"Harold, I sure as hell do know what I'm saying. I've been living with this for two weeks. I mean I've *known* about it for two weeks. I just never thought it could happen to me. Cuckold. Most women don't like it that much, and to go out and meet a man not just once, but three times . . . I was just floored, Harold. Absolutely stunned. She came and told me. I didn't even catch her or suspect her. She told me she's been unfaithful. Do you know what that can do to a man, Harold?"

"But, Wally, she came and admitted to you that she made a mistake. She confessed. Now if you go ahead and get a divorce, it's not going to help you or her — and it sure as hell isn't going to do the company any good. I'd have to let you go, Wally. You helped make up the company policy about divorce."

"To hell with the policy! I'm not some clerk. I'm a vice-president. I've worked fifteen years for this company." He stood and walked around the room. "The dam-

370

nable part of it is I still love that woman. What would I do without her? What the hell would I do without the kids? What could I *tell* them? Just what would I do to earn a living? Your salaries aren't that good that I can afford to retire in luxury."

Harold rubbed his chin with his left hand. What the hell was going on? This was the second such situation in two weeks. He let Wally sit down before he went on.

"Look, Wally, I can't afford to lose you. Patch it up. We've got a couple of shaky marriages of long standing in the company, but they never divorced. They give the appearance of a marriage. That's what I'm asking you to do. And Becky evidently loves you or she wouldn't have confessed. You still love her, so don't let your stupid pride get in the way. So she made a mistake. Be a little forgiving. Some men make mistakes, too, get out of line. If you ever had another woman in the past, Wally, that would rather balance out the problem with Becky, wouldn't it?"

"Hell, Harold, that's different. I'm a man."

"Right, you're a man, not a stud horse. If Becky had caught you in bed with another woman, she would have been furious, right?"

"I guess so."

"And just because she didn't catch you means you're pure as the driven snow? Come on, Wally. The Christian thing to do is turn the other cheek. Tell her not to do it again or you'll break her arm. Then make sure she never gets itchy again. Take care of her so she gets all she wants at home."

Wally stood. "All right, Harold. I'll have a long talk with Becky. She promised me she'd never do anything like this again, and the hell of it is, I believe her."

Harold looked up. "Fine, Wally, fine. Have that talk tonight, *after* you get in bed."

They both chuckled.

Harold probed. "Wally, did she say who the man was?"

"No, that she wouldn't tell me. Said she didn't want me trying to kill him and getting killed myself. Why?"

"Oh, nothing, really. I wondered if it might be someone inside the company?"

"Somebody we both know?"

"It's a chance. I've had another similar situation. The employee was on a lower level, and said his wife had done this sort of thing before, several times before, and there was nothing I could say that would stop him from divorcing her." He sighed. "You might as well know. That's why Simon Walker from purchasing quit last week. He was down to

San Diego for two weeks and got back three days early and surprised his wife. It was a real surprise when he found a man in his bed with his wife.

"Simon never did see the man's face because he went through an open window carrying his pants. On the dresser, Simon found a key that looked familiar. He tested it and it fit the front door of this building."

Wally whistled in surprise. "Damn, that is interesting! How many front-door keys are checked out?"

"Over fifty, every top-ranking executive in the building has one, including me and you. So that doesn't help much. My advice to you is to take this lump which was no fault of your own, and then just keep her so busy she won't have time to wander."

At last Wally nodded. "Okay, boss, you win. But I'm going to keep such a tight rein on her, she'll think she's wearing a chastity belt!"

Randy Pemberton came back to the building late that night. It was just after eleven when he unlocked a back door and went up to the accounting department. He used a small candle and found the desk he wanted. He removed the lower drawer and took it to his own office, where he transferred everything in the drawer to an identical one which he had hired built for him at an enormous fee. The only difference in the new desk drawer was a secret compartment built into the back. He put the old drawer in a paste-board box, sealed it, then took the box to the trash bin where it would be picked up just after midnight.

The drawer with the secret compartment he took to accounting and fitted it back into the desk. Then he went through two more locked doors to a small holding safe, and with another pair of keys, opened it. He took out a thousand dollars in used paper money, relocked the safe and closed all doors the way he had found them. He put the money in the secret compartment in the desk drawer and closed it carefully. The finish matched perfectly. No one could ever tell there had been a switch made.

Randy laughed quietly as he pulled his gloves on tighter and went down to the back door. He checked carefully to be sure there was no one around, then went through the door into the alley. He drifted through shadows to a street two blocks away, where he had left his carriage.

He drove through several streets then, along Market and past the Pemberton Mercantile. It was still the biggest and best store in town, five floors of fine merchandise from all over the world. Too bad, in a way, but it simply had to be done. They had to be shown!

Two blocks farther down, he turned to the left, drove another block and parked. He tied the reins, took a valise from the buggy and walked back toward the rear door of the Mercantile. It simply had to be done.

The old key still fit. Randy let himself in the freight entrance, and listened, but could hear no bells, no kind of alarms. There had been none here when he did his one week of "guard" duty with old man Fawcett during his executive know-it-all training. He was only now beginning to realize how complete and valuable those two years had been. He knew a great deal about every part and operation of the firm. How things were done, where people were, what procedures were followed. It was perfect. He could rip this company apart with ease!

Randy decided he would go around Fawcett's hideaway on the second floor and make sure the old man didn't know anything was happening until it was too late.

He went silently up the stairs to the top floor of the huge store. In the men's clothing section, he gathered a large quantity of paper, clothes, paper boxes, anything that would burn, and piled it under a shelf filled with more boxes. This he splashed with coal oil from a two gallon can which had been in the valise.

One stinker dropped into the oily paper produced a quick fire as the flames shot up, igniting other parts of the storage room. The fire began to burn intensely. Randy closed the door to the back room so the fire would reach a peak intensity before it could break out and be seen.

Randy raced to floor three where he did the same thing in women's clothing. He had sloshed the coal oil around and taken a stinker off the packet when a voice shouted behind him.

"Drop the fire match or I'll shoot!"

Randy recognized the voice of old man Fawcett, the guard. How in hell had he sneaked up like this?

Randy held his hands steady and turned. When Fawcett saw it was Randy, a company vice-president, he began lowering the gun. In that split second, Randy whirled and threw the two gallon can of coal oil at him. The old man couldn't dodge the can, nor did he have time to bring up the gun and fire. The can hit his chest and drove him backward, making him drop the gun.

Randy jumped forward, picked up the

gun, then ran back and struck three stinkers, dropping them into the oil-soaked cloth and paper. The fire gushed up at once.

Fawcett crawled toward the door. Randy ran to him and kicked Fawcett in the stomach, rolling him on his back.

"Where are you going, old man? Trying to sneak out? You just might not make it. You might get trapped trying to put out the fire."

Randy pulled a fire extinguisher off the wall. He never had learned how to use one. Fawcett cowered on the floor.

"Son, you don't know what you're doing, what you're saying. Help me out of here and I'll stick by you. Say you was hurt and out of your head. Help me, son!"

Randy laughed. "You think anyone would believe a crazy old coot like you? Your word against mine? I'm a Pemberton. Remember that." Still, it sounded like too much of a risk to take. His plan had called for him getting in and out without being seen. This changed things.

Randy knew what he had to do, and he didn't shy away from the task. He was thinking the whole thing through carefully, trying not to overlook any possibility, any way out. No, there was none.

The display rack should be about right. He tipped it over on the second try and watched it crash down on Mr. Fawcett. One of the shelves grazed his head, and the old man didn't move.

Good, Randy thought, easier for the old man that way. Randy dropped the fire extinguisher near the body and found his can of coal oil. It had spilled out half of the fluid on the floor, so Randy dropped another stinker sulphur match into it. The fire caught slowly, then built, running along the line where the oil had drained down the wooden floor.

Behind him, the women's wear section was totally engulfed in flames, and the heat was intense. He ran down the stairs to the first floor. Toward the back he set another fire in the paint section, opening five gallon cans as he had at the warehouse. When he ignited the paint, he knew that no fire department in San Francisco could stop the blaze.

With the big building blazing on at least three floors, Randy took his valise and the empty coal oil can with him and unlocked the freight-entrance door. He paused, looked, saw nothing and slid outside. He heard nothing unusual. Certainly, he could not hear any of the hand-cranked fire sirens. Good.

Slowly, with no hurry and a kind of cold

deliberation, he moved from one patch of shadow to another down the alley. When he was clear of the alley, he walked more quickly toward his buggy.

By the time he got to his official residence, it was past midnight. He put the horse away, then put the coal oil can and the valise in the basement. He undressed, got into bed and lay there thinking. By morning, one of the foundations of the Pacific Steamship and Trading Company would be gone. The company would have suffered its most tragic loss in history. Not only would the Pemberton Mercantile be totally gutted by flames of an "undetermined origin," but a long-time employee would have died trying to quench the blaze.

Randy had never liked the talkative old man anyway. If he'd stayed out of the way tonight, he would still be alive.

It was more than an hour later when Randy awoke to the wail of half the fire sirens in San Francisco. He listened to them and decided there were more hand-cranked sirens than he had ever heard before.

He turned over, smiled, and went back to sleep.

CHAPTER SEVENTEEN:
A MESS OF MORALS

The day Martha was arrested would live in her memory for all time. They were gentlemen about it, but she was taken to the city police station, her name recorded in a book, and a file card made out with her name and address and offense. Then she was taken before a judge who found her guilty of interfering with the legal duties of a fireman. In this case, the judge determined that the safety of the city was at stake since the firemen she interfered with were performing a much-needed drill in fire-hose training. Therefore, she was guilty of a misdemeanor and the fine was set at twenty-five dollars. Martha paid the fine and left, but by the time she got back to the park, all the women were gone.

As she rode home in the hired cab, she decided she would tell no one about being arrested. Then she remembered a reporter in the background, smirking through the whole thing, and she was sure that she would make the front page of the *Bulletin* tomorrow. So she told everyone, including Allen, who was shocked at first, then gradually saw the humor in it. They both decided there was nothing wrong with being arrested or even going to jail, if your cause was a good one.

That had been a week ago. The newspapers had played it up as much as Martha thought they would, and dozens more invitations poured in for Sue to speak, as well as unsolicited contributions for the suffrage treasury. One woman sent them a hundred-dollar bill, but would not give her name.

Sue was booked for the next month with speaking engagements, and she and Martha decided to postpone the next "event" until the invitations slowed down again.

In place of immediate action, they worked on a local city ordinance to give women the right to vote. Martha called one of the company lawyers she knew, Haliburton Saunders, to a meeting at their home. At first, he was amused at their "antics," as he called them. But as they talked, and Sue showed him the downright unfairness of it all, he changed his mind and pledged his wholehearted cooperation.

They worked out a legal, fair and airtight city ordinance giving women the right to vote on any issue concerning the city government, including city and county officials. At the same time, the ordinance also made women eligible to run for any elected city or county position. The women were delighted.

Several days later, Martha forgot her elation totally. She sat in her buggy on Market Street, crying silently into her handkerchief. She had heard the sirens the night before and knew that it must be a huge fire. But she had no idea what it was until she drove down Market Street and saw the ruins of Pemberton Mercantile.

She looked out at the jagged, gutted, blackened remains of the big store where she had worked so hard, and she couldn't stop the tears. Her driver had stopped, waiting for her word to go on. She had tried to find the fifth floor where some of the offices had been, but it was completely gone. Some of the floors below had burned away completely and sections of the top floors had sagged, then dropped into the inferno. Part of the building had slid to one side, crushing a small harness and saddle shop next to it.

A policeman strolled past and she called to him.

"Officer, was anyone hurt in the fire last night?"

"Officially, I can't say, ma'am. But I did hear that the old night guard had been found. Begging your pardon, ma'am, his body was found. But no one else seems to have been caught. Just the usual twisted knees and sprains by the smoke eaters."

"Thank you, officer."

Martha dried her eyes, and told the driver to continue up Market Street to the Pacific Steamship Building. She asked the driver to wait and went inside. Her father was in his office and delighted to see her.

"It's been weeks since you've been down here," Harold Pemberton said. "You saw the Mercantile?"

She nodded.

"A shame. We have no way of knowing how it started. One of the firemen said he found a fire extinguisher in a death grip in Ivor Fawcett's hand. Evidently he was trying to put out the blaze, but couldn't. They can't even tell which floor it began on."

"I'm so sorry about Mr. Fawcett. I used to say good night to him almost every evening."

"He was a fine man. We'll make certain

that his widow is well taken care of."

"Was it a big money loss?"

"Over a million dollars. Our fire insurance will cover part of it, maybe half."

"We're going to rebuild?"

"Of course." He motioned to the chair. "Sit down a minute, could you, Martha? I want to ask your advice on another matter. You know, I've made out my will. My attorney said it was absolutely mandatory to have an up-to-date will that's all legal and proper. So I did."

"Daddy, we don't want to talk about that."

"Yes, Martha, we need to. There's one thing I've learned in this life and that is that no one lives forever. I certainly won't be the first. No, my will is made, and my stock in the corporation will go to my family. To Penny, to you, to Randy and to Abigail. Do you think it would be a good idea to divest myself of those portions of the stock that will come to you and Randy now, so you both could vote them, and so you could take a more active role in the company?"

"No."

Harold looked at his daughter. "Just a no, that's all?"

"Daddy, I don't think you should give out the stock and the money and the responsibility. It could lead to proxy fights and family dissension and all sorts of problems. And I don't think Randy is ready for it. I really don't. I've seen him in heavy stress situations, and I think this would not be good for him."

"Stress? He's gone through my executive-training program, the full two-year course. He came through with absolutely outstanding results. He's worked in fifty-two separate departments and divisions of the company and he's done a fine job with each one."

"Daddy, I can't approve. That's my feeling. Randy isn't ready for that much financial responibility. As for me, I won't accept any stock transfer now. I want you to run the company just as you have always done. I don't want to be on the board of directors. Period."

Mrs. Tausch, Harold's secretary, tapped on the door and came in. "There's a problem in accounting, Mr. Pemberton. Mr. Schwartz is here and he's worried. I told him you were busy but I'd ask if you could see him this afternoon."

Martha rose. "I do have to go, Father. Thanks for talking with me. And remember how I feel on that matter."

"Please stay, Martha. This shouldn't take long, and you'll get to see some of the top echelon workings of your company. Mrs.

Tausch, tell Joe to come in."

Joseph Schwartz was a heavy-set man, with drooping jowls, a large nose and eye glasses. His back seemed stooped from perpetually bending over account books and ledgers. He smiled at Martha and nodded, then turned toward his boss, and laid a folder on the desk.

"Mr. Pemberton, I just can't figure this any other way. Fredericks showed 4,860 dollars in the safe last night, all checked in and double approved. This morning when the safe opened, there was a thousand dollars missing. Everything had been checked and double-run. There's no doubt. His books showed a cash income of $4,800 for the day, and that much was put in the overnight safe. This morning he's a thousand short."

"Have you taken care of it, Joe?"

Joe Schwartz sat down in the chair beside the big desk. It was plain that he'd been there before. He was also unhappy about something.

"Yes, we checked it out, have been working on it all morning. You know that ex-Pinkerton man we hired to head up guard and internal security, Eugine King? Well, I got him right on it and we went around and around. I told him that Fredericks was one

386

of my best men, absolutely trustworthy. He wanted to go through Fredericks' desk, his house, his bank account. I told him no, but finally gave in on the desk. We got Fredericks into my office and they almost tore that desk apart. Then they compared the drawers and discovered one with a built-in secret compartment. The packet of fifty twenty-dollar bills was in that compartment.

"Fredericks? He's never given us any trouble before. Now we'll have to change all the locks. Funny, though, I still have my doubts."

"That he took the money?"

"Yes. He was so stunned, shocked. He simply couldn't believe that there was even a secret compartment in that drawer. Then the Pinkerton guy had us both out there while he opened it, and there was the money."

"If there's any doubt about him, don't make any charges. Just quietly let him resign and we'll forget it. We haven't really lost anything." Harold Pemberton sighed. Why the hell was he having all this trouble right now? He hadn't experienced anything like this in twenty years.

"Oh, Joe. Did you compare the drawers in the desk?"

"Yes, sir. They looked good on the outside,

the color and type of wood and the finish. But inside the mortise and tenon joints were made differently. Oh, it was a skillful job. I do some woodworking as a hobby, and the drawer was expertly done. The Pinkerton man said the wood was newer, much newer in the secret compartment drawer. Which just means that Fredericks was smarter than we thought."

"Did he admit taking the money?"

"Admit it? No, he was quick and firm in denying it. He also was quietly furious, said someone was trying to get him fired."

Harold rubbed his chin. "Joe, transfer Fredericks to some non-critical job where he handles no money, and don't discharge him. And no police charges. I want to talk to him. And put some independent detectives on him and see if he has had any troubles with his family, wife, finances. Check his bank if he has an account, and see if there is any desperate need for money, any history of gambling, women, even opium. Go the whole route. We don't want to crucify an honest man. How long has he been with us?"

"Twelve years. He's the fourth man in my department."

"Let's be certain he's guilty before we sack

him. Thanks, Joe, for bringing this right to me."

Joe stood, knowing when he was dismissed. He nodded at Martha and left the room.

Harold stood and walked to the window. Why did he always look out over the bay when he was troubled? He wasn't sure, habit, probably, but it seemed to help.

"Daddy, no wonder your employees are so loyal. You could have pressed charges and had that man thrown into prison. You're the finest man I know."

He turned and thanked her, then told her the other troubles he was having with top executives and their wives.

"This morning, two more of my top men came in with short letters, written in different hands, on different kinds of paper, but both naming the wives as cheating on their husbands.

"Both the women denied it. The letters gave dates and places and the men admitted to me that they couldn't be absolutely sure what their wives did that day, but neither of them could imagine their wives cheating on them. I'm wondering if it is a plan of some kind, a plot by a sick mind trying to poison our whole firm. How better than to get the top men fired because of our rule about divorce?"

"Oh, Daddy, who would be that cruel, and that unhappy with you? You haven't fired anybody lately who might be mentally upset, have you?"

He shook his head.

"It could be chance, just everything piling up all of a sudden."

"I hope so, Martha. I truly hope so."

He came back from the window. "Of course, the family does have one of its members with an arrest record." His eyes twinkled.

"Yes, and I would do it again if they were endangering my women marchers."

"And you didn't even have a parade permit."

"We didn't know that we needed one. But from here on, we'll be straight and firm on legal grounds. We have a legal advisor."

"A woman?"

"There are no women lawyers I know of in San Francisco. No, a man, and a liberal, a right-thinking man. Something like you, Daddy." She stood. "Don't worry about this other. I'm sure it will all work out in the long run." She went around the desk and kissed her father's cheek the way she had done since she was old enough to remember. He patted her shoulder and Martha went back out into the bright San Francisco sunshine. Neither of them remembered that there was another family member with an arrest record. True, the arrest had been made in Mexico. But all the same . . .

A week after the big fire, and while the demolition workers were still tearing down the last of the blackened hulk, Martha and Susan Stone went to the regular meeting of the city board. Their legal representative, Haliburton Saunders, had obtained an agenda spot to present a matter of utmost importance. Since Saunders was a member of the bar, and a man, he did not need to give them the subject.

Mr. Saunders took the floor as the women watched, and launched into a two-minute, carefully worded message about freedom, equality under the law and the right of every adult to have a voice in his or her government.

"And so, gentlemen, it is with a great deal of pleasure that I present to this august body a proposed city ordinance giving equal voting rights to both men and women, with identical rights in all areas of residence and citizenship as now stated in our charter. It is my hope that the board will give due and careful consideration to this document, and that we may soon see it enacted into law to continue to make San Francisco the leader in establishing personal rights for all its citizens."

There was a thunderous cheer from the fifty women who had packed into the board room. All of them were from the suffrage association. Chairman of the board, Arthur Milligan, stared at Saunders for several seconds, then rapped his gavel and began to move to the next item on his agenda.

Mr. Saunders cleared his throat. "Mr. Chairman, may I ask that the matter I so submitted, and now give you in writing, be acted upon at once by the board or referred to committee for study?"

"You may ask, Mr. Saunders."

"Then I do so ask, Mr. Chairman."

"Very well, Mr. Saunders. The matter of the woman's voting-rights ordinance will be referred to our committee on legislation."

"Mr. Chairman, now that the matter is on the agenda and placed with a committee, I believe the matter is open to discussion."

Chairman Milligan nodded, a sour expression showing.

"That being the case, Mr. Chairman, I yield my discussion time of five minutes to Miss Susan Stone."

There were cheers as Sue walked to the front of the room and faced the city board.

"Thank you, Mr. Saunders. It is always a pleasure to talk to the board, and I look forward to the day when one, just one, woman will be elected as a member. But until that time comes, all women will unite to make our wishes, yes, our demands, known since this is the only way we will improve our lot and lift ourselves out of the semi-slavery mode we are now trapped in.

"I wonder if you men have any understanding of the legal and everyday discrimination that all women suffer? For example, on election day, we sit home and let our husbands, brothers, fathers and uncles go to vote and *determine for us* who our new President will be, who our new senators and representatives in Washington and Sacramento will be. We even stand by and let the men on this body vote concerning our taxes, our way of life in our very own city. We are totally disenfranchised. We are mere observers in the total arena of government and law. And this ordinance, giving San Francisco women the right to help determine their own destiny, is one law that this board has a moral obligation to pass."

Martha had heard the same ideas before, dozens of times now, but at each outing, Sue seemed to adapt them anew, to put them in a different light, and always to season them just right pointing them at the particular body to which she was speaking. She was a remarkable woman, truly outstanding.

Later, Martha was surprised when the chairman's gavel hit the solid oak pounding board in front of him.

"Time is up, Miss Stone, thank you," Chairman Milligan said.

"I ask for two more minutes to sum up," Sue said.

The chairman, a lawyer himself, looked at her with surprise, then in a monotone, answered, "Request denied. We move on to item four on the agenda, the dedication of twenty-four streets in the Fulton area."

"Mr. Chairman, I demand two more minutes as a common courtesy," Sue shouted.

"Miss Stone, you have had your say. Another outburst like that and you will be escorted from the premises."

"You and your authority. Let the little people talk for a change. You talk up there all the time. I won't move a step and I won't be quiet. I have a sacred cause, the cause of every woman in this city, and I can't be quiet. I don't care what you say, women will gain the right to vote. Perhaps not today, maybe not next week. Perhaps not even in my lifetime, or yours, Mr. Chairman. But we will get the vote."

The chairman signaled to the back of the room, and two policemen came down the aisle.

"Yes, yes, call in the police. Let them beat me, and strangle me, and take me to their jail and molest me. You men all stick together. Where are all the women police? Yes, we should have women police, too. Women will get the vote. You just wait and see."

The two policemen stood in front of her.

"Miss Stone, will you leave quietly?" the chairman asked.

"Hell, no!" Sue screamed. "They'll have to drag me out of here. I'm going to talk as long as I can and as loud as I can. There's no way you can stop me except by knocking me out or killing me. Yes, you'll have to kill me!"

One policeman touched her shoulder.

"Did you see him strike me? This officer assaulted me. I'll have an assault and battery suit filed against you next week. Mr. Saunders, watch this closely. Get the names of these two officers. We're going to sue them and the city."

The officer had jerked his hand back and stepped away.

"Officers, remove the woman. You have a

legal right to clear this room of all undesirables, and Miss Stone is certainly that. Carry her out of here if you have to!"

One of the policemen grabbed her around the waist from behind. The second uniformed man reached for her legs, but was kicked in the shoulder and then the shins. She kicked him once more before he caught her legs and lifted her. One of her arms pulled free and slammed into the officer's face. He yelled and caught her arm.

All the way down the aisle Sue was screaming.

"You're denying me my civil rights! Let me speak! Women must have the vote to stop these kinds of crude, male repressionist acts. Men are desperate. Look how they are assaulting me. That cop touched my breast! I'll sue you double, you beast! Every woman here, listen, this could happen to you next! Not even inside a building is a woman safe. What is our city coming to? These men should be horsewhipped." Susan was quiet for a moment as she reached down and bit the policeman on the arm. He howled and Sue laughed.

"Take that, you monster. Attack me, will you? Touch my breast, will you, you rapist! Help, rape! Help! These men are trying to rape me!" Sue clawed the closest officer's cheeks with her fingernails. Then they were through the doors.

Martha sat in the back row, shivering. She was frightened and angry. Furious, but frustrated. She had to get out of there and go to the police station. She had to get bail put up and get Sue out of jail. She motioned to Haliburton Saunders and they slipped out of the room. Half of the women followed them. Quietly she and Saunders left by a side door and went in his buggy to the police station where they arranged to have Sue released.

She was charged with disturbing the peace and assault on a police officer. The latter was a serious felony and would require a jury trial. The bail was set at a thousand dollars.

Martha hurried to her bank, wrote out a draft for the amount and had it verified and the authorization notarized. A half hour later Sue was released, still shouting.

Saunders shook his head and she stopped. Outside, she sagged against Martha who helped her into her carriage. The driver took them to Sue's home and Martha told him to wait for her.

She leaned against Martha all the way to the house and then asked her to come inside. There Sue fell into a chair.

"God, but that was exhausting! Sometimes I think I could have been a great actress. I seem to get my best ideas, my best words in a crisis situation, when I'm in the spotlight and especially when somebody is dragging me out of a room."

"Could I get you a cup of tea?" Martha asked.

"Yes, could you, dear? I'd appreciate it."

Martha went to the kitchen, found the tea and turned on the small gas plate. When she got back to the living room, Sue met her with two cups and a pint of whiskey.

"I think I need a short jolt of encouragement."

She took half a cup of tea and poured in a long shot of whiskey and sipped it. "This is the only way to drink tea, believe me. I've never been arrested before, Martha. It's no fun, is it? I guess you know that. I felt so confined, so closed in. They actually *locked me* in a room! I don't think I've ever been locked in anywhere before." Sue shrugged out of the dress and pulled it over her head. She wore a shift under it but her figure showed through plainly.

Martha rose, surprised, uncertain, somehow disturbed by all this, especially the disrobing. "I think I'd better go, Sue. I want you to get into bed and have a good long nap. You'll feel better with sleep. Tomorrow, you come by my house and we'll do some planning on our next move. The voting ordinance was a good tactic. It puts them on the defensive."

Sue nodded, hardly hearing what Martha said. She wanted to pull off her shift, take off her underclothes and stand there naked and wanting. But dear Martha simply wouldn't understand.

She walked with Martha to the door and said goodbye with a semblance of normality. Once the door closed, Sue leaned against it and rubbed her breasts. She shook her head, ran into the living room and pulled on her dress. She washed her face, and put just a touch of redness on her lips, then she went out the back door and across the alley. She only hoped that Paula was home today, and that Paula was alone.

A few moments later Sue knocked on Paula Hendricks' back door and beamed when the tall woman opened it. She stretched up to be kissed and Paula touched her lips with her own, smiling.

"Yes, sweetheart, I'm here and I'm alone and I'm lonesome. You couldn't have come at a better time."

Paula reached for Sue and the small woman leaned against her, smiling. Already she was sensing that soft, wonderful glow of being wanted and needed and the thrill of desire swept in and blotted out everything else.

CHAPTER EIGHTEEN:
A TARNISHED PENNY

Penny had been working at the hospital more than a month now. She enjoyed the contact with the people, expecially the men's ward where there were always comments about how pretty she was. One of the patients kissed her one day as she bent close to him to see if he were asleep. His hands caught her head and held it as he kissed her lips, then he let go of her at once.

They both giggled and he did it again. Then she leaned away and told him he was a naughty boy. Two days later, in the same ward, another man touched her breast as she helped smooth out his covers. He did it on purpose and, when she looked at him, he glanced away. If he'd been honest about it, she might have let him feel her again.

She was in the small linen closet on the second floor today folding pillow cases when a young doctor looked in. Penny had seen him around the hospital often. He was about thirty, red-headed and single. She'd heard he was an outstanding doctor.

"Oh, I was looking for Nurse Jenkins."

"Dr. Knapp, I don't believe you," Penny said, smiling. "Come in. Maybe Nurse Jenkins is under these pillow cases somewhere."

He laughed, stepped in and closed the door. "Penny, isn't it?"

"You know very well, my name, Dr. Knapp."

"Yes, that's true, I do."

"You thought since Nurse Jenkins was off this morning you could sneak up here, trap me and steal a kiss, right?"

"Why, of course not! I'm busy making my rounds, and I just wondered . . ."

"You wondered what, Dr. Knapp?" She put down the pillow cases and stood, trying to stretch her breasts tightly against her pink uniform.

"I thought maybe we could have lunch toether sometime. You get off at noon, right?"

"That's true. But I am sorry you weren't trying to steal a kiss. I would have liked that."

He looked up quickly, his eyes not quite believing her. "You wouldn't mind if I tried to kiss you?"

"Of course not. I wouldn't have minded two minutes ago, and I wouldn't mind right now." She walked a few steps toward him. He grinned, looked at the door.

"Go ahead, lock it, Doctor. If you'd feel safer."

He pushed the bolt in, locking the door and stepped toward her. "Penny, I . . ."

Before he could finish she reached up and kissed his lips softly, then pulled away.

"Now that wasn't much of a kiss, Penny."

"Think you can show me a better one?"

Now his smile broke through. He put his arms around her and pulled her close, then bent and kissed her lips hard and held the kiss a long time.

Penny felt the fire burning into her lips and relaxed against him, hoping that the kiss would never end. He was the most handsome man she had ever seen, certainly ever kissed. He ended it, but still held her.

"Not bad, but nothing really happened," she said.

"What did you expect to happen?"

"You know, skyrockets, stars, explosions."

"That's all make-believe," he said.

"Let's try it again."

This time he kissed her, holding her so tightly that her breasts pushed hard against his white doctor's coat. When their lips met,

Penny's parted slightly and her tongue probed at his and, just for a moment, he opened his lips. Then he broke off the kiss and stepped back.

"Penny, I can't do that. I mean, you're the prettiest girl I've ever seen, and you kiss great, but . . ."

"But you don't want to do anything else?"

"Penny, it isn't that . . ."

"You're a doctor and I'm just a little pink lady."

"No Penny. You're ten times the woman most of them are, but . . ."

Penny caught his hand and kissed it, then drew it to her breasts. She wasn't sure what she wanted him to do. All she felt was a lot of wanting. He let his hand lay there quietly.

"Dr. Knapp, doesn't that mean anything to you?"

"Oh, Penny, it means a great deal! It means too much. There is no way I can do anything more than kiss you, believe me. I'd like nothing better than to tear off your clothes and lay you down right here, right now!"

Penny took his hand and pushed it under the jumper and inside her blouse on top her bare breast. He almost cried out in surprise and delight.

"Penny! You shouldn't be doing this."

"Why not? What is it hurting? I like the feel of your hand there. You're a doctor. Is there anything wrong with that? Will I get sick if you fondle my breasts?"

"Of course not, but something far worse for you could happen, and you know what I mean. Time enough for that after you're married, Penny. Now, let me ask you something. Could I come courting?"

She held his hand on her breast and shook her head. "No, you're too old. But I like you, and I'd like you to kiss me again."

He did, and his hand started to move, to rub slowly.

She broke off the kiss, stepped back, and quickly took off the jumper and shrugged out of her unbuttoned blouse. Her breasts came free, jiggling and bouncing in the soft gas light of the room.

"Penny, Penny, don't do this. You've got much of your life ahead of you. Don't spoil it this way."

"I'm not spoiling a thing, Dr. Knapp." She stepped to him, put her arms around him and held tight.

"Dr. Knapp, do I have to ask you? Please, right here, right now. I'll never tell a living soul!"

"And what if you get pregnant? Girls do, you know."

"I won't. My sister said she had one hell of a time getting pregnant. I probably will, too. Besides, you're a doctor. You'd know what to do."

He bent and kissed her breasts, then pushed her away and ran to the door and unbolted it.

"Penny, you're a Pemberton, remember? The word has been spread that anyone who touches you, anyone who deflowers you will end up on a marble slab down in the funeral parlor. I don't want to go that way. I'll call on your mother and see if I can have her permission to come courting." He stared at her breasts, then her face.

"God, but you're beautiful! I wish I could. Oh, Jesus, but I wish I could take you right here!" He shook his head, slipped out the door and was gone.

Penny sighed, pulled up her blouse and buttoned it, then put on the jumper. Damn it to hell! She practically raped the poor boy and he still wouldn't do it to her. What did Martha call it — intercourse? She sighed again, stacked the pillow covers on the table and went back to the ward. She had to finish her rounds with the books. Then it would be time to leave.

The rest of the morning, she judged each man she met, wondering what he would look like undressed, if he would be the one to take her to complete satisfaction. When her time was over at the ward, she hung her jumper in the closet provided for the pink ladies, and walked slowly to the front steps. She hoped she would see Dr. Knapp again, but she didn't. Perhaps she should let him come courting, make him put in the time, and then turn him down cold. That would serve him right. She had felt so ready today, and he had come looking for her. Damn him!

She tried to put it out of her mind when she saw the buggy with Arturo driving. Arturo was a Mexican, about eighteen, she guessed. He had a natural way with horses and was the best driver they had. Each day at noon, he came to pick her up and take her home. Today, he had the buggy with the winter side curtains still on it, a hold-over from the rainy stretch of weather they'd had.

"Hello, Arturo," she said. Very early she had learned to be polite and considerate of the servants. Her father insisted on that. She learned that this was the best policy for happy workers. They did a better job and it made for a more relaxed household as well.

"Morning, Miss Penny. Cure everyone today?"

Penny bantered back a comment and

stepped into the jump-seat buggy. In this rig, the driver had a small seat up in front just forward of the half top and side curtains. Penny felt so penned in by the curtains. On impulse, she asked Arturo to drive down to the bay. He chose the closest part where there weren't docks and ships. They sat there a moment looking out over the water. Suddenly she thought about Arturo, and wondered if he might be talked into helping her.

Penny sat in the rear seat and looked at the boy. He was young; maybe he would get excited easily. She leaned forward and tapped him on the shoulder.

"Arturo, could you come back here for a moment? There's a spring that is coming up through the seat cushion."

"Yes, Miss Penny." He tied the reins and stepped to the ground, then opened the side curtain and leaned forward.

"I don't think you can see it from there. Step inside and I'll show you."

He nodded and climbed into the buggy kneeling on the floor boards so he could be closer to the seat. When he got in the curtain fell closed behind him. Arturo looked up questioningly at Penny Pemberton.

"Arturo, I want to talk to you. Tell me, do

you think I'm pretty?"

"Oh, yes, Miss. About the prettiest girl in all of San Francisco."

"And my . . . my figure, Arturo, what do you think about my figure?"

Arturo frowned. "Really not my place to say, Miss Penny."

"Arturo, I asked you a question. Now you answer me or I'll have to talk to Father about you."

Her tone was sharp and he drew his lips tight for a moment, then spoke. "Miss Penny, you're a beautiful woman. You have a slim waist, and good hips. A perfect figure of a woman."

"What about . . . about my bosom? Is it big enough?"

Arturo blushed. She could see it in the shaded coach.

"Yes, ma'am, that's just perfect too."

"Arturo, scratch my back. Right there." She took his hand and placed it on her back. He rubbed it a little.

"Yes, Arturo, that's good. Now, more to the side, here." A moment later she moved his hand forward again, then took it and placed it over her right breast. "Arturo, I itch right here, rub it for me."

He hesitated.

"Arturo, I could get you discharged, you

know that?"

"Yes, miss."

"Then, go ahead." She watched him rub her gently, then a little more, but he stopped. "More, Arturo, until I tell you to stop." She watched the bulge in his pants get larger and larger. He gave a little moan and quickly she unbuttoned her blouse and thrust his hand inside.

"Oh, Arturo, that feels so wonderful. Do you like to do that, Arturo?"

"Yes, miss! Oh, yes!"

She reached toward his crotch, found the bulge and rubbed it. For a moment, she fumbled with the buttons there.

"Arturo, open up your pants."

He shook his head. "No, Miss Penny. Then I would for sure be fired. I need the work."

She bent forward and kissed his mouth hard, her tongue washing his lips. But he wouldn't part them.

"Arturo, you open your pants or I'll tear my blouse and run screaming to Mother and tell her you tried to rape me coming home. And don't think I won't do it. Now, you open them!"

Arturo scowled, then shrugged. For him this job probably was over, anyway. Why not show this fancy one? He unbuttoned his fly and let the turgid penis spring out.

Penny gasped. "It's so big, so huge! You mean that big thing would actually go in . . ." She shivered. "No, it couldn't be . . ."

She reached toward it, then pulled her hand back. "Have you ever . . . I mean, has it ever been . . ."

"Yes, Miss Penny, I've slept with a girl. I've done it."

"Oh . . . is it difficult? I mean, how does a person learn how to do it the very first time?"

He laughed. "Little Penny, it is easy, very easy."

"Arturo, do it with me, right now! Here. You and me!"

He laughed and shook his head. "No, Miss Penny. You are a *Pemberton.* Don't you know what that means? I could be shut out and never get another job in the whole state. I would be beaten up and probably killed if your family found out. I would be hounded and pushed around for years."

"But don't you want to?"

"I always want to, every time I see you. But Arturo knows he can't." He rubbed her breasts. "Just a little play, a feel, then we go home, no?"

"But I'm ordering you to have intercourse with me."

He laughed again, looked outside to see if anyone was around.

She reached down and grabbed his penis. He yelped and then pushed his hand between her legs and rubbed up her parting thighs to her crotch where his fingers searched and probed through the silk cloth protecting her.

Penny thought she was going to explode with delight and passion and wonder. His hand felt so exciting there. She hoped that he would never move it. She began to wiggle on the seat and her hand kept on his long thing and pushed it back and forth. Then Arturo's finger found what it was hunting, something small and hard at her crotch, and she did explode, sailing out into the void of the stars, shooting past the galaxy and winging off into outer space, watching new worlds born and old ones detonate into sparks. At last, she circled and came back to her own planet and into the jump-seat buggy where Arturo was kissing the tears on her cheeks and pushing his hard thing back into his pants and buttoning up.

"Miss Penny, you ever say a word about this and I'll deny we ever came here. You make up a good story why we're a half hour late getting home. This is your part of it, you hear? You say anything at all, even that

I touched your tits and I'd get my ass fired in a minute. You appreciate what I did for you, you protect me, you really understand?"

She could hardly hear him, let alone know what he was saying. But she nodded and he got out and drove quickly toward the big Pemberton mansion, praying to God that they wouldn't be too late. Just before they got there, he turned and went through his warning again. Told her to say there was an emergency at the hospital and she worked later than usual. This time, Penny had come far enough back to her normal senses so she did understand, and she loved Arturo for trying to take care of her. But she also hated him for not putting it inside of her. Or maybe she loved him even more for that. She wasn't sure. But one of these days, she would go ahead and find out what it was all about — all the way — and then she would know. Then the nagging, the urging, the wanting to know, to experience it would be satisfied once and for all, and she could think about something else for a change.

Friday afternoon of that same week, on April 20, Penny told her mother she was going down town shopping and would be gone most of the afternoon. She wanted to start working on her clothes for her European trip, even though her father was against her going. Penny had Arturo drop her off near the best shops, and told him to be back at the same place at 4:30. She went into one of the stores and, as soon as Arturo drove away, she walked back to the street and hailed a hack. She gave him an address just off Meriweather Street, but she had no idea where it was. Penny was surprised when the rig stopped, since it was so close to the downtown business district.

Penny paid the driver and walked up to the door of the small house and knocked. No one answered and it was locked. She went to the back and tried the door. It was locked, too, but the window in back had been left open. Penny found a box to stand on and crawled through the opening.

Inside, the rooms were about what she expected. Comfortable without being extravagant. The liquor cabinet was well stocked and so was the pantry. She'd hoped the twin-girl whores would be there, but evidently they had the day off, or were out on the town. It might be better this way, after all.

Penny toured the rooms again, marveled that Randy could keep such a love nest so close to the downtown office, and have it a secret so long. A month ago she hired a pair of good private detectives to chart Randy's movements. They worked twenty-four hours a day, and now she had a complete sheaf of daily reports on Randy, including all of his activities for the past month. She knew all about his twins and the dozen or so other women he had brought here, although she didn't know any of their names.

Penny wrote a note at a small desk, sealed it in an envelope, and put Randy's name on the outside. She took it with her when she went out, leaving the front door unlocked.

A block down the street, she found a young boy, about twelve, who said he would deliver the letter to Mr. Pemberton, at his offices, personally for the offered quarter. Penny felt sure he would.

She returned to the small house and waited. By her lapel watch, it was exactly an hour and five minutes after she sent the boy off with the note until she heard a buggy pull up at the back door. A moment later, Randy burst into the living room. Her back was toward him.

"My God, are you sure that you're really pregnant?"

Penny turned slowly. She was impressed at the look of terror on his face. When he saw Penny, his expresson turned to raw anger and fright as he swore and lashed out at her.

"Penny, what the hell are you doing here? Who sent that note? You? I should have you whipped and run out of town in a whore wagon."

"Sweet brother, I don't love you, either. But if either of us ever wants to get our hands on any of the really big money involved in the family company, we had better be more discreet, especially you and your very own whorehouse here. It took me a month to find it, but I'm sure if Father tries, he could do the same job in a week.

"Now, big brother, shut up, sit down and let's talk. I'm not about to try to reform you, or change your habits. But let's try to work together, instead of your ignoring me. I'm almost twenty years old, damnit, and I want you to treat me with a little respect."

Randy sighed. "Sure, baby sister, you want respect. Is that why you put on that sexy nightgown that's much too small for you? I can see it under your robe. Is that why you found out about this place, so you could blackmail me into something? Sure, you're all heart, little sister, worrying about me. Now what's your gambit? Are you the one who really is pregnant and you want me to hire some thugs to beat up some guy and then drop him in the ocean ten miles out?"

Penny laughed. "No, no, no. Randy. I'm not looking for anything like that." She eyed him with a new respect. "You are right, though, about my not wanting to talk to you at home. And there is something I want."

"Money?"

"No, I get all of that I want."

"What? You want some guy beat up?"

"No."

"What the hell is it, then?"

She opened the wrapper that covered the nightgown and Randy sucked in his breath. The sheer nighty covered only her vital parts but he could see right through the thin silk. She was remarkable, her tiny waist and flaring hips made him put his hand to his crotch, and when he looked at her thrusting breasts, he began to rub himself slowly.

"Jesus, so that's it. You want safe big brother to frustrate himself and teach you about sex?"

"Yes, damnit!" Slowly she pulled the nighty off and stood before him, naked.

"Holy . . . Look, little sister, you get me worked up, I might not be able to stop."

"Randy, talk sense. I'm your sister."

"Yeah, but with a sexy, great body like yours . . . Jesus, I must be dreaming. Yeah, I am dreaming."

417

"Take off your clothes, Randy. Let me see what a man looks like. I've never seen a naked man in my life."

"Jesus! I'm getting out of here right now." He started for the door, but she grabbed his arm. He hadn't tried very hard to get away. She took off his jacket, then his tie and shirt. She unbuckled his belt and opened the buttons on his trousers and let them fall down.

Randy sighed, and told her to step back. He pulled off his underwear and stood there watching her.

"My God, a man is beautiful!" she said, her hand going to her mouth.

He moved toward her.

"No, Randy. You're my brother and we can't touch each other. That's the rule. We can't touch each other. We just talk and look."

Randy scowled, stunned at the thought of it, then he nodded.

"All right, but let's go into the bedroom where we both can sit down, at least."

She watched him for a moment, then agreed, and went to the bedroom where she had changed clothes. She picked them up and put them all on a chair, then sat on the edge of the bed.

"What's it like, Randy, making love?"

"Marvelous, wonderful, like you want to

do nothing else for the rest of your life."

He sat on the bed. She couldn't take her eyess off his crotch.

"How does anything that's so big, ever get in . . ."

"Don't worry about that. It just does. There's plenty of room. Things expand and stretch. There's no problem, believe me."

"Could I touch it?"

"You said no touching." Randy was holding himself back. He didn't know how long he could. She was a sex toy if he'd ever seen one, just begging him, asking him, pleading with him to take her. But anyone who got her the first time would have to take her by force. Why not keep it in the family?

No! That was unthinkable! Ridiculous! He had to get dressed and out of there. Damn, this could really blow his whole plan to get even with his father for the cruel hoax he had played on them with Martha. If she was a bastard, maybe he was, too, and Penny! Who could say? He had to get through this and continue his campaign against the company. It was really starting to move now. Executives were dropping like cuckolded flies!

He had worked out his whole program to bring down Pacific Steamship a year ago — exactly what he had to do and with a timetable. So far, it was moving along just fine. There was no way little sister was going to mess up his plans. Now all he had to do was start up, tell Penny to go to hell, put on his clothes and get out of there as fast as he could. He didn't even care if Penny was still there when the twins got back.

Penny said something and her breasts swung toward him. He stared at them and then down at the golden triangle of blonde thatch at her crotch and he groaned. His resolve crumbled. An erect penis has no conscience.

Penny realized her mistake a moment before he came at her. Randy was not emotionally mature enough for this sort of temptation. She had just decided to move off the bed and dress when he slammed into her shoulder, knocking her backward and almost at once he fell on top of her.

"You little bitch! You fucking little whore! How long have you been selling it? This old story about wanting to learn about sex is the oldest whore come-on in the world. Didn't you know that? I found you out. Five will get you a hundred that you're the one pregnant already and want someone to blame. Well, you won't blame me. I've never made anyone pregnant in my life. I keep trying. Now, you take it, you whoring bitch!"

She was crying, but she was sure he didn't notice. Penny wanted to scream but it wouldn't help. She was aware of his hands on her breasts, on her neck, of his fingers squeezing around her throat, then the searing, surging pain as he moved forward, penetrating her. She realized his hands had loosened from her throat but everything was dark and fuzzy and she wasn't sure what happened after that for a few moments.

A minute later, she was crying. It was terrible, ugly. It shouldn't be like that. This wasn't making love, this was animal lust. She didn't want it, but there was no way she could stop him. He was heavier and larger than she and there was no way she could throw him off.

But she wouldn't get pregnant. Martha had said it took only one time, but Martha had said it was hard for her to get pregnant. Penny knew she wouldn't be impregnated easily, either. And Randy had said he'd never fathered a child.

Penny wailed and cried and tried to throw him off, but she could not until he was finished and then he rolled to one side. She pushed and kicked him until he fell off the bed to the floor. That brought him back to his senses. He rose and looked at her.

"My God! What have I done? My own

sister? What have we done, Penny? You never should have come here. I'm not the kind of man you can tease that way. I should kill you. Strangle you and burn down the house. No one would ever know, would they? But I won't. Now get your clothes on, you whore. I'm going to dress and then burn down this damned place. It's brought me nothing but heartache and trouble and evil and danger."

Penny dressed quickly, fearful for her life. She ran out the back door as soon as she was dressed and watched from half a block away as flames spouted from the small house a short time later. He must have set it afire in a dozen places. By the time the fire department got there, the house was almost gone.

Penny picked up her skirts to keep them from the dirt of the street and walked toward the business district. She found a cab and went downtown where she walked into a sweet shop and ate candy for half an hour. All the time she was thinking, worrying, wondering. She was strangely unmoved by her first sexual experience.

At last she decided to keep up the lie of shopping and went out and bought three dresses she didn't really want and a new hat. Even that didn't help.

Was it over now? Could she get back to

doing something besides worrying about sex and men? She decided that she could. She would take more interest in the hospital work. Perhaps she should take the training and become a nurse.

When Arturo came past the place where he was to meet Penny, he found her waiting with a stack of packages. She didn't say a word as they drove home, and Arturo was just as pleased. He was still uncertain how to treat her, so kept it as formal as possible. He still couldn't believe he had gotten that close to her. Perhaps he wouldn't lose his job after all.

Penny sat looking out the buggy, remembering. That's all there was to it? She had been dreaming and worrying and wondering about it for years, and that's all there was to making love?

CHAPTER NINETEEN: RANDY KNOTTED

All the rest of the afternoon Randy berated himself. Stupid, stupid, stupid! It was a dumb, ridiculous, outrageous thing to do. Yet he had been trapped. To make love to your own sister was unthinkable. Yet he had done it. He hadn't meant to, as God was his witness. He hadn't wanted to. In fact, he was a breath away from leaving the house three times.

He had watched his house burn after he sent Penny away. The flames seemed to cleanse his soul a little, to burn away some of the guilt, to make it something he could live with. He faded into the background so the firemen never saw him.

Randy had gone directly back to his townhouse after the fire. The horror of what he had done with Penny kept coming back, and only after he drank half a bottle of gin did he get to sleep.

The next day he heard at work that Henley Jones, the third mate from the *Sea Swallow,* was missing. He had simply vanished and someone wondered if he had been shanghaied. He was the third mate who had given Randy such a bad time on a cruise to Hawaii and back. Randy listened, and smiled, and sent a hundred dollars to the tavern owner as a bonus.

Two weeks later, on May 10, he realized he had heard nothing from Penny.

About eleven that morning, a messenger came with a note for him. He opened it with annoyance, and looked in surprise at the neat handwriting — a woman! God, he hoped it wasn't another note like the one he got from Penny. That would be too much to stand. He glanced at the signature and saw "Amelia." His spirits soared as he looked back to the start of the message and read it slowly.

"Mr. Pemberton. Would you be so kind as to share my lunch with me today? There is a small park only two blocks from here where I usually go and eat on sunny days. We can watch the gulls and the birds and maybe see the bay. If you would care to go, let's meet on the front steps at five after twelve. Amelia."

He ran to his small bath in his inner private room and quickly shaved again.

Then he checked his suit and wished that he'd worn the brown one. Too late for that now. He called in the shoe shine boy and had his glistening shoes polished again. Then he sat near the window and waited.

Randy had no thought of trying to get any work done. He hadn't accomplished a single thing since Amelia's note came. He was still angry at Penny for what she did. Damn her! Spy on him, would she? Set detectives to follow him? Well, they could damn well follow him today and record the whole extravagant, bawdy, scandalous picnic lunch on the green.

Penny! He didn't want to think about her.

Instead he thought of Amelia, of the delicate, soft quality of beauty she had. Quickly he forgot Penny. Amelia was the most perfect thing that had ever happened to him. He had never known another woman like her. He had no idea how old she was. It didn't matter. She was perfect.

Randy met Amelia at the appointed time. He had waited there from five till twelve just to be sure not to miss her. When he saw her coming down the steps, he felt his palms go sweaty and such a large lump rose in his throat that he wondered if he would be able to speak.

She wore a spring print dress, and he saw

now that she did have breasts, and a small waist and boyish hips. Her red hair picked up the sunlight and sparkled through it as she almost skipped down the steps. She carried a paper sack in one hand and a purse in the other. Her smile was pleased, gentle and at the same time, provocative. He couldn't explain it. He loved her.

"Good morning," she said.

He nodded, not sure he could speak.

She smiled and pointed. "It's right down this way two blocks. I hope you don't mind walking."

"No, that's fine." He wanted to add that he had known how to walk for years, but couldn't manage it.

The park was little more than a vacant lot two blocks over from Market Street. They couldn't really see the bay from there, but there were some pigeons and small birds that waited for crumbs from the lunch crowd. Someone had mown down the weeds and grass and it did look a little like a park.

Amelia found a spot covered with clover and sat down gracefully, spreading her skirt around her and using part of it as a tablecloth, then she opened the sack and took out cloth napkins for both of them, and three small sandwiches each and fruit and some hard candy.

She looked up impishly. "I'm sorry the wine steward forgot to put in the wine I ordered. We'll just have to make do with the drinking fountain across the street."

Randy laughed. It broke the tension, and suddenly he was talking normally, the way he usually did. He complimented her on the sandwiches, thanked her for asking him to come to lunch with her.

"I thought after your invitation to lunch, it might be all right to return the favor — and not look like I was being too forward." She looked at him and he was surprised at the depth of meaning she put into the next few words.

"Mr. Pemberton, I truly do admire you, and I must admit that I am smitten with you. I know a girl is not supposed to say or even hint at such a thing, but it's been such a long, long time. I've been wishing you would talk to me or ask me out or ask if you could come courting for over three years now. It seems that you're so unnaturally shy when you're around me, that I thought I better make some response. I wanted you to *know* how I feel about you. If you don't feel the same way, then so be it. I won't mention it again, and I won't bother you and take you away from your four-course lunches."

He felt a tear roll down his cheek. He was so moved he couldn't say a word. He wanted to reach out and hold her, to kiss her and kiss her again. He wanted to tell her how he longed to take her in his arms and tell her what she meant to him. But he knew he could not do those things there in the park.

"Amelia, you have no idea how happy it makes me to hear you say those words. I've loved you from afar for too long, afraid you would reject me, afraid that you might laugh at me. You're right. Usually I am so choked up when I see you that I can hardly talk. I hope the more we are together, the more I can overcome that small problem." His hand reached out and touched her fingers. Then they clasped hands tightly and smiled at each other.

"Amelia, I think I have loved you forever. It may sound silly and trite, but I mean it." He blinked back tears, and she lifted his hand and tenderly kissed it.

Randy cleared his throat before going on. "I understand you have lost your father, so I will be coming to speak to your mother soon about a very important matter."

"May I ask what it is about, Mr. Pemberton?"

"No, Miss Borcherding, you may not ask. That's between your mother and me. When we come to some decision, then you will be properly informed."

"You wouldn't even tell me just a little bit about what it might concern?"

"That's highly irregular. It just isn't done that way, Miss Borcherding. I'm sure you understand that."

She watched him, not sure now if he were teasing her or not. Then she saw the start of a smile at the corner of his mouth but it promptly vanished. She was more confused. What did he mean? Would he be talking to her mother about marriage? What else would he want to talk to her about?

He began speaking of other things then, about the business, the terrible fire, how they were working hard on rebuilding. She didn't have a chance to press him about the visit to her mother. But how could it be for any other reason? It had to be about marrying him.

"It's time I was getting back."

"You shall be late today. I'm going to see to it. And then I'll walk in with you and your immediate superior will have a near heart attack when I make an excuse for you. It should be fun."

Amelia smiled, yes, it might be interesting at that. She had never been late before. Perhaps she wouldn't have to worry about working in the accounting department, or anywhere else, for very much longer!

They ate the sandwiches, and the apples, and even the hard candy. Amelia picked up all the wrappers and the apple cores and put them in a city trash basket. Then they walked to the drinking fountain and tried the clear water. All of the other lunchtime eaters had vanished. Randy led her slowly back to the office.

Then she understood. He *wanted* her to get back late. He wanted to show her that he had some authority, to throw his weight around a little. It was the unreasoned brag of a grownup little boy. But what harm could it do?

They walked into accounting a half hour late and Mr. Auten scowled at her, then glanced up and saw Randy Pemberton's smiling face just behind her. Mr. Auten flushed away the scowl and replaced it with surprise and then respect.

"Good afternoon, Mr. Pemberton."

"Yes, hello. Miss Borcherding was working with me on a special problem. Sorry I couldn't tell you that I would be needing her. I trust her coming in now will cause you nor her any great problem?"

"No, Mr. Pemberton, no trouble at all. Miss Borcherding is one of our best work-

431

ers. We're glad she could be of some help to you."

"Fine, I'll remember that." He turned and, without even looking at Amelia again, walked out of accounting.

Amelia almost giggled as she went back to her desk. She was aware that half the others were whispering about her, but she didn't care. Soon, very soon now, her business career just might come to an end!

Thursday night of the next week, on May 18, Randy went into accounting at five minutes before five, spoke to Mr. Auten a moment, and then walked directly to Amelia's desk.

"Miss Borcherding, would you close up your desk and come with me, please?"

"Yes, sir."

Five minutes later, they were in Randy's fancy buggy, moving away from Market Street.

"Now, Miss Borcherding, if you'll tell me how to get to your home, I'll be glad to take you there."

"Mr. Pemberton, did I *invite* you to my home?"

"No, I'm going to see your mother, to ask for your hand in marriage and her blessing. Does that meet with your approval?"

"Oh, my, yes, Mr. Pemberton. Yes, indeed,

it does!"

"Have you mentioned the possibility to your good mother?"

"Indeed I have not, Mr. Pemberton."

"You had your doubts, then, Miss Borcherding?"

"I never count my chicks until they peck through the shell."

"Yes, a good rule. Any number of events might transpire, faulting no one, of course. Yet such a match might not happen."

"This one will," Amelia said sliding closer to him on the buggy seat. "For we both want it. What can possibly stand in our way?"

"Puny man is no match for destiny, dear child. Destiny wields the scythe with the grim reaper only his chore boy."

The Borcherdings lived in half of a house rented from the owner, on Fairway Street. The house was not much larger than the others on the block, and it was the kind of neighborhood where the extra money would be helpful. They parked in front and went in the side door.

"Mama, I'm home," Amelia called out, after closing the door. A small woman with gray hair tied in a bun at the back of her head came in from the other room.

"We have company, Mama. This is Mr.

Randy Pemberton. Mr. Pemberton, this is my mother, Ruth Borcherding."

She looked at him carefully. "Have you come calling before, young man?"

"No, ma'am."

"Just what are your intentions toward my daughter."

"That's what I'd like to talk to you about."

Her face was serene, small glasses perched on her nose and she looked at Randy now by lifting her head to see through them.

"Well, you're big enough to keep her in line. Let's talk."

Mrs. Borcherding sat in a rocker and waved the others toward a well worn couch nearby which had a blanket draped over it.

Randy looked at Amelia, who shook her head.

"No, sir. I'm not leaving. This is about me, about us and I'm staying."

Randy laughed gently and smiled at her. Then he turned to Mrs. Borcherding.

"You have a remarkable daughter here, Mrs. Borcherding. I've been watching Amelia for five years now, and at last I've decided it's time that I marry her."

"You got any money, son?"

Amelia giggled and turned away, embarrassed.

"Yes. I'm a vice-president and will one

day be on the board of directors of the Pacific Steamship and Trading Company."

"That's the great big company? The one that lost the Pemberton Mercantile down town? Looks like you lost all your money."

"No, ma'am. The fire loss was about a million dollars. The corporation is valued at slightly more than forty-five million dollars. One quarter of that is rightfully mine."

"Then you're telling me you're rich?"

"I will be some day. Right now, I have all the money I want, or need."

Mrs. Borcherding looked at Amelia. "Is all this he's telling me true? He could make it all up."

"It's true, Mother. I have been watching this young man around the company for five years, now. And he *is* a vice-president and the son of the founder of the company."

The old woman shrugged. "Do you like him, daughter?"

"Yes, very much."

Randy looked up quickly and their eyes met, and that's when she knew it would be all right.

"And do you want him, want him in your house, in your bed?"

"Yes, Mother, very much."

The older woman stood, went to a cupboard and brought back a small bottle and three glasses. She poured two fingers of apricot brandy in each glass and passed them around.

"Then let's get on with it. You ready to set a date?"

Randy was on his feet, smiling. He looked at Amelia and realized that he'd never been more excited, more delighted about anything in his life.

"Mrs. Borcherding, there is one small point I'd like to make. I'd like this to be a secret marriage for the first four months. We would be married quietly and legally by a judge. Then later this summer we will have the formal announcements and I'm sure my mother will insist on a huge ceremony and celebration and a church wedding. But I've waited five years to make Amelia my wife. I'd like to marry her next week."

Her mother looked at Amelia. "You know about this?"

"No, Mama. But it's all right with me. We will be married and then later we'll be married again. It doesn't matter to me, I just want to be sure to get married to Mr. Pemberton."

"I don't like it. Seems sneaky, underhanded." She held up her apricot brandy and drank it. "But it's you getting married, not me, girl. So do it any way you want."

An hour later, and after three more toasts with the brandy, Randy went to the door with Amelia.

"Are you happy?" he asked her.

"Oh, yes, so very happy, and now, impatient."

"It won't be much longer. Could I ask my bride for a kiss?"

She nodded and waited for him to lean down, for his lips to touch hers. She didn't respond at first, then she pressed forward gently so he would feel it and then leaned away, a soft glow was spreading through her with a flush of excitement and satisfaction when she realized that she was engaged to be married the very next week. Friday afternoon, she would become a bride. It was almost more than she could bear. She put her arms around Randy and hugged him. When their lips parted, she still held him. "Randy."

He leaned down. "Mr. Pemberton, I am going to be the best wife any man ever had."

He kissed her once more, tenderly, and went out the door.

A week later, on May 25, Randy had made all the arrangements including the legal ones and had certain items "delayed" for a few months so public notice of the marriage would not be made. Then, in the private chambers of Hamilton S. Rassmussen of the superior court, he and Amelia were married. Only Mrs. Borcherding and a court witness were there to make it legal, and the judge signed the papers and assured Randy he would hold everything for four months before he put them on file. Randy was sure the judge thought there was some devious plot involved but he didn't have the nerve to ask a Pemberton.

Randy bent to kiss Amelia as the judge watched. Then they hurried out a side door and into the buggy. Randy had considered seriously where to spend their wedding night. He was almost set on using a hotel, but at last decided on his townhouse. He gave all but two of the servants the weekend off. Now he drove straight to the house, not as large or luxurious as his father's, but adequate, with its sixteen rooms. It faced the bay and had a fine view. He put the buggy away himself, then carried Amelia to the rear entrance and over the threshold.

She wore a simple white dress and a cap and veil, and now she smiled up at him, her arms around his neck.

"I haven't understood why it has to be kept a secret, darling Randy, but if you say so, then that's the way it shall be. After the weekend, I'll go back to my mother's house.

I shall give notice at work, be there for two more weeks, and then I shall be home, waiting for you."

She let him put her down and she turned excitedly. "Now, show me around your grand house! We will live here by the end of the summer, you said. That will be marvelous. I'm so excited that I can hardly wait to move in."

He led her through the house and the last place he showed her was the bedroom. The bed was a huge four-poster with giant carved posts. The mattress was a soft goosedown featherbed that was a delight to sleep on.

When Amelia turned to leave he put his arms around her.

"Let's stay here a while," he said, and she smiled in understanding and reached up to be kissed.

They undressed with their backs to each other, and not once did Amelia peek. She kept her undergarments on and slid into the bed covering herself to her chin.

Randy took his time, letting her watch if she wished. He stripped naked and turned toward her. She had been watching and when she saw him turn, she smiled at him in frankness.

"You are beautiful," she said, tears coming to her eyes. "Just, simply beautiful!"

He slid into bed and put his arms around her and kissed away her tears.

"Darling Amelia, you never have to cry again. I am here to take care of you, to protect you, to love you. I'll always be here."

She relaxed and stopped crying and shivering, pressed against him and soon everything was fine, and she welcomed his closeness, his caresses. It all seemed so right; so natural, and when he moved over her and entered her, it was not painful or terrible. It was the most wonderful feeling in the world, as if she had been waiting for this moment for as long as she could remember.

When she knew she was going to be married, she went to the library and read everything she could find about marriage, parenthood and pregnancy, including the restricted books. She forgot now what it said about pregnancy, but it was something about there being an ideal time for conception. She wished she could remember it. Somehow she felt she must be near her best time. Wouldn't that be marvelous if she could become pregnant on her wedding night!

CHAPTER TWENTY:
WHAT A WOMAN'S FOR

The weeks sped by. There was still a goodly number of engagements for the "speaker's service" the suffrage association had set up. Two women handled it now, making dates, keeping track, assigning different women in place of Susan when she was booked, and generally making the whole thing work like a well oiled watch.

Despite more printing bills and expenses, the association now had almost two thousand dollars in its treasury. The money came from speaker fees, new members and donations.

Sue looked at the membership total and sat down suddenly where she was visiting in Martha's parlor.

"Have you seen the totals lately, Martha? We now have over four hundred and fifty members. I'm amazed!"

"Just shows what a good speaker can do for a cause," Martha said.

Sue shook her head vigorously. "No, not true, Martha. We had struggled for over a year here in town and we still had only seven members. Then you joined. It was your push, your organization and your getting us those spots before the city board that did it. Showmanship and organization."

"How are the branch chapters doing?" Martha asked. "What about the new one in Sacramento?"

"It's taking off like a newly planted weed," Sue said. "I just hope this boom continues."

"It will. Now what we need is to plan our big rally. You said you received a letter from Susan B. Anthony and she won't be able to get to the West Coast at any time this summer. So we have to forget about using her. You will be our star speaker, and we'll try to get Governor Irwin. It can't hurt him any way to say a few words. I should be able to talk him into it."

"The governor? You know him? You continually amaze me, Martha. I've made a list of some of the committees I think we need."

"Let's try for Carpenter's Hall for the meeting," Martha said. "It isn't too busy and I think we can get it for a nominal fee. I know the wife of the man who runs it and we should be able to get a lower price to rent it."

Susan watched Martha. She was totally captivated by the woman, by her business sense, by her efficiency, by her beauty and the total seductive power of her figure. But Sue knew that it could never be. Martha was too male-oriented ever to think about anything else. Sue shook her head to clear out such maverick thoughts and plunged ahead.

"Martha, I'll want you as general chairman, of course. And I hope you can enthuse as many of your society friends as possible. Maybe make some of them honorary co-chairmen. This would give us good coverage in the society section of the paper. How many people will that hall hold?"

"Just over five thousand. It has a small stage at one end, more of a platform, but the acoustics are good and your voice will carry to the last row."

"Good. I'll work up some kind of a twist, some kind of an attention-getter. I don't know what it will be, but we'll want to enthuse these women. One thing we will need is a huge membership committee to sign up every woman in the room."

"And no men allowed, except the governor and policemen. I'll get in touch with Governor Irwin today if he's still in town. I don't see why we should have any trouble getting him to come. Even though Bill Irwin is a Democrat, my father has been a good political friend of his, and this will be a simple political debt to pay back."

They talked another hour, laying out procedures and plans, and set up another meeting for the next afternoon when Sue would bring the top committee chairmen she had picked.

As she was getting ready to go, Martha frowned at Sue.

"Pardon me for asking this, Sue, but how do you get along? You don't work. You aren't married. Do you have an independent income?"

Sue hesitated. "No, not actually. I have a small pension my father left me, a monthly payment. The house is free and clear, so it doesn't take much to keep me going."

"Thank you, Sue. I only wondered. I hope you don't think I'm being too inquisitive."

"Not at all. We'll all be here tomorrow about two."

As Sue walked down the sidewalk to the street, Martha made up her mind. She should be in better circumstances. Martha would establish a trust fund in the name of the association, and a thousand dollars would be designated to be paid yearly in ninety-dollar-a-month installments to the director of the association. By putting five thousand dollars in the bank, it would earn interest and should pay about six years. She would go down and set it up at the bank that afternoon. Then, at the next meeting, Martha would have Sue named as director of the association as well as president.

The next morning, Martha made contact with Governor Irwin who was still at the Belmont Hotel, and won his pledge to speak at the rally. They talked about dates and finally established June 18, which was the only time the governor had available until sometime in August. That left them less than two weeks to get ready, but it was what they had to do.

Martha hosted the meeting that afternoon and they made the detailed plans, mailed letters of invitation to all branches and chapters and urged even those out of town in Sacramento and Los Angeles to form caravans and come to the meeting to show their solidarity.

Each member of the group in San Francisco would pledge to bring ten women with her and to invite a hundred more. They would work the whole city, with block chairmen, and try to get the hall overflowing with women.

Martha set it up along the lines of a political campaign, and by the end of the first week, they had over five hundred block chairmen who would come and guarantee to get everyone on their block interested.

Martha did some quick calculations and knew the hall would not hold all 5,000 but she wanted it to be stuffed so full that women flowed into the lobby and then into the street outside. What a story that would make for the newspapers. It would give women some real political power, some punch!

She told Allen all about it. He smiled, nodded, and went back to reading the *Chronicle* and the *Bulletin*.

"Listen to me," Martha scolded. "Don't you care what we're doing?"

Allen put down the paper and looked at her with a touch of surprise. "Of course, I care what you're doing. I think it is long overdue, but you indicated early that there was no place for any men in your movement. So I'm helping you by not hindering you. I'm not saying you can't give some trust fund five thousand dollars. I'm helping by standing aside and saying that you have the right as a person to activate this project you feel so strongly about."

Martha sat beside him, kissed his cheek and closed her eyes.

"I'm sorry, darling. I didn't mean to snap at you that way. I'm just working so hard trying to make this a success."

"It happens on June eighteenth. That's a Monday night. How did you pick that day?"

"Governor Irwin will be in town that day and it was the only open evening he had. We wanted him before the end of the summer."

Allen caught her hand. "If there is anything I can do behind the scenes and with a little influence, just tell me."

"I'll do that, kind, good husband," she said, then kissed him.

The next week was a whirlwind — attending teas, urging more participation in the rally. They got some newspaper space but not much. She answered a million questions, stood up to a woman's irate husband and generally exhausted herself.

Sunday afternoon, she collapsed in a tub of bubbles and hot water and soaked for an hour. She had done everything that she could. From here on, it was up to the block captains and the out-of-towners.

Martha sat in her bedroom in a wrapper, going over the whole thing. It was set as well as it could be. She could not visit each branch captain and urge her to bring out her people. They had a chain of command.

Sue told ten women what she wanted, and they each told ten more, and each of them told their specified ten more. That brought their coverage up to 1,000 persons, and they could contact each one of them in two days. The system worked well.

Sunday night, Martha lay back on her soft feather bed and tried to relax. She couldn't, and she knew that she probably would sleep very little until it was all over Monday night.

As she lay there Martha wondered how Penny was getting along. She hadn't seen her in more than a month. Her mother said Penny had seemed to settle down a little. She was taking more interest in her work at the hospital, and a young doctor there had started calling on Sunday afternoons.

Martha remembered her own teen years. It had been either total glory or tragedy with absolutely nothing in between. She knew that girls hadn't changed, and neither had boys. But Penny was in a perfect position: young, pretty, smart and with wealthy parents who could support her until she could find exactly the right rich young man to marry. And Martha was sure that Penny would do very well in life. She was a little impulsive now, but all the Pembertons were. Yes, Penny would do just fine.

Martha was right about Sunday night. She

dozed only to waken, trying to remember if she had taken care of some detail. She woke Allen four times. Each time, he mumbled something about trying to relax and dropped off to sleep at once. Martha had to work at falling back to sleep.

She was up at five-thirty, helping the cook in the kitchen. There was nothing else to do at that time of morning and she couldn't even close her eyes again. Three times, she laid out clothes she wanted to wear that day, and three times, she changed her mind.

For a while, she stood watching little Hal in his small bed in the nursery. He slept on his stomach, both hands over his head as if he were being held up. He moved, made a small mewing noise and turned over, spilling the light cover to the floor. She put it back, kissed his forehead, and went into the parlor.

The weather would be warm that day. Not even the usual low morning fog was shrouding the hill. She could see the sun breaking over the ridges to the east. Martha sat in the big chair and rocked as she stared out over an awakening San Francisco. From her seat by the window, it was the most beautiful city she had ever seen. So peaceful and she was so comfortable. She slept.

Allen woke her when he walked into the

parlor two hours later, not knowing where she was. She jumped, rubbing her eyes and laughed at his surprised expression.

"I couldn't sleep, so I was walking around."

"Go back to bed and take another nap," he said. "You'll need it before this day is over." He was ready to go to the office.

"I might try that nap idea, right after breakfast."

She had fresh strawberries, cream and sugar and two slices of toast. Then she did go back to bed and slept until noon.

That evening Martha was at Carpenter's Hall at seven. The program did not start until eight, but already women were entering the big chamber to be sure of a good seat. She saw a dozen buggies with banners on them parked along one street. The banners said the rigs were from the Sacramento Suffrage Association.

Martha hurried inside and found Sue pacing the floor.

"I just know we won't fill the hall. I can just feel it. The newspaper people will be here and we'll look ridiculous."

Martha turned Sue around and found the manager's office. There, they sat down, and Martha poured Sue a cup of coffee.

"Sue, it is going to be fantastic. I know. I

can just feel it. All you have to do is go out there and give your ten-minute talk — or fifteen minutes, knowing you — and then introduce the governor. You do remember his name, don't you?"

"I think so. At least I will when the spotlight hits me. We will turn down the house lights when the speakers are on, won't we? Oh, Martha!"

She slumped against Martha in a pretended faint that could have been the real thing as far as Martha was concerned. She caught Sue and held her.

Sue loved it, then blinked open one eye.

"Think I'll make it, doctor?"

Martha tilted her straight and let her go.

"You'll make it. You're an old trouper. This is about the three thousand eight hundred and seventy-sixth speech you've given in the past month, so relax."

Martha went to a special room at the side of the building where Governor Irwin was holding court. A man at the door almost wouldn't let her in. She told him who she was, but that didn't mean a thing.

"Governor Irwin, who is this idiot on the door?" Martha screamed.

It brought a gasp from the man holding the door. She shoved it open and walked past him.

Governor Bill Irwin stood in the middle of the room, but had turned at the shout and laughed when he saw Martha.

"Martha, Martha, I see you're still surprising people. That idiot at the door is my son, Charles. Charles, meet Martha Pemberton Cornelius, one of the brightest young women I've ever known."

Martha ignored the offered hand and nodded at the young man. She turned back to the governor.

"Mr. Irwin, you realize that none of these men will be permitted in the auditorium, don't you?"

"I'd heard that rumor."

"We can't allow you in there unprotected, governor," said a large man standing beside him.

"Protection from these mere, pitiable, non-voting women?" Martha asked. "You think we might strangle him or rape him?"

That brought a laugh, with the governor leading it. "Martha, how about two men just below the speaker's podium. We can keep them out of sight."

"Governor, I told you no men, no retinue, and it has to stand. If you'd rather disappoint five thousand women who are politically active and control their husband's ballots . . ."

"Martha, be reasonable. Just two men."

"All right, two. They can be at the doors on either side of the platform, but out of sight."

"I think that will be all right, Leon. Martha, we'll do it your way. This is your night. I'll have the rest of the men here go out the side door when they leave so they won't cause a stir in the lobby, all right?"

"Thank you, Governor Irwin, I'll be in to give you a five-minute call before we're ready for you to go on."

Martha let the governor kiss her hand. He smiled, asking to be remembered to her father, and then she was back in the lobby, watching the women arrive. Most of them had walked or come by buggy and carriage. She saw several women she knew from her mother's circle of friends. And then, of all things, her mother came into the lobby. She looked a little lost and out of place without Harold there to guide her. Martha ran up, caught her hand and hugged her, then led her to the best seat in the house, reserved for special guests.

"Martha, dear, I do hope you know what you're doing here."

"Yes, we do, Mama. It's the right thing."

"Well, I don't see what's wrong with things just the way they are. I'm certainly contented this way."

Martha kissed her mother's cheek. "Yes, Mama, I know. Millions of women are. But millions more of us want something besides the three B's — babies, bonnets and bathtubs. I'll see you when it's over. Did someone drive you here?" Her mother nodded, looking around now, and Martha went back to the lobby.

The house was filling slowly. It was almost a quarter past seven, and Martha had a sinking feeling.

Back in the lobby, more women poured in. The evening was mild and it had been a sunny day, so there was no bad weather to keep the women home.

By a quarter to eight, almost every seat in the house was filled. It would be a sellout. Martha found two women from her chapter and posted them at the doors to stop admitting people when the seats were all filled. The doors and windows would be left open so those outside would be able to hear.

Her plan worked and soon every seat was filled and women were standing in the packed lobby and more on the steps and around the windows on the side.

Promptly at eight, Sue Stone walked to the speaker's platform and received a standing ovation from the 5,000 women in the big hall. It took five minutes to calm the crowd, and Sue knew that the meeting was a success already.

Martha stood near the side doors, just off the platform, and watched. It was wonderful. The suffrage movement was now launched on firm ground, with massive support. The fight would be long and hard, they would be lucky if they got any new laws passed, or the constitutional amendment that Susan B. Anthony was talking about, for another twenty-five years. But it would come eventually, and part of the reason was this meeting tonight!

Martha felt the first thrill of success as she listened to Sue quieting the throng. It was going to go well.

"My good friends and future women voters of California," she began.

The hall exploded in spontaneous applause again. She quieted them. "We have gathered here tonight to hear our honorable Governor William Irwin. But before he speaks, it's my privilege to position you a little on just where the fight for women's suffrage is today, how it is moving and how you can help.

"First, the mother of our movement, Susan B. Anthony, sends us her warmest regards and is sorry that she can't be here with us tonight. She is leading a march in Washington, in our nation's capitol, and planting the seeds there that someday should grow into a huge suffrage tree that will cover all of us.

"We are only starting here in California. We are building a statewide organization. We need your support. First we are approaching individual cities — coaxing, threatening, cajoling — urging them to pass city or county suffrage laws that apply to elections in those jurisdictions. Our first long-range goal is a California state law such as those now in effect in the territories of Wyoming and Utah. Sooner or later, there will be a constitutional amendment proposed by the Congress of these United States, and then we will really have something to fight for."

Again cheers and clapping thundered through the big hall.

Martha listened carefully, then went and rapped on the governor's open door. He came to it himself.

"I think you better come up now, Governor, she's almost finished."

They went to the edge of the area masked by short wings of the platform and listened.

"I heard everything she's said," the governor told Martha. "My door was open and her voice carries very well."

"Governor Irwin, I know you probably can't endorse our cause, but I hope you will give us some 'down the road' encouragement. Sooner or later, women are going to get the vote, so you might as well help us along a little now. As a professional politician, you must know how the times are changing, how women are moving into business, finance, becoming doctors, lawyers."

Governor Irwin smiled. "Martha, if I can't walk this tightrope and say something you women want to hear without getting all the men voters mad at me, then I really don't deserve to be your governor."

A moment later, Sue wound up her talk, and introduced the main speaker. A few women clapped. Then the applause died until Sue led it and the governor felt properly welcomed.

Martha was disappointed. The governor talked for almost a half hour and said very little. He touched vaguely on women's rights, their right to strike out into education and law and into medicine, but he never once mentioned voting. When he was done, the applause was sparse.

Sue went back on the stage and began selling the idea of the Suffrage Association and memberships, and sent assigned women into the audience with pads and papers and membership cards to sign up the women. They also took pledges from women who would volunteer to head up new chapters in outlying areas of the state and others who could travel and help establish more branches.

The business session lasted for almost an hour. Before it was over, Sue rallied the women with a chant that almost brought the rafters to swaying.

"We're voters but they won't let us vote! We're voters but they won't let us vote! We're voters but they won't let us vote!"

Then the meeting was over. A thousand women tried to crowd down front to shake Sue's hand. Others shouted encouragement to her and waved their new membership cards. A half hour after the meeting ended, Martha pushed her way through the crowd to Sue and began leading her away.

"Please, let us through. Miss Stone is very tired. She must go now and get some rest. Yes, we thank you for your support. Please help us all you can."

It took Martha fifteen minutes to get Sue to a side door and then to Sue's buggy. Women were still clustered around the entrance, hoping Sue would come out that way. Martha did not know what happened to the governor.

Sue sat in her buggy and sighed.

"Martha, could you drive me home? I don't know if I could get this rig there or not."

Martha took the reins and flicked them against the horse's back, but it sensed an unfamiliar hand on the leathers and didn't budge. Sue spoke quietly to the animal and it moved forward. Martha drove slowly down the street, careful not to miss the turns to Sue's house. She was two blocks away from the right street when another buggy came up quickly behind them, and a second one cut in front of Sue's horse and stopped, blocking their way. They were wedged in between the two rigs, unable to move.

Panic shot through Martha, but she kept a firm grip on the reins. She couldn't even scream when two men appeared at each side of the buggy. All four men wore head masks.

"So this is the little bitch who wants to vote?" one voice asked.

"Well, show her how we vote," another voce said. He caught Sue's wrist and pulled her toward the side of the buggy. Martha grabbed the buggy whip and smashed it across the man's masked face. A hand behind Martha closed around her body and gripped one breast, holding her immobile.

"This one, too?" a gruff voice in her ear, asked.

"Hell, why not, bring her, too. She can watch. But you know who she is, don't you? Don't muss with her ass or it's our neck in a noose. This little bitch — she's the one we're really gonna get."

The next few moments were a madhouse of flying arms and legs as both women silently fought the men. At last two men grabbed each of them, and carried them into the separate buggies.

Martha was forced into a buggy and then held on the seat by one man as the other drove.

She had no idea how long they drove or where they were. They stopped in an alley. With one hand over her mouth, the men led Martha into a dark, empty house. One room had been fixed with black curtains over the windows, a mattress on the floor and two coal oil lamps burning. Martha watched as Sue was carried in. She was still struggling, had lost her hat, her jacket was off and one sleeve of her blouse torn away. They pushed her down on the mattress and she sat up.

"You bastards!" she spat at them. "If one of you so much as touches me again, I'll hunt you down and have you castrated. You goddamned scum, keep your hands off me!"

"My, my, she does talk foul," one of the masked men said. He was the tallest, had a hood over his head and now dropped down and mocked Sue.

"Miss Stone, you're always talking about women's rights. Well we figure it's about time you know what a real woman is for. A female's job is to lay on her back with her legs spread apart and take all a man can give her. That's what she's for. Before tonight's over, you're going to know what you've been missing all these years. Then we'll see how your campaign goes."

As he talked, two men slipped up behind Sue, grabbed her arms and pulled her flat on her back. The man speaking jumped forward and pinned her legs and another man came into the scene and began taking off Sue's clothes. All the men wore full head masks and dark clothing. Martha saw now it would be almost impossible to identify any of them.

Martha turned away. Someone still held her, and he was now tying her to a chair. She didn't even remember she had been put in a chair. This whole thing was so ugly, so terrible. Sue kept screaming at them until they gagged her with a handkerchief.

Then they held her and ripped off the last of her underclothes. Martha turned her head. They couldn't make her watch. She began crying softly, the sobs came but the sound couldn't drown out the low moaning wails from behind the handkerchief.

One after another, the men opened their pants and lowered themselves over her, and Susan's desperate shrieks and screams penetrated right through the cloth gag.

When the fifth man lifted away from her, there was no one holding Sue. She lay on the mattress, turning her head from one side to the other, sobbing through the gag. Her hands and feet, now free, remained where they had been pinned as if she were still held spread-eagled by the rapists.

The last man slid out the doorway without a word and the room was quiet except for Susan's sobbing. Martha looked down and realized that Sue did not understand that the men were gone. Martha knew she had to get free, to untie the ropes. She found the knots and undid them as fast as she could. When she was free of them, she stood, picked up what was left of Sue's clothes and went to the mattress. Kneeling beside Sue, Martha began to talk softly, low as she would to her baby.

"Sue, it's all right now. They're gone. All

of them are gone. We're alone, Sue, just you and I. Sue! I'm going to untie the gag from your mouth. Do you understand, Sue? It's me, Martha. I'm going to help you. Sue, now just a minute and the cloth gag will come out of your mouth."

Martha took the cloth away, and Sue's eyes came open for the first time and she saw Martha. She started to swing her fist at the form over her, then stopped and let a new burst of tears stream down her face. Sue whimpered and sat up, leaning against Martha who put her arms around the woman and rocked her back and forth like a sick child.

"It's all right, Sue. They've gone. They can't hurt you any more. Let's get your clothes on. Here, help me."

It took Martha a half hour to get her dressed. Sue wouldn't say a word. She sat rigid, hardly moving, until Martha convinced her that it would be all right.

Once she had Sue dressed, Martha didn't have the slightest idea what they could do. Martha had lost her purse somewhere in the struggle, and Sue did not have hers. They had no money. It must be nearly midnight, and she didn't know where they were. Martha left Sue sitting on the mattress and, using one of the lamps, found the back door of the house. Outside there was moonlight shining. To Martha's complete surprise, Sue's horse and buggy were tied close to the back door. The men had relented and shown a modicum of pity after being so brutal to her.

Martha went back and persuaded Sue to stand, then walked her slowly to the buggy. It was a chore getting the small woman up to the high seat, but once that was done, Sue regained a little of her composure and sat upright, gripping the sides of the rig.

Martha realized there was only one place she could go, directly to her own home. She drove down the alley to the street and headed in one direction, hoping she would recognize something. After two blocks, she saw that they were still generally in Sue's neighborhood. She found a cross street she knew, followed it, and a few blocks farther on, recognized where she was.

When they arrived at the back door of Martha's hilltop mansion, Arturo came out quickly with a lamp and lighted their way to the side door. He then put the horse and rig away.

Allen met them at the door.

"Martha, where have you been?" He stopped. "Whatever has happened?"

She shook her head at his questions and

helped Sue toward the stairs and into the first guest room on the second floor. Martha laid Sue on the big bed, pulled off her shoes and then spread a light quilt over her. She wiped Sue's brow with a wet cloth and, a moment later, the little suffragette dropped off to sleep.

Out in the hall, Allen paced the varnished floor, a million catastrophes bombarding his mind.

Martha slipped out of the room, motioned Allen to their bedroom and sat down, now totally exhausted herself. She told Allen about it from her first talk with the governor. When she was done, she realized she had been pacing the length of the bedroom.

"Now, Allen, what on earth shall we do? If we go to the police and swear out a rape complaint, it would open Sue to scandalous publicity. Even with my testimony, it could be considered a publicity stunt, to get more newspaper space for the Suffrage Association. But those men must be punished."

"There was no way to identify them?"

"None, absolutely none. We never saw their faces."

Martha sat down, and leaned her head on Allen's shoulder.

"Allen, I don't think we should file any charges. Instead, I'm going to see if Johnnie

Laveau would like to try a little detective work. If he finds out who the men are, he can use some of his famous magic on the culprits, and they'll wish that they had never been born!"

CHAPTER TWENTY-ONE:
END OF A REIGN

As tired as Martha was, and as emotionally drained, she got very little sleep that night after the suffrage rally. Five times she was up when Sue cried out in the darkness. Martha went to her and talked to her as she would a small child, calming her fears, re-assuring her.

Martha didn't believe that Sue ever came fully awake during her siege of terror. She wasn't sure if Sue had ever come out of the daze she had been in after the rape.

As soon as it was light, Martha sent one of the drivers to Dr. Luther Stewart's home with a note. The doctor came right away to see Sue.

The moment Martha entered the guest room, a little after seven, Sue was awake. Her eyes were wild for just a moment, then they settled and she half-smiled at Martha.

"Did that really happen last night, after we left the hall? Or was it just a bad dream?

It was a dream, wasn't it, Martha?"

Martha came to the bed and smoothed back Sue's hair. "Some things just happen, Sue, that we can't control. It wasn't a dream, it was all real, but what we have to do now is try to forget it, not to think about it, and go on, move forward. Do you understand what I mean?"

Sue looked at her with wide eyes that reflected her remembered terror. This time, it took longer for Sue to beat it down, for her eyes to focus on Martha, and then she nodded.

"Yes, Martha, I think I understand, and I'll try hard. Are they all gone? Where am I?"

"You're at my house, Sue, in a guest room. We came here last night. I have our doctor here to see you. He's Dr. Stewart, and he's been looking after me since I was a little girl. I want him to examine you and talk with you, would you like that?"

"I don't need a doctor."

"Well, let's just talk with him. We won't say anything about last night, just that you've had a terrible shock and are feeling sickly."

For a moment, Sue's eyes started to panic again, then they settled.

"Yes, yes, that's all right. But I won't let

him examine me, you know, down below."

"That's fine, dear. I'll bring him in."

By noon, Sue was almost back to her old bouncy self. The doctor had taken her pulse, looked in her throat, listened to her heart and suggested she have a spring tonic. He said she was perfectly healthy, but that she should get more outdoor exercise.

Sue and Martha had lunch, with Sue still in a robe. They ate from trays in the guest room. The salad and melon slices pleased Sue, who played the sick little girl staying home from school. After lunch, she looked at some clothes Martha loaned her. The dress was too large, but it would do until she got home. She slid out of the wrapper and stood there in her chemise looking at the dress. She dropped it and walked to where Martha sat.

"Martha, dear Martha, I don't know how I can ever thank you. If you hadn't been there last night, I probably would still be on that mattress, half out of my head, or I'd have run naked into the street. I don't even like to think about it!"

Martha stood and kissed Sue's cheek. "It's all right now, Sue. It's all over. And you're going to go on, stronger than ever. But I don't think we should report this to the police. What could we prove? It could look like a publicity stunt. I have a good friend working to find out who the men are, and when we find out, we will punish them."

Sue's arms went around Martha and she reached up and kissed her hard on the mouth. Then Sue's hand fell to Martha's breasts and she fondled them.

At Martha's look of astonishment, Sue broke off the kiss and clung to Martha. "Oh, Martha, darling, I'd much rather have you making love to me. Those men were so brutal. Please, make love to me, Martha!"

Gently Martha loosened Sue's arms from around her and stepped back. She had never been so shocked in her life. She stepped back another two feet.

"Sue, when you're dressed, I'll see that your buggy is ready." Martha turned and fled. She had no idea that Sue . . . The woman had never given a hint that she was that way before, or else Martha had been too blind to see or understand it. To come right out and ask . . .

Martha hurried to the kitchen and told the cook to have the driver hitch up Miss Stone's buggy. Then Martha went to the library and stood looking at the books. She was offended, shocked, disappointed. Was this *why* Susan Stone was such a good suffragette? Were the leaders all that way? What about Susan B. Anthony? Was she married, a mother, or single, and did she have leanings like Susan Stone did? Martha was confused.

But one thing was clear. She was through working with Susan in the suffrage movement. It was off to a good start now and should continue with its own momentum. Martha was sure that the rest of the committee leaders were not that way. Most of them were married and mothers.

Martha turned and walked back to the guest room. Sue sat on the bed, dressed and crying.

"Sue, your buggy is ready. I'll be turning over the treasurer's books of the association to you. I'm sure your group will do very well from here on."

Tortured eyes came up pleading with her. "Martha, if it was what I did and said . . . I mean I can't help how I feel about you. I'll be careful. I won't ever touch you again. Please don't quit us. We need you."

"I'm sure you'll do very well, Miss Stone. Now, if you'll follow me, I'll show you where your buggy is." Martha turned and, without looking back, left the room and walked down the stairway to the side door, where the buggy was hitched and the horse waiting.

Martha let Sue walk past her, said good-bye in a neutral voice, and hurried back into the house. She watched Sue get into the buggy and drive away. When she was certain the buggy was gone, she gave a big sigh and went to her room and collapsed on the bed. She was suddenly so sleepy that she knew she would drop off standing up if she didn't lie down. And by sleeping, she wouldn't have to remember Sue's hands and think about what she said and did. A moment later, she was sound asleep.

Less than a mile away, on that same June day, Harold Pemberton paced his office. He had been talking with Randy about the retail division when he had an urgent visit from Kettering Jamison who headed the legal staff on corporate matters. They had talked privately for ten minutes, then Jamison left. Randy went back inside to find his father furious.

"Now, Jamison! He was the last person I ever imagined might think about divorce. I've never had anything like this happen in the thirty years I've been in this business. It's outlandish! Do you know, Randy, that there have been eight of my top corporate executives or vice-presidents considering a divorce because of wandering wives? Eight of them!"

Randy sipped at a glass of port wine his father had poured for him earlier. He chuckled inwardly at the pain his pranks had caused his father. This was the first real benefit he had seen from his series of seductions.

"Father, perhaps it's time you considered softening your policy about divorce."

"No! Absolutely not! I'm against it, and no one shall work for me, especially in a leadership position, who can't even maintain his own marriage. Absolutely not! That's one of the guiding principles of the whole Pemberton system."

"It was only a suggestion, Father. Does that mean you'll be firing half of your corporate executive staff? That doesn't sound like very sound management."

"Of course it wouldn't be. That's why I'm so furious. I'm caught between the fire and the frying pan. Either way, I burn myself. Either way, the company loses. I just can't imagine what the women these days are thinking of. These are females in their forties, some of them in their fifties. Sometimes I think all this women's suffrage and women's rights is going to break down our whole moral structure, ruin the family, and that would be tragic since families are the basic

building blocks of our whole social structure."

"Have we lost any top men so far, Father?"

"Yes, one. Simon Walker. He said his wife
had been unfaithful to him several times in
the past. He'd had a lot of trouble with her
running wild, and this was the final straw.
He told me he was divorcing her this time
no matter what I said. His resignation is ef-
fective at the end of this month. I've been
able to hound the rest of the men and keep
the marriage intact at least temporarily.
Sometimes it seems like the only thing I do
anymore is talk to couples about how to get
along with each other and to stay married."

"The women caused all this mess?"

"In every case, it's the woman stepping
out on her husband. Isn't that bizarre? The
women are playing around. That's un-
natural, almost as if it were planned. But
those damn women! What do they want?
They should know they can get more than
they want right at home from their husbands. Then they go out hunting more, or
get involved and cause me trouble, and the
company pain. Randy, there is simply no
way we can afford to lose those eight men.
We just can't!" He stood and pounded his
desk. "I'll order those men not to divorce
their wives, if I have to. By God, I'll even

give them a bonus to stay together, so I don't have to fire them. A lot of money always helps."

He sat down suddenly, frowning. Harold Pemberton swallowed hard. "Damn those women. I should get them all together and give them a sound tongue-lashing. Really scold them. Remind them that . . ." Harold Pemberton grabbed his chest and cried out in sudden pain. He slumped over his desk, his hand reaching out to Randy for help.

Randy jumped up and ran to the desk.

Harold lifted his head. "Oh, god, it hurts. Chest. Get the doctor, quick." His head flopped forward and rested on his hands on the desk.

Randy ran to the outer office.

"Father's had some kind of an attack! He wants the doctor! Quickly!" Randy was shouting, and Mrs. Tausch dropped her pencil, jumped and ran out of the room and down the steps toward the doctor's office. Dr. Stewart's office was in the building right next door.

Randy hurried back into the other room and looked down at his father. He lay against the chair, gasping for breath, his hands clawing at his chest. A low moaning cry such as Randy had never heard before surged from his father's lips. It was a tortured, hideous sound, half animal, a desperate appeal for help, a scream of anger and frustration that life could treat a human being so badly.

Randy opened his father's jacket and shirt, but still the hands clawed, the face now a mask of pain and fury. His voice rose higher and higher in a screaming crescendo. Then all at once he stiffened, doubled up in his chair, and he gasped. He fell back against the leather, his head rolling to one side, his eyes staring straight, the only sound now a soft wheezing as his last breath gushed from his lungs.

Randy stood, looking down at his father, not wanting to touch him, afraid that he was dead. He did not want to face the thought that this man he had hated so long was now dead. A growing fury built in him as he realized that now there could be no more vengeance. He would be denied the look on the old man's face when he faced ruin, when he knew, *knew* for certain, that Randy had brought down both him and the company. Harold Pemberton would never know about that plan now, and Randy damned him for that final trickery.

But there was something else for Randy to think about. He was the heir, he now controlled this whole damn company and, depending on how the will split up the Pemberton stock, he was a millionaire! The family would retain the stock, he was sure. His mother and Penny would get some and Martha a small share, but the controlling portion must surely be his. He would talk to the legal section just as soon as he could and get a copy of the will.

Randy turned as the doctor rushed into the office. Randy motioned Mrs. Tausch back and closed the door.

The doctor was looking for a heart beat. He pushed his ear hard against Harold's chest and listened. He looked into Harold's eyes, then slowly closed the eyelids.

"Would you describe exactly what happened, Randy," the doctor said.

Randy told him as well as he could what occurred from the first onset until that last terrible death rattle.

Dr. Stewart sighed, and sat down to write some notes on a pad that he took from his bag. "From what you said, Randy, I'd guess that it was his heart. It just gave out. The symptoms all seem to be there, the chest pains, shortness of breath, the terrible pain, clawing at the chest, then the stiffening." He shook his head. "Your father was only fifty-one or fifty-two. It seems early to go with a bad heart." The doctor stood. "I'll take care of the undertaker and such. You'll want to close the business for the rest of the day, I would expect."

"Yes, Dr. Stewart, we will, and thank you. I'll have Mrs. Tausch tell everyone."

He found Mrs. Tausch crying at her small desk. She knew he must be dead and the confirmation brought more tears. He told her to notify all sections to close for the rest of the day, and all day Wednesday, but they would re-open Thursday morning. Back in his own office, Randy couldn't help but be a little angry. He had been so close, the plan so near to completion to blow the company apart. But his father had won again. He always won. This time, however, he had to die to do it. Still, Harold Pemberton had won. Randy kicked the desk leg and went out to get his buggy. Someone had to tell his mother and Martha and Penny, and he was the only one.

The funeral Friday afternoon was attended by some of the most important people in the state, including Governor Irwin and his wife. The casket was left open and hundreds filed past to take one last look at Harold Pemberton. The eulogy was long and carefully spoken by Reverend Engle during the Presbyterian service. Randy never knew there were so many flowers in

San Francisco. The church was banked with them, and hundreds more floral wreaths and arrangements surrounded the open grave.

His mother broke down at the cemetery and he helped her to a chair. Then after the short graveside service, he led her to her carriage. Randy patted her hand and told her not to worry about a thing. He would run the company just the way his father had.

His remark brought no reaction from his mother, because she had not understood what he said. She wanted only to get home and cry herself to sleep and dream of all the years she thought she and Harold would have left together.

The Monday after the funeral, the principal heirs received copies of Harold Pemberton's last will and testament. There were few surprises for Martha or her mother. Penny was pleased that she received one fourth of the entire estate, including one fourth of the voting stock in Pacific Steamship and Trading Company. But she fumed because she would not be permitted to vote the stock until her twenty-first birthday. Until that time, her mother would exercise her voting rights for her.

Each of the four participants received identical one-fourth shares of the estate, which infuriated Randy. There was no question in his mind that he should have fifty-one percent of the stock. A controlling interest should indisputably be his. Now he must convince his mother of any move he wanted to make. She could kill any issue she did not like. Even if both he and Martha wanted something, their mother could block it with her and Penny's fifty percent and a tie vote. He fumed silently, sure that he had to do something to gain legal control of the firm just as quickly as possible.

Martha noted with pride that there was a trust fund of 20,000 dollars established, with payments of 50 dollars a month to go to Maria Consuela Lucinda Valdez, of Todos Santos, Baja California.

On Tuesday, June 26th, 1877, the four heirs met at the Pemberton mansion. Martha had called the meeting and Allen was with her. They assembled in the library, and Randy at once assumed command.

"I know losing Father has been a shock to all of us, but there are urgent matters at the company that simply must be taken care of at once. Many legal matters that can't wait. I'm sure both Martha and Allen can appreciate that. We must quickly designate someone to be the acting president or operating manager of Pacific Steamship and Trading. We simply must have an operating head of the corporation until the board of directors names a new permanent chairman of the board and president, both positions that Father held."

Martha had not said a word yet, but now she spoke. "Randy is absolutely right. There must be a president, and an interim or acting president can serve legally just as well. So I move that we name Randall Pemberton acting president of Pacific Steamship."

Randy looked up, too surprised to speak for a moment. He had known with certainty that Martha would fight him for control of the company. She had never liked him and that Mexican trip had convinced her she was right. And it had established his absolute hatred of her. Now she was nominating him to be president!

Martha's mother promptly seconded the motion. Martha had spent two hours that afternoon convincing her mother that they should put Randy into the temporary position now. They would let him try his wings. And since both of them were thoroughly convinced that he would fail, it would be a simple matter to move him out of the temporary position by replacing him with a permanent president.

Randy beamed when the two women gave him their votes. That was enough. He laughed.

"Well, I wasn't campaigning for the spot. But it looks like Mother's fifty percent of the vote and Martha's twenty-five percent would outvote me even if I voted against myself, which I'm not going to go. It looks like I am then officially elected as interim president of Pacific Steamship and Trading Comapny, Inc."

His mother looked at him sternly. "Randall, now you listen to me. I want you to promise me that you'll continue the business and general principles that Harold has always followed. They were good enough for thirty years. I want you to maintain them."

"Now, Mother, of course, I'll keep the general policies. That's only good business practice. And the whole purpose of a business is to make money. I'll run the firm the way Father would have. Naturally, each man has a little different style, a different way of doing things. So there may be some small changes in procedures and operations. But the main point is that the business will function and it will continue to show a profit."

Martha smiled at him, and Allen nodded sympathetically.

Penny sat beside her mother and glared at Randy the whole time. She had not said a word to anyone since she came into the room. Now she looked at Martha and inclined her head a few inches, but her face remained an icy mask of aloofness.

"Well, then, I guess that ends the meeting. I better get down to the office and light a midnight lamp and start to get things in order. There will be some legal papers for all of you to sign tomorrow to make this action official. Legal will be getting in touch with you." He went to his mother and kissed her on the cheek, waved at the others and left.

When the front door closed behind Randy, Mrs. Pemberton turned to her eldest daughter. "Martha, I just hope to heaven that you know what you're doing."

"I do, Mother, believe me. We talked it over. We want a smooth transition of management. Penny and I talked this afternoon, after you and I did. We all feel that Randy simply is not fit to take over the position as permanent president. So we put him in as interim head to fill the gap while we decide who should run the company. Isn't that what we decided, Penny?"

Penny knew Martha was only drawing her into the conversation to make her feel better. But in spite of her knowing that, she was glad she was asked. She bobbed her head. "Yes, Martha, that's what we decided. Randy is a strange person, and I don't think he should be permanent president. He could blow up the whole firm, bring it to ruin."

Allen had been smoking his pipe and listening. He blew a perfect smoke ring and watched it lift toward the ceiling.

"Martha and I have had some serious talks about who should run the Pemberton firms. We both agree that it should be a Pemberton. Mr. Pemberton used to talk to me about that. Said he liked me but he hoped I never ran the company. He always wanted a Pemberton to be in firm control. So Randy is in there now, and if we think he needs to be replaced, it is my strong suggestion that Martha should take over."

Penny laughed.

Mrs. Pemberton looked at Allen in amazement.

"Yes, Mrs. Pemberton, true. Technically, she isn't a Pemberton by name, but that is easy to change. We go to court and ask that her name be legally changed to Martha Pemberton-Cornelius. It's legal. And she is a Pemberton, and talented and experienced enough to run the firm. Frankly, who else is there? Mr. Pemberton thought he had twenty years to groom Randy or bring along a replacement if Randy didn't work out. His time was cut short, and so are our candidates. I certainly don't know enough about the whole operation of the combined businesses to take over the reins right now. I might be able to learn enough in three or four years, but we are talking about a massive multi-structured corporation, with combined assets of well over forty-five million dollars. That is big business and big trouble if you do the wrong thing.

"None of the five top vice-presidents have a broad enough background to run Pacific Steamship. Each of them is an expert, a specialist in one line, but not on the overall. They simply are not smart enough, experienced enough, or good enough master executives to apply their skills in varying circumstances to make the business prosper. So I think we should be serious about considering Martha as the new and permanent chairman of the board and president of the corporate structure."

Mrs. Pemberton sighed. She did not like business. She wished that it would go away and let her get back to her literary society. She reached for Martha's hand.

"That young man of yours may be right, Martha. I've never told you how I admired and was so proud of your accomplishments with the Mercantile. You have a spunk and a drive that I simply never had. I think you'd make a marvelous president of our firm, and if your name is Pemberton-Cornelius, so much the better. Tomorrow I'll have a legal document drawn up giving you my voting proxy for both my stock and that of Penny's that I vote. That means you'll control seventy-five percent of the stock and the company. Now, if you don't mind I have a fascinating book that I simply must finish reading before my society meeting next week."

Martha touched Penny's arm. "Penny, is that all right with you? Do you want me to vote your stock?"

"No, but there's nothing I can do about that. What I want is money. I want to control my money. And I want to go to Europe right away, next week."

Martha hugged her. "Penny, don't be so anxious. There will be all the money you'll need, or want, and all the trips to Europe you can stand."

Wednesday morning, after the impromptu board of directors' meeting, Martha went down to the corporation headquarters building on Market Street. The first thing she saw when she came in the door was a notice printed in large letters. It announced to one and all that Randall Pemberton was the new interim president of the firm and head operating officer. His jurisdiction began that morning, June 27, 1877. He would expect all officers of the firm and workers at every level to continue to perform their duties as in the past, and to help the company toward even greater successes in the future.

Randy certainly didn't waste any time. She went to the fifth floor, to Allen's office.

"You must have seen the quaint little notice," Allen said.

"Yes."

"He had it read to every employee this morning at the start of the work day, and notices will be sent to every ship and outlying office and company. This lad believes in taking over quickly and letting everyone know it."

"Has anything else surprising happened?"

"Those divorces that your father has been so worried about. Randy talked this morning to each of the eight men involved and gave them a pep talk about the firm. He said their personal lives were of no concern or any proper business of Pacific Steamship, and he didn't care if they were divorced a dozen times or had ten mistresses, as long as it didn't interfere with their work performance and their operating of Pacific Steamship."

"Now that is a change of style. Divorce is not forbidden. Anything else?"

"Just the usual — everyone is going to be fired, and all of Randy's drinking buddies will replace them."

"That sounds normal enough." Just then, Leslie Hanks came in.

"Leslie, this is my wife, Martha. Martha, Les Hanks, our land procurement, buildings and supplies vice-president."

Martha waved. "Hello, Les. We fought a lot when I was with the Mercantile."

Les tried to smile, but it wouldn't break through. "Yes, we did, Mrs. Cornelius. And usually, I lost. I really lost this time. I stopped in to say goodbye. Your brother just fired me. I'm out, through, finished. And I don't have a single idea why he cashiered me."

CHAPTER TWENTY-TWO:
THAT SPARK OF LIFE

When Martha came home just before lunch-time, she found Johnnie Laveau waiting for her. He grinned, flashing his white teeth.

"This mon plenty glad see, Miz Cornelius."

Martha gave him a quick kiss on the cheek and sat down smiling. Johnnie was still as handsome as ever, crafty, amazing and efficient. Since her marriage, Johnnie had been working at the job of his choice, back to sea for over a year. Then he moved to the docks where he could still be around the ships, and have the comfort of shore life.

But when Martha needed him for a special assignment, Johnnie jumped.

"Have you found anything, Johnnie? I know trying to locate five men in a city of this size, with nothing to start with, is extremely hard."

"This mon shor say plenty yes! Johnnie and friends sit in saloon, listen. Johnnie hear much. Was tall man long time here live? Or come from other place?"

Martha thought back to that night of terror. She remembered the tall man who had talked more than any of the others. Now she realized there had been a difference in his speech.

"Johnnie, how could I have forgotten it. He did talk differently — with some kind of an accent — a drawl, a Southern accent. You've been in the South, Johnnie. You know how they talk."

Johnnie's teeth flashed in another grin. "Good, much good! Big tall fella me hear. Much drink all bottle, talk all time. Tonight Johnnie give fella extra bottle. Then Johnnie talk with him in alley."

"Johnnie, remember I don't want you to kill him or anything like that. But I do want the five men to pay a price for what they did to Sue." That's when another face suddenly came through for Martha. The rape had been a hundred times worse for Sue than it would have been for her. Since Sue was a homosexual, she would have a special heightened horror of a man even touching her, let along having intercourse with her. Sue had suffered more than Martha would ever be able to imagine.

"Johnnie, if you could use your magic in

some way, so that every day those men lived they remembered what they did and would suffer a little because of it, then justice would be done."

Johnnie grinned, bowed sharply and ran out of the house.

Martha turned her thoughts back to the company. That first morning, Randy fired his unattractive secretary and brought in a young girl who could barely read and write. But she was bosomy and beautiful. Next he had fired Les and two more key men. Martha and Allen had worried over that for a while, until Allen figured out what could be Randy's reasoning.

"Randy went through a training period of two years, working in almost every department in the company. He did work for those three, as one of the lowest men in their sections. It could be that Randy builds up a hatred for anyone in authority over him. Not a conscious hatred, perhaps, but a festering, insidious growth that, when it has a chance, breaks out. I wouldn't be surprised if he hated your father for the same reason, a rebellion against authority."

"Then he might fire all fifty department heads."

"He might, but he undoubtedly liked some of the men, got along with them. No,

I'd guess he would go after only those few he thought the firm could spare and whom he hated the most."

"Which means that basically my brother is not very well mentally."

"There's a chance he has let some of these angers and hatreds get the best of him. We'll just have to wait and see."

A week later, Martha sat in her bedroom at home, looking over a sheaf of papers that Allen had spread out in front of her.

"He is going too far, Martha. After only a week he has fired six top men. He has demoralized half the firm. We have lost one big shipping contract because Randy didn't like the looks of the man who came to sign the contract. Our ships are tied up at four wharves here in town because of problems Randy has brought down on us for no good reason."

Martha looked at the reports. "It certainly is serious, but do you think it's enough to make him step down?"

"Martha, we don't need any legal reasoning. This isn't a court case. You have the votes, you can become chairman of the board and president just because you want to. As for me, I think these are definitely serious enough charges to topple him."

"What else is he up to, Allen?"

"I've had two reports from people in my department that Randy has met them outside of work, and pumped them for anything about me that he might use to effect a dismissal. He's trying to lay a trap for me so I'll have to resign. Tonight, just as I got into my buggy, two blonde girls — twins, I think — ran out of the shadows and jumped into my buggy with me. One began kissing me and the other opened her dress, exposing her breasts. A moment later, there was a blinding light. When my eyes came back to normal, I saw a photographer trying to fold up his tripod. I pushed the girls away and ran after him, caught him and tore his camera apart, ruining the photographic plate. That's one bit of evidence he won't have."

"Allen, that's just terrible!"

"Well, it wasn't all that bad. One was a good kisser and the other a beauty." Allen laughed and ducked the pillow Martha threw.

"Martha, I think it's definitely time you move in as president and chairman of the board. Let's do it just as soon as possible, before he bankrupts the whole company."

"How do we do it?"

"Bring signed proxies with you for your mother's votes and we go to the office and call an official board of directors' meeting. Randy won't be invited. We have you nominated to be permanent president and chairman of the board and then adjourn the meeting. You vote your seventy-five percent of the stock and it's done. The legal department then draws up minutes of the meeting, and it's over except for the paper work."

"Should we do it tomorrow morning? Oh, no, tomorrow is a holiday, July fourth. We can do it Friday. Will you come with me?"

"Yes, of course. Now don't start getting cold feet. This is a big job, but you know enough about the firm and how it works in all its parts. You can do it. I'll be around to give you what help I can. Now, we both better get to sleep."

They settled down in the bed and turned out the lamp. A few minutes later, his hand moved over and touched her leg.

"Hey, is it too late?" he asked.

She rolled toward him, smiling. "Darling, it's never too late."

Friday morning, everything went according to plan. The legal maneuvering was done, the documents drawn and Martha signed them in the correct places. Martha had also named Allen treasurer of the corporation. Then they walked into Randy's outer office.

Allen waved the buxom secretary back to her chair and opened the big door, walking in unannounced with Martha beside him.

Randy was in conference with three men.

"Gentlemen, we have important business with Mr. Pemberton," Martha said. "Could you excuse us, please?"

The men gathered papers and, with knowing looks, left the room. The last one out closed the door.

"Randy, the board of directors held a special meeting and named the permanent officers of the corporation," Martha said.

Randy leaned back in the big chair, smiling. "Good, good, this interim label can be a little bit of a drawback."

"You won't have to worry about that any longer, Randy," Allen said. "Martha has been elected the new corporation president and chairman of the board. You're still a member of the board of directors, of course."

Randy's face whitened as he felt the full impact of the statement. "Cashiered, without any defense? You can't do that!"

"We did it, Randy," Martha said. "You have been doing a terrible job of running this business. We had to move you before you took the whole company into bankruptcy."

"But who voted? Who was there? Why wasn't I there?"

"Seventy-five percent of the stock was voted, and it all went to Martha. We cast your twenty-five percent in opposition."

"No, no, it isn't legal." Randy walked around his desk and glared at them. "You planned this all along. You were out to get me. Let me make a few mistakes, then pounce on me. It isn't fair!"

"Randy, was it fair the way you have been firing people without any cause?" Martha asked. "We'll find a spot for you in the organization where you will fit in, where you'll be happy."

"No, by God! I won't resign!"

"You don't have to, Randy. Martha voted you out of office at the board of directors' meeting. You know how easy that is."

Randy turned his anger toward Allen. "Cornelius, you sneaky son of a bitch. You're the one who poisoned her mind against me. I know how you operate. You rich Eastern bastards are all the same. I knew lots of you guys at Harvard."

"Randy, calling names isn't going to help matters at all. You're out as president. You're on the board of directors, but you have no corporate assignment yet," Martha said. "I'll send some movers in to help you take your things out."

"No, by God!"

Randy had moved back behind the desk now as if trying to protect it. "You wanted Father to win, didn't you? Both of you were working with him, and against me all the time. Oh, I knew it. Father would get you on his side. I knew that all the time, but I didn't let on. He had to die to beat me this time, and now you try to beat me again, but it won't work. Everyone will understand. Everyone will know that I had to do it."

Martha was still seated. Allen rose from the chair, a curious expression on his face.

Randy opened a side drawer and pulled out a gun, a long-barreled six-shooter like cowboys used.

"Well, you won't get away with trying to cheat me! First, you, Allen, and then my darling sister."

Randy lifted the heavy six-gun and aimed at Allen, who dodged to one side just as the gun fired. Allen then leaped forward and dove across the big desk, skidding toward Randy as he lowered the gun to fire again. The second slug slammed into Allen's thigh and ripped downward. But Allen hardly felt it. He was so angry, so outraged that he crashed into Randy and they both toppled backwards over the desk chair.

As they fell to the floor, the gun flew from Randy's hand. Allen's smashing right fist connected with his brother-in-law's jaw, reducing him to wailing, screaming hysteria. On the floor, Allen sat on Randy's chest and hit his jaw once more, this time knocking him out and leaving the room in sudden and strange silence.

The door opened cautiously, and the secretary's blonde head peeked inside.

"Miss, would you have someone go get a doctor? Dr. Stewart in the building next door," Allen said. "It seems that Mr. Pemberton has had a sudden touch of hysteria."

Martha ran and knelt beside Randy, saw that he was still breathing and looked at Allen's left leg where a dark red bloodstain spread on his trousers. She pulled up his pants leg, but couldn't reach the wound. A moment later, she took a pair of scissors from the big desk and cut open his trouser leg. The bullet had entered at the midpoint of the front of his thigh, tore through the inside, missing the bone and came out the back. It made an ugly wound and blood poured out. Quickly Martha tore a strip off one of her petticoats, ripped it in half and pressed the cloth against both sides of the wounds. She looked up anxiously at Allen who sat on the carpet now, his back against the desk.

Rows of small beads of sweat sprinkled his forehead. He motioned to the six-gun lying six feet away, and held the compresses in place as she got the weapon and gave it to him. Allen dumped the remaining solid cartridges from it and put them in his pocket. The six-gun he put back in the drawer.

By the time Dr. Stewart came running up the stairs, the bleeding had almost stopped.

The medical man looked at the wound. "Who is the nurse?" Allen pointed at Martha. "Well, you should come to work for me. If you hadn't put those bandages on there and stopped the bleeding, you could have been a widow by now." He checked the compresses and then looked at Randy.

"He got hysterical, Dr. Stewart, so Allen had to hit him."

"Was that before or after he shot Allen?"

Neither of them said a word.

"Now, come on, you two, don't you think I've ever seen a gun-shot wound before? Nice small hole on one side and a big one on the other? I saw more bullet holes than I cared to back in sixty-three and sixty-four."

He opened his bag and took out some strong tape and bandages. By the time he had the leg cleaned and bandaged securely,

Randy was starting to moan.

"Martha, we don't need to report this to the police, as long as you'll guarantee that we can put Randy in the hospital for observation for a few days. Hysterical? Yes, if he was waving a gun around. I think it best we keep him in the controlled section for a while. We'll admit him under another name, so there won't be a lot of publicity."

"Thank you, Doctor Stewart. I don't know what this family would ever do without you!"

That afternoon, Randy was taken to the violent ward at the hospital. Allen went home to learn how to use his crutches. And Martha moved into her new office, where she had been to see her father so many times. She visited all of the executives on the fifth floor and told them of the change in management. Each one looked relieved. She said there would be a meeting the first thing Monday morning so she could be briefed on what was going on, what needed to be done, and what their aims and goals were. They would all work together, cover any losses of the past weeks and move ahead.

Next she talked to personnel and got a list of the names of everyone Randy had fired during the past two weeks. She sent them all letters, asking them to return. Their dismissals would be reviewed with the intention of reinstating them to their previous positions.

Back in her new office, Martha had all of Randy's things boxed up and moved to a vacant office. She began going through the paper work that had piled up in several pasteboard boxes. It seemed that Randy had done little during the past week except select persons he would fire.

Martha worked all through Friday and the weekend in her office, sorting out things that needed to be done at once, trying to make heads or tails of the stacks of work. By Sunday evening, she had made some semblance of order. She would have to find a good secretary, too, somebody who would work closely with her, almost an administrative assistant.

At home, Allen was *garumphing* around, learning how to walk with the crutches, and bound and determined to get back to work on Monday if he had to crawl. He spent half of the next two days learning how to get in and out of his buggy in spite of the clumsy crutches and his stiff leg.

Monday went well for Martha. She knew a little about her job and most of the departments, and she and her staff worked together realigning priorities, and laying out specifics for each group to work on immediately.

Tuesday, a note came by messenger from Dr. Stewart, telling Martha and Allen that Randy had been released that morning. Randy had behaved in an absolutely normal manner in the hospital, so there was no reason to hold him. He didn't seem to remember the shooting, and Dr. Stewart didn't remind him of it. But Dr. Stewart said he could not guarantee that Randy wouldn't become violent again if he were angered.

The first thing Randy Pemberton did when he left the hospital was to go home. He took a bath, had a cigar and checked his calendar. He had ten more days until he would announce his engagement to Amelia. They would have everything just right, and the best for the wedding and the pre-wedding social events. They would spend money as though he were a millionaire, which, indeed, he was.

Vaguely, he remembered something about the office, about the business, but evidently it wasn't important. He didn't want to go to work today, so he decided he wouldn't. After all, he had been in an accident of some kind, and had been in the hospital.

Randy readied his town house and then went to visit Amelia. He would have her to lunch at the house, and then exercise his husband's prerogative that afternoon. It would be long and slow, delicious and exciting!

Amelia was at her mother's home when he arrived, and soon they were in his buggy, rolling toward the town house. She was wearing the spring print dress he loved and he noticed how well it set off her figure.

They hurried through lunch and went upstairs to the master bedroom, and slowly undressed each other.

Amelia kissed his bare chest now as she lay on top of him in a teasing pose that surprised Randy. She was not one of the whores from the peep houses.

"Darling Randy, I have a surprise for you."

"What is it?"

"This is something special that I know is going to make you very, very happy. I'm so thrilled and ecstatic that I can hardly believe it sometimes. I couldn't wait to tell you."

He kissed her throat and then her chin and her lips, his hands busy lower down.

"Little sweetheart, what is your surprise?"

"Do you remember our wedding night, when we were together and it was fabulous, the most wonderful, fulfilling experience of my life? Making love with my husband is . . . is . . . There is simply nothing to compare it to in the whole world. That night I had the feeling that I wanted something to happen, and darling, it did."

He stared at her, a puzzled, irritated frown on his face.

"What happened? We were married, we made love."

"Yes, that, but now, I know something else happened on our wedding night, too. Darling, I'm pregnant! I'm going to bear you a son, an heir, someone who can carry on the great Pemberton line. I knew you'd be so happy since you're the last male and I thought . . ."

She winced as he pushed her off him and jumped out of bed.

"You what? You're pregnant!"

"Yes, darling, as near as I can tell it happened on our wedding night. Isn't that wonderful?"

"Wonderful! You Goddamned little whore!" Amelia gasped, but Randy went on. "It isn't wonderful. It's terrible! I don't *want* a son. I don't *want* to continue the Pemberton line. I'd just as soon wipe it out right now, the way I'm going to wipe out the Pemberton business and fortune! I hate the

504

Pemberton name! I hate everything about it! Don't you understand that?"

He lunged at her but she scurried off the bed and stood, naked and shivering, on the other side, her face jumbled with uncertainty and surprise.

"But Randall, I thought you'd be delighted with a son."

"How many times do I have to scream at you that I'm not?" He seemed to calm down a little. "Amelia, I think you'd better put on your clothes. Our plans have been changed. Yes, dress quickly!" He pulled on his trousers and shoes and his shirt, but didn't bother with his tie or coat.

"You see, my dear, there is going to be a tragic accident here today. Yes, tragic. This beautiful little town house is going to burn down, to go up in smoke."

"Oh, no! It's so beautiful. We must save it!" Amelia said.

"We can't." He broke a stinker off a bunch from his pocket, scratched it and let the sulphur flames eat into lace curtains at the window. They flashed fire, burning into the heavy drapes and shooting upward to the wooden ceiling.

"Oh, no. Randy, don't!"

"It's all your fault, Amelia. I trusted you, and you let me down. I must have told you

I couldn't get anyone pregnant, and then you tell me that I have. It's all your fault. Your fault!"

The flames dropped to the floor and burned at the carpet.

"Randy, don't do this, please. Put out the fire."

"Ha! It's your fault you're pregnant. You should have thought of that before. There are ways *not* to get pregnant."

"But I *wanted* to have your baby, your son!"

He tried to hit her, but stumbled. She had her clothes on now and darted for the door. He tripped her and she fell hard against the bed but bounced up, and opened the hall door. He raced after her.

Amelia stopped near the bannister by the stairs, not sure what to do, sure that he could catch her if she only ran. He saw her and came on, running, glad he had her cornered. She stood facing him now and he hurried, reached for her, ready to try to push her backward over the bannister.

But just as he came to her she dropped to the floor and moved toward him. Her shoulder hit his knees. His momentum carried him forward over her body. Randy screamed as he fell, and he saw too late that he had miscalculated.

There was only the edge of the bannister to grab at, but he missed it and he screamed again as he dropped over the side and plunged fifteen feet to the floor below.

Amelia shivered. Then she stood and looked down at him. For a moment, she had a feeling of dizziness and stepped back. Randy was not moving on the tile floor below.

Amelia sobbed as she looked back at the burning bedroom, then below at her husband. She forgot the fire and hurried down the steps. At one side, she found Randy. He still had not moved. Now was her chance to get away while he was unconscious! She looked closer, and saw his head at a strange angle. A seepage of blood came out of his mouth. He lay face up, his eyes open, but they didn't move either. Fearful, trembling, she bent closer. His neck must be broken! Oh no!

He was not breathing!

She knelt beside him and tried to find a pulse beat on his neck, but could not.

For one long, terrible moment, she wanted to scream, but her throat tightened up and prevented it. She must put out the fire! She ran back up the steps to the bedroom. But the moment she looked into the room, she saw it was impossible. Flames filled the whole room, the carpet blazed, smoke gushed out of the room. It was an inferno.

Amelia hurried down the steps, found the two servants in the kitchen and sent one of them running to report the fire. She and the cook hurried out the back door and watched in despair as the Randall Pemberton town house spouted more and more smoke and flames. Now the fire broke through the roof and spewed from several windows. It was far too late to save the house.

Amelia sat on the grass and cried. How had it happened? Why had it happened? All because she told Randy that she was pregnant and was going to bear him a son. Why had he become so instantly, insanely furious? Was he actually mad, out of his mind? Had Randy lost his senses before he . . . She couldn't bear to think of it.

By the time the horses pulled the heavy fire engine up the hill to the town house, it was fully aflame. The men could not even get inside. They worked to keep the houses on each side from catching fire.

Amelia sat across the street now and watched it burn. It was the most terrifying sight she had ever seen. Slowly she realized that it also was a funeral pyre, because no one had pulled Randy's body from the house.

She watched as her whole future burned up before her eyes. She had lost a husband before she'd gotten to know him; she had lost a beautiful house, she had lost enough money to take care of herself for the rest of her life. Surely, the Pemberton family would find some way to discredit and nullify her marriage to Randy. Now she had only the judge's word. Randy had kept the marriage license and certificate, which probably burned up in the fire.

Amelia turned and began walking home. Tear tracks showed plainly on her cheeks. There was nothing for her now. She walked and tried to think it through. Her purse had been burned somewhere in the bedroom. She couldn't even hire a cab. She walked, her head down, dry tears on her face, an ache in her heart, that she had never known before.

Desperation was in her eyes, but then she looked down and her whole face softened and smiled and her hands folded over her abdomen, protectively, guarding that one part of Randy that she still had, that one small spark of life that no one could ever take away from her!

CHAPTER TWENTY-THREE:
A BAD PENNY

Martha sat in her buggy, looking out at the still-smoking ruins of Randy's town house. No one knew where Randy was. He wasn't at the office. June, the cook, sat across the street, but she was babbling, crying and incoherent. A few phrases came through and Martha had figured out that Randy and a girl had been there for lunch. Then a fire started and she heard a scream. The girl came down to the kitchen and sent Lonnie for the fire department. She hadn't seen Mr. Pemberton since she fixed the lunch.

Martha told June to go home and wait. They would continue her wages and take care of her.

The hulk of the house still smoldered as the firemen threw water on the few remaining uprights that hadn't burned. The two brick chimneys stood two stories high, looking like naked skeletons against the sky.

Hundreds of people milled around. It was

the biggest spectacle of the month. Martha stayed in the buggy as Allen continued talking with the firemen. A moment later, Martha heard a shout and saw a fireman run out of the blackened house with something in his hand. He showed it to someone, and the two men went back into the remains on the first floor. The second story was entirely gone.

Martha wondered what else could happen to the family. It had been a tragic few months. She watched Allen limping toward her across the street and she thought his face looked grim. He didn't look up, his eyes on the ground as he came to the rig and strugged with his painful leg as he got up beside her. He took the reins and began driving at once.

"What is it, Allen? What did they find in there?"

He looked up at her and swore just under his breath. "Martha, they found Randy. He's dead. He died inside the house. They can't tell much. His body was badly burned. There will be a complete investigation and they'll want to talk to all the servants tomorrow. Randy had let everyone off today except one driver and the cook."

"Randy is gone! Are they sure it's Randy?"

"The fire captain said he'd seen Randy

many times and he was almost sure it was him. Positive identification will be made later. They found Randy's wallet under his body. We better get right home and tell your mother."

Martha tried to cry, but couldn't. She thought of all the times when they were growing up, all the fun they had, the good times and the bad. But that was before Randy had changed so. It was just before Mexico he seemed so different. She wasn't sure how or why it had happened. Maybe what Allen said about him was true. Somewhere, somehow, he'd learned to hate any and all authority. And finally, Randy simply hated too much.

Two days later, they learned that it had been Amelia Borcherding with Randy in the house. She came forward when police asked for information. She said she thought everyone knew, and that she would be glad to tell them what had happened. First, she told them that she and Randy had been secretly married since May twenty-fifth, when Judge Hamilton Rassmussen performed the ceremony. The judge had delayed the public recording of the ceremony at Randy's request. But it was all legal and proper.

Amelia's story came out slowly. Martha

sat beside her and put her arm around her and smiled.

"Amelia, you're a part of our family now. We'll take care of you. We'll protect you. Just relax and tell us exactly what happened that day."

She did, leaving out nothing, telling them how Randy said he hated the family, the family business and the family name.

Later the medical examination proved that Randy had suffered a broken neck. But his death had ultimately been due to the fire and the lack of oxygen.

Martha had Amelia move in with her and Allen until they could arrange for a new house to replace the one that burned. Amelia was Randy's only heir under the law. What was his was now hers.

Two weeks later, Johnnie Laveau paid a visit to Martha. She took him to show him her roses and Johnnie told her the good news.

"This tall mon, he the one. So far Johnnie find three friends. One more to go."

"You are positive these are the men? You're sure they are the ones who hurt Miss Stone? There can be no room for a mistake."

"Yes, mon. They brag about it, Miz Cornelius."

"And you have something in mind for

them? Something that will pain them?"

"Oh, yes, mon, Johnnie sure do!"

"I'd rather not know what it is, Johnnie. Just be sure that it is a just punishment, a punishment that fits the crime."

When Johnnie left, he rode his horse down a road to the sparse outskirts of San Francisco, where he had put up a strange-looking shack years ago. He had signs and symbols on the door and the children in the area were frightened to death of the place. Everything inside was just the way he had left it. He looked at the cat in a cage, a black female he would need one of these days.

Today, he worked on five small dolls. Each was about a foot long. All but one had a lock of hair that had been snipped off a real person. Each of the dolls was male and had replicas of genitals. Around the scrotum of each doll he had tied a fine silken thread. Now he tightened it a little more on each one.

He took the four dolls and made a series of chants and motions over them. Then he moved to a small tin and dropped in some incense which he lit. He smiled at the scent of the fumes that wafted up.

Johnnie checked the silken threads again and lifted his voice in a soft chant:

"Eh! Eh! Momab hen hen!

Canga Bafie te.
Danga moune de te.
Canga do ki li!"

Johnnie carried the four dolls to the corner of the hut and removed several boards from the floor. He put the dolls in the earth and covered them carefully. As he put back the floorboards, he hoped that tomorrow he would be able to add the fifth doll to the others.

Johnnie left his small house and rode back to the city, stopping at the Lighthouse Saloon, which was far enough away from the docks to have seamen and locals in a good mix of customers. Johnnie bought a mug of rum and moved to the back where he slid into a chair near four regulars who drank and talked softly.

One man stood, his face screwed up with pain and headed for the privy out back. Another man watched him go, shaking his head.

"I know how you feel, friend. I ain't never had nothing hurt this way before. It's like my balls was on fire all the Goddamned time. Like somebody was puttin' 'em in a vise."

The taller of the men stood, tears now in his eyes. He slammed his fist down on the table, upsetting a mug of beer.

"Dammit, I'm not going to do this any-more. It's got to have something to do with that Goddamn Stone bitch."

"You gonna go and ask her if she's got the crud or the blue balls or the swollen dick fever or something?" another voice asked. "Not me. I'm staying just as far away from that small bitch as possible. Jesus, how did I ever let you bastards talk me into that anyway? Must have been crazy. Oh, Christ!" He jumped up and headed for the back door.

Johnnie drank his rum slowly, listening, a smile working across his brown features.

"I went to a damn doctor and asked him what was the matter. He punched and felt a minute and said damned if he knew. Sug-gested I just lay off women for a while. Hell, I could have told him that."

Johnnie kept looking for the fifth man, but he was not there, nor did he come in during the next hour. Johnnie needed a lock of the man's hair or a fingernail, a bit of flesh, anything from his physical body. He had been lucky and gotten snips of hair from the first four one night last week when they'd all been falling-down drunk. He was afraid the fifth had vanished.

Johnnie finished his second rum and listened to the agonies of the four men. He would loosen the silk thread after a week, allow them a week without pain, then tighten it up again. He could loosen it every other week to make half their lives to be lived with a constant mysterious painful pressure on their testicles. He was sure if they all stayed in San Francisco, he could maintain his control over them. Some day, he would tell Miz Cornelius. She would appreciate the exquisite type of torture they were suffering. And indeed, what better punishment could there be to fit their crime?

Johnnie smiled to himself and went outside to his horse. Four out of the five was a good average.

Penny had wanted to go see her big sister for over a month. She didn't know what to say or how to bring it up, but now it had to be done. She went on Sunday afternoon because she knew the family would be home. Penny found Martha sitting in the rose garden dousing her favorites with a mixture of soap suds and onion juice.

"It's a very fine agent to use against the aphids," Martha said. "They don't like the strong smell of the onion juice and the soap glues it on the leaves and stems. Of course, sometimes the roses smell a little like onions, but they lose the odor after a day or two." She patted the green grass beside her.

"Sit down and rest yourself, Penny. I haven't seen much of you lately. You're looking just marvelous, so pretty and fresh. How is everything going at the hospital?"

"Oh, the hospital? Yes, it's fine. No, it's dull and a lot of work." She paused and looked up at her sister. "You said once that we could have a talk, about boys . . . and sex."

"Yes, Penny, and I'm sorry that I never invited you over for an afternoon. I've just been so busy lately."

"I know. The company." She turned, determination on her young pretty face, her blonde hair curling over one shoulder. "I've been talking to that friend of mine, and she says that it's absolutely certain that a girl is pregnant if she misses her time, you know, her bleeding. I told her she was all crazy."

Martha smiled. "Well, Penny, this time your friend is right. When a woman is pregnant she doesn't have any bleedings, and so that's one positive way of telling that she is pregnant. Sometimes a bleeding will come a week or two late because of any one of many problems, but if you miss two times, then it's for sure."

"I don't believe you! Why should you know everything?" Penny jumped up, angry, hands clenching, swinging the purse she carried. She stalked up the grass walkway, then returned.

"Why should I believe you just because you tell me? I should go talk to a doctor. Dr. Stewart would give me the real facts. Maybe that's what I should do."

"Penny, come back and sit down. It's nothing to get so excited about. Is this friend of yours pregnant?"

"Her? Uh . . . no. I don't think so. She was just telling me what she heard her cousins and her aunts talking about. No, she's not pregnant. She says she's never done it, so she can't be." Penny at last sat down beside her sister again.

"Martha, you're real sure that after missing twice a girl has to be pregnant. What about missing three times?"

"Yes, I'd say that means she should go right to a doctor. They can tell for sure. Who is your friend?"

"Huh. Oh, it doesn't matter." She slumped against Martha and all at once began to cry. "Martha, I'm just so miserable. Sometimes I wish I could die. I mean, what's the use? Everything seems so hard, and nobody has time to help me."

Martha put her arms around the sobbing girl and rocked her.

"Penny, you are a beautiful young woman, with so much. Don't you realize that? You have suitors. What about that young doctor? I hear he's handsome and a great doctor as well. You don't have to worry about money or working, so you can just sit back, wait and take your pick of all the rich young men until you find a real love match."

Penny pushed away from her sister, and glared at her. She jumped up and without a word walked to the end of the garden. She stood there, fists clenched, her purse under her arm. She glared at Martha for a long time, then slowly walked back. She sat down six feet from Martha, and spread her skirts carefully around her.

"Martha, I don't have time to wait and pick out an exciting young man to marry. Right now, I am three months pregnant! Three months and I'm starting to show it!"

Martha gasped and her eyes went wide. "Oh, Penny! I'm so sorry. How . . . Look, don't you worry, dear Penny. Mother and I will work out something. You could move to San Diego with Mother until your time, then come home. Who is the father? Will he marry you?"

"No. He . . . he can't marry me." Penny was sobbing again, but she held up her hand when Martha started to go to her. "No, you stay right there. I caused this mess, and I can take care of it myself. I don't need your help. I know you want to help, but I know how to solve the whole thing."

She opened her purse and took out a small hand gun, a Derringer, Martha had heard them called. It was so small a man could hide it in his hand.

"Penny, put that down. That's no solution. Think what it would do to Mother. You'll only be pregnant for another six months, then you have the rest of a glorious life ahead of you. Fifty or sixty or seventy years! Think of that, Penny. Now, put the gun on the ground and come over here so we can plan out your trip. We'll go see Mother this afternoon and tell her, then make plans for that European trip you wanted. Yes! You and Mother can tour Europe. You can stay in Paris until the baby is born. Paris has excellent doctors, and you'll be fine there. Then you can put the baby up for adoption. How does all that sound?"

Penny didn't seem to hear any of it. She looked at the gun, quite calmly checked to see that there were bullets in it, and then she put her finger on the trigger. Tears came again.

Martha started to crawl toward her, but

Penny shook her head.

"No, Martha, you stay right there. It's too late now to do anything about it. I've been wicked and evil and now I must pay the penalty." She looked up at the sky, then at the grass and the roses. Penny leaned forward to smell a pink rose. At that moment, she shot herself through the head just over her right ear.

The explosion of the gun made a surprisingly loud roar in the garden.

Martha screamed and crawled to where Penny lay. The force of the bullet had pushed Penny against the rose bush. Before Martha got to Penny she heard Allen coming toward them. He knelt beside Penny.

"Oh, my God!" he said, and touched her blood splattered face, then he checked for breathing but couldn't find any. He pressed his fingers under Penny's chin for a pulse. There was none.

Martha cried silently against Allen's shoulder.

"She was so young, and so beautiful. Why couldn't I have talked her out of it? At first, I thought she was only trying to scare me so she could have her way and go to Europe. I never had any idea she was serious about . . ."

Allen helped Martha from the grass and

walked with her inside the house. He sent one of the drivers to the police station, then waited in the garden for them to arrive.

CHAPTER TWENTY-FOUR:
AFTERMATH

Martha and Allen read and re-read the diary they had found in Penny's room. It was a complete record of the last six months of her life, her dreams, her loves, her sexual experimentation and how she reacted to each. It included the daily reports from the detective agency and its surveillance of Randy.

"You know what this information must mean Allen," Martha said. "Penny didn't put it all together, but I can. It was Randy who must have burned down the Pemberton Mercantile. And he killed poor old Mr. Fawcett, the night watchman. This report says Randy was seen entering the building at 12:15 a.m. and leaving it at 1:34 a.m. on the morning of the fire."

"Yes, that seemed to fit the pattern," Allen said. "He hated the company and, from what Amelia said, he screamed that hatred at her for several minutes before he set fire to the room and then fell over the bannister. His whole idea must have been to kill Amelia and her unborn child and have them burn up in the house, a tragic accident."

"Poor Randy, why did he hate us all so?"

"We'll never know, Martha. But it's my guess that the warehouse fire we had several months back was Randy's work as well."

They went on reading, Martha handing the pages to Allen as she finished them. She started on the next and shuddered.

"Oh, my God, that poor girl!"

Allen picked up the pages and read:

"Today I discovered what 'it' is all about. Today I was raped by my brother, Randy Pemberton. I went to his secret love nest near Merriweather Street to talk to him. I wanted him to show me himself and educate me about men. I underestimated his ability to control himself. When I disrobed in front of him and asked him to do the same, he became tremendously excited, knocked me down on the bed and entered me. I was shocked and horrified, stunned. I knew he had done it inside of me and I prayed that I would not get pregnant. If this is what intercourse is like, then I'm not going to look forward to it anymore. I was revolted and frightened and there was much pain."

Allen put down the closely written page

and touched Martha's shoulder.

She turned and leaned into his arms, tears on her cheeks.

"Martha, Penny wasn't just pregnant, then, she was carrying her own brother's child! That's why she couldn't bear to live. That's why no one could have talked her out of doing what she had already decided to do. It wasn't your fault that you couldn't stop her. Nobody could have stopped her. The total blame lies with Randy Pemberton."

They clung together for several more minutes until Martha felt she could sit alone. She wiped the tears away and rubbed her head.

"Poor Penny. She wanted to know about sex and love so badly, and when she found out, it was too late for her. How could such a strong man as my father beget children who became so tragically confused about life? I just don't understand it."

Martha closed the diary and vowed that she would lock it away in a bank-safe box until there was no more possible need for it legally. Then she would burn it page by page so there never would be more shame brought down on Penny.

In the newspaper accounts of her suicide, there was no mention made of her pregnancy. But Dr. Stewart had assured Martha and Allen that Penny had been three months pregnant at the time of her death.

A week later, Martha and Allen were having a candlelight dinner in the main dining room. They used a small table so they could reach across and touch hands.

Allen finished his dessert and looked out at the gas lights blossoming around San Francisco. He reached for Martha's hand.

"You know that flurry of infidelity our top management experienced recently? I did some checking. Actually, I asked two of the women I know best to come to my office with their husbands' permission. We had good, long talks, and when I felt I was on safe enough ground, I asked both, individually, if the man they had become involved with was Randy Pemberton. In both cases, the women could not hide surprise, and soon admitted it was Randy. I went on to tell them about the conspiracy Randy had played out, explaining to each that she had been carefully and expertly seduced with a specific purpose in mind. When I was sure about Randy, I told all seven of the men involved, and I think I smoothed things over. Those marriages will never be as strong as they were, but the men at least understand it was not just a casual fling, but that their wives had been masterfully and mercilessly courted and seduced for a purpose."

Martha sipped her wine and stared at Allen over the top of the glass.

"I'm proud of you, Allen, for clearing that up. Several of those couples must be feeling much better tonight about their marriages."

They were silent for a while, both thinking about the whole span of events that had touched them so tragically. Now they were grateful just to be whole, happy, and alive. Martha knew that from now on she would savor each moment of life that she was allowed, because she knew life could be cruel as well as beautiful and it could end so quickly.

"Amelia picked out her new house today," Martha said. "I was along with her, and honestly, she looks so fragile and shy, but she is a dynamo. She has a sharp mind, and she bargained like a gypsy. Afterwards, she apologized to me, saying she still is haunted by poverty, still thinking that she must get the most value for every penny she spends. The house is just three doors down from the one that burned, and is almost the same size. She refused a much larger house, saying she wouldn't know what to do with all the rooms, and that it would cost a fortune for furniture. Then she laughed and said she had forgotten again that she *could* spend a fortune on furniture if she wanted to.

"I am totally impressed by Amelia Borcherding Pemberton. When the bank opened Randy's safe box for the lawyers, they found the marriage license and certificate, and Amelia was delighted. She's going to be a strong member of our family, and there is still a chance that her child will be a boy to carry on the Pemberton name in spite of Randy."

They moved from the table and sat in front of the bay window that opened onto a glittering view of San Francisco's shimmering lights. Every day, there were more gas lamps on the streets, other lights showing up all over the city.

Allen put his arm around Martha. "I know we made a bargain not to talk about the business at home, but I think you should know that everyone I've spoken to on the fifth floor is pleased and delighted with the way you've taken hold of the business and are moving it ahead. There is no doubt that Pacific Steamship and Trading Company is about to start on one of the biggest spurts of growth in our history."

"Thank you, sir," she said and kissed his lips softly. Then she let him return her kiss and she caught his hand. "I'd like to have a serious discussion with you upstairs," she said.

"In which room?"

"In our bedroom."

"I think I have an appointment open tonight."

A short time later, they lay close together as Martha played with the hairs on Allen's chest.

"I've been building up my strength all week," he said. "I've seen you hopping around here, and chirping like a mother bird making her next nest. It is about that time again, isn't it?"

She kissed his shoulder and nodded. "And we've come to your most likely time of the month to get pregnant?" he asked.

She kissed his cheek in affirmation.

"Six days in a row, once a day?"

Martha giggled and snuggled against him.

"Well, I guess I can put up with it, if you can guarantee the result."

Martha shook her head and let him kiss her lips. "Sir, in this area of production, about all you can do is plant your seeds and hope that one of them grows."

Allen laughed softly. "That sounds good enough for me."

Martha lay there in the serenity of expectation and love and warmth, and hoped that she could conceive a daughter, and then after that one more son. Then she would devote herself to both the business and her family, and they would watch both grow at the same time.

Martha hoped that years from now, when she had grandchildren, she could look back and know that this night was a whole new beginning for the Pemberton-Cornelius family, and that from here on it would be joy, and peace and quiet assurance that the heartbreak and tragedy were all behind them. From now on, she prayed, they would glide down a peaceful stream of happiness.

She kissed Allen and held him tightly. Whatever happened, they were together. He was her one true love, her life, and hand in hand they would meet life, whatever it brought them.

Martha leaned up to kiss him.

The employees of Thorndike Press hope you have enjoyed this Large Print book. All our Thorndike, Wheeler, and Kennebec Large Print titles are designed for easy reading, and all our books are made to last. Other Thorndike Press Large Print books are available at your library, through selected bookstores, or directly from us.

For information about titles, please call:
  (800) 223-1244

or visit our Web site at:
  http://gale.cengage.com/thorndike

To share your comments, please write:
  Publisher
  Thorndike Press
  10 Water St., Suite 310
  Waterville, ME 04901